—THE—
WHISPERING
SHAD◉WS OF
SAVANNAH

JENNY ELAINE

ISBN: 9780578980744

In memory of my great-great grandmother, who was diagnosed with sclerosis and had to spend the last twelve years of her life in a mental hospital.

Books by
Jenny Elaine

Rose of Savannah Series

The Healing Rose of Savannah
The Whispering Shadows of Savannah

A Shady Pines Mystery Series

Secrets From The Past

Through the years, women have been looked upon as being the weaker sex, with all of our strengths and abilities often forgotten during moments of weakness. In the early days, a woman could endure the extreme physical pain of bearing a child, only to be sent away when she later suffered from postpartum depression. A woman's voice didn't matter, and countless women were sent to mental institutions for reasons such as: novel reading, religious matters, laziness, imaginary female trouble, fever, and jealousy. However, just like Vivian and Eva, the two main characters in this story, a woman may have trials and struggles, but she also possesses an inner strength that pushes her to go on even when it feels hopeless. Let us never forget, overlook, or underestimate our inner strength. Let us find a light in the darkness, a song in the silence. Let us stay strong and endure life's battles, so that one day we can look back and say, "I am an overcomer."

PROLOGUE

May 1944

I tiptoed quietly down the long corridor, the blinding darkness of the night so thick and heavy, I found it to be almost suffocating. I paused for a moment and took a deep breath, trying to calm the erratic pounding of my heart as it beat a wild rhythm within my chest. I didn't know what would happen if they caught me, but for the sake of my sanity, I knew I had to at least try to escape.

I began walking again, my nerves coiled tighter than a rattlesnake ready to strike. I'd been trapped in this nightmarish pit for three months...or had it been longer? I'd lost track of time. Each minute, second, and hour all bled and ran together, creating one large blur in my mind. Everything happened so fast, and yet my time here had crept by agonizingly slow.

As I made my way towards the light under the door at the end of the hallway, I began to wonder if I would truly be free once I escaped, or if this place would always own a small part of me.

I was almost there; I could see the sliver of light drawing closer. Just a few more steps and...

Suddenly, the door behind me squeaked open. "Oh, Vivian," a shrill, childlike voice sang out, echoing loudly off the bare walls. "Where are you going, Vivian?"

I stopped, knowing I'd been caught. Shoulders stooped, I turned in defeat just as the overhead lights flipped on.

1

Vivian

October 1941

I strolled along the sidewalk, the cool, early morning breeze ruffling the dark tendrils that fell around my face. It wasn't very often that Savannah was graced with such beautiful weather, and I'd told Father that I wanted to walk to work this morning, instead of riding with him as I usually did.

Sighing with contentment, I smiled as I watched a Cardinal flitting back and forth amongst the branches of a live oak tree, the red of its feathers bright and bold against the green leaves and silvery strands of Spanish moss. The city was just beginning to awaken, and I could hear voices and laughter drifting through the open windows of the homes that I passed, the smell of freshly brewed coffee blending with the familiar scent of saltwater that always floated gently along the breeze. Orange and gold mums lined the steps leading up to brightly painted front doors, adding their brilliant splashes of color to the wrought-iron gates and brick buildings that were shaded by massive oaks.

I loved the city in which I lived, and sometimes during my early morning strolls, it felt like I was taking a walk down the paths of history. I could see southern belles with their hoop skirts and lacy bonnets stepping from a horse-drawn carriage to attend a ball or afternoon tea, and I could hear the *clip-clop* of horse hooves trotting along the cobblestone streets. I often wondered what it would be like to step through the portals of time, to meet those that came before us, to see how life was once lived.

As I rounded the corner and my family's restaurant, The Park Bench, came into view, I thought of all the history that existed in just this one building. My great-grandfather first bought the two-story home in the early 1800s and spent months restoring it for his new mail-order bride, Priscilla, who would come all the way from Maine. Story had it that when she arrived in Savannah, Priscilla hated the heat, mosquitoes, and sand gnats so fiercely that she was on the verge of leaving, but when she toured the city and saw the beautiful home her fiancé had made for her, she fell madly in love and decided to stay. She later wrote in a letter to her cousin that she couldn't imagine living anywhere else.

The house was passed down among the family until it reached my father, who eventually turned it into a restaurant. The business thrived almost immediately, and I was practically raised in the kitchen, where I spent many hours beside my mother learning how to cook. I grew to love the hustle and bustle of running a business, of learning what works and what doesn't. It was thrilling to create a unique experience and atmosphere that people would walk away from with a smile on their face and a promise to come back.

When we had to close the restaurant during the depression, I was devastated to think that we might lose the building entirely. All I could think of was how much Priscilla loved this place, and how her heart would be broken if it were lost by our family. Those years during the depression were very long and hard, but we managed to hold on to the building, and when we could finally open back up in '39, I was thrilled.

"Glad to see you could make it," Cook said when I arrived through the back door of the kitchen.

"I'll admit that I was lollygagging a bit," I replied, smiling as I slid into an apron.

Mother no longer worked full time, and Father hired "Cook", as we called her, to help me in the kitchen. She was a large, middle-aged women with a very loud opinion, but we respected each other and she'd learned that although I was only twenty-one, I could run the kitchen as efficiently and effortlessly as could any experienced and trained professional.

"Heard from your friends lately?" Cook asked as I pulled out a large bowl from the pantry and began cracking eggs.

I knew she was referring to my two closest friends, Savannah Rose and her cousin, Maxine, who had been in Hawaii the last few months, and I nodded my head.

"Yes," I replied, retrieving a whisk from a nearby drawer. "I actually just received a letter from both of them yesterday. They're working hard at the hospital in Honolulu, but it seems like they're having a good time, and Hawaii sounds absolutely beautiful."

I missed them a great deal, which Cook could clearly hear in my voice, and I wondered how long they would have to be gone. Life had been so fun and exciting when they were here, with the three of us attending dances and parties together, and things just hadn't been the same since they left. I was more thankful than ever for my job at the restaurant that had kept me busy and my mind occupied the last few months.

Later that afternoon, I was chopping celery in the kitchen when a knock sounded on the restaurant's back door.

"Who on earth could that be?" Cook sighed

"I'll get it," I said, wiping my hands on my apron as I hurried to open the back door.

"Hello," a handsome, young man greeted me, smiling as he politely tipped his hat. "My name is Howard McCombs. I recently bought my uncle's farm just outside of town, and I was wondering if the owner would be interested in talking with me about supplying produce for the restaurant. I promise to provide delicious and fresh produce at a very competitive price."

"Well, Howard McCombs," I replied, smiling in return at the obviously well-rehearsed speech, "I'm the owner's daughter, and I'm sure he would love to talk with you."

Howard's eyes brightened, and I showed him through the kitchen and into my father's office. Not long after, he returned to tell me that Father agreed to give him a month's trial. His face was flushed with such excitement that I couldn't help but laugh.

"What's so funny?" He asked, tilting his head inquisitively. He wasn't much taller than me, and had a wide, dazzling smile and brown eyes that sparkled. His shoulders were quite wide and strong, and his hands were tanned and roughened from farming. He was, however, dressed to a T, without a wrinkle in his crisp, white shirt, and every inch of his curly brown hair was combed neatly into place.

"Your exuberance is contagious, I guess." I shrugged, returning to my cutting station.

Howard moved to stand beside me, clearing his throat as he leaned one elbow against the counter. "You know," he said, "I'm new to the area and could use a tour guide. You wouldn't be available tonight around five o'clock, would you?"

"Hmm," I pursed my lips together, "I've never been a tour guide before. What exactly does the job entail?"

Howard made a show of tapping his chin thoughtfully. "It would involve taking me to the second-best restaurant in town, because obviously this one is the best, and then a nice walking tour through some of your favorite spots; you could even show me the best place in town for ice cream. I would pay for everything, of course."

I cut my glimmering green eyes over at Howard and smiled, my heart fluttering a bit in my chest. "I think I could handle that," I said, attempting to keep my tone calm and nonchalant.

"Good," Howard grinned. After getting my address, he stood to his full height, said he'd pick me up at five o'clock and walked out, whistling a tune.

"He certainly is a smooth talker," Cook stated, cocking an eyebrow at me.

I left work early and hurried home, excited and a little nervous about my date. I hadn't gone out with many men before, and asked Mother to help me with my hair. At five o'clock sharp, the doorbell rang, and I smoothed my hands down the golden yellow dress I was wearing, quickly checking my lipstick in the mirror before I opened the door.

It turned out to be a wonderful evening. Howard was talkative and charming, and my nerves were soon forgotten as we ate at a local seafood restaurant and later toured the city. I showed him some of my favorite spots, which included a few of the peaceful, picturesque squares that Savannah was famous for. Canopied by giant oak trees and filled with little walkways, benches, and fountains, the squares were also surrounded by magnificent mansions built in the 1700s. These beautiful monuments from the past still lived and breathed, speaking softly of the lives that once dwelled within their walls. The homes were now filled with new people who were creating their own stories, and the lights that glowed from the windows spoke of time moving on, while somehow continuing to stand still.

We strolled along the sidewalks, and I showed him the house in which Juliette Gordon Low was born, stating proudly that she was the founder of Girl Scouts of the USA. The home, which was built in the early 1800s in the neoclassical, Regency style, stood tall and grand, with two staircases leading up to a front door that was surrounded by six, majestic columns. I told him a bit about "Daisy" Gordon Low and of what a talented artist she was, and then we walked on to get ice cream sundaes at Leopold's. We talked and laughed and discussed our visions for the future, and by the time he took me home, I was exhausted but completely taken with Howard McCombs.

"I'd like to see you again soon," he said as he walked me to my door. "Would that be alright with you?"

Turning to smile at him, the light from the porch lamp reflecting off of his brown eyes, I nodded and said, "Yes, I'd like that very much."

He leaned down and gently kissed me good night on the cheek, and my heart skipped a beat. I hurried inside the house, and as soon as I entered my bedroom, I began spinning around like a ballerina, arms outstretched and dress billowing out about my calves like a giant, golden sunflower.

"Goodness, you must have had a good time tonight," Mother stated from the doorway, her eyes sparkling as she laughed at my silly antics. I'd gotten my green eyes and tiny figure from her, and I'd always adored the two dimples in her cheeks when she smiled.

Grinning, I pulled Mother into the room and closed the door. "Oh, Mother, I did," I said, sighing as we sat on my bed.

I told her all about the wonderful evening and of how much I liked Howard. She listened with a small, knowing smile on her lips, and suggested that I invite him over for supper one evening.

"I'd like to get to know this young man who has you so starry-eyed," she said.

Feeling giddy, I put my arms around her neck and hugged her tightly, thankful for the relationship we had. She was always so supportive of me, of my dreams and ideas, and I didn't know what I'd do without her. Being raised without siblings, she'd known that I would need not only a mother, but a friend, and she'd been the perfect combination of both.

"I'll ask him when he takes me out again," I promised, and for the rest of the night, I laid awake, staring up at the ceiling with a huge smile on my face.

2

Vivian

In late November, Howard asked if I'd like to go out to his farm for a sugarcane grinding.

"What is that, exactly?" I asked.

It was a Sunday afternoon, and we were sitting on the front porch of my parents' house drinking sweet tea. Howard had been to visit me twice since our first outing, and I was excited that he wanted me to see his farm.

"All the neighbors get together and harvest the sugarcane crops, and then that night we grind the sugarcane and have a party," he explained. "There will be food, music, and dancing, and just a lot of fun. Please say you'll come."

This would be the first crop he would harvest at his new farm, and I could sense his excitement. Smiling, I nodded and said, "I would love to come."

When Friday afternoon arrived, I drove fifteen miles out of town and turned down a long, bumpy dirt road. The area was calm and peaceful, with old farmhouses and barns dotting the landscape as I passed, and cows grazing lazily among green, grassy fields. I arrived at Howard's farm and pulled in through the gate, noticing that the men were still in the fields across the road, cutting down what remained of the large, grassy stalks of sugarcane with cane knives. It looked like hard, grueling work, and I wondered how the men held out all day long.

I stepped from the car, slowly taking in the farm Howard had recently purchased from his uncle. It was a beautiful spot, but still needed a lot of work. The two-story house needed painting and a few repairs, as well as the barn, and an old, broken-down tractor lay in the yard by the well. It was a charming place, and I knew that once Howard finished with the repairs, it would be the perfect country setting.

I entered the house and walked down the long hallway that led to the kitchen, glancing into each room as I passed. There were three bedrooms, a small sitting room, and I was surprised to find that there was even a tiny bathroom. Most of the old farmhouses didn't have indoor plumbing, but I was pleased that this one was the exception.

Floorboards groaned beneath my feet as I walked, telling me a story of the families and lives that once occupied this dwelling, and I touched the old wallpaper that peeled from the walls, picturing in my mind how everything would look once Howard was finished with the repairs and renovations. When I finally reached the kitchen, I found the large room filled with smiling, chattering women, and when they turned to look at me curiously, I cleared my throat and introduced myself. Howard's aunt and uncle were still living on the farm until after the harvest, and his aunt immediately hurried to my side to give me a hug.

"I'm Celia, Howard's aunt," she said, pulling back to smile at me. "It's so nice to meet you."

Celia was a short, plump woman in her mid-fifties, with large, wide-set eyes and graying brown hair. She wore an old plaid dress with an apron that was splattered with flour, and I noticed a sprinkling of the powdery substance on her nose, as well.

I was ushered into the kitchen, handed an apron, and put to work. I'd arrived early just for this reason, and I dove in to the preparing of fried chicken, mashed potatoes and gravy, macaroni and cheese, butter peas, green beans, and biscuits with gusto. By the time the men were done and waiting in the front yard with rumbling stomachs, we'd just finished putting the last apple pie in the oven and began carrying the food out to the awaiting tables.

"Vivian, I didn't realize you would arrive early," Howard said, pulling me off to the side as he washed his hands and face in the well. He smelled of dirt, sweat, and hard work, and his clothes were filthy, but I barely noticed.

"I wanted to help with the cooking," I told him, smiling.

Reaching up to wipe a bit of flour from my chin, Howard said warmly, "I'm glad you came. You look beautiful."

The evening passed with a lot of laughter and stories of other harvests and parties from the past. The people were simple, without giving much thought to the world outside of their farms, and I found them to be very kind and charming. They were different from the people in the city, and when I looked beneath the slowness of their speech and the dirt under their fingernails, I quickly realized how intelligent they were. In this small group of hardworking neighbors was a world of knowledge, such as what herbs will cure a cold, how to rebuild an entire piece of machinery, or how to know when it's going to rain. One lady was a midwife, and she spoke of all the difficult deliveries she'd overseen the last twenty-five years, and a man in his mid-thirties told me he'd designed his own tractor and built it from scrap metal.

Having lived in the city my whole life, I hadn't been to the country very often, and found it fascinating how these people lived, and also how the sugarcane was harvested and ground. I watched as the men put the stalks between two huge rollers as a mule went round and round, causing the rollers to squeeze the juice from the cane into buckets underneath. I found myself to be quite lacking in the knowledge of how farms were run and operated, and told Howard so.

"I never really thought about how the sugar I use daily at the restaurant is made," I told him as we walked along the dirt road, taking a quick break from the others. "It's a lot of hard work, isn't it?"

"It is," he nodded, "but I'm so excited to finally have my own farm. Can you imagine how it would be to plant your crops, work hard and put your heart into it, and then just a few months later reap the benefits? I didn't plant this sugarcane crop, but I can only imagine how rewarding it must feel."

We rejoined the others then and danced around a bonfire as a few of the men climbed up on the old, broken-down tractor and played tunes on their banjos and fiddles. It was a wonderful night, and I was sad to see it end.

As everyone said goodbye and Howard walked me to my car, I sighed with contentment. The air was crisp and cold, and millions of stars twinkled from the sky; I'd never seen so many stars in my life. I gazed up at them, not noticing the look of warmth in Howard's eyes as he watched me.

"As beautiful as those stars are, they don't hold a candle to you," he breathed, his voice low as he stepped closer and took my hand.

Blinking, I met his gaze, my heart skipping a beat at the look in his eyes. He leaned over and kissed me then, his lips soft and warm, and I felt my eyes flutter closed of their own accord. I'd never been kissed before, and I thought it must be the most wonderful feeling in the world.

We courted for nearly a year before Howard asked me to marry him, and our months of courtship flew by. He wanted the farm to be well established before we started a family, but I didn't mind waiting. I wasn't lonely anymore, and the time we spent together was happy and without care. Howard spent every other Sunday with us, and we would sometimes go to picture shows or on picnics in the park. My parents loved him, and when he finally got down on one knee and proposed in August of '42, I readily accepted.

I hadn't been prepared, however, for the emotions I would feel when it was time to leave my parents, the restaurant, and childhood home behind. I cried when I said goodbye, but consoled myself with the fact that we would only live fifteen miles from town and I would still be able to see my parents and friends quite often.

"My baby is all grown up," Father said just before walking me down the aisle, his voice choked with emotion. "I'm going to miss working with you every day, Vivvy."

I was going to miss it, too, but we had so many plans, Howard and I, and couldn't wait to begin our life together. When we arrived at the farm after the wedding, I climbed from the car and gazed at our new home, my eyes taking in the newly renovated, two-story farmhouse with delight. It was painted yellow, as per my request, with a wraparound porch, white shutters, and gleaming white spindles. Two rocking chairs bumped along in the breeze on either side of the front door, and a white picket fence stood proudly around the yard. I couldn't wait to plant flowers along the edge of the fence and porch, and could already imagine how beautiful it would look come spring when the roses and azaleas were blooming.

As Howard picked me up and carried me over the threshold, a feeling of contentment washed over me as we entered our new home. I thought of all the happiness we would share, of the love and laughter that would fill each room. I imagined what our children would look like, and how exciting it would be to become a mother someday.

The morning after our wedding, I went to the window and looked out at our beautiful farm, feeling both nervous and excited about this new adventure ahead of us. I knew it would take some time for me to get used to the farm life, but I was determined to do my very best. Whatever came our way, though, good or bad, rain or shine, I knew we would face it together, and I had no fear of the future.

3

Vivian

February 1944

I often reflect on the early days of our courtship and marriage, trying to draw strength from the memories. Less than three years had passed, and yet it felt like a lifetime, and I wondered what it was about growing older and the passing of time that can make one change so drastically. We'd been so happy in the beginning and after our sweet baby, Howard Junior, was born, but then things started to change.

Five months ago, a massive hurricane stormed through the East Coast, destroying our sugarcane crop in one fatal swoop. We lost a lot of money, but I was thankful that we had enough in our savings to see us through another year. Howard, on the other hand, was devastated by the loss, and I understood because I know how difficult it is to pour yourself into something only to see it fail. When I tried to offer him comfort, however, he pushed me away and said it wasn't about the work or the effort of planting the crops, but the money we'd lost.

"At least we still have our home," I'd tried to tell him, as it could have been destroyed in the hurricane as well.

Nothing I said seemed to help, and he continually grew more distant and moody until I began to feel like I was married to a stranger. He started going out a couple of nights each week with no explanation of where he was going, and began receiving strange phone calls at random times during the day and even sometimes at night. I tried to ask him about it, but he told me it was nothing. I wondered if he was having an affair, but had no proof.

I went into town one afternoon and spoke to Mother about our problems, feeling down and frustrated and just needing to talk. Father was at work, and we sat in the living room on the same old sofa that had been there for as long as I could remember, and I told her everything.

"I just don't know what to do," I told her, tears sliding down my cheeks. "Do I suggest we sell the farm, and try something different?"

Mother sat next to me, gently rocking Howard Junior as he slept, and sighed heavily, her eyes filled with concern. "I think you should try to talk to him again about what's going on," she said. "And if he wants to sell the farm, you both know that you'll always have a place at the restaurant."

Blowing my nose, I sat back against the soft cushions and said, "I don't understand why this is so hard."

"Marriage is hard sometimes, honey," Mother said gently. "You have to work at it, tend to it, and care for it, just like you do with that little garden of yours. Just let him know he has your love and support, and I'm sure he'll come around."

Feeling better, I left my parents' house and drove back home. As I bumped along the narrow dirt roads, I looked past the blurred scenery next to the car and out at the brilliant blue sky that touched upon fields of green and gold on the horizon. I thought of how much like life that was and realized that sometimes you have to look past what you're going through and know that beauty and peace wait just ahead.

When I arrived back at the farm, I noticed that the bank manager, Mr. Manson, was pulling in behind me. Climbing from the car, I smiled and waved, wondering why he'd come all the way out here to see us.

"Would you like something to drink?" I asked him as we walked inside.

"No, thank you," he shook his head, smiling politely.

Howard entered the room then, and I excused myself as I hurried upstairs to put Howard Junior down for his nap. When I came back downstairs, I overhead Mr. Manson state we were behind on our mortgage payments. My eyes wide, I stood and listened to Howard's terse, defensive responses, my stomach clenching with worry. Why were we behind on the payments? It just didn't make sense.

When Mr. Manson left, I stepped into Howard's office and asked him about it.

"You need to just let me worry about that," he snapped, his face red as he ran his fingers through his hair.

"But, Howard, I don't understand why we're behind on the payments," I persisted. "What have you been doing with the money?"

"That's none of your business."

"How can you say it's none of my business?" I questioned, my temper flaring. "I'm your wife, Howard."

"Yes, you are, but if I'd known what a nag you'd be, I probably wouldn't have married you," he stated angrily, slamming his hand down on his desk.

The blood left my face as I stared at Howard in shocked silence, my eyes wide with hurt. Through all the hard times we'd endured the last five months, he'd never spoken so harshly to me before.

"Well," I finally said, clearing my throat, "whether you like it or not, you did marry me, and I have a right to know what's going on."

"Nothing is going on, Vivian."

"May I see the bank book, then?"

Howard grew even angrier then and refused to show me, stating in loud tones that if I didn't trust him, I should just leave.

"Maybe I will," I said, tears forming in my eyes.

Just then, Howard Junior began to cry, and Howard said, "Yes, and maybe you should take him with you. All he does is cry."

I ran upstairs and into the baby's room, slamming the door behind me. Tears streamed down my cheeks as I picked up Howard Junior and cradled him against my chest, wondering once again what had happened to the man I'd married. What had gone wrong between us? I'd thought that whatever came our way, we'd be able to make it as long as we had each other, but now it seemed he no longer wanted me around. Had I failed somewhere along the way? Had I not tended to the marriage, like Mother said?

The baby hiccupped then, and I looked down at him, his sweet little face a blur through the tears. I bent my head and kissed his cheek, breathing in the soft scent of baby powder, and somehow felt comforted by this sweet, sixteen-pound bundle of joy. He couldn't speak to me, he couldn't offer words of encouragement, but he loved me and needed me, and right then, that was enough. I felt stronger and more at peace as I sat in the rocking chair and began to sing a soft lullaby, my words weak but my spirit willing to keep fighting for our family; if not for me, then for him.

Later that night, the telephone rang, piercing the stillness of the night like a siren. With a sigh, Howard threw back the covers and went downstairs to answer. I lay there silently, half-listening through the fog of sleep that still floated through my brain and wondered who would call at such a late hour. I could hear Howard talking downstairs, and a moment later, he returned and flipped on the lamp beside our bed.

"What's wrong?" I yawned, sitting up to watch as he got dressed.

"There's a problem down at the shipyard with one of our shipments," he answered, his voice clipped.

My stomach clenched at his tone, and I sighed inwardly; he apparently was still angry with me.

"Do you have to go now?" I asked, glancing at the clock. "It's almost two in the morning."

"I know what time it is, Vivian," he snapped, hurriedly slipping the brown leather belt through the loops on his pants. "And yes, I have to go now."

After he'd gone, I tried to clear my mind and go back to sleep, telling myself I didn't need to think about the argument and all of our problems right then. I'd just begun to relax when a sound from outside jarred me fully awake, and I lay there for a moment, listening. After a moment, I climbed out of bed and walked to the window to peer out, my eyes searching the shadows below. The moon moved from beneath a cloud just then and shone on the barn, illuminating the weathered wooden door as it

20

creaked back and forth in the breeze.

Howard must have forgotten to close it, I thought, sighing inwardly as I slipped into my robe and headed downstairs. My house slippers made a soft *swooshing* sound along the hardwood floors as I walked, and I slowed my gait when I neared the nursery, tiptoeing by so as not to awaken the baby. I heard the door bang against the side of the barn once again and hurried outside, the cool air causing me to shiver slightly.

Thick clouds moved over the moon as I crossed the yard, and I wrapped my arms tightly around my waist as everything grew inky black, a chill creeping up my spine. I lay the blame for my tense nerves on the argument with Howard and thought I'd better heat myself a glass of milk when I got back inside if I wanted to get any sleep tonight.

I finally reached the barn, the massive silhouette looming up before me like a giant, black mountain, and I quickly pushed the door closed, flipping the latch into place. Suddenly, I had the strange feeling that I wasn't alone, and I stood very still and quiet, my hand resting on the latch as I listened. An owl hooted in the distance and wind rustled through the trees, but I realized that something else was missing; the crickets and frogs were completely silent, and I knew it wasn't simply due to my presence. A chill raised the hair on the back of my neck, and I told myself to run into the house, but I was too afraid to move.

Just then, a twig snapped loudly nearby, and I felt the warmth of a body step up behind me. Before I could react, one hand clapped painfully over my mouth while the other gripped me firmly around the waist, and I was slammed back against a firm, broad chest.

"Don't fight, and I won't break your pretty little neck," a harsh voice whispered in my ear.

I felt the blood leave my face as my heart pounded loudly in my ears. I could hear footsteps and muffled voices coming from behind in the direction of the house, and I realized there was more than one man. Who were they, and what did they want? My mind swirled like a feather in the midst of a tornado, and I fought the feeling of panic that rose within my chest.

Just then, the man spun me around to face the house, and I felt my eyes widen in horror at the scene before me. Two men were dousing the house in what appeared to be gasoline, and before my mind could process what was happening, they lit a torch and flames quickly began shooting up the wooden frame, lighting up the dark sky like the rising of the sun at dawn.

My heart pounding, I turned into a wild woman, kicking and biting as hard as I could to get away. With a howl, the man released my mouth, his hand quickly moving to clutch my arm in a death grip.

"Why, I oughta…" he growled.

"My baby!" I screamed, trying to jerk my arm away. "My baby is in there!"

21

I heard the man gasp, and his grip loosened just enough for me to make a run towards the blazing inferno. I could feel the heat slapping against my skin, but I didn't care; all I could think of was saving my baby.

"I ain't heard nothin' about no baby," I heard one man exclaim. "Let's get out of here!"

Before I reached the door, I was jerked back and dragged across the yard. I cried and fought with all of my strength, but to no avail. I could hear the baby crying, and thought that my heart would break into a million pieces if I didn't get to him.

"We won't be responsible for two deaths," the man hissed.

"Let me go," I sobbed, still struggling. "Please."

The last thing I remember was hearing a siren off in the distance, and then a sudden, horrible pain in the back of my head as everything went black.

4

Vivian

Someone was patting the side of my face and calling my name, and I turned my head away and grunted, my eyes slowly drifting open to find the blurred face of my husband staring back at me.

"Vivian, what have you done?" He cried, and I stared blankly up at him, wondering why there was black dust all over his face.

"Step back, Mr. McCombs, and let me have a look," another voice said, and I suddenly realized there were many unusual sounds all around that were slowly making their way through the fog in my brain. Footsteps, men talking loudly, the crashing of timber, the roaring of an engine. What was going on?

"Can you sit up, Mrs. McCombs?" The man asked, kneeling down before me. He took my arm and gently helped me up, placing his hand on my back to support me when everything suddenly began to spin.

"Wha-what's happened?" I muttered, reaching up to hold my throbbing head.

I looked at the man kneeling before me and realized he was a police officer. I then glanced over his shoulder, and through the shadows, saw what remained of our home. It lay in a smoldering heap just a few yards away and I blinked, the memory of what happened flooding back into my head like a tidal wave.

"Oh, my God," I whispered. I tried to stand, to run to what was left of the house and find Howard Jr., but the officer stopped me.

"My baby, where is he?" I cried, my eyes pleading with both Howard's and the officer's as I fell back onto the ground.

Neither of the men would meet my gaze, and with a sick feeling in the pit of my stomach, I knew the truth.

I began to shake all over, violently and uncontrollably, like a reed in the wind. "No, no," I moaned, shaking my head as tears flooded my eyes and the most horrible pain I'd ever felt in my life rushed over me. I couldn't think or breathe and quickly turned my head to the side as the contents of my stomach came gushing out.

"Take a deep breath, Mrs. McCombs," the officer said, patting me gently on the back, but I could barely hear him over the ringing in my ears.

23

I felt hot and cold all at once, and lights began to flash before my eyes. I could hear the officer speaking, but couldn't understand a word he said. Slowly, everything faded away, and I melted to the ground in a dead faint.

When I awoke several hours later, I was lying in my old childhood room. Blinking away the fog in my eyes, I looked to my right to find my mother sitting next to me in a rocking chair, her chin touching her chest as she softly snored. I glanced around in confusion, taking in the familiar dressing table and mirror, chest of drawers, and pink floral wallpaper. I felt as if I'd stepped back in time somehow, and memories of my childhood suddenly swept through my muddled brain. I closed my eyes and could hear the giggling of schoolgirls during sleepovers, and smell the roses Mother grew in the backyard. I could see myself running barefoot through the grass at night during the summer, laughing and chasing lightning bugs, and I could feel the warmth of my father's arms as he held me in his lap and read to me. There was something so comforting about childhood, of being innocent and carefree, and I found myself wanting to hold on to those memories instead of facing life in the present. I didn't, however, know why.

"Honey, are you alright?"

Mother's soft voice brought me back to reality, and I opened my eyes to look at her. I could see worry written heavily upon her face, and noticed the swollen, red circles around her eyes.

"What's happened?" I whispered, my throat sore and dry. I knew in my heart that something was terribly wrong, but couldn't seem to grasp hold of the truth that lay just beyond my reach.

Suddenly, I thought I heard Howard Junior crying, and I sat up in bed to go to him. The room began to spin, and I clutched my pounding head as nausea swept over me. Mother stood and hurried to my side, her hands soft and cool as she gently stroked my back.

"It's going to be okay, honey," she said, her voice soft, but I didn't miss the pain that laced her words.

A sudden flash appeared before my eyes just then, and I saw our house engulfed in flames. I heard my screams mingling with the baby's, and I squeezed my eyes shut as everything came flooding back with painful, mind-shattering clarity. A sound like I'd never heard before passed my lips; it was the sound of deep, soul-wrenching pain, and I felt my body clench and tighten as I curled into a ball and sobbed.

I heard the bed creak and felt Mother's arms wrap tightly around me, pulling me against her chest as she rubbed my hair and gently rocked me back and forth. The pain in my chest was suffocating, and I gasped for air as hot tears poured continuously down my cheeks. It felt as if every nerve in my body was being pricked and prodded by needles, and the visions in my head of my sweet, precious baby that I would never see again were almost more than I could bear.

Mother and I sat there for nearly an hour, clinging to each other as our tears mingled together. I finally reached the point that I was so drained I could no longer cry, and with an aching heart, I laid back against the pillows, feeling empty and utterly depleted of life. Mother stood and wiped her eyes, her fingers trembling and face pale. She'd lost her only grandchild, and I knew that her heart was broken, not only for herself but also for me.

After a moment, she took a deep breath and asked if I could eat something, and I shook my head.

"No," I whispered, my throat raw and swollen; I didn't care if I ever ate again.

Without saying a word, Mother left the room and returned a few moments later with a cup of hot, chamomile tea.

"Please try to drink this, honey," she said, her eyes pleading. "I don't want you to become dehydrated."

Not wishing to worry her further, I forced the tea down, wondering for a moment if my queasy stomach could hold it.

"How long was I asleep?" I asked, handing the empty cup of tea to my mother as I leaned back against the pillows once again.

"About ten hours," she replied, sitting next to me to rub my arm gently. "After you fainted and they brought you here, we called Savannah and told her what happened. You were coming around and starting to cry again, and we asked if there was anything she could do. She called Zachary Holt, that young doctor she works with, and he came right over and gave you a sedative."

I had no recollection of that happening, and it gave me such a strange feeling. How could I have been so dazed that I had no memory of seeing the doctor and receiving a shot? I was, however, grateful that Mother made the call, as I knew I didn't have the presence of mind to make it myself. Savannah Rose Danes was my best friend and the closest thing I'd ever had to a sister, and she deserved to know what happened.

"Where is Howard?" I asked as I pushed myself back down between the covers, my head pounding and eyes heavy.

"He and your father have been helping to clear out what's left of the house," Mother replied, her voice soft as she tucked the quilt around my chin and shoulders.

I felt more tears prick the backs of my eyelids, and I heaved a deep, shuddering sigh. We'd lost our home and all of our belongings, but I'd gladly have given it all away if I could just hold my son in my arms once again.

"Get some rest, honey," Mother said, leaning over to kiss my forehead. Her presence alone comforted me, and it wasn't long before I drifted off into a deep sleep.

As I slept, my dreams were like visions from the past. I saw myself working alongside Howard to keep the farm going, my hands gaining calluses from tending to the animals, planting a garden, and growing our own vegetables. I canned jellies, preserves, marmalade, peas, carrots, and corn, and even found the time to do all the cooking, washing, and mending. Life was busy, but we were happy, and when I discovered I was pregnant, it filled me with an overwhelming sense of joy. In my dreams, I could clearly feel the tiny flutters growing in my stomach and hear Howard's laugh when I couldn't decide on a name for the baby and voiced my frustrations to him.

"If it's a boy, just name him after me," he said, smiling. "It'll be simpler that way."

"And if it's a girl?" I asked, my lips pursed.

He shrugged. "Name her after your mother."

Satisfied with both answers, I sat back in my chair and nodded, smiling as I gently rubbed my growing belly.

In a flash, my dreams jumped forward four months, and I found myself walking slowly around the nursery, rocking my tiny newborn baby as I softly sang a lullaby. Howard stood in the doorway watching us with a warm smile on his face, and when I gently placed the baby in the crib, Howard came over and kissed me. We stood there together with our arms around each other and watched as Howard Junior slept, and I leaned my head against my husband's shoulder, sighing with contentment.

That was the last happy memory Howard and I had together, and in my dreams, I watched him turn and walk away.

The next morning, I was awakened by the sound of the doorbell ringing. After a moment, my parents peeked into the room to tell me the police had arrived and wanted to know if I could answer a few questions. I nodded "yes" and pushed myself up into a sitting position, immediately grabbing my head as it spun wildly.

"Give us a moment, and then bring them here into her room," Mother told Father as she rushed to my side. "I don't think she's strong enough to get up just yet."

After forcing a few sips of water down my throat, Mother helped me straighten my hair and slip into a bed jacket. She'd just finished tying the strings at my neck when Father showed Howard and the police officer I'd seen before into the room.

"Hello, Mrs. McCombs, I'm Officer Wright," the police officer said, his shirt rumpled from a long night. He was quite tall, with dirty-blonde hair and a five o'clock shadow, and I gauged him to be around my age. "Are you able to answer a few questions?"

I nodded "yes", and Officer Wright pulled a small notepad and pencil from his pocket. "Can you tell me what happened night before last?" He asked, a lock of hair falling across his forehead.

Taking a deep breath, I slowly began to tell the story. I tried to block out the images as I spoke, knowing that I wouldn't be able to finish if I didn't. When I told Officer Wright about the three men, he looked surprised and asked if I'd recognized any of them.

"I couldn't see their faces," I said, squeezing my mother's fingers when she reached to take my hand. "It was too dark."

"Were any of their voices familiar to you?"

When I shook my head "no", Officer Wright hesitated a moment before he asked, "Mrs. McCombs, do you walk in your sleep?"

I blinked, caught off guard by the unexpected question. "Yes, sometimes," I replied hesitantly, glancing around the room. Everyone was staring at me with a strange look in their eyes, and through the fog in my brain, I felt a sense of unease creep over me.

"Your husband tells me you often have dreams that seem very real to you," Officer Wright continued, watching me closely. "For instance, he said you sometimes "see" things that aren't really there, like snakes in your bed or on the floor."

"That's true," I nodded, my cheeks flushing with embarrassment. I hurriedly added, "Once I wake up, however, I always realize it was just a dream. What...what does that have to do with anything, though?"

"Vivian," Howard spoke up, stepping closer to the bed, "there was an empty can of gasoline lying on the ground next to you. Officer Wright is having it checked for fingerprints, but there is little doubt of how that fire was started."

I stared at my husband, trying to process the meaning behind his words. "Howard, what are you saying?" I finally asked, my stomach clenching.

"I think you know what I'm saying," he replied, returning my stare.

"Howard, this is absurd," Mother interrupted, her voice strained. "There is absolutely no way Vivian could have done this, even if she was asleep!"

My eyes widened, and I felt the blood drain from my face. "You...you think *I* set that fire?" I asked my husband in a strangled whisper.

"There was no one there but you," he said, his voice rising defensively.

"But those men were there," I cried. "How else would you explain this bump on my head?"

"When you woke up and realized what you'd done, you fainted and hit your head," Howard stated matter-of-factly.

"That's not true!" I glanced frantically around the room, hoping that someone would believe me.

"I'm sure it isn't, honey," Mother said, gently patting my hand.

"Howard," Father stepped in, "don't you think you're going a bit too far?"

"Vivian," Howard sighed, ignoring my father, "you're making this very difficult. We know you can't help it, but you've suffered from this…problem…since you were a child. You need help."

"What do you mean by that?" I wanted to know, almost afraid to hear the answer.

Before Howard could respond, Officer Wright cleared his throat and said, "I don't think we need to continue this conversation right now. I have all the information I need, and Mrs. McCombs should get some rest. I'll be back in a couple of days."

I nodded and watched him go, feeling frustrated and completely helpless. How could Howard accuse me of such a thing? Mother gave me a hug and told me not to worry, and Father kissed me on the forehead. Howard walked out without another word, and after they'd all left the room and closed the door, I laid back against the pillows, exhausted as my mind spun in a thousand different directions. I *did* walk and talk in my sleep sometimes, and often suffered from very vivid dreams, but I always knew I'd been dreaming when I woke up. Didn't I?

I paused, my stomach sinking. No, I didn't. Howard was right; I did confuse my dreams with reality at times. But could I have really been dreaming the night before last?

No, I thought, shaking my head firmly. I couldn't make myself believe I was responsible for killing my baby. As I laid back down, however, and pulled the covers up to my chin, I fought against the tiny trickle of doubt that floated in the back of my mind.

5

Vivian

The next day, Savannah Rose came by the house to see me. She walked into my room and, without a word, sat on the edge of my bed and pulled me into a hug, her eyes filled with tears.

"I'm so sorry, Vivian," she whispered, gently rubbing my back as I cried against her shoulder.

I could still remember the look of worry in her eyes as she helped me deliver Howard Junior on that dark, stormy night five months ago. It was right in the middle of an incoming hurricane, the same one that destroyed our crops, and Savannah had stayed by my side the entire time. It was a long and difficult birth, and I'd thought that both myself and the baby were going to die, but we made it through and I could clearly remember the joy and happiness I'd felt when I held Howard Junior in my arms for the first time. How was it possible that only a few months later, and with just the flick of a hand, he was gone?

"I can't believe this has happened," I said in a broken voice as I pulled back to wipe my eyes. "What am I going to do, Savannah? And now the police think that I'm responsible."

Savannah looked at me with a startled expression, her dark eyes filled with confusion. "What?"

I explained what happened, and how Howard told the police I'd been sleepwalking and dreamed the whole thing. Once I'd finished, Savannah stood to her feet and began pacing around the room.

"I can't believe this," she exclaimed, her cheeks flushed. Spinning to look at me, she asked, "And the police actually believe him?"

"I'm afraid so," I nodded, sniffing. Lowering my voice, I added, "Many people don't understand this "problem" that I have, even my parents. I heard Father tell Mother once when I was young that there might be something wrong with me."

"Sleepwalking is something that many people don't understand," Savannah sighed, coming back to sit beside me. "But there's nothing wrong with you, and I don't believe for one second you were asleep and set fire to your own house."

"But what if my fingerprints are found on that gasoline can?"

29

"They won't be. Think about it, Viv," Savannah said, her gaze intense. "It's possible that you heard a noise outside and, in your sleep, went out to close the barn door. I also suppose that you could have dreamed those men into existence because you've always had a very vivid imagination and you can be a little jumpy, especially at night. But setting fire to your own house makes no sense, because what would be the reason behind it? It's not as if you were dreaming of lighting a candle or starting a fire in the fireplace. I just don't believe you did it, Viv, and I honestly can't understand how Howard could."

I paused, thinking over what Savannah had said. Often when one was acting out a dream, there was a reason or meaning behind it. For instance, I once dreamed that I was hungry and went into the kitchen to open a box of cookies. When I woke up the next morning, cookies were scattered all over the house. Savannah was right; I had no reason to set that fire. But still I wondered…

"Howard and I had a fight that night," I told Savannah. "What if, in my sleep, I was upset and trying to get back at him?"

"Do you really believe that?" Savannah asked, cocking an eyebrow.

I hesitated, finally heaving a sigh as I shook my head and said, "No, I don't."

"Don't worry, Viv," Savannah said, reaching out to squeeze my hand, "those men were real, and the police will realize soon enough that you're telling the truth."

I hoped she was right, but I could feel something dark and ominous creeping towards me; I just didn't know what.

The next day, I pushed myself from bed and, with Mother's help, dressed all in black and drove with my parents to the cemetery. Howard and I had agreed to have a simple graveside service for Howard Junior, and as I stood and listened to the preacher's voice drone on and on, I found I couldn't tear my eyes away from the tiny casket that held the remains of my son's body. Was this really happening? I found it hard to comprehend that I would never touch my baby's soft curls or hear his sweet little laugh ever again. I'd never hold his hands as he learned to walk, or teach him the ABC's. I wouldn't hear his first words or watch him later graduate from high school and possibly even college. A life had been extinguished in one horrific moment, and I suddenly knew that my heart would never be the same.

I reached out for Howard, needing to feel his strength and comfort, but he stepped away from me, his expression cold. As they lowered the casket into the ground, I didn't realize how hard I was crying until Father wrapped his arm around my waist and all but carried me from the cemetery. I didn't want my baby to be left behind in that deep, dark hole, and when we finally made it back home, I was almost delirious. Mother quickly mixed something in a glass and forced it down my throat, and in just a few moments, I drifted off into a fitful sleep, cradled in her arms like a child.

Two days later, Savannah Rose stopped by for another visit. I hadn't moved from my bed since Howard Junior's funeral, and I knew I must have looked utterly frightful by her expression when she stepped into my room and saw me.

"Honey, you need to go outside and get some fresh air," she told me, her eyes filled with concern. "Are you eating?"

I shook my head, my eyes filling with tears. "I'm not hungry."

Without a word, Savannah took a brush from the vanity and began running it gently through my dark, tangled tresses. After a moment, she said softly, "Do you remember the Christmas dance we had back in '40?"

"Yes," I slowly nodded my head, a slight smile pulling at my lips as I remembered. "You were watching everyone else dance because you didn't know how, and Connor surprised you with a kiss under the mistletoe."

"How did you know I couldn't dance?" Savannah gasped, leaning around to look at me.

Chuckling, I said, "Maxine and I both knew you couldn't dance, but don't worry; I don't think anyone else did."

"Neither of you ever told me that," Savannah said, a smile in her voice. After a moment, she sighed and said quietly, "I miss her so much."

Before I could reply, there was a loud knock on the front door, and moments later, Officer Wright, Howard, and another man carrying a black medical bag entered the room with my mother in tow. I immediately noticed the ashen look of worry on her face, and I felt my stomach clench.

"I'm sorry for the interruption, Mrs. McCombs," Officer Wright said, pausing in the doorway when he saw I had company.

Savannah began to step away, but I grabbed her hand and asked her to please stay. I didn't know what kind of news Officer Wright would bring, and I needed the extra support.

"It's fine, Officer Wright, please come in," I said, my stomach suddenly in knots. I hadn't seen Howard since the funeral, as he refused to stay here and had been sleeping in the barn on our property, and I didn't like the look on his face. His eyes were cool and distant, and his lips pressed into a firm, unwavering line.

"Mrs. McCombs, we got the results back from the gasoline can," Officer Wright said, stopping to clear his throat. My eyes were glued to his face, and I didn't realize that I was gripping Savannah's hand so tightly that her fingers were going numb. "We didn't find any fingerprints at all, which I'll admit is a little strange, but I'm sorry to say there is no evidence that

31

anyone else was there that night. We searched the grounds and found no footprints, and there were no tire marks that didn't match the tires on your husband's car."

"Maybe Howard set the fire then," Savannah stated, her eyebrow cocking defiantly when Howard turned to glare at her. I knew she was angry at him over the sleepwalking accusation, and I wasn't surprised at her attempt to defend me.

"I received a phone call, which the operator will confirm, that took me away from the house," Howard snapped, his cheeks growing red. "And Officer Wright saw me on the highway; I actually followed him to the house."

"How convenient," Savannah sniffed.

"Yes, he's telling the truth," Officer Wright nodded. Sighing, he turned back to me and said, "Mrs. McCombs, I'm going to have to write in my report that the circumstances surrounding the fire are suspicious, but since we don't have any evidence and we can't prove anything, there won't be a trial and the case will be closed. However, your husband has spoken with Dr. Abbott here and…well, I'll let him explain."

The physician stepped forward and, nodding stiffly at me, he said, "Mrs. McCombs, after talking with your husband and realizing what a dangerous threat your situation poses not only to yourself but to those around you, I have suggested that you be sent to a hospital where you can receive the proper care and treatment for your…problem."

I felt Savannah stiffen next to me, but I didn't quite understand what he meant. "A…hospital?" I asked hesitantly.

"Yes," Dr. Abbott nodded. "And your husband agrees."

"Where is this hospital, Doctor?" Savannah questioned, her fingers tightening around mine.

"Just a few hours from here in Martinsville."

Both Savannah and my mother gasped, and I felt the blood drain from my face. "No," I whispered, shaking my head. The Martinsville State Hospital, once known as the Idiot and Lunatic Asylum, was one of the largest and worst asylums in the country. I'd heard the horror stories of women sent away by their husbands over simple, ridiculous reasons that had absolutely nothing to do with true insanity; I also knew that they rarely ever returned home.

"You can't be serious," Savannah stated in a strangled tone.

"It will be for the best, Vivian," Howard said stiffly, barely meeting my gaze.

"Howard, please don't do this," Mother begged, stepping forward to touch his arm. "She can stay here with us if…if you don't want her with you."

"Hazel, she is my wife and I'm doing what I feel is best," Howard snapped, jerking his arm away from my mother.

32

"Best for whom?" Savannah asked, her jaw clenched.

Ignoring her, Howard turned to me and said, "Get dressed. The doctor has some people outside waiting to take you."

"Now?" I gasped, panic rising in my chest.

Howard nodded, and Doctor Abbott said, "The sooner we get you there, the sooner they can start your treatments, Mrs. McCombs. I'll go outside and tell the orderlies to come in and get you in a couple of minutes."

As he turned and walked from the room, I began to tremble all over. "I won't go," I said, my jaw clenched as I clutched the covers between my fingers.

"You have no choice," Howard stated coolly.

"I can't believe you're doing this," Savannah hissed, and I realized my mother was crying. "This isn't even legal; you must go before a judge first."

"I've already acquired the correct documents and signed all the papers, so that won't be necessary," Howard snapped, turning his glare on Savannah. "She's a danger to herself and everyone else."

"That's not true and you know it," Savannah returned angrily.

"Howard, please don't send her away," my mother pleaded, the desperation and pain in her voice breaking my heart.

His face set in stone, Howard marched over to my side and snatched the covers away. I jerked, my breaths coming in quick gasps, and I could feel a wave of hysteria clawing at my heels. As soon as he took hold of my arm and tried to pull me from the bed, something inside of me snapped, and I began to fight with every ounce of strength I could muster. I kicked and clawed, the room spinning like an out-of-control top. I was absolutely terrified of going to an asylum, and the only clear thought in my mind was to get away from him and find some place to hide.

From the corner of my eye, I saw two men in white uniforms step into the room. They immediately ran to Howard's aid and twisted my arms behind my back, quickly restraining me with a straight jacket. I jerked and thrashed, but it was to no avail; I could barely move in the bindingly tight contraption.

"Better keep her in that thing," Howard told them, wiping a stream of blood from his lip as he stepped back. "She's a wild one."

I couldn't think clearly as they pulled me from the room; all I could do was cry and beg them not to take me. My mother was sobbing uncontrollably, and I saw Savannah rush to her side and help her into a chair.

"Mother, Savannah, please help me!" I screamed as the men drug me outside. I was beginning to feel light-headed and knew that if I didn't calm down, I was going to faint, but I was beyond the point of any rational thought.

Just before they shoved me into the back of a black car, I heard Savannah call out and I turned, my hair falling wildly across my face as I searched frantically for my friend.

"At least let me tell her goodbye," Savannah begged, and with a sigh, the two men stopped and nodded.

Wrapping her arms around me, Savannah hugged me tightly. I was so dazed that I almost missed her hurried, whispered words, "Don't worry; Zachary has connections in Martinsville. I'll talk to him and see what we can do to help you."

The men pushed her away and shoved me into the back seat, slamming the door in my face and locking it. I sat there, trembling like a leaf, and watched through the window as Savannah waved goodbye, her expression that of agony as she stood on the sidewalk and watched us drive away.

6

Eva

February 1939

I walked alone through the thick, dark forest, my shoes softly crunching the snow beneath my feet and leaving a long trail of footprints in the path I'd forged. I breathed out slowly, my breath forming a white cloud around my face, and I stopped to watch as a rabbit hopped daintily through the snow just ahead. The forest was peaceful and quiet, as it always was, and I felt a tear of sorrow trickle down my cheek at having to say goodbye.

This place that was called "The Black Forest" was my home, it always had been, but everything was being turned upside down and Papa was afraid for us to stay. Hitler had been molding and shaping my beloved homeland to fit his evil agenda for years, and we could clearly see the effect his rule was taking on the German citizens. The gradual ostracizing and persecution of the Jews, the new laws and speeches, the burning of books…it was all leading to one end, and both of my parents knew it would be war.

My parents met while Father was deployed during World War I. My mother was sixteen and father nineteen, and Papa always said she was the most beautiful thing he'd ever seen. A year later, right after the war ended, they were married. They'd planned on moving back to my father's home in Savannah, Georgia after my mother graduated from school the following year, but circumstances kept preventing it. First, my grandmother became ill and they stayed to help care for her, then I was born and they didn't wish to travel with a small child. Four years later, my mother became pregnant once again, but miscarried and was very ill for quite some time. They finally decided to stay until I was grown and out of school.

I felt a dusting of fresh snow fall onto my shoulders from the branches above, and I looked up, barely able to see the sky through the thickness of the trees. This past winter had been a rough one, to say the least. With the shortage in coal, the nights were long and miserably cold, and I became very sick. One night in December as I was lying before the dying fire, shivering with fever, I heard Father tell my mother he was growing worried for our safety and that we needed to leave before things got any worse. Both of my mother's parents were gone, and since my father was an American citizen, it wasn't very difficult to gain passage for the three of us. So, the day to leave had finally arrived, but I wasn't ready to say goodbye, and was frightened about moving to a new country.

I could hear Papa calling to me then, his voice echoing off in the distance, and with a sigh, I turned and followed my own footprints back out of the forest. As I said goodbye to this shaded, branch-covered haven that had been my playhouse since I was a little girl, I wondered how it would be to live in America. Would my father's mother like me? I'd never met her before, but Papa spoke so fondly of both her and his childhood home that I couldn't help the niggling of curiosity in the back of my mind. Perhaps it wouldn't be so bad after all; perhaps I might even grow to love it, just as Papa did.

February 1944

Papa used to say perseverance will get you where you want to go in life, but sometimes, like today, I just wasn't so sure. Oh, Papa, if only you were still here, I thought, my heart clenching.

I stood outside of a local supermarket, twiddling my fingers as I tried to gather the courage to go in and ask to speak to the manager. My swollen feet throbbed painfully inside the old pair of high-heeled shoes I wore, and my stomach pinched with hunger. I'd been out every day this week, walking from this place to that, searching fruitlessly for a new job after losing the one I had at the laundromat when it closed. This would be my fifth stop today, and my body ached with exhaustion.

Taking a deep breath, I stepped inside and made my request, my voice trembling only slightly. The young man behind the counter nodded and hurried across the store, leaving me to stand there anxiously waiting for what felt like hours instead of mere minutes for the manager to emerge from the back. I often wondered why time seemed intentionally to stand still during moments of stress, and in my mind, I saw a mighty hand reach through the clouds to grasp hold of a giant clock, wrapping its fingers tightly around the ticking hands and forcing their movements to come to a stop.

After a moment, I finally saw the manager step from his office, and I held my breath. He walked towards me, stopping along the way to speak to a customer, and I swallowed nervously, my throat as dry as sandpaper. For a quiet, timid person such as myself, it was very hard to converse with total strangers and ask them for a job, but I was doing my best. My family needed me, bills were demanding to be paid, and I could feel desperation clawing at my heels. If only someone would say "yes" and give me a chance, I would feel that I could breathe again. So far, however, I wasn't having any luck.

The manager was approaching once again, and I rubbed my sweaty, trembling hands down the sides of my dress, my heart beginning to beat faster the closer he came.

"How can I help you?" He asked me in a direct, no-nonsense tone of voice.

I swallowed past the lump in my throat, my mind suddenly striking a blank as I struggled to remember the speech I'd recited over and over all week. When the manager raised an impatient, questioning eyebrow, I cleared my throat and said in a small voice, "I...I'm in search of a job, sir. Would you happen to have anything avai..."

"No, we're not hiring right now."

He turned and walked away, leaving me to stand there helplessly, my mouth still open in a muted question, as tears of frustration gathered in my eyes. Turning, I walked slowly back out onto the street, the bell jingling above the door with false cheerfulness as it closed behind me. I stood there for a moment, feeling lost and dejected, and noticed an empty storefront next to the supermarket. I stepped under the shadow of the awning and leaned against the boarded-up door, tears dripping down my cheeks and shoulders stooped in defeat as thoughts and worries filled my mind. If I couldn't find a job, what would happen to my family? To my precious little boy, who was relying on his only parent to take care of him? I wasn't qualified to do very much, I knew that, but I could learn. It seemed, however, that no one was willing to give me a chance.

For me, making a good first impression was difficult, especially when most people detected my German accent and took an immediate disliking to me. We were in the middle of a long and horrible war with Germany, and many of the people here had lost loved ones overseas, so I couldn't blame them for their dislike and prejudices.

Oh, what am I going to do?

I felt like a failure and was spiraling towards complete and utter despair when the sweet face of my little son suddenly flashed before my eyes, and I knew I couldn't quit. I had to keep trying; there was no other choice.

Wiping my eyes, I heaved a sigh and continued on my way, hoping that I would find something soon. About an hour later, I noticed the flashing lights of a restaurant's sign just up ahead, and as I neared the large, two-story building, it was all I could do to put one foot in front of the other. I stood across the street for a moment, so tired I could barely hold my head up, and whispered a soft, desperate prayer under my breath before I crossed the street.

Stepping inside of The Park Bench, the smell of food wafted past my nose and I stopped for a moment, savoring the heavenly scent as my stomach rumbled loudly. I hadn't had anything to eat since breakfast, and it was now almost supper time; I couldn't, however, afford to buy myself anything to eat. Noticing that the hostess was eyeing me curiously, I quickly smoothed down my light blonde hair and stepped up to her wooden stand, asking in a small, soft voice to speak with the manager.

I anxiously awaited as the girl went in search of a "Mr. Parker", trying not to dwell on the doubts running through my mind. This was one of my last resorts; if I didn't get this job, we would soon have no money with which to buy groceries. *Think positive*, I told myself. Wrapping my arms around my waist, I leaned against the wall, thankful for the quick moment of rest; I was so tired and hungry that my head was beginning to spin.

A moment later, a gray-haired man in his early fifties stepped from a side room and beckoned to me. My legs trembling, I followed him into the large office and sank down into the chair that sat opposite a beautiful mahogany desk, my hands clenched tightly in my lap.

"I'm Mr. Parker, the owner," the man said as he circled around the desk and sat down. "How can I help you?"

I hadn't expected to see the owner, and felt my eyes widen. "I…I'm Eva Beckett," I said, forcing myself to speak slowly in the hope that Mr. Parker wouldn't notice my accent. "I stopped by to ask if…if you have a job opening? I will do anything, Mr. Parker; cook, serve, wash dishes. Anything." I forced myself to stop, hoping that I hadn't sounded too pushy or desperate.

"Are you a good cook?" Mr. Parker asked, his dark eyes studying me closely.

Blinking in shock, as I'd expected him immediately to turn me down just as everyone else had, I nodded and said, "Yes, sir, I-I believe so. My grandmother, Mrs. Hamilton, has taught me how to make many of the popular Southern dishes."

Mr. Parker looked at me in surprise. "Mrs. Thomas Hamilton?" He asked.

"Yes, sir. Do…do you know her?"

"I knew her husband," he replied with a nod. "He and my father were quite good friends." Leaning back in his chair, Mr. Parker continued to study me curiously for a moment, and I had to force myself not to fidget. "Where are you from?" He finally asked.

Feeling my hopes crash onto the ground, I tried to maintain a neutral expression as I said softly, "Germany." When he raised his eyebrows, I quickly added, "But I've lived here for five years. My father, as you must know, was an American, and my husband is…was…as well. I'm a good cook and a hard worker, sir, if you'll just give me a chance." I stopped then, realizing that I sounded like I was pleading for my life in front of a jury. My cheeks flushing, I glanced down at the floor in embarrassment, knowing that my fate was doomed.

"Do you have any family besides your grandmother?" Mr. Parker asked.

"Just my mother and little son," I replied in a small voice.

"What of your husband and his family?"

"My husband died almost a year ago," I said softly, glancing up at Mr. Parker. "His family lives in Connecticut; they didn't approve of the marriage, so I've never met them."

Mr. Parker said nothing for a moment, and the silence was so loud it was deafening. Finally, he sighed and said, "Would you agree to a trial run of a week? My assistant chef had to leave last week, and I'm very much in need of a new one. Because of the war, I'm afraid that I can't pay much, but I send leftovers home with the staff, and you would have Sundays off."

I couldn't believe my ears. He was going to give me a chance? Swallowing past the lump in my throat, I nodded and said, "Yes, sir, a trial run will be just fine with me, as well as everything else you mentioned."

Pursing his lips, Mr. Parker stood and reached across the desk to shake my hand. My fingers trembled as he clutched them in his large hand, and as I turned to leave, I hesitated before saying quietly, "Thank you, Mr. Parker, for this opportunity. I appreciate it more than you know."

Mr. Parker walked around the desk and stood before me, his face solemn as he said, "I recently lost my grandson, and my daughter…" he stopped and cleared his throat. "Well, you're about her age. I can see that you need a job, and I wouldn't want your little son to suffer. Come in tomorrow morning at seven, and we'll see how the next week goes."

I walked slowly from the restaurant, two silent tears slipping down each cheek as I suddenly felt overwhelmed with emotion. My little family was on the verge of going hungry and losing everything, and I whispered a prayer of thanks that someone was finally willing to give me a chance. I only hoped that I'd do a good job and please Mr. Parker, as well as the rest of the staff.

It was almost dark by the time I turned down my street, and I waved to my neighbor who lived on the corner.

"Hello, Mr. Fernsby," I called out to the elderly gentleman.

"Hello, young lady," he replied, lifting his hand. "My grandson arrived today. Would you like to meet him?"

Smiling, I nodded and walked up to his house, ignoring the exhaustion that was weighing heavily on me. Mr. Fernsby had told me that his grandson would soon be moving in with him once he moved from Brunswick to work in the Savannah shipyards, and I was flattered that Mr. Fernsby wished to introduce us; many of our neighbors weren't so kind and accepting of my mother and me.

As I climbed the front porch steps, Mr. Fernsby opened his screen door and called out, "Kirk, come meet one of our neighbors."

A moment later, a man in his late twenties stepped out onto the porch. He wore a short sleeve, button-up shirt that was open and revealed a stained white t-shirt underneath. His hair was cut short, and his eyes were the same deep shade of brown that I imagine Mr. Fernsby's used to be. With a cocked brow, he looked at his grandfather and then at me, his face expressionless.

"H-hello," I said when Mr. Fernsby introduced us. "It's very nice to meet you."

Kirk immediately noticed my accent and, his eyes narrowing, he simply said, "You, too," and without another word, turned and walked back into the house.

The screen door slammed shut in my face and I flinched, my cheeks burning at the obvious rebuff. I'd expected Kirk to be as kind and friendly as his grandfather, but I really couldn't blame him for disliking me; he had, after all, lost his younger brother just a few months ago to the German Nazis.

Clearing his throat, Mr. Fernsby turned to me and said apologetically, "He's still a bit tired from the move. I'm sure once he's rested up, he'll be in a better mood."

Smiling kindly, I patted my neighbor on the arm and said, "I'm sure you're right."

After bidding Mr. Fernsby a good night, I walked on down to my house, hoping that Kirk would be good to his grandfather. The old gentleman had been living by himself since his wife died five years ago, and he needed someone to help look after him. He'd been lost since his wife's death, something I could well understand.

As I walked down the small driveway that led up to my house, my mind traveled back to the moment I'd received the news of my husband's death.

"Mr. Beckett was involved in a car accident," the police officer told me, hat in hand. "I'm sorry to say that he didn't make it."

I could still feel the wave of pain and shock flood over me as I'd stood frozen in place, my head spinning as the officer continued to explain what happened, his voice drifting further and further away. Paul was dead? I couldn't believe it, nor could I accept it to be true until I was forced to identify his body. The officer had to carry me from the room, as seeing the broken, lifeless body of my husband was just too much for me to handle.

I'd cried for days, unable to eat or sleep. All that kept running through my mind was the day we'd first met. I'd been in America for only a few months when he nearly ran me over with his car on Broughton Street; I still wasn't accustomed to the street laws and signs, and had stepped right out in front of him. He'd immediately stopped and jumped from the car, asking anxiously if I was okay; it didn't take long for him to ask me for a date.

"Let me take you to lunch," he'd said, his deep blue eyes sparkling as he smiled. "I won't take no for an answer. I did, after all, almost run you over, and I'd like to make it up to you."

I could still feel the rush of warmth flooding my cheeks over the invitation; I'd always been very shy and inhibited, and receiving the attention of such a fine-acting man led me to feel quite flustered and uncertain. Without saying a word, I'd simply nodded my head in agreement, smiling timidly up at him as he took my arm.

We went to a nearby diner and stayed until almost supper time, talking about our lives, hopes, and dreams. I'd always preferred to listen to others rather than do much talking myself, but Paul had such an easy way about him that I found myself opening up and feeling relaxed in his presence.

I discovered that he was from Connecticut, and in town on business. His family owned a very prosperous shipping company, and Paul said that they had many connections and ties in Savannah. When we finally left, he drove me home and asked to see me again during his next visit. Two months later, he stood on my doorstep with a bouquet of roses. The courtship was quick, lasting only three months after that, but neither of us needed more time to know that we wanted to get married. Paul had to go home one last time before the wedding, and when he returned, he had a suitcase in hand.

"I'm moving to Savannah and getting a new job," was all he would say.

After a bit of prodding, he finally told me of his parents' objections to the marriage.

"My whole life they've planned everything out for me, which included my marrying Jeannette Hollins," he said, sighing. "She comes from a very prosperous, wealthy family, and our union would have been quite the trophy for my parents to sit on top of the mantle. When I told them I was going to marry you, they said that they would disown me, but I don't care; they're not going to dictate my life anymore. If all that matters to them is money and titles, then good riddance."

I'd felt terrible about the whole thing, as I knew his parents objected because I was simply a poor immigrant girl with barely a high school education, and they wanted better for their son. I couldn't blame them, and when I tried to tell Paul that maybe we shouldn't get married after all, he wouldn't hear of it.

"I've never felt about anyone the way I feel about you," he'd assured me. "You're all I want in this world, and if I can't have you, then I'll have nothing."

We got married two weeks later, and spent a glorious honeymoon in Helen, Georgia. The charming little mountain town was so peaceful and beautiful that I almost hated to leave, and I simply adored the Bavarian-style buildings. Paul and I took picnic lunches up to the Anna Ruby and Raven Cliff waterfalls, and even went swimming a couple of times in the cold water. It was a sweet, precious memory that I would never forget.

Shortly after we were married, Paul and I discovered that I was expecting a baby, and we were both overcome with joy and excitement. I hadn't expected to become pregnant so soon, but I'd always dreamed of becoming a mother, and Paul was over the moon when Davey was born and he had a son. We'd both had such wonderful plans as new parents, of raising our son in a happy, healthy home, and it crushed me to think that Paul wouldn't be here to help carry them out. I still, however, wanted to do the very best that I could for our son, even if I would have to do it alone.

I sent a letter to my in-laws after Davey was born, hoping to patch things up, but they never responded, and Paul never spoke to them again. It broke my heart, but there was nothing that I could do, and when Paul died right after Davey's second birthday, I sent them the watch he'd said his father had given him, and a couple of pictures we'd taken during our marriage. I'd still yet to hear from them.

I pushed the gate open, walking up the driveway and onto the front porch, thoughts of Paul's deep blue eyes and contagious laugh still heavy on my mind. It had been a hard year without him; he'd been my strength and my rock, the one I'd come to lean on after Father's death, the one that I knew would always take care of us. Now that he was gone, I realized every time I looked into our son's face that it was now up to me to see about our family. I only hoped that after losing my first job, I wouldn't let them down again.

7

LEON

You've been doing such a wonderful job that I feel you are perfect for the position of Senior Loan Officer. Are you interested?"

Eyes wide, Leon (pronounced Lee-uhn) Danes stared at his employer in surprise. He'd been wishing for a promotion for months now, but had little hope of receiving one anytime soon with the war and many hardships everyone was facing. He could hardly believe his ears; all of his hard work was finally paying off.

"Yes," he nodded eagerly, standing to shake his boss's hand, "I would be thrilled to accept the position."

Later, as he drove home, Leon's mind was filled with plans for the future; with this promotion, he would finally be able to afford the payments on that little house he'd had his eye on. Ever since his father died when he was a teenager and his older brother, Connor, joined the Air Force, Leon had stayed home with their mother and done his best to help out. Right after college, he got a job at the local bank and had worked there ever since, adding part of his paycheck to the money Connor sent home every month to help pay the bills. He'd worked hard and was grateful for the promotion, but it hadn't always been easy. Life itself had, in fact, been quite hard.

When America joined the war in '41, he was unable to serve his country due to a mild case of asthma he'd suffered from since childhood, and so he'd thrown himself even harder into his work, striving to overcome feelings of failure as he watched Connor and many of his friends leave the city to join the fight, some never to return. When his brother was reported as missing in action, he realized that he was slipping into depression, something he'd never experienced before in his entire life. He'd always been so happy-go-lucky, with a ready smile and sunny disposition, but as everything around him began to change and crumble, he started changing, too. He slowly began to withdraw from his friends and family, keeping mostly to himself and saying little when around others. He was miserable, and hadn't known how to get out of the deep, dark pit he'd suddenly found himself buried in.

Then, during a huge lapse in judgement, he made a dreadful mistake. While walking Savannah Rose, one of his oldest and dearest friends, home from work one day, she commented on the change in his attitude and asked what was wrong. Like a spoiled child, he allowed all of the pain and bitterness he'd been feeling to flow freely from his mouth, never once stopping to realize that what she'd been through far outweighed his own problems. He said some incredibly stupid and insensitive things, they got into an argument, and before he knew what he was doing, he told her he loved her and then proceeded to force a kiss upon her.

She'd rejected him, and he couldn't blame her. It was a shameful thing to do, and if only he could turn back time, Leon would never have done such a thing. He'd known in his heart that Savannah didn't return his feelings, and in sharing the way he felt, he'd placed a mark on their friendship.

When his brother was discovered alive and returned home the following month, it didn't take long to realize that Connor was the one Savannah loved. When they announced their engagement shortly after, Leon found himself struggling with how to handle the news, and after the cheers and celebrating had died down, he excused himself and disappeared to the back porch, wishing to get his thoughts in order. It wasn't long before Connor sought him out, and Leon forced himself to offer a smile and "congratulations".

"I'm not going to beat around the bush, Leon," Connor had said, his gaze steady as he looked closely at his brother, "but I saw the expression on your face when we announced the engagement this evening, and I wanted to talk to you."

Stuffing his hands into his pockets, Connor took a deep breath and let it out with a loud whoosh before continuing. "I didn't realize until now how much you cared for Savannah Rose. I'm sorry, Leon, I never intended to hurt you. You're my brother and someone that I have a great deal of respect for, and I don't want this to create a wedge between us."

Leon had stood there in surprised silence, a wave of guilt and emotion suddenly washing over him at the selfish way he'd been acting. Connor was not only his brother, and a good one at that, but he had always been one of Leon's closest friends and someone he looked up to. Connor deserved the very best, and if he was the one that Savannah wanted, Leon decided right then and there that he would be happy for them.

After the conversation with Connor, it felt like a mighty weight was lifted off Leon's shoulders, and as the weeks passed by, the dark cloud of depression finally began to disappear. He grew accustomed to seeing Savannah and his brother together, and slowly realized that his feelings for his soon to be sister-in-law weren't what he'd originally thought them to be. He'd always had a crush on her, but when he started going through such a dark time, her presence, her familiarity and friendship was something he began to lean on, and he'd ended up magnifying those feelings into something greater than what they really were. Once he finally realized that, he began to feel at peace, and when he watched her and Connor get married three months later on a chilly afternoon in December, he'd felt genuinely happy for them. He didn't know if there was that certain special someone out there for him or not, but he was glad now that it hadn't worked out with him and Savannah.

Connor volunteered to go back overseas in January, and he shipped out two weeks later. It had been hard to tell him goodbye again, but everyone hoped and prayed he'd be back soon. Leon missed his brother a great deal, and he wished he were here now to share the good news with.

As Leon turned down the street he'd grown up on and parked in front of his mother's house, he pulled his thoughts from the past and quickly climbed from the car, eager to tell everyone about his promotion. It was the first Friday of the month, and as had recently become the habit, everyone was gathered at his mother's house for supper. Savannah would be there, as well as her aunt and uncle, Raymond and Debra Coleman; they'd been the Danes' next-door neighbors Leon's entire life and were both very dear friends.

As soon as Leon walked inside, his smile faded. From the tight, somber expressions on everyone's faces, he knew something was wrong, and it looked as if Savannah had been crying.

"What's going on?" He immediately wanted to know.

"Vivian has been sent to Martinsville," Leon's mother, Emma, told him.

Leon felt his eyes widen in shock. "What?" He cried. "Why?"

Taking a deep breath, Savannah slowly explained everything that had happened that morning. As she spoke, Leon found himself going from shock, to horror, and finally to anger.

"How could Howard do this to her?" He wanted to know as he paced around the room. Leon had known Vivian since high school and she didn't deserve this, especially after everything she'd been through. "Isn't there anything we can do to help her?"

"I'm going to talk to Zachary tomorrow," Savannah said, sighing. "He has connections with the asylum, so I'm hoping he can do something."

The meal was unusually quiet that evening, as everyone's minds were filled with heaviness over the news of Vivian, and after they'd all gone home, Leon realized he'd forgotten to share his good news.

8

THE SHADOW

He walked along the busy street, taking in the many sights, sounds, and smells. Shoppers hurried all around, some stopping to look in store windows filled with various items of clothing, while others went inside to buy, and a few peddlers dotted the sidewalk. Car engines, the occasional honking horn, excited chatter, and the clicking of heels against the pavement met his ears, and when a young man jumped out to take his picture, he quickly turned his head and pushed past. With a scowl, he crossed the street and pulled the collar of his trench coat closer around his face, taking a deep breath of the cool, salty air.

It was Saturday, and a busy day for Savannah. He had his own set of purchases folded inside of the paper bag he carried and was glad that he only had one more stop to make.

The bell jingled above the door of the five and dime store as he walked inside, and after only a moment of searching, he found exactly what he'd been looking for.

"I'd like to buy this," he told the man at the counter as he handed him the little pocket knife.

"That'll be ten cents," the man said, folding a bit of brown paper around the knife.

He threw the money onto the counter, took the knife, and headed back out to the street with a satisfied smile. Everything was in order now, and he could shortly begin with his plan.

9

Vivian

After being dragged from my parents' home, I was taken to the train station where the orderlies led me to a private box car. The other passengers glanced at us curiously as we passed, their eyes widening when they noticed the straight jacket. Once inside the private car, the orderlies took the jacket off, and for the entire two-hour ride, I sat shivering in the seat, my nerves so taunt that I was on the verge of hyperventilating.

When we arrived in Martinsville, I was once again led to an awaiting car, my eyes darting back and forth but my brain hardly able to focus on the sights and sounds around me. We drove out of the city and into the country, the passing pine and pecan trees whirling by in rapid blurs of color.

Twenty minutes later, we drove through a large, wrought-iron gate with a sign that read "Martinsville State Hospital". I turned in my seat and watched as the gate closed behind us, shutting us in like a prison, and it felt to me like the entire world was being closed off.

There were many buildings of various shapes and sizes scattered all around the property, most with bars on the windows. The hospital grounds were huge, like a city in itself; nurses and patients walked about, and I spotted several men out working in the fields as we passed, hoeing and planting. I stared out from the back seat of the car, my stomach churning as I clenched my hands nervously together in my lap, hardly able to believe this was really happening.

We finally pulled up in front of a large, one-story building and went inside. I soon discovered that this was the reception ward, and as the two orderlies talked with the lady at the front desk and handed her my papers, I looked around the huge "waiting room", quickly realizing I wasn't the only one brought in that day; there were at least ten other people sitting in the chairs that lined the walls. One man was talking to himself and laughing, an older lady cried and moaned pitifully, two gentlemen were sitting in the corner playing chess, and the others were scattered about the rest of the room.

One orderly took my arm, led me to an empty chair, and told me to wait.

The young woman I sat beside glanced up from the magazine she was reading and eyed me curiously for a moment.

"You look terrified," she stated matter-of-factly.

"I...I suppose that's because I am," I stuttered, uncertain of what to say to this woman. She was quite attractive and very well put together, with not one hair out of place, and although she seemed friendly enough, I was afraid to trust anyone.

Suddenly, a young man who'd been sitting quietly in the far corner began to shriek, the ear-piercing sound echoing loudly throughout the room as he hit the back of his head against the wall over and over with a resounding thud. Eyes wide, I watched as two male nurses hurried from a room to my left and grabbed the boy roughly under his arms, dragging him from the room and slamming the door behind them. About thirty seconds later, the muffled, echoed screams from the other room suddenly stopped.

"Better hold yourself together or they'll do the same to you," the girl said to me, shaking her head.

"Do what?" I asked, almost afraid to voice the question.

"Electroshock therapy," she replied. "They do it as a form of treatment, as well as when patients get out of hand or become too hysterical. They strap you to a table and hook you to a machine that sends electric currents through your brain and causes you to go into convulsions; it's very effective in calming people down. I just hope they remembered to put something in that poor boy's mouth or he may no longer have a tongue."

I stared at the woman in complete horror, my eyes going back to the door of the room they'd taken the boy into. How could this possibly be happening? Surely, I was dreaming.

"What... what happens after the treatment?" I asked in a choked voice.

"It works very well for some people, but often they lose their memory, which can be both good and bad," she replied, shrugging. "Sometimes, if it's done too much, it can damage the brain and the patient becomes almost like a zombie. Unfortunately, though, they don't have any say in the matter."

"It ain't as bad as the drug, though," a middle-aged woman from across the room spoke up after apparently overhearing our conversation.

"Drug?" the woman beside me asked curiously.

"Yep," the other patient nodded, "it was before the electric shock. They'd give you a shot that would send you into such convulsions you'd sometimes break your back."

Determined to keep calm and not allow myself to become hysterical, I cleared my throat and said, "You...you both seem to know a lot about what they do here."

"Yeah, this is my second visit," the woman beside me said with a sniff, while the other lady ignored my statement altogether.

I turned to look at the young woman, blinking in surprise. "Oh?"

"Yes, apparently I have some sort of hysterical personality disorder or something," she rolled her eyes, laughing loudly. "I'm supposed to be cured, but my husband seems to think otherwise. He says I'm not a good wife and that I like the attention of other men too much."

Before I could comment, one of the male nurses came out to retrieve her. With a dazzling smile, she stood and said in a low, smooth voice, "Hello, Carl, have you missed me?" and moved to stand closer to him.

Without a word, and his stony expression never changing, "Carl" motioned for her to go into the room. With an annoyed sigh over his lack of response, the young woman sashayed past him, her tight skirt emphasizing the movement of her hips.

I sat in that waiting room for over five hours, the clock on the wall ticking unusually loud. They brought in more patients, and I was beginning to think I would faint from hunger when I was finally called back to be evaluated by a doctor. I was led into a small room and told to sit on the cold, metal table which rested in the center of the room with a bright light overhead.

After a silent, middle-aged doctor had drawn a few vials of blood, listened to my heart, and took my blood pressure, he stepped back to jot down some notes and, taking a deep breath, I cleared my throat and said, "I'm not crazy, Doctor."

"I'm sure you're not," he stated drolly, as if he'd heard those words many times before.

He then checked my temperature and shone a bright light into my eyes. After scribbling a bit more in his notepad, he proceeded to question me about the sleepwalking. "How long have you suffered from this condition?"

"Ever since I can remember," I replied in a low voice. I hated I had no control over something that I did involuntarily in my sleep, something that others called a "condition". It made me feel helpless and hopeless, and like there was something very much wrong with me.

"Have you ever caused yourself or anyone else physical harm during these episodes?"

"No," I shook my head.

"And you say you weren't asleep the night your home was set on fire?"

"No, I was awake," I said with assurance.

"Have you been unhappy in your marriage?"

I blinked, caught off guard by the question. "N-no," I stammered, glancing away. "My marriage isn't perfect and we've had a few problems lately, but I haven't been unhappy."

"What sort of problems have you and your husband been having?"

I hesitated, uncertain of how much information I should share. "My... husband has been acting strange the last few months, and I recently found out that he hasn't been paying our mortgage. When I tried to ask him about

49

it, he refused to tell me what he's done with the money."

"So, you argued?"

"Yes," I nodded, wishing I could see the notes he was taking.

"Did you wish to hurt yourself or your husband after the argument?"

"No, of course not," I replied, shaking my head.

The doctor continued to take notes, showing no reaction whatsoever to my responses.

"How did you feel about being a mother, Mrs. McCombs?" He asked after a moment, his gaze steady as he watched me over the spectacles that rested on the end of his nose. "Tired? Trapped?"

"No," I stated firmly, my voice trembling a bit. "I love being a mother and I love...loved my son. He was the best thing that's ever happened to me."

"Before your son died, were you ever depressed? Did you cry often?"

I could feel pricks of frustration nagging at my already taunt nerves, and I had to force myself not to burst into tears. It was obvious this man, along with my husband and the police back home, believed I'd either purposefully or subconsciously set that fire and killed my son due to depression or some sort of mental breakdown. The fact that I couldn't prove my innocence, at least not while I was trapped in this place, was the most frustrating of all.

"I cried sometimes," I finally whispered, "but only when my husband and I argued."

The doctor studied me silently for a moment, and I forced myself to meet his gaze and not squirm under the scrutiny. Finally, after what seemed like hours, he nodded and said, "That's all for now, Mrs. McCombs. We'll get you settled in and talk more later."

I was sent back to the waiting room for another hour until a nurse finally came inside and told me to follow her. Utterly exhausted, both physically and mentally, I walked slowly outside and followed the woman down a path until we reached a three-story brick building with lights shining from the windows. I was taken inside and assigned to "Ward F36", and as I followed yet another nurse to said ward, I noticed there were many rooms with small windows in the doors. I glanced through one of those windows as we passed by and caught sight of a barren, isolated room with a mattress lying in the middle of the floor. I almost missed the woman who sat huddled in the far, right-hand corner, her eyes cast downward in a sightless stare as she rocked back and forth on her heels. The sight made me shiver, and I wrapped my arms tightly around my waist as I hurried after the nurse.

After traveling to the second floor, I was shown into a large room with about twenty-five beds lining the walls and a nurse's station in the middle. I was immediately struck by the stench of unwashed bodies and drew back, trying not to gag as I quickly took in my surroundings. Most of the beds were unmade, trash and dirt were scattered about the floor, and women of various ages milled about, some talking while others kept to themselves. I was taken to a bed that had a single nightgown folded on top of the pillow, along with one pair of underclothes.

"Supper is in an hour," the nurse said after giving me a rundown of the rules. "Just follow the others when you hear the bell ring."

I sank down onto the small cot that now belonged to me and looked around, my mind barely able to comprehend that this was all really happening.

"Well, well, looky here," a raspy voice loudly spoke out and I glanced up, a feeling of wariness coming over me as a woman with blonde, frizzy hair stepped toward me, a smirk on her face. "What's your name, honey? We need to welcome you right and proper, don't we girls?"

The other women in the room cackled out, eyeing me like a pack of wolves. Swallowing, I said, "My name is Vivian. Vivian McCombs."

"Such a pretty name for a pretty lady," the woman said, reaching out to run a finger down the side of my face.

Jerking away, I stood up and faced the woman, my legs trembling as I hissed, "Don't touch me."

The woman laughed, her teeth yellow and cracked, and I had to force myself not to cringe.

"Not very nice, are you?" She asked cynically. Suddenly, the smirk slipped away and a hard look came over her face. Her eyes glinting, she stepped closer and said in a low, daunting voice, "You'd better come off your little high horse, honey, or you'll find yourself in a real bad spot."

Before I could reply, another voice called out, "That's enough, Doris. Leave the girl alone."

Snickering, Doris turned and sauntered away, and I realized my rescuer was the night attendant. The two women eyed one another for a moment, and I didn't fail to notice the look of warning the attendant gave Doris. With a clenched jaw, Doris walked across the room and sat on her bed.

I slowly sank back down onto my cot, trembling all over. How was I ever going to survive in this place if I couldn't make it through the first night?

"Hello," a voice from behind spoke softly, and I turned to see a young woman of about nineteen or twenty smiling politely at me. She was terribly thin with dark rings around her eyes, and I immediately noticed the look of hopeful yearning on her face, as if she'd been waiting a long time for someone to come along and befriend her.

"Hello," I replied hesitantly, trying to keep my voice from shaking.

"I'm Maisie," she said, tucking a strand of long, chestnut brown hair behind one ear. "Your name is Vivian?"

"Yes," I nodded.

"That's a pretty name," she stated kindly. "Are you from around here?"

"No," I replied, shaking my head, "I'm from Savannah."

"I'm from Atlanta," she said, coming closer to sit down on the bed next to me. She had light brown eyes, high, prominent cheekbones, and her skin was very pale. Lowering her voice, she said, "Try to stay away from Doris. She picks on every newcomer, and I don't think she liked the way you stood up to her."

"Okay," I agreed, sighing; I'd only just arrived and already made an enemy. "How long have you been here, Maisie?"

"About five months," she said softly. "Would you mind if I ask why you're here?"

As if I'd known her my whole life, I spilled out my entire story to Maisie, tears slowly seeping down my cheeks as I relived each and every horrible memory. She reached out and gently took my hand, her eyes filled with compassion.

"I am so sorry, Vivian," she said once I was finished. "It's obvious you didn't set that fire, and it honestly seems to me that your husband may know more about it than he's letting on. I have no doubt the police will figure it all out, though, and you'll be out of here in no time."

The supper bell rang then, and Maisie took my hand and told me to follow her lead. I'd been starving until then, but as I walked along beside my new friend, I suddenly felt sick to my stomach. Was she right about Howard? I hadn't thought about it until she mentioned it, but he *had* been acting strange, as if he'd wanted to get rid of me as quickly as possible. Were Maisie's suspicions about my husband correct? If that were the case, then he knew those men I saw were real and that they were responsible for setting the fire that killed our son. But why would he lie and cover up for them?

I followed Maisie and the rest of the women downstairs to join the other patients in a large, open room that smelled of food and soured mops. Several long dinner tables with benches filled most of the space, and as our supper was already waiting for us, everyone piled onto the benches and began eating.

The food, which consisted of chicken, boiled potatoes, a vegetable, and a slice of fruit, was bland but filling. As soon as I started eating, the woman across from me began to talk to herself and laugh. I glanced up at her, my brow furrowing as I watched her pick through the food on her plate and drop bits of it onto the floor.

"Don't bother saying anything to her," Maisie whispered when she noticed where my attention was directed. "She does this at every meal, and they always make her clean it up afterwards."

I gazed around the room, my food forgotten as I took everything in. Some women ate properly, wiping their mouths with a napkin after every bite and keeping their elbows off the table. The others, however, made my stomach turn; some ate with their fingers, some dripped food all over their chin and clothes, and others that looked deathly thin and frail sat with their arms folded, refusing to eat at all.

After supper, they directed us to return to our ward. I sat on my bed across from Maisie and asked, "Why are you here, Maisie? If you don't mind my asking."

"Not at all," she shook her head. "I have epilepsy, and my family thought that perhaps I could find some help here. My mother didn't want me to leave, but Father insisted."

"Is there anything they can do for the epilepsy?" I asked.

"I don't know," Maisie shrugged, sighing. "Although I don't have attacks very often anymore, I've been this way since I was a child. I was hoping that I'd finally grown out of them, but when my grandmother died suddenly five months ago, I became very upset and had an attack. The doctor back home doesn't know how to treat me, and the only doctor I've seen since my arrival here was the one that examined me when I arrived. From what I understand, they're very short staffed because of the war, and there is only one physician per six hundred or more patients. Who knows if I'll ever get treated, and honestly, that's fine with me."

I nodded in understanding, my mind going back to the screaming boy in the reception ward earlier.

That night, after the lights were out and everyone was settled in their beds, I lay perfectly still, terrified of going to sleep as I listened to the soft snores and random moans that drifted through the darkness. I knew from experience that, after a stressful day, I was more apt to have a nightmare and walk in my sleep, and I didn't want the night-watch nurse to catch me and make a note of it. I was also terrified of getting murdered in my sleep, and although Maisie assured me they kept the more dangerous patients in different, secluded rooms, I couldn't seem to stop jumping at every sound, especially after my run in with Doris.

Turning over, I sighed softly, the heaviness of my situation weighing down on me like an enormous boulder. How could Howard have done this to me? He'd been so loveable and charming during our courtship and early months of marriage; I could remember all the times he'd brought me flowers and written me sweet little love notes. Where had that man disappeared to, and how had he come to hate me so? It hurt, this feeling of betrayal and abandonment, and I wondered if Howard intended to leave me here forever, all alone and forgotten.

Finally, well after midnight, I gave in to the exhaustion that clung to my body and drifted off to sleep. I lay in one position all night, utterly still and quiet, but my dreams were filled with visions of my sweet baby, and when I woke up once around three a.m., I was crying hot, silent tears.

The next morning, at seven a.m. sharp, the ringing of the bell jerked me

53

awake, and the nurse announced that it was time to wake up.

"Good morning," the woman who slept in the bed to my left greeted me with a bright smile.

"Good morning," I responded with a hesitant smile of my own.

I saw that her gaze was drawn to the table that separated our beds and, having noticed the ribbon I'd taken from my hair and placed on the table the night before, her eyes grew bright as she pointed to it.

"That's pretty," she said. Her voice was high-pitched, like that of a child, and yet she looked to be in her early thirties. She sat on the edge of her bed and swung her feet back and forth, constantly twirling the end of her greasy blonde hair around her forefinger. I also noticed a baby doll half-buried beneath the covers that she apparently slept with. "I never had nothin' so pretty."

"Thank you," I said kindly. "I'm Vivian. What is your name?"

"My name is Ruby," she replied, bouncing up from her bed to take my hand. "You're new, so I'll show you where the ladies' room is."

Ruby all but dragged me from the room in the same direction where everyone else was going. The ladies' room, which consisted of five toilets, a row of sinks and three showers, was even more filthy than the ward where we slept. Trying to breathe through my mouth, I waited for my turn to relieve myself and change back into my dress, cringing as the women behind me kept pushing me to move forward. Some women stood at the sinks washing their faces while the others didn't even bother; they just stood off to the side with their arms crossed, a blank, glazed-over expression on their faces. I also noticed that many of the women didn't even change from their stained, raggedy nightgowns.

"Good morning," Maisie said with a smile as she passed by on her way out. "I'll save you a seat beside me at breakfast."

After the morning meal, everyone had to go back to their wards so the workers could clean up the breakfast dishes. I took a lukewarm shower, as there was hardly any hot water, pinned my hair back, and brushed my teeth with one of the many toothbrushes that lined the sinks. Afterwards, I asked Maisie if we could go outside for a walk.

"Leaving the building is an earned privilege," she told me. "Once you're here for a while and if you're well-behaved, they'll start allowing you certain privileges such as more freedom, occupational therapy, etcetera. Until then, we're forced to stay locked inside and entertain ourselves."

Before I could reply, a woman suddenly screamed, and I spun around just in time to see a large mouse running across the floor. With a shriek, I jumped onto my bed, watching in disbelief as several of the women chased after it, laughing and squealing as if chasing a ball or some toy. Before they could catch their prize, however, the poor, frightened creature ran between the beds and disappeared through a small hole in the wall. Some women moaned with irritation at losing the primary object of their game,

54

while others shrugged and walked away. Sighing, I sank down onto my bed, wondering what else would happen in this place that would take me by surprise.

For the rest of the day, we roamed around the building with nothing to do. Rocking chairs were scattered about while thin, frail women rocked endlessly back and forth with blank stares on their faces. Most were barefoot and looked as if they hadn't cleaned themselves in weeks, and when I asked Maisie about it, she said, "A lot of these women refuse to take showers, and some of them are even afraid of water."

After lunch, I went over to one of the barred windows and gazed out, longing to be outside. Maisie joined me after a moment, and I pointed out the patients who were roaming freely about the grounds.

"Those are the lucky, privileged ones, I assume?" I asked.

"Yes," she nodded, the sunlight glinting off of her light brown eyes.

"Do any of them ever try to escape?"

"I don't think so, at least not very often. There aren't enough attendants to keep a close eye on everyone, but we're fenced in with guards at every gate, so there's not much hope of escape. One patient managed it a few months ago; I heard they found his body in the swamp three days after his escape."

Eyes wide, I looked at Maisie and she said with a shrug, "Although it was rumored that he was murdered, no one knows the details of how he died."

Shaking my head, I peered to my right at the building across from us and blinked, a bit taken aback when I noticed the windows were filled with the thin, ghostly silhouettes of other patients staring back at me. They didn't wave or smile, they simply stared, their faces void of emotion and full of emptiness.

When I asked Maisie if they were locked inside, as well, she replied, "Yes, but those patients are in isolation rooms because they're a danger to themselves and others."

I glanced back then, wanting to cry at the hopelessness I saw in the eyes that gazed back at me, and I suddenly felt an enormous wave of compassion for all the people locked inside of these walls. I knew that many of the medical terms used for the mentally ill really existed, but how many of these people were simply like Maisie and me? Not insane, just possessing a condition or health problem that others didn't understand or know how to treat. How many were sent away by family members who, in shame, would later pretend they'd never even existed?

"That building there through the trees," Maisie said, interrupting my thoughts as she pointed, "is the main medical center. They also have a chapel where they hold weekly services, and a gymnasium for dances."

"They hold dances here?" I asked in surprise.

"They do," Maisie nodded, "but not everyone may attend. It's so odd here, Vivian. This place is like a town in itself. There are about 10,000 patients here, and several hundred employees."

After a moment, Maisie announced she was going to lie down until the lunch bell rang, and I turned to follow her, accidentally bumping into a woman who stood behind me.

"I'm sorry," I apologized, glancing up at the woman.

When our eyes met, the severe look of hatred in her gaze startled me, and I instinctively took a step back.

"You!" she screamed, pointing a finger at me. "You're the one!"

Confused, I began backing away from the woman, noticing that the chatter in the room hadn't ceased a bit, as if everyone was used to this sort of behavior.

With what sounded like a fierce growl, the woman began charging at me, flailing her arms and shouting that I was trying to kill her.

"She's helping them," she cried, her eyes wild as she again pointed at me. "The shadows are trying to kill me, and she's helping them!"

My heart pounding, I leaped backwards, slamming painfully into the wall as the other patients jumped out of the woman's path, their expressions wary but not surprised. Within seconds, the woman was upon me, her hands tense as they reached out to wrap around my neck. She was much larger than I, her fingernails long and sharp like that of a falcon, and her black hair flew wildly about in tangled, frizzy curls. Before I could react, Maisie grabbed my arm and jerked me away just as two male attendants appeared seemingly out of nowhere and tackled the woman to the ground. They quickly restrained the overwrought patient and dragged her, kicking and screaming, from the room.

As the echoes of the woman's shouts died down, everyone seemed to shrug the incident off and returned to their previous activities, while I stood rooted in place, pale and shaken.

"Are you okay?" Maisie asked, her voice gentle as she touched my shoulder.

"What…what happened?" I asked, my throat as dry as sandpaper.

"She's schizophrenic," Maisie explained. "People like that see and hear things that don't exist, and sometimes they become hysterical and violent. You'll learn soon enough who to stay away from, but you won't have to worry about her for a while; she'll be placed back into isolation after this incident."

As I followed Maisie back to our ward, I was trembling all over. I felt the sting of hot tears pressing against the backs of my eyes, but forced them to stay down. I was too afraid of showing any sign of emotion, but in that moment, I wanted to be home more than anything, where I felt safe and things were normal. I was quickly starting to wonder, however, if life would ever be normal again, and realized that in order to survive in this place, I would have to toughen up and be prepared to protect myself at any given time.

10

Eva

Affter my trial week at The Park Bench was complete, Mr. Parker announced I was officially hired. I was thrilled, to say the least, and had to force myself not to burst into tears of gratitude. Instead, I smiled widely and thanked him, my heart squeezing inside my chest with thankfulness. If not for this job, I don't know what I would have done.

I hurried home, my steps lighter than they'd been in a long time, and not even the frown I received from Kirk could dampen my spirits for long. He was in his grandfather's front yard cutting some shrubs when I passed, and the way he stopped and glared at me was a bit unnerving, but I refused to allow him to dishearten me. Instead, I simply smiled at him as I passed and hurried on my way.

I was so eager to tell my family the good news, I almost didn't notice that the "For Sale" sign which had been resting in front of the house next to mine was gone.

I hope whoever bought it will be good neighbors, I thought as I hurried inside.

"Mommy!"

The sound of the sweet little voice and toddling of footsteps rushing through the house brought a smile to my lips, and I held out my arms in anticipation as my three-year-old son, Davey, ran to me as fast as his chubby little legs could carry him. Launching himself into my waiting arms, Davey laughed with the boisterous glee of a child and wrapped his little hands around my neck, squeezing tightly.

David Paul Beckett was the light of my life. He looked almost identical to me, with his white-blonde hair and soft blue eyes, but now and then I would see a glimpse of his father in a certain look or expression, and it would catch me so off guard that all I could do was pull him into my arms and hold him close. It broke my heart that he would never remember his father, but I did my best to talk about Paul and show Davey pictures of him often. I also had a picture of Paul's parents, and his younger brother, Asher, that I kept in a special photo album for Davey. He didn't remember Asher, as it had been nearly two years since he'd seen him, but I was suddenly reminded of the first time we met...

Paul and I had just returned from our honeymoon a few days prior, and I

58

was in the kitchen baking a cake when the doorbell rang. I hurried through the house and opened the front door, my eyes flying open wide as I gasped and said in a breathless voice, "Oh, my, you must be Paul's brother!"

He'd stared at me for a moment, a slow smile spreading across his handsome face. "Yes," he'd finally said, chuckling, "I'm Asher. You must be Eva."

"Ash!" Paul had cried from behind, and I quickly jumped out of the way as he rushed past to pull his brother into a bear hug. "What are you doing here?"

Slapping Paul on the back, Asher pulled away and grinned at his brother. "Well, I came to talk you out of this crazy marriage," he'd said, "but after meeting your lovely wife, I see now why you can't live without her."

Asher stayed with us for nearly a month. I'd always wanted to have a sibling, and seeing Paul and his brother together was very special. When he left, I was sad to see him go, but he came back to visit many more times until he joined the military in '42 right after Pearl Harbor. He wrote to us faithfully until one day his letters just stopped. Paul received a telegram from his cousin shortly after telling us that Asher was missing in action and presumed dead. Paul's heart was broken, and I finally understood how it felt to grieve for a sibling.

Shaking my head, I pulled myself back to the present and smiled, kissing Davey on the cheek as we walked toward the kitchen. "How's my boy today?" I asked, wiping a couple of what appeared to be cookie crumbs from his chin.

"Good," he replied, reaching up to twirl a strand of my hair around his finger. "I eated all my peas," he added proudly, his words a bit garbled but clear enough for me to understand.

"That's wonderful," I congratulated him, stepping into the kitchen to find my mother and grandmother standing at the stove making supper.

"Eva, I'm glad you're home," my mother greeted me, glancing over her shoulder with a smile.

"Hello, Mutter," I said, using the German word for "mother" as I kissed her on the cheek.

"Honey, you must be so tired," Nana spoke up, her ever-watchful eyes scanning my face. "Sit down and we'll bring you a plate when it's ready."

Nana was my father's mother. I met her for the first time when we moved here five years ago, and was instantly struck by her soft, genteel manner. Daddy said that's how a true Southern lady acted, and I instantly fell in love with her kind smile and big heart. Her one goal in life was to see to her family's needs and comforts, and ever since I got a job, she went out of her way to pamper me. After Paul died, she sold her house and both she and Mutter moved in with me, and I was so grateful for their company.

"Yes, ma'am," I smiled at Nana, adding, "but before I do, I have some good news." When both women turned to look at me expectantly, I told them I got the job.

"Das ist wundervoll!" Mutter cried. Although she had quite a thick accent, Mutter still spoke very good English. When she was excited or emotional, however, she never failed to slip back to her roots. Rushing to my side, she pulled me into a hug and said, "I am so proud of you."

"Oh, honey, I'm thrilled to hear that," Nana cried, tears immediately popping into her eyes. "If there weren't such a shortage of sugar, I'd make you a cake to celebrate."

"We have some honey," Mutter said, her eyes bright as she turned to look at Nana.

While the two excitedly began discussing recipes they could use the honey for, I sat down at the table and helped Davey color a picture of barn animals.

"What color is that?" I asked him, pointing to the red barn.

"Wed," he instantly replied, and I couldn't help but smile as I ruffled his blonde hair.

Later that night, after I'd put Davey to bed, I fixed myself a glass of warm milk and carried it back to my bedroom, my eyes falling upon the many photographs that lined the walls. One was of my father when he was a little boy, and I reached up to touch the cool glass gently, a wave of sadness passing over me. I missed him so much. I could remember how he would take me fishing when I was little, and read to me at night before bed; he was the one who taught me to dance, and to also never give up, even when life gets hard. He'd always been the one to take care of us, to protect us and see to our needs, and when he suddenly passed away from a heart attack a year after our arrival in Savannah, mine and my mother's worlds were shattered. I'd been so thankful to have Paul to lean on, but now that he was gone, too, life just wasn't the same.

With a weary sigh, I turned and walked to my room, the milk in my glass now cold.

The next morning, I pushed away the doubts in my mind and decided to try something new; I put on a pair of overalls, gathered a few tools of my father's, and headed outside. It was Saturday, and the restaurant was closed due to a leak in the roof, and since I couldn't afford to hire anyone, I was going to try my hand at a few necessary repairs around the house. A couple of shutters were drooping, one of the porch steps was wobbly, and the lock on the front door was broken. So, I grabbed the tools and tried my best to feel positive, although I had no idea what I was doing.

"I'll call you when breakfast is ready," Nana said when I entered the kitchen.

"Thank you," I replied, smiling at her as I took a few quick gulps of coffee.

Once outside, I sat the toolbox down on the ground and glanced next door, noticing that there was a vehicle parked in the driveway. I hoped they wouldn't come out and see me, as I looked a fright; I'd pinned my hair back in a hurry, and the baggy, paint splattered overalls were an old, worn-out pair of Paul's. I certainly didn't want my new neighbors' first impression of me to be a bad one.

For a long moment, I stood staring at everything that needed to be done, feeling a little overwhelmed. It was hard not having a man around the house, and I didn't have a clue how to fix and repair the things that were broken. If only I'd asked Papa or Paul to show me a few things, maybe I wouldn't feel so inadequate.

Sighing, I reached into father's old toolbox and pulled out a hammer and a few nails, eyeing the drooping shutter with uncertainty. I tried for nearly twenty minutes to repair it, but with no success. Each time I hammered in a nail, it would either bend or the heavy shutter would force it back out. I was just about to give up and start in on the porch step when I heard a door to my right open and close. Distracted, I glanced in that direction and, as I wasn't paying attention to what I was doing, completely missed the nail I'd been aiming at and hit my thumb with the hammer. I jumped back with a yelp of pain, tripped over the toolbox, and flailed wildly about in an attempt to catch myself before finally crashing to the ground in a very unladylike, dusty heap, a loud *harrumph* passing my lips when my backside connected with the hard earth.

Dazed, I sat there for a moment, shaking my head as stars floated before my eyes. I heard footsteps hurrying in my direction, and then a pair of strong hands wrapped around my forearms and hoisted me up before I could utter a sound.

"Whoa there," a male voice said next to my ear as his hands steadied me, "are you alright?"

Turning my head, I found myself staring into a pair of heavily lashed hazel eyes. "Y-yes...I think so," I replied faintly.

"You took quite a tumble there," he stated, making no effort to move back.

Stepping away slowly, I brushed my hair out of my face and cleared my throat, trying to ignore the throbbing pain in my backside.

"I-I wish I wasn't so clumsy," I said, my cheeks burning with embarrassment. "Thank you very much for helping me up."

"You're quite welcome," he smiled. Suddenly, his eyes twinkling, he bowed at the waist with exaggerated flourish and said, "Leon Danes, at your service, madam."

Blinking in surprise, I smiled awkwardly and said, "I'm Eva. Are...are you my new neighbor?"

"That I am," Leon nodded. He was quite handsome and much taller than me, with curly brown hair and a wide, friendly smile. "I have little furniture, but I brought the few things that I do have over this morning." He glanced down at my overalls and then back up at the shutters, asking, "Were you attempting to nail that back into place?"

At my nod, he chuckled. "Your husband not much of a handyman?" He asked, and I realized he must have seen the ring I still wore on my finger.

"My...my husband died last March," I said softly.

Leon's eyes widened. "I'm so sorry," he said, cheeks flushing. Clearing his throat, he pointed to the nail that had fallen to the ground and said, "Not trying to tend to your business, but that nail isn't going to work. Do you have any bigger ones?"

I picked up the pack from the toolbox and showed him. "Those will work," Leon said, rolling up his sleeves as he took the pack of nails from my hand.

"What...what are you doing?" I asked in surprise.

"Being a good neighbor," he winked. "It won't take me long to fix this."

"Oh, no," I shook my head, "I couldn't ask you to do that."

Smiling at me, Leon said, "You didn't ask, I volunteered. I'd really love to help; please let me."

I hesitated for a moment, knowing that I needed the help and yet hating to impose on my new neighbor, especially since I'd only just met him. He didn't, however, seem to mind, and with a grateful smile, I finally said, "Alright, thank you very much."

Leon had both shutters fixed in ten minutes; he'd just finished putting in the last nail when Nana stuck her head out the door and announced that breakfast was ready.

"Oh," she said, her eyes widening in surprise when she saw Leon, "I didn't realize we had company."

I quickly made the introductions and added, "I was having some trouble with the shutters, and he offered to fix them for us."

"How nice," Nana smiled warmly. "Would you like to join us for breakfast?"

Leon agreed, and we all went into the house. I hurried to my bedroom, changed into more respectable looking clothes, and quickly rejoined everyone in the kitchen.

"Who you?" I heard Davey ask as I pushed the kitchen door open.

"I'm your new neighbor," Leon smiled down at him. "My name is Leon."

"Mr. Leon helped me fix those old, droopy shutters, Davey," I said as I helped him into his chair.

We said grace and then dug in to the grits, toast, scrambled eggs, and bacon Nana and Mutter prepared. After receiving my first paycheck, it was nice to have such a delicious and filling breakfast, compared to the milk and toast we'd been eating for the last month.

As we ate, Davey asked Leon question after question, his excitement at there being another male in the house quite obvious.

"Davey, why don't we let Mr. Leon eat his breakfast first, and then you can ask him a few questions?" I finally told him gently.

Davey nodded, and I was grateful that he was apparently on his good behavior.

"Mrs. Hamilton," Leon said after a moment, addressing my mother, "I see that the beautiful brooch you're wearing has a sapphire in it. That was my late father's birthstone."

Mutter, who'd been eating in complete silence, gently touched the small brooch she always wore, her expression softening as she smiled. "My husband gave it to me," she replied.

I could see by the look in Leon's eyes that he was surprised by my mother's thick accent, which was why she'd made a point to be so quiet, and I held my breath in apprehension. Many Americans hated Germans, not that I could blame them, and the snide remarks and looks of disgust we'd received from so many in the community hadn't been easy to adjust to.

"Well, he has excellent taste," Leon stated, smiling warmly.

I slowly let out the breath that I was holding, my spine relaxing back against the chair. "My father actually died four years ago," I explained in a soft voice.

Leon stilled, his fork full of eggs stopping halfway to his mouth as he met my gaze. "I am so sorry," he said, his eyes full of sympathy. "I know how it feels to lose a father; I was a teenager when mine died."

"Those that we love are often taken too soon," Nana spoke up, reaching over to pat my hand.

"Yes, they are," Leon nodded in agreement.

After breakfast, Leon insisted on helping me with the rest of the repairs. Davey asked if he could help, too, his eyes bright with excitement, and before I could respond, Leon took his hand and said, "Of course you can; I'd love to have a helper. Come on, let's go find that toolbox."

I went outside and watched as Leon patiently showed Davey the different tools and explained how to use them; he even let Davey help him hammer in a few nails.

"This is fun," Davey said exuberantly as he carefully watched and copied Leon's every move. I couldn't help but smile when Leon bent over on his right knee, placing his elbow onto his left, and Davey did the same thing, only a bit more clumsily.

When Davey almost tipped over, I caught his arm and said with a chuckle, "Why don't you let Mr. Leon work while you go play with your train?"

With a sigh of disappointment, Davey nodded and turned to go inside, his shoulders stooped.

"Thanks for your help, Davey," Leon called out to him. "I couldn't have done nearly as good of a job without you."

A smile brightening his face, Davey waved goodbye and skipped into the house, the screen door squeaking and slamming shut behind him.

"Thank you for that," I told our new neighbor, smiling down at him.

"He seems like a great kid," Leon said as he dug through the toolbox in search of a screwdriver. Looking up at me, he added with a grin, "I have to say, though, he talks way more than you do."

My cheeks flushing, I crossed my arms and said, "I talk…sometimes."

His eyes twinkling, Leon chuckled and said, "Tell me about yourself then."

Blinking, I shuffled my feet awkwardly for a moment before I asked, "What would you like to know?"

Sitting back on his haunches, Leon pursed his lips in thought. "Hmm," he said, scratching his chin, "how about…what do you like to do for fun?"

"These days?" I asked, raising my eyebrows. "Sleep."

Leon looked at me in surprise, bursting into laughter. "I didn't expect you to say that," he said, shaking his head, "but now that you mention it, 'sleep' has certainly become more fun the older I've gotten."

Smiling, I said, "I enjoy swimming, and picnics, and bike riding, but I rarely have time to do those things anymore."

"I know what you mean," Leon replied as he moved over to the front door to fix the broken lock. "But we should all take the time to do something fun now and then, don't you think?"

I nodded my head in agreement, and as he worked and we continued chatting, I decided it would be nice to do something in return for Leon's kindness.

He'd just finished with the lock on the front door when I asked, "What is your favorite dessert?"

"Is "all of them" an acceptable answer?" Leon chuckled. Standing to his full height, he stretched his back for a moment as he considered my question. "I think that peach cobbler is probably my favorite. How about you?"

"Apple strudel," I immediately replied. "Mutter makes the very best."

"I don't believe I've ever had that before," Leon stated. "What is it?"

After I'd described the decadent, mouth-watering dessert, he rubbed his stomach and said, "That sounds amazing. I'd love to try it sometime."

The next morning, I left a fresh apple strudel on Leon's door stoop with a note of "thanks" for all of his help. I also left another on Mr. Fernsby's porch, as I knew he loved Mutter's strudels, and hoped that it would help to soften up his grandson a bit, as well.

11

ASHER

The night was black and cold, and the mission was to drop over four tons of highly explosive bombs on one of the largest arms factories in Germany. Asher Beckett was a top turret gunner, and his job was to protect against overhead attacks, as well as monitor the engines and fuel.

"We're getting closer, boys," the pilot alerted over the radio. "Get ready."

Asher was unusually nervous that night, and as they neared the target, he could feel every muscle in his body tense. Only a matter of seconds passed as they readied the bombs, but it felt like an eternity; the sooner this job was done and they could get out of there, the better.

The bombs were released, and their explosions lit up the night sky like fireworks on the fourth of July. Asher kept his eyes trained ahead and above, his trigger finger ready as the pilot turned and headed back towards the base. Seconds ticked by slowly as they flew away from the fiery destruction they'd left behind, and with each moment that passed, Asher felt himself relax bit by bit. Perhaps they were going to make it, perhaps...

Suddenly, the plane shuddered violently as it took an unexpected spray of bullets from a German night fighter down below. The left wing immediately combusted into flames, and Asher heard the navigator say over the radio that the pilot was dead and his instrument panel destroyed. Asher and the other gunners did their best to ward off the attacker, but when another rain of bullets pierced the B-17's hard shell, the navigator no longer responded, and they knew that all hope was gone. The bomber was going down, and there was no other option but to parachute out...right into enemy territory.

Asher and the other gunners left their positions to gather at the forward escape hatch, and one by one they jumped from the mighty steel bird as it spiraled wildly towards the ground. The noises inside the plane were deafening, but as soon as Asher jumped, counted to five and pulled the rip cord, everything became eerily, deathly silent.

The air was icy cold and stung the skin on his cheeks as he floated down towards a dark and unknown abyss, and he wished more than anything for a cloudless sky. They'd flown a good bit out of the city before they were attacked, and Asher braced himself for a hard landing.

Within seconds, he crashed through the tops of the trees, his parachute getting caught in the branches. He winced as bark and wood pierced his skin, and stifled a yelp of pain when his knee connected with the solid trunk of the tree. He hung there for several moments, suspended and dangling in the air as he waited for his buddies to help him down. He was afraid to call out, as they were now in enemy territory, and breathed a sigh of relief when he heard the crunching of leaves as someone approached.

Just then, a flashlight shone directly into his eyes, and his stomach sunk when he heard the words, "Wer ghet dahin?"

He soon discovered, once they cut him down from the tree, that they'd landed only a few yards away from a German patrol.

That was over a year ago, the day they'd been captured and taken to a German POW camp, and it was a day that would forever weigh heavily on Asher's mind. Being forced to surrender to one's enemy was like handing your soul over to the devil, and the long months spent in captivity were sucking the very life out of Asher and the other prisoners. He tried to hold on to thoughts and memories of better times, and one particular image stayed in his mind day and night: the image of a beautiful, blonde-haired and blue-eyed angel that had stolen his heart the first day he met her. Would he ever see her again? He hoped so, and that hope was one thing that kept him going.

Life at the camp wasn't easy, to say the least. The guards were cruel, food was scarce, and the quarters cramped and uncomfortable. After being in the military, it was difficult for the men to live in such filth, and they did their best to keep clean with cold showers and the few supplies they were given from The Red Cross. The POW camp was small and several miles from civilization, and Asher would sometimes just stand outside and watch for any planes that might fly overhead, his heart yearning to be up there with them.

It was early one Thursday morning, and the men had just lined up outside to be counted. As they waited, Ethan, one of the gunners from his squadron, stepped up beside him and whispered, "There's talk of escape, and Watson wants to know if you're interested?"

Asher glanced down the line, noting that the guards weren't close enough to overhear their conversation. "Sure," he replied in a low voice. "How?"

"A tunnel," was all Ethan would say.

Asher sighed inwardly, wondering why Watson thought this attempt would be any different from the others he'd heard about. Since the camp was built on top of a very sandy subsoil, it was almost impossible to construct any type of substantial tunnel, and the barracks rested a good two feet off the ground so guards could easily detect any digging. How, he wondered, did Watson think he could successfully pull it off?

"We'll build the tunnel entrance in the drain sump in one of the washrooms," Watson told him later.

"How will we fortify it?" Asher wanted to know.

"With boards from our bunk beds, as well as anything else we can find around the camp."

Watson was a master engineer and Asher didn't doubt his ability, and the more he listened to Watson's plan, the more he believed it could work.

"Once we escape, how will we make it to the border without being caught?"

"Ethan thinks that one of the guards will help us get falsified papers," Watson said. "You speak German, don't you?"

"A little," Asher replied, nodding. "Eva, my sister-in-law, taught me."

"Good," he said. "If we get stopped and questioned, you can speak for all of us."

For the next three days, plans for the tunnel were secretly discussed and drawn up, and scraps were collected with which to build and fortify the walls of the escape route. It would take months, a lot of careful planning, and would be a highly dangerous mission, one that could get them killed if they were caught, but the men were determined to at least try because in their minds, being in a prison camp was the same as being dead.

12

Vivian

I'd been at Martinsville for two weeks when Dr. Zachary Holt came to visit me, just as Savannah said he would. I followed the attendant to the visiting area, my eyes searching for a familiar face. I didn't know Zachary well, but he had always been very kind and polite to me, and just being near anyone that was a link to home gave me a feeling of hope.

I finally spotted him sitting at a table to my right and hurried in his direction, the friendly smile on his face when he saw me instantly putting me at ease.

"Dr. Holt," I said as he stood to take my hand. "Thank you so much for coming."

He nodded, a lock of reddish-brown hair falling across his forehead. "Of course," he replied, reclaiming his seat after I'd taken mine. "I'm just sorry I couldn't come sooner."

"How are my parents?" I immediately wanted to know.

"As good as expected," he said, reaching up to loosen his tie a bit. "They wanted to come with me, but the train fare is a bit too much for them right now. They said that they'll come as soon as they can, and they also sent a letter."

He reached into the pocket of his navy blue suit coat and withdrew the letter, handing it to me after receiving clearance from one of the nearby guards. I clutched the envelope in my hand, wishing desperately to see my parents. How had it only been two weeks since I'd left home?

"Are you okay?" Zachary asked, his aqua blue eyes studying me closely.

"I'm trying to be," I replied, sighing. "I just want to go home; it's difficult staying continually cooped up in one place with nothing to do, and on my second day here I was nearly attacked by a schizophrenic woman who thought I was trying to kill her. If I wasn't crazy before, I fear I will be soon. Can't anyone convince Howard to get me out of this place?"

"Well," Zachary hesitated, clearing his throat, "that is a bit of a problem. You see, after you were taken away, Howard disappeared. We've searched and searched, but no one seems to know where he is."

I stared at Zachary in surprise. "Have you checked with his family? His immediate family are all gone, but his aunt, uncle, and a few cousins live in South Carolina."

"We called them, but they said they haven't seen or heard from him since your wedding."

"How strange," I muttered, Maisie's words once again flitting through my mind.

"Don't worry, Mrs. McCombs," Zachary said, his voice kind, "we'll keep looking for him."

"Please, call me Vivian."

"Only if you'll call me Zachary," he replied with a smile.

I nodded, smiling in return. "It's a deal." A thought struck me then and, tilting my head to the side, I asked, "Do you come here often?"

"I normally only come once or twice a year to demonstrate the newest advances in medicine and surgery to the young medical students who intern here at the medical center," he replied, leaning back in his chair to casually cross one leg over the other. "You see, I went to college with the head surgeon there and we're good friends. Now that you're here, however, I plan on coming at least once a month to check on you. I know many people here, Vivian, and I'm going to do my best to make certain they treat you well."

"Thank you so much," I told him, touched by his show of concern for a woman he barely knew. "That really means a lot to me."

Nodding, Zachary reached down and retrieved a package that rested at his feet, handing it to me. "I already received clearance to give you this," he explained. "It's just a few things your mother and Savannah thought you might need. If you can let me know of anything else, I'll be happy to bring it to you during my next trip here in a few weeks."

"At least once a month…during my next trip here in a few weeks."

Zachary's words hit me hard, and I felt myself cringe inwardly. Would I really be here that long? *I may be forced to stay here forever*, I thought, swallowing hard against the sudden lump in my throat.

"I don't think I'll need anything else, but thank you for your kindness, Zachary," I said, forcing myself to smile as I took the package from him.

"Alright," he said, standing to his feet. "Well, I have a meeting with one of the head doctors here, and I shouldn't be late."

"Thank you again for everything," I said, clutching the package against my chest as I stood to walk out with him.

Once we were outside, Zachary stopped and put on his blue Fedora hat, tilting his head to look down at me. "As I said earlier, I have to make another trip here in a few weeks, so I'll stop by and look in on you," he said. "We're doing the best we can to find Howard, and I have no doubt that we'll have you out of here in no time."

I bid him farewell and went back to my ward, where I sat in one of the rocking chairs and opened the package from home. As I looked through its contents, tears welled up in my eyes at the thoughtfulness of Mother and

Savannah, and I felt a wave of homesickness pass over me. Inside the box, I found a small bag of toiletries, extra underclothes, a couple of books, and several sheets of paper on which to write home. There were also two letters inside, and I immediately tore into them, devouring the words like I was starving.

"*I can't believe this has happened,*" Mother wrote in her familiar, slanted handwriting. "*Your father and I are beside ourselves, and we're doing the very best we can to find Howard and get you home. Don't worry, sweetie, I'm sure this will be over soon. Your father said to tell you to be strong, and that he loves you. So do I, honey, always remember that. No matter what happens in life, I'll be on your side, fighting for you.*"

I leaned my head back against the rocking chair and cried, cradling Mother's letter against my chest. I missed them both so much, and just reading their words was a source of comfort to me. Would it really be over soon, as Mother said? I wasn't certain, but I clung to hope as if it were a rock in the midst of a raging sea.

"*Do you remember all the good times we had when we were younger?*" Savannah wrote. "*Well, they're not over yet; we still have plenty of good times left to share. We're all looking for Howard, and I'm certain he'll be found any day now. Don't worry, Viv, this will all be over soon. I just know it.*"

With a sigh, I folded the letters and put them back in the box, planning to respond to them both immediately. As I went in search of a pen or pencil, I wondered where Howard could be, and a sudden memory floated through my mind. It was from the morning after our wedding; we'd just finished eating breakfast, and were standing together on the front porch looking proudly out over the farm.

"*This is where we'll raise our children and grow old together,*" Howard had said, pulling me close with a look of warmth in his eyes.

I could remember that moment as clearly as if it had happened yesterday, but the feeling of love and excitement of starting our life together was now gone, and I wondered yet again if I'd ever be able to go home, or if I was simply holding on to false hope and a lost memory.

A few days later, I'd just finished eating breakfast when a tall, middle-aged attendant approached me.

"Vivian McCombs?" She asked.

"Yes," I nodded hesitantly.

"Follow me, please."

My stomach clenching anxiously, I followed the lady outside, across the hospital grounds, and in through the back door of a large, rectangular shaped one-story building. I paused just inside the door, my eyes widening in awe as I surveyed the largest, most spectacular kitchen I'd ever seen. The attendant continued walking, and I had to hurry to catch up, my eyes taking in the huge stoves, refrigerators, and shelves upon shelves of plates, pots, and pans as we walked. Workers scurried back and forth, carrying trays filled with dirty dishes, and the clanking of silverware reverberated loudly throughout the enormous room and blended in with the constant chatter and pitter-patter of feet.

"You used to work at a restaurant, right?" The attendant asked, interrupting my thoughts.

Pulling my gaze away from the hustle and bustle of our surroundings, I looked back at the attendant and nodded. "That's right."

"I thought so," she said, pursing her lips. "You'll be working here five days a week, from seven in the morning 'til three o'clock in the afternoon. This is a privilege that you've earned for good behavior, so don't mess it up."

I blinked, surprised at the woman's words. A privilege such as this usually wasn't earned for several months, so how had I grown so lucky? Only a few days ago, Maisie had earned her first privilege of gardening twice a week, with the promise that, if she continued to be well-behaved, she could gradually work her way up to five days a week.

Suddenly, it hit me; Zachary had arranged this for me, bless his soul. When I saw him again, I made a note to thank him for this favor.

The attendant led me to a woman who was writing the lunch menu on a large board that hung from the wall and introduced us.

"This is Mrs. Dobson," she told me. "She's worked here for over twenty years and is in charge of the kitchen. Mrs. Dobson, this is the young woman you were asking about."

With that being said, the attendant turned and walked from the room, leaving me to fend for myself.

"I was told that you used to work in a restaurant?" Mrs. Dobson asked, smiling politely at me.

"Yes, ma'am," I replied, nodded.

"Did you ever do any cooking?"

"I did most of the cooking for years until we finally hired someone to help," I said.

"Wonderful!" she said, a smile brightening her face. She then pointed over my shoulder to a woman sorting through a large crate of vegetables and said, "That's Alice. Go on over and introduce yourself, and she'll tell you what to do."

With a nod, I pushed my way through the other workers and tapped "Alice" on the shoulder. She turned to look at me, her pale blue eyes surveying me quickly from head to toe. She was a large woman, in her mid-fifties, with curly gray hair and soft wrinkles around her eyes and mouth. Before I could say anything, she smiled broadly and said, "You must be the new girl. Violet, or something like that?"

"Vivian," I corrected with a smile.

"Oh, yes, I'm terrible at remembering names," she said, laughing.

"Mrs. Dobson sent me over," I explained. "I was a cook for several years, and she said you would tell me what to do."

"You cooked in a restaurant?"

I nodded, and Alice's face lit up. "Honey, that's wonderful news," she cried, her eyes sparkling. "I used to own a restaurant, and up 'til now most of the cooks here are just housewives and have little experience cooking for crowds."

She pointed to one of the vegetable crates and said, "Since I'm sure you're quick with a knife, help me slice these up and once the breakfast dishes are done, we'll start cooking lunch."

An hour later, I stood at one stove with a wooden spoon in hand, my forehead beaded with sweat as I stirred and seasoned the massive pot of vegetable soup. Alice stood at the stove next to mine doing the same thing, her cheeks rosy red from the heat as we chatted.

"You said you used to own a restaurant?" I asked, her outgoing, friendly personality putting me at ease.

"Oh, yes, I had a great big, boomin' restaurant," she nodded. "I miss it."

"Why did you leave it then?"

Alice glanced at me in surprise. "You don't know who I am?"

"No," I replied, looking at her quizzically. "Aren't you an employee here?"

Throwing her head back, Alice burst into laughter, her shoulders shaking with mirth from the obvious joke I'd made, although I was quite uncertain what that joke was.

"Oh, honey, you're cute," she snickered, wiping tears from her eyes. "I'm Alice Layne, the woman accused of poisoning her husband three years ago."

My mouth dropped open as I stared at Alice in shock. I'd read about the case in the newspaper, but had no idea this was the same woman. I hadn't even realized they had sent her to Martinsville.

"I...I'm sorry, I didn't know..." I stammered.

"Oh, don't fret your pretty little head about it," she said, waving a hand at me. "They wanted to execute me, but figured it would be best to declare me insane and send me to an institution since they had never executed a woman in Georgia. I'll have to admit, though, it's not so bad here sometimes."

Alice continued to chatter on and I did my best to listen, but all I could think about was why would they allow a woman accused of poisoning her husband to work in the kitchen? I shook my head, sighing inwardly; this place just kept getting more and more strange.

13

Eva

"Goodbye, I'll see you all tomorrow," I softly called out to the rest of the staff at The Park Bench as I put on my hat and gloves.

I heaved a sigh when no one bothered to respond and reached for my sweater. I loved my job here, but the people I worked with were just like everyone else; they resented my heritage, and although they never said anything unkind to me, I could feel tension in the air anytime I attempted to make conversation. They also didn't approve of the position Mr. Parker had given me as assistant chef. It gave me a bit of authority, something I was very uncomfortable with, and Cook would often force me to give the other employees "orders", which didn't make things any easier for me. I wasn't the type to order anyone to do anything, but when I would politely ask them to chop vegetables or mention that we needed extra pots washed, I received hard looks and eye rolls. I wondered if they would ever truly accept me.

"Here, let me help you with that."

Startled, I looked up to find that Jackson, one dishwasher who had recently begun working at the restaurant, had walked up behind me and was reaching for my sweater. He picked it up and held it out for me to slip my arms into, his hands resting lightly on my shoulders longer than necessary.

"Thank you, Jackson," I said, taking a step back as I buttoned my sweater.

"You're very welcome," he smiled, his dark eyes warm as he moved closer once again.

Clearing my throat, I said goodbye and stepped around him to go out the back door. He was the only person who had made any attempt to be nice to me, and while I was very grateful for it, I sometimes felt uncomfortable whenever he was near. I couldn't quite put my finger on why, but as I always tried to be positive about others, I simply decided that I just didn't know him well enough yet.

As I walked home, I wrapped my sweater tighter around me and shivered. It was getting late, and the "March winds" were living up to their name as fallen leaves blew across the sidewalk and overhead branches rustled back and forth in the breeze. I saw a stray piece of paper blow out of a nearby trash can, and I'd just picked it up to place it back into the container when I noticed someone walking toward me. Peering through the dim lighting, I saw it was a man wearing a dark trench coat, his hat pulled so low over his face that I couldn't make out any discernable features. I assumed at first that he was just walking home from work, but when he stopped and simply stood there watching as I threw away the scrap of paper, I felt a sudden chill creep up my spine. Although I couldn't see his face, I could feel his eyes boring into me and, wrapping my sweater tighter around my waist, I turned and hurried on my way, my ears listening for the sound of his footsteps.

There they were. Glancing over my shoulder, I saw that he'd also begun walking again, and noticed that he kept his pace the same as mine. It seemed he was following me, but why? With a sense of foreboding, I quickened my stride, my eyes fixed on the corner just up ahead. That was my street, and if I could only reach the corner, I planned to run the rest of the way. I could hear his heels clicking along the pavement as he, too, walked faster, and I fought the urge to scream. Surely I was overreacting; why would he be following me?

When I finally reached the corner, I turned and broke into a run, the lights of my house bouncing before me as I drew closer and closer. I saw Leon standing in his front yard talking to a man that I didn't recognize, and I called out his name, relief flooding my body when he saw me and hurried out onto the sidewalk.

"Eva, what's wrong?" Leon asked when I reached his side, out of breath. He stepped closer and took my arm, as if afraid that I might faint. The man he'd been talking to made his way to where we stood, concern etched upon his handsome face as he studied me.

"A man," I said breathlessly. "A man was f-following me."

Leon glanced over my shoulder, searching the growing darkness with concerned eyes. "What man?" He wanted to know.

I turned to look, my breath finally slowing a bit, and I found that the street behind me was deserted. The man was gone.

"I...I thought he was following me," I said uncertainly, my voice shaking.

"Who was he?" Leon's friend asked, stepping closer. "Have you ever seen him before?"

His gaze was direct and searching, but kind. "No, I don't think so," I said faintly. "He was a stranger."

I turned to look back at Leon, my face flushing with embarrassment. Apparently the man wasn't following me after all and while I was relieved that he hadn't been, I was also humiliated for running down the street and causing such a spectacle.

"I don't see him now," Leon said, his brow furrowed. "I guess you scared him away when you called out to me."

"Perhaps he wasn't really following me after all," I said, glancing down at my feet. "I probably just let my imagination run away with me." I looked at Leon's friend then and gave him a small, shy smile. "I apologize for interrupting your conversation."

"It's quite alright," he kindly assured me.

"You did the right thing, Eva," Leon told me, touching my arm. Gesturing to his friend, he said, "This is Doctor Zachary Holt. He was making a house call in the neighborhood and stopped by to share some news about a friend of ours he recently visited."

I reached out to shake the doctor's offered hand, not failing to notice the unusual color of his eyes. Mine, my mother's, and Davey's eyes were all a soft, baby blue, but I'd never seen such bright aqua eyes in all my life. They were the exact shade of the Mediterranean Sea on a sunny day and were filled with warmth and kindness.

"It's very nice to meet you," Zachary said pleasantly, "and I'm glad that you're alright." He then turned back to Leon and said, "I'll be returning to Martinsville in a few weeks, and will continue to keep you and your family posted."

Leon and I waved to Zachary as he left, and I found myself wondering about their mutual friend in Martinsville.

"Come on, I'll walk you inside," Leon said to me with a smile, still holding my arm as we turned and made our way up to my house.

"Have you and the doctor known each other long?" I asked.

"About a year, maybe a little less," was Leon's reply. "He works with my sister-in-law."

We'd reached the porch, and I turned to look at Leon. "You have a brother?"

"I do," he nodded. "His name is Connor."

"How nice," I said, smiling. "I always wanted siblings."

"Yeah, he's the best," Leon replied, stuffing his hands into his pockets. "When Father died, he really stepped up and took care of Mother and me. He's a pilot in the Air Force."

"He sounds like a wonderful person," I said, not missing the obvious pride in Leon's voice. There was something in his eyes, though, that caught my attention. It was a look of disappointment, and I wondered what he was disappointed in.

"He is," Leon replied, nodding. "If it wasn't for my asthma, I'd be serving, as well."

Ah, so that's it. He feels like a failure for not serving his country.

I hesitated for a moment before I said in a soft, gentle tone, "You know, my father used to say that God gives us all unique talents and abilities, and we should do the best we can with the gifts He gives us. We can't all pilot

75

a fighter jet or shoulder a gun in the trenches, but we do the best we can in the place we're in. Can you imagine if you were deployed and hadn't been here the last few years to assist the people who have come to you at the bank for help? Families could have lost their homes, children would have gone hungry, and businesses would have closed down. You've saved lives, Leon, just in a different way."

Blinking, Leon stared at me for a moment, apparently surprised by my words. When he said nothing, I felt my cheeks flush and hoped that I hadn't overstepped myself somehow. I rarely spoke out in such a way and immediately berated myself, wondering what on earth had come over me.

Before I could apologize, Leon shook his head in amazement and said, "You must be very intuitive, Eva Beckett, to know I needed to hear that." Glancing down at his feet, he sighed and said, "I've felt so guilty for not being able to join my fellow countrymen in this war that I never even thought about all the people right here in my own city that I've helped. I need to have more faith in myself, don't I?"

He glanced up at me and I nodded, smiling softly.

"Thank you, Eva," he said, his face relaxing as the disappointment I'd seen earlier began to slip from his eyes. Grinning playfully, he added, "You won't start charging a fee for all of your wonderful words of wisdom, will you?"

"Oh, no, I wouldn't think of it," I laughed lightly.

The foyer light flicked on then and I heard Davey yelling that he could hear voices outside.

"I'd better go in," I told Leon, reaching for the door handle.

"Be careful coming home tomorrow," Leon cautioned. "If there are any suspicious characters hanging around the restaurant, give me a call and I'll come get you."

"Okay," I nodded. "Thank you, Leon."

"Thank *you*," he replied warmly, reaching out to squeeze my arm.

I opened the front door and stepped inside, glancing back out to watch Leon walk away. His head was held high as he whistled a cheerful tune, and I couldn't help but smile. It seemed I had actually made a friend in this town, after all, and I was very grateful for it.

Later that night when I went to bed, I found that I couldn't sleep. Thoughts of the stranger who followed me home were keeping me awake, and I finally climbed out of bed and made my way into the kitchen. When I opened the door and stepped inside, I was surprised to find Nana sitting at the table reading a day-old newspaper.

"You can't sleep either?" I asked, keeping my voice down as I tied my robe around my waist.

"No," she sighed, shaking her head. Her hair, which was normally worn up in a neat, tidy roll, was down and braided and a bit disheveled, and she wore a loose-fitting housecoat with tiny pink flowers. Nodding towards the stove, she added, "I warmed a pot of milk if you'd like a cup."

My eyes brightening, I walked across the kitchen towards the stove, my house slippers sliding softly across the wooden floor. After I'd helped myself to a mug of milk and added a bit of honey, I sat at the table next to Nana and took a sip, the warm, sweet liquid slipping satisfactorily down my throat.

After a moment, I looked at Nana and asked, "Nana, how did you and Grandfather meet?"

Looking a bit surprised by the sudden question, Nana folded the newspaper and laid it back on the table.

"Well, now, that's an interesting story," she said, a sparkle forming in her eyes as she smiled at me. "When I was seventeen, I took the train from Bloomingdale to Savannah to attend a party. It was the middle of July, and I remember they had made an enormous tub of homemade ice cream, so I fixed myself an ice cream cone. Your grandfather was part of the band; he played the drums. During one of his breaks, he came up to me and asked for a lick of my dessert. Can you believe that?"

Huffing, she shook her head and we both laughed, her face more animated than I'd ever seen it. I loved hearing about our family's history, and couldn't believe that I'd never asked her about this before. I'd only "met" Grandfather through his letters, as he had already passed away when we came to live here, but hearing Nana talk about him, I felt like I really knew him. Through her eyes, I could see his face and hear the sound of his voice, and I leaned my elbows over onto the table and cupped my chin in my hands as I listened, completely entranced as she spoke.

"I almost said "no" because, well, you know how I am about my ice cream," Nana continued, chuckling, "but there was something about the twinkle in his eye and dimple in his chin that just got to me. So, I shared my dessert with him, and he told me all about himself. By the time the ice cream was gone, we were both head over heels for each other. He drove me home later, and you know something?"

I shook my head. "What?"

Leaning toward me, she tapped my arm and said with a smile, "We were married for almost fifty years, and he kept my return train ticket in his wallet until the day he died."

"That is so sweet, Nana," I replied, sighing softly. "It sounds like you two really loved each other."

Taking a sip of her milk, she nodded and said, "We surely did, honey. We had our ups and downs, just like any couple, but I was the apple of his eye and he was mine. I'll always miss him."

We talked for nearly an hour, with Nana telling me story after story of her childhood, her parents, and of Grandfather and their life together. I loved these little trips down memory lane, these fascinating snippets and peeks into the past, and I could clearly see each picture that Nana painted with her words.

When I heard the clock strike midnight, I stood up and, with a yawn, took my empty mug to the sink. "I think I understand now why Davey gets so sleepy when I read to him," I said, chuckling. "After so many wonderful stories, I think I'm finally ready to go to sleep." I washed the mug and put it away, walking back to the table to kiss Nana on the cheek as I softly added, "I'm so glad that we all live together. Thank you, Nana, for everything you do for us."

Her faded blue eyes filling with tears, Nana squeezed my hand and said warmly, "You're a special girl, Eva Beckett, and I'm so thankful that I have you, your mother, and Davey. It's not always easy getting older, you know, but it gives me comfort to know that I'll always have the three of you by my side."

Smiling, I gave her another quick hug and we both went to bed. As I curled up beneath the covers and began drifting off to sleep, I thought of Nana's stories, and my dreams were filled with dances, warm summer nights, and ice cream cones.

14

Vivian

The next couple of weeks passed quickly, and I found myself falling into a routine. After completing my shift in the kitchen, I would meet Maisie in the garden or in our building to do laundry and a bit of sewing.

"Are you sure they're not working you too hard?" Maisie asked once, her eyes filled with concern.

"No, not at all," I assured her. "If I didn't have something to occupy my time, I'm afraid I truly would go crazy. Besides, I'd much rather they put me to work than sedate me or try something worse."

In the month that I'd spent at the hospital, I hadn't thought that anything could surprise me any longer. I was, however, very wrong. It was a Friday afternoon, and we'd just finished with the lunch crowd in the cafeteria. I went out to gather the tea pitchers when one of the male patients began vomiting on the floor. His name was Anthony, he was in his mid to late fifties, and suffered from severe depression. I'd learned that after several shock treatments, he could no longer remember the last ten years of his life, and his behavior was mostly like that of a child. I rushed to his side, concerned by the sick, green look on his face.

"Anthony, are you alright?" I asked, resting my hand on his back.

"My…my belly is…is hurting," he mumbled, holding his stomach pitifully. "I…I'm sorry, Miss Vivian."

"I'll clean up this mess, don't worry," I assured him.

When I returned moments later with a rag, I saw that two male attendants stood next to Anthony, disgust on their faces.

"Don't bother, missy," one of them said, snatching the rag from my hand and thrusting it under Anthony's nose. "He'll clean up his own mess. Won't you, Anthony?"

Nodding, Anthony took the rag and began to clean up the vomit, his hands trembling.

"I can do it," I stated emphatically. "He's much too ill to…"

The two men guffawed loudly, cutting me off. One of them sneered at me and said, "You're all "ill" in this place, and I'm tired of dealing with Anthony's pathetically weak stomach. Maybe if he has to clean up after himself, he'll decide to toughen up a bit."

"Yeah, and why don't you just eat that rag while you're at it?" the other attendant said, shoving Anthony with his foot.

Anthony's face was flushed with embarrassment, and I thought I saw tears in his eyes. The two men continued to bully him, and I was on the verge of giving them both a piece of my mind when Anthony picked up the soiled rag and began putting it in his mouth.

"Anthony, stop," I cried, stepping toward him.

One attendant grabbed my arm, his eyes glinting as he said, "Leave him alone."

I stood there and watched in horror as Anthony attempted to swallow the rag and began to choke. I fought against the attendant, completely helpless as Anthony's face grew red and garbled, strangled sounds began emerging from the back of his throat.

"He's going to die!" I screamed, but all the two attendants would do was stand there and watch with smirks on their faces.

The cafeteria was almost empty, except for a few remaining stragglers, but no one paid us any attention. It all happened in just a matter of seconds, but it felt as if time stood still and everything moved in slow motion. The noises faded into the background as all of my attention was directed on Anthony, and when his face began to lose its color and turn blue, I thought that my heart would burst.

"Mrs. Dobson!" I screamed, hoping someone in the kitchen would hear me, but it was too late. I watched Anthony slump to the floor in a lifeless heap, his eyes fluttering closed as the rag hung partially from his mouth.

Mrs. Dobson and Alice came out just then, their eyes widening at the sight before them, and the attendant quickly released my arm.

"They killed him," I whispered in a broken voice, tears streaming down my cheeks.

"What are you talking about?" One attendant asked incredulously. "Anthony was an idiot; everyone knows that! He stuffed that rag into his mouth and swallowed it before we could stop him."

Looking at the two men in disbelief, I shook my head and said, "That's not true, and you know it."

"Vivian, come on back into the kitchen with me," Alice said, glaring at the two attendants. When I protested, she took my arm and said firmly, "Now, Vivian."

Once back in the kitchen, I turned to Alice and said, "Alice, those two men intentionally let Anthony die. They forced him to eat that rag!"

"I don't doubt that for one minute, but remember, honey, you're just a patient here," Alice said, stepping closer and lowering her voice. "You can't go around accusing two workers like that, especially when one of them has friends in high places, unless you want to end up on the table getting shock treatment for "hysteria" and "delusions"."

I couldn't believe that was true; surely someone would believe me. It was outrageous to think that those two men would go unpunished!

Later that afternoon, I saw one of the doctors enter the kitchen, and I had a feeling he was looking for me. He was known as "Cruel Cadle", and I felt my stomach clench when Mrs. Dobson called me to a side corner where Dr. Cadle waited.

"I hear that you've been a bit hysterical over the incident with one of the male patients this afternoon," Dr. Cadle said, his icy blue eyes cool and steady as he studied me. He was in his late forties and bald on top, with a fringe of thin, brown hair at the nape of his neck.

"Well, it was certainly no picnic to watch *Anthony* die after being forced to eat that rag," I stated, seething over the fact that he wouldn't even call Anthony by name.

"From what I hear, no one forced the patient to do anything," Dr. Cadle retorted, his jaw clenching. "In fact, the two attendants tried to save his life, but it was too late."

"That's not true," I stated, ignoring the look Alice was giving me over the doctor's shoulder. "Those two men basically murdered poor Anthony."

"I don't think you really mean that."

By the tone in Dr. Cadle's voice, I knew I'd overstepped myself. Was it so wrong to tell the truth in this place, or were the patients considered so much less than human that their word counted as nothing?

"I'm sure that Vivian is just upset," Mrs. Dobson spoke up. Looking at me, she said firmly, "Once she has calmed down, she'll forget everything she thought she saw."

Dr. Cadle looked at me and, raising an eyebrow, asked, "Is that true?"

I hesitated, wanting to fight for Anthony and for the truth, but I was slowly realizing that no matter how I felt or how hard I fought, my voice didn't count. In this place, none of our voices mattered.

Sighing, I gave one tight nod and said stiffly, "Yes."

"I certainly hope so," he said, adding pointedly, "for *your* sake."

Dr. Cadle turned and walked away, and I had to force myself not to call out to him, to announce that they wouldn't continue getting away with such crimes.

"I hope you really will forget and move on," Mrs. Dobson said. When I looked at her and she saw the frustration in my eyes, she sighed and reached out to touch my arm. "I'm sorry, Vivian. I know how hard it is here, but sometimes we just can't do anything about it. You're a good worker, though, and I don't want anything to happen to you."

Nodding, I said, "Thank you for stepping in the way you did, Mrs. Dobson; I have a feeling I was headed for "treatment" if you hadn't."

Smiling, Mrs. Dobson patted my arm and walked away. I learned later that she and her husband had a lot of political pull at the hospital, and if not for that, I'd never have been given the chance to "calm down".

For the rest of the day, all I could think of was Anthony. He'd been such a pitiful, gentle soul, and what happened wasn't fair. How many others before him had suffered the same fate? And how many more would follow?

There was an area just past the grove of pecan trees where Anthony's body would be taken. A lonely, desolate place with thousands of small, numbered markers dotting the grassy landscape. This is where those who didn't matter were taken, the ones who didn't have anyone that cared enough to retrieve their bodies and take them home to be laid to rest. These poor souls weren't even allowed the last privilege of having their names written upon their grave markers. A number was all they were given, it was all that was left; just a single row of digits to tell of the broken, forgotten lives buried beneath the surface.

That night, I re-read my most recent letters from home, the words giving me comfort and strength. Mother wrote about the birdhouse in their backyard, and how the bluebirds had come back to build another nest. She then told me of a new quilt she was making, and I smiled as I read her sweet words:

"I'm using all of your favorite colors," she wrote, *"so when you come home, you'll know that I was thinking of you every second while you were away. I'm not the best quilter in the world, but at least you'll know I made it with love."*

She continued with updates from the restaurant, her thoughts on the new Sunday School teachers at church, and descriptions of how rainy and wet the weather had been. Father wrote the last paragraph, and I couldn't help but smile at his constant use of capital letters and slightly messy handwriting.

"I've hired a new assistant chef," he wrote. *"She's painfully shy, but I can tell that she has a very big heart, just like you. She's a wonderful cook, and I can't wait for you to meet her when you come home. I miss you, honey, and I hope you're doing well. Your mother and I pray for you every night. Let us know if there is anything you need, and we'll do our best to send it to you."*

Smiling softly, tears gathering in my eyes, I folded the letter and gently placed it back in its envelope. He wished to know if there was anything I needed, but the thing I needed most wasn't something that could be sent in the mail. I needed to go home.

15

Eva

Wednesday morning, I sat in the Candler Hospital waiting room, my worried eyes watching my son's every move. When he woke up that morning complaining of a sore throat, I immediately called Mr. Parker and explained that I couldn't come in until after lunchtime. I then hurried to the hospital with Davey in tow, my stomach clenched with worry. It was May, not even summer yet, but the weather was already quite warm and all I could think of was polio.

We were called back quickly and led to a room where the doctor was waiting for us. As soon as we stepped through the door, I realized that our doctor was Leon's friend, Zachary Holt.

"Hello," he greeted us warmly. "It's nice to see you again, Mrs. Beckett." He then squatted down before Davey and reached out his hand. "Davey, I'm Dr. Holt. It's nice to meet you."

Like a little man, Davey shook the doctor's hand and stated that it was nice to meet him as well. Zachary helped him onto the examination table and began to gently rub his hands along Davey's throat.

"Has he had any other problems, Mrs. Beckett?" Zachary asked, glancing over at me.

"No," I shook my head. I sat in a nearby chair, my hands clenched nervously in my lap. "He hasn't been coughing or running any fever, but I wanted to get him checked before any of that got started."

"You did the right thing."

I sat and watched as Zachary did several of the "polio tests"; he told Davey to turn his head from side to side, touch his chin to his chest, and wiggle his toes. Davey performed all three actions with no problem. Zachary then shone a light into Davey's eyes and ears, and told him to stick out his tongue and say "ah". After peering down his throat with the light for a moment, he nodded and stepped back, placing the little light back into his coat pocket.

"It appears that your son is suffering from inflamed tonsils," Zachary told me. "He'll probably need to have them removed at some point, but I don't recommend it now."

I blinked, almost afraid I'd heard him wrong. "So...so, it's not polio?" I asked hopefully.

"No, Mrs. Beckett, it's not polio," Zachary shook his head, his smile reassuring. "I'll send a nurse in to administer a shot, and then you can take him home. You should keep him in bed for the next few days, and feed him only soft foods until his throat gets better."

"Thank you, Doctor Holt," I said, sighing with relief.

"You're quite welcome," he replied. "But please, call me Zachary." Turning back to Davey, he said, "Take it easy now, okay?"

Davey nodded solemnly and, with a departing smile, Zachary left the room. I sat back in my chair and closed my eyes, so relieved that I wanted to weep for joy. I knew that tonsillitis was serious, as well, but at least it wasn't the dreaded polio.

"I not wants a shot," Davey suddenly spoke up.

Glancing at him in surprise, my stomach sunk when I saw the frown on his face.

"It will make you feel better, honey," I tried to reassure him, hoping that he wouldn't act out with the nurse. He was normally very well behaved, but just like any other child, he had his stubborn moments, and I prayed that this wouldn't be one of them.

"No," he shook his head, his lower lip poking out.

Just then, a young nurse came in carrying a tray. She was tall and slender and strikingly beautiful with long, dark hair and sparkling black eyes.

"Hello there," she said, smiling at the both of us. She sat the tray down and said to my son, "You must be Davey. My, what a handsome young man you are. My name is Mrs. Danes, but you may call me Ms. Savannah, if you'd like."

"Hi," Davey said, smiling shyly at the pretty lady, and I hoped that his earlier concerns were now forgotten.

Savannah turned to look at me then and said, "You must be his mother?"

"Yes, I'm Eva," I replied, nodding. I paused a moment before asking hesitantly, "Are you by chance any relation to Leon Danes?"

"Yes, as a matter of fact, I am," Savannah said as she rolled up Davey's sleeve. "He's my brother-in-law."

"He and I are neighbors," I explained, watching her every move and hoping that Davey wouldn't cry too much over the shot.

"Oh, you must be the neighbor he helped with the shutters," she said. When I nodded, a bit embarrassed, she added, "He was so happy when he realized what wonderful neighbors he has. He even told us what a fantastic cook your grandmother is."

"He's been very kind to help us," I said, smiling.

"He also told us about your husband," Savannah said softly, her eyes filled with sympathy as she looked over at me. "I'm so sorry, Mrs. Beckett."

"Thank you," I replied, swallowing past the sudden lump in my throat at her kindness. "And please, call me Eva."

"Alright, and my name is Savannah," she stated.

Savannah readied the shot and, holding it up for Davey to see, said, "Sweetie, this is going to feel like a pesky little bee sting, but I know you're tough and can handle it. Right?"

Davey nodded bravely and, much to my surprise, hardly cried when Savannah inserted the shot. I, however, felt a little light-headed.

"Good job, honey," I congratulated him once it was over. I then looked at Savannah and said sheepishly, "It seems he did better than I did."

Noting my pale face, Savannah chuckled and said, "Oh, that's normal. At least you didn't faint like the last mother did."

She helped Davey from the table and as we walked out, she laid a hand on my arm and said, "You know, the hospital is holding a dance this Friday night at the local Masonic lodge to raise money for war supplies. My husband, Connor, is in Europe, and my family keeps telling me I need to go out and do something fun to get my mind off of missing him so much. I'd love to support the war effort, but I don't want to go to the dance by myself. Would you like to go with me?"

I blinked, looking at Savannah in surprise. "Oh…I don't know," I said falteringly, my cheeks turning pink. It was a very thoughtful request, but I wouldn't know anyone there; I was painfully shy and always felt awkward around strangers.

"At least think about it, please," Savannah persisted. "It will be a lot of fun, and both Leon and Zachary will be there."

I hesitated, not wishing to tell Savannah "no". I hadn't received such a kind invitation since coming here, and I *would* know at least three people there. Unable to resist the pleading look in Savannah's eyes, I finally smiled and nodded, agreeing to go.

"Oh, good!" Savannah cried with excitement. "I have a car, so I'll pick you up around seven."

Before I could say anything else, she pulled me into a quick hug, said that she hoped Davey would feel better soon, and hurried off in the opposite direction.

Carrying Davey out on my hip, I hailed a taxi and waited for it to pull up. Just before I climbed into the back seat, I caught a glimpse of a lone figure standing across the street. The shadows of an overhead tree covered his face, but it appeared that he was looking directly at me, and I immediately thought of the man that seemingly followed me home that dark, windy night only a couple of weeks ago. Fighting off a feeling of unease, I quickly climbed into the taxi and closed the door, giving the driver my address. As we drove away, I glanced back to find that the shadowy figure was gone.

16

THE SHADOW

He watched as Eva climbed into the back of the taxi, a slight smile pulling at his lips as he turned and walked away. She'd spotted him beneath the tree, but he was so covered by the shadowy branches overhead that he knew she hadn't seen his face; he'd have to make certain it stayed that way. When he saw the look of apprehension in her eyes, he knew she was thinking of the night he followed her home from work. It was almost like he could read her mind, and he liked that; it gave him a feeling of power.

Thoughts of that cold, windy night flashed through his mind then, and he chuckled under his breath. She was terrified when she realized she was being followed, and the way she ran, as if he couldn't catch her if he tried, was almost comical. He'd enjoyed toying with her, and seeing the look of fear on her face was thrilling, but he'd have to keep himself more hidden from now on; he couldn't risk her seeing his face.

As he walked along the sidewalk, the sound of her voice played over in his head. She spoke with a soft, lilting accent, and although she tried to disguise her German roots, they were there nonetheless; she couldn't hide from them, no matter how hard she tried. Most everyone these days hated the Germans and Japanese, and she was no exception.

When he turned the corner, he bumped into a young boy collecting metal scraps, and his hat tumbled to the ground.

"Hey, watch it, kid," he snapped, shoving the boy out of the way as he reached down to retrieve his hat.

The boy backed away, his eyes wide, and the man's lip curled in disgust as he continued on his way down the street. He didn't like kids, he never had; he found them to be a bother and a nuisance. His father had felt the same way about him when he was a kid; he could still remember the painful beatings and feel the sting of a sudden, unexpected backhand across the face as proof of his father's dislike.

Sighing, he shook thoughts of his miserable childhood out of his mind and wiped the frown from his face. He had other, more important things to think of, and refused to allow himself to sink into that rabbit hole of memories just now. Instead, he thought of Eva, and began making plans for the next time he would see her.

17

Vivian

It was hard to believe I'd been at Martinsville for six weeks, and I could barely grasp that so much time had passed since my baby's death. I thought about him all the time, and still dreamed of him nearly every night. I sometimes wondered if I'd ever stop thinking I heard him crying, or quit pausing at noon with the thought that I needed to feed him. Would the pain ever go away?

I was grateful for my job in the hospital's kitchen; it kept me busy, which was something I craved and needed now more than ever. I wasn't one to just sit still and watch the world go by, and even after Howard and I were married, I worked just as hard on the farm as I did at the restaurant. By pushing myself now and focusing on the tasks at hand, I could distract myself a bit from dwelling too much on my situation. It wasn't easy, however, when a patient became overwrought or violence erupted. As with Anthony, the violence wasn't always just between the patients. I did my best to keep quiet, do as I was told, and stay under the radar, but I wasn't always so lucky.

I was working in the kitchen one afternoon kneading a huge mound of dough when another worker bumped roughly into me. She'd been carrying too many trays and hadn't seen me, and our collision caused her to drop the trays onto the floor with an explosive, ear-piercing clatter. When I turned to see who it was, my stomach sunk when I realized it was none other than Doris. I'd stayed out of her way as much as possible since my arrival, but she'd recently begun working in the kitchen two days a week, and I knew our paths would eventually cross.

"You did that on purpose!" she cried, grabbing me by the arm. Her face was red with anger and her nostrils flared open wide like that of a crazed horse.

Forcing myself to stay calm, I shook my head and said, "No, I didn't. You bumped into me."

Her eyes narrowing, Doris jerked me closer and snarled, "*You* bumped into *me*, and if you try to say otherwise, I'll slam your teeth right down…"

"I don't think you will, Doris," another voice interrupted from behind, and I blinked in surprise when I saw a pair of hands reach out to take hold of my offender's arm. I glanced over Doris's shoulder to see that my protector was none other than Alice.

Doris hesitated, turning around to look at Alice. The two women's eyes met as they sized each other up, and the steely look in Alice's gaze made Doris shrink back. She let go of me and, clearing her throat, mumbled "sorry" before walking away.

"Thanks, Alice," I said, smiling gratefully at my defender.

"Stay away from her," she warned me. "They never discovered who did it, but I know for a fact that she beat an attendant nearly to death once; she's truly one of the crazy ones."

"I'll do my best," I replied, sighing. Cocking an eyebrow at Alice, I added, "But she did back away from *you*."

"That's because she knows I'm crazier than she is," Alice replied with a loud cackle, winking at me.

Alice walked off, and I returned to my dough, making a mental note to remain on her good side and stay out of Doris's path.

Later, while I was making icing for a chocolate cake, one worker came over and said in a low voice, "Remember Jimmy?"

My brow wrinkling, I had to think about it for a moment before it dawned on me. "Oh, yes, the patient that would bring chopped wood over, right?" When she nodded, I asked, "He got released a couple of weeks ago, didn't he?"

"He did, but he's back."

I wasn't surprised; he had a severe case of paranoia and always frightened me a bit when he came around. "What did he do this time?" I asked, as I knew that he'd been in and out of the hospital for years.

"He suspected his wife was having an affair, and hid in the closet until she came home," the girl said, her eyes bright and voice animated as she told the story. "When she brought another man home with her, he stepped from the closet and shot them both right through the heart; he'll be staying in the section for the criminally insane now."

She walked away then, and I stopped what I was doing for a moment, a chill racing down my spine. What a terrifying thought that a potential murderer had stood in the same kitchen as me; I'd even talked to him a few times! And how horrible that his wife's life could have been spared if they hadn't released him. Between the incident with Doris and the news of Jimmy, I was reminded once again of the people by which I was surrounded.

Once I'd finished working in the kitchen, I went in search of Maisie and finally spotted her sitting alone on a park bench under a small grove of oak trees. She held what appeared to be a crumpled up piece of paper in her lap, and it looked as if she'd been crying. Distracted, I hurried toward her, failing to notice the two women creeping up quietly behind me.

Before I knew what was happening, someone grabbed my hair and yanked me backwards, slamming me painfully to the ground. Stars floated before my eyes as one woman straddled my legs while the other held me down by the shoulders, and with a sinking feeling in my stomach, I realized the one before me was Doris.

"Alice ain't here to help you this time, girly," she snarled. Her eyes were wild like a mad dog, and a sneer curled her lip as she loomed over me. Reaching into her pocket, she withdrew a pair of scissors and held them out for me to see. "Maybe this'll teach you a lesson."

She opened the scissors, the silver blade catching the sunlight as she lowered it toward my throat. My heart pounding, I struggled frantically and tried to call out for help, but no one was around. No one, except for Maisie.

My young friend launched herself at Doris with a fierce scream, knocking the much larger woman off as the two tumbled to the ground. The patient that held me by the shoulders leaped to her feet and fled through the trees, leaving me to push myself up and stumble towards Maisie and Doris, my head swimming. They were struggling over the scissors, and with a gasp, I saw Doris was on the verge of piercing Maisie's stomach with the sharp blade. Grabbing her by the hair, I yanked the woman away with all my might, barely dodging the fist she aimed at my kneecap.

I suddenly heard several yells heading in our direction, and both Doris and I froze. Shoving me backwards, Doris jumped up and ran, her wild hair steaming out behind her like the straw from a witch's broom. The attendants saw her and immediately gave chase, while another hurried towards Maisie and me. After explaining what happened, we were taken back to our ward and told to stay put.

Maisie and I sank down onto our beds, both shaking and weak from such an experience, and I grabbed Maisie's hand, thanking her profusely for coming to my rescue.

"I'm just glad I was there," she said, sighing. "I believe she was going to kill you."

"Yes, so do I," I agreed, my stomach clenching.

About an hour later, two attendants came into the room to tell us that Doris had been caught.

"We spoke to Mrs. Dobson, and she confirmed that you've never been a problem, and also that Doris had it in for you after a minor mishap earlier today," one of them told me. "So, there won't be any punishment on your end."

"What about Doris?" Maisie asked.

"We have put her back into isolation," the other lady replied. "She was allowed some freedom to work in the kitchen on a trial basis, but she'll most likely stay in isolation permanently now."

I hope so, I thought after they left. Because if she wasn't, I feared she really would kill me if given the chance.

After the attendants were gone, a sudden thought struck me and I grabbed Maisie's arm, my eyes brightening with excitement.

"You didn't have an epileptic attack, Maisie!" I cried. "You were under a great strain and did just fine; perhaps you really *are* growing out of them."

Her eyes widening, Maisie said, "You're right! I can hardly believe it." Her face falling again, she glanced down and said, "I just wish my father could see that I'm doing better."

Taking her hand, I asked gently, "Did you receive a letter from home today? I noticed you looked upset earlier."

Nodding, she said, "Yes, from my sister. She's getting married next month, and I won't be able to be there for the wedding. Oh, Vivian, I miss my family so much. If only Father would let me come home!"

I nodded in understanding, giving her hand a compassionate squeeze. "Maybe your father and my husband will come to their senses soon, and we'll both get to go home," I said, although I feared Howard would never allow me to leave this place. If, that is, they ever found him.

Saturday afternoon, the asylum held its first dance since my arrival. Maisie wouldn't go, as loud music often brought on an attack, so I went alone. I didn't care to dance, but was curious to see what it was all about.

The gymnasium was filled with well over a thousand patients when I arrived, some dancing, while others watched from the sidelines. I stood in the entranceway for a moment, taking it all in with wide eyes. There were at least five hundred patients dancing, from awkward shufflers to smooth Fred Astaire types, and their clothing ranged from work clothes to party clothes to somewhere in between. One lady wore an outlandish hat from the 1910s, and I spotted an eccentric looking old man wearing a tuxedo with a monocle over his eye. The entire scene was a sight to behold.

I noticed an elderly lady with dementia whom I'd met once in the cafeteria sitting alone, and I went to sit beside her.

"Hello, Mrs. Wainwright," I spoke to her, smiling.

She looked at me suspiciously and asked, "How do you know my name?"

"I helped you find a seat in the cafeteria a few days ago," I explained.

"Oh," was all she said, and I knew she didn't remember. After a moment, she looked at me and asked in a small voice, "Would you mind telling me where I am?"

"You're at the hospital in Martinsville," I stated kindly, my heart going out to her. There were so many here that were just like her; lost, helpless, and confused. I wondered if Mrs. Wainwright's family ever came to visit her, and if they did, would the poor soul even recognize them?

A man who appeared to be in his late thirties approached me then and shyly asked if I wanted to dance. When I hesitated, he said, "I won't step on your toes, I promise," and the hopeful look in his eyes caused me to pause and reconsider.

"Oh, well, I suppose one dance won't hurt," I finally agreed.

The music was slow, but thankfully my partner didn't try to pull me too close. "What's your name?" He asked. "Mine is Winston."

"I'm Vivian," I told him. I looked him in the eye as we spoke, a common trait of mine, and he glanced away as if nervous or uncertain. "Where are you from, Winston?" I asked after a moment of awkward silence.

"Albany," he replied, clearing his throat. "I suppose you're wondering why I'm here."

I wasn't, but felt that he wished to tell me, so I nodded.

"I was in the Army when Pearl Harbor took place," he began, his voice low, "and I immediately got deployed. I was gone for a year, and I guess…I guess I wasn't capable of handling the stress of it all. When they sent me home, I tried to work on the railroad for a while, but everything was just different; *I* was different. I felt sad and lost all the time, and the constant talk of the war just made it worse. I started drinking so much that I lost my job, and finally my family had enough and saw that I came here. Pretty pathetic, isn't it?"

I'd heard of other men who came back from war this way; depressed, on edge, and unable truly to connect with others around them anymore. It was a sad thing, and I felt a wave of compassion for my dance partner.

"No," I told him, my voice kind. "I think this world gets to be a little too much for all of us sometimes."

He looked at me in surprise, and I saw a flicker of hope in the depths of his tired, gray eyes. "Thank you, Miss Vivian. That makes me feel a bit better," he said, and I thought for a moment that he was going to smile, but the look quickly disappeared.

The song had just ended when a familiar voice asked from behind, "May I have this next dance?"

I spun around to find Zachary standing there with a smile and an outstretched hand.

"Zachary!" I cried in surprise, placing my hand in his. "I didn't know you were here. How did you find me?"

"Well," he said, pulling me into his arms as the music started playing once again, "a couple of the nurses mentioned a dance in the gymnasium, so instead of sending someone to find you, I thought I'd just check myself; I figured you'd be too curious not to be here."

"You figured right," I chuckled. "I just had to see it for myself."

Zachary met my straightforward gaze and smiled. He was much taller than me, and his shoulders were surprisingly broad for a doctor. He kept a respectable distance between us, and I noticed that there was something about him that always put me at ease. He embodied a sense of calm and a genteel, down-to-earth charm, and although he was quite handsome, there didn't seem to be an arrogant bone in his body. He was also quite a good dancer, considering the slight limp he had from a childhood injury.

"Has anyone heard from Howard?" I asked hopefully. "Mother said y'all were still looking for him in her last letter."

"Unfortunately, we still haven't been able to locate him," Zachary sighed. "We won't give up, though. Your parents, Savannah, and even her in-laws are doing everything they can. In fact, when I last spoke with Leon Danes, he wanted you to know you're in his thoughts and prayers."

"How nice of him," I said, smiling. Leon and I had been friends since high school, and it was nice to know that I still had some support back home.

Suddenly, the girl dancing next to us fell to the floor with a moan, her entire body jerking violently, and we quickly jumped back. Most of the other patients ignored her and continued dancing, but I stared in horror as her eyes rolled into the back of her head and drool began oozing from the corner of her mouth.

"She's having an epileptic attack," Zachary said, immediately rushing to the girl's side. A couple of other patients joined him, and they pulled her away from the stomping feet of the crowd, her body tense and shaking.

Nurses were on the scene in seconds with a stretcher, and I stood by, watching as they picked her up, placed her onto the stretcher, quickly tied her down, and wheeled her away.

After witnessing such a scene, I stated I was feeling a bit shaky and wished to sit down. Nodding his head in understanding, Zachary took my hand and led me to a nearby chair.

"Would you like something to drink?" He asked with concern.

"Oh no," I replied with a wave of my hand, "I'll be fine in a moment."

Zachary sat beside me, his eyes drifting around the room. "Are you doing okay here in Martinsville? Are they treating you alright?" He asked after a moment.

"Some treat me better than others, but I'm doing the best that I can," I replied.

I decided not to tell him about Doris; I didn't want my family to be any more worried about me than they already were, and I went on to tell him about my job in the kitchen. "I actually sort of enjoy it," I said, shrugging my shoulders with a slight smile. "It reminds me of the days when I worked at my family's restaurant."

"Do you miss those days?" Zachary asked, crossing one ankle over his knee as he leaned back in his chair.

"Sometimes," I nodded. "I loved working there, and I had big plans of expansion when I took it over some day."

"Why didn't you continue working there after you were married?"

I was a little surprised at the question, as most men didn't want their

92

wives to work, and Howard had been no exception.

"Well, we lived too far out of town for one thing," I replied, "and there was so much to do at the farm. Plus, Howard didn't want me to keep working."

"Hmm, that's too bad," Zachary said. "Especially since you obviously loved it so much."

"Well, if I ever get out of here, maybe I'll go back," I replied, sighing wistfully at the thought.

I suddenly noticed a young man and woman step away from the crowd and sneak outside, and when I pointed it out to Zachary, he said, "I've heard that couples sometimes manage to escape and get married. It always seems to end in disaster, though, which isn't surprising."

It wasn't surprising in the least. The patients here were lonely and looking for someone to love them, but often weren't capable of having solid, long-term relationships. Whether it was from their mental condition, or because they were never shown love and didn't understand how to have a relationship, I didn't know.

"Miss, would you help me?" A small voice to my left asked, interrupting my thoughts.

I glanced over to find Mrs. Wainwright standing there, her shoulders hunched as her faded blue eyes searched my face.

"Yes, dear, what's the matter?" I asked, standing to my feet.

"I...I can't remember your name, but I'd really like to go to my room," she said weakly.

I reached for her purse and retrieved the small slip of paper with her information on it. It listed her name, age, and which ward she was assigned to; there should have been someone escorting her, but I didn't see any extra nurses around.

"Yes, I'll take you there now," I said, smiling kindly at her.

Zachary came along, both of us holding on to Mrs. Wainwright's elbows as we slowly walked across the grass. We'd just entered her building when a young female attendant saw us and came over.

"What do you think you're doing by bringing her here?" She addressed me, her tone sharp and disapproving. "You're supposed to let a nurse do that."

"Mrs. McCombs was only trying to help, as there didn't seem to be anyone escorting Mrs. Wainwright," Zachary stepped in. "I'm Doctor Holt, a friend of Mrs. McCombs, and if there is a problem, then I suggest you take it up with Dr. Hagan; he and I are good friends."

Zachary spoke in a kind, yet stern tone, and the attendant immediately became contrite. "There's no problem, Doctor," she said, forcing a smile as she took Mrs. Wainwright's arm and led her away.

"Thank you," I said, smiling gratefully at Zachary as we walked back outside.

93

"You're quite welcome," he replied. Turning to look at me, his eyes were a bit regretful as he said, "I've got to be going. Is there anything I can do before I leave?"

"No," I shook my head, wishing he didn't have to go so soon; it was nice being around someone from home. "You've helped me so much already. Will you give my love to my parents and Savannah? And please thank Leon for his kind message when you next see him."

"I will," he nodded.

I watched him walk away and sighed, feeling as if he were taking "home" with him. I hoped and prayed that they would find Howard soon; I may be surviving in this place and trying to remain positive, but what I hadn't told anyone was the toll it was taking on me. Being away from home in a place full of such sadness, violence, and negativity was draining the life out of me. The longer I was here, the more thankful I was for Maisie; I often felt that her friendship and having someone to talk to were the only things keeping me sane.

18

Eva

When the evening of the dance arrived, Davey was better, but not completely well yet. I was going to call Savannah and explain that I couldn't attend the dance with her after all, but Nana and Mutter insisted I go.

"We'll stay and see about Davey," they both said. "It's been far too long since you've had any fun, so go out and enjoy yourself."

As I got ready, Mutter came into my room and asked if I'd like help with my hair.

"Yes, please," I nodded, sitting eagerly in front of the vanity mirror. I always did a good enough job with my hair, but Mutter just seemed to have the magic touch.

"I remember the first time your father took me dancing," she said, a smile in her voice as she gently ran her fingers through my hair.

Looking at her in the reflection in the mirror, I asked, "Will you tell me about it?"

I'd heard this story countless times before, but it never grew old and Mutter never grew tired of telling it. I loved listening to her speak. Her voice was so soft and lyrical, and I could see my childhood and our beautiful homeland reflected in her words.

"I was so young," she said, shaking her head as a dreamy sigh passed her lips, "but I knew he would be the man I married someday; the war was long and hard, but just being in his presence gave me such joy. I can still see him standing there in his uniform, holding an enormous bouquet of flowers when I opened my front door. I don't know why he liked me, to be honest, because I barely spoke a word the whole way to the dance."

"He liked you because he could see how beautiful you are, on the inside and out," I said, smiling at her in the mirror.

Her cheeks flushing a bit at the compliment, Mutter gently rolled and pinned my hair up on the sides, her fingers as light as a feather. "I don't know about that," she said with a small laugh as she fluffed the ends of my hair. "Your father certainly was handsome, though, and I loved how he spoke so fondly of his homeland and this beautiful city we now live in."

"You were nervous, too, when we came here, weren't you?" I asked, recalling the butterflies I had in my own stomach when we arrived in Savannah.

Nodding, she said, "Yes, and even though I miss Germany sometimes, I wouldn't go back. This is our home now."

I felt the same way. We may have had our fair share of struggles here, but there was something about this place, this city, that soaked deep into your soul, the way paint soaks into a canvas. The vibrant colors and details had somehow woven their way through my veins, forever sealing and binding within my heart like a promise, and I knew I would never be happy living anywhere else. I loved Germany and always would, but like Mutter said, this was our home now.

"You look beautiful, der Liebling," Mutter said, pulling me away from my thoughts as she leaned around to kiss my cheek.

The doorbell rang at five minutes past seven and, after telling everyone goodbye, I hurried through the house, my heels clicking against the hardwood floors. I was wearing a soft, blue dress that matched my eyes perfectly, but I hoped no one would notice how old and a bit worn the dress was; I'd had it for years and couldn't afford to buy a new one. I'd worn it only on special occasions, so it was still in good shape…even if there was a small stain at the bottom and a patched tear under the arm.

When I opened the door, Savannah smiled at me and, lacing her arm through mine as we walked towards her car, said, "Your hair looks amazing, and I love your dress! I'm so glad you decided to come. I really wanted to go tonight, but hated to go by myself."

My heart immediately warmed at Savannah's kind and thoughtful compliment, as I knew she hadn't missed how out of style my dress was. It seemed that she could tell how uncertain I felt and was attempting to put me at ease. I'd never had many friends and hardly knew what to say, but I quickly felt my nerves calm in her presence as we drove to the Masonic lodge.

"How is your husband?" I asked when she mentioned his name.

"He writes as often as he can," she replied, her voice becoming a bit wistful, and I could tell that she missed him very much. "He seems to be doing well; he just misses home. I try not to worry about him too much, but after what happened last year, I just can't help myself."

At the look of question on my face, she explained, "His plane was shot down, and he was listed as missing in action for several months. It was a very hard time for us all, and when he suddenly returned home in September right in the middle of a hurricane, we discovered that he'd almost died in the plane crash and was saved by a German couple who took him into their home and nursed him back to health."

"That's amazing," I said, captivated by the tale.

"Yes, it is," she nodded, smiling as she added, "it was during that hurricane when I realized for the first time how much I loved him."

By the time she'd finished with the story, we were pulling into the parking lot of the Masonic lodge. As we walked inside the large, two-story building, the party was just beginning. Lights were strung from the ceiling, chairs lined the walls, and a large table in the corner was piled high with sandwiches, cookies, and punch. The room was filled with so many laughing, chattering faces that I immediately took a small step behind Savannah, feeling a little overwhelmed by all the people. I always felt uncomfortable in large crowds, especially when I hardly knew anyone.

A band was setting up in the corner, and I noticed Leon standing in the crowd talking to a very pretty young woman.

"That's Lucy Michaels," Savannah said when she saw me looking Leon's way, her lips pursed as she watched them. "She asked him to escort her tonight."

"That's nice," I replied with a smile.

Her brow cocked, Savannah looked at me and said, "You say that now, but just wait until you meet her."

I wasn't sure what she meant by that and I didn't ask, but as I followed Savannah through the crowd, I looked back at Lucy and wondered why Savannah apparently didn't like her.

Savannah took me around and introduced me to so many people that I couldn't have remembered their names if I'd tried. Some were friendlier than others, and although I made certain to speak as slowly and plainly as possible, some still detected my accent and I immediately felt their walls go up. Trying to make conversation with complete strangers was exhausting, but when I knew they didn't like me, it became doubly hard.

There were several soldiers milling around who were home on rotation, and I caught a glimpse of Zachary standing by himself and sipping on a glass of punch. He caught my gaze and smiled, a sandwich in his hand as he waved to me.

Someone called Savannah's name then, and she hurried across the room, stating that she'd be right back. As soon as she left, the band began getting their instruments ready and the men immediately began asking ladies to dance. I moved to stand against the wall, my stomach clenching nervously. I'd taken ballet in Germany, but the only man I'd ever danced with was Paul and I felt anxious about dancing with a stranger now; I only hoped that I wouldn't embarrass myself too badly. I saw a young soldier heading in my direction and I took a deep breath, blinking in surprise when another soldier pushed him out of the way and got to me first.

"May I have this dance?" He asked, his eyes twinkling.

I nodded, shyly taking his hand as we joined the other couples on the dance floor and waited for the music to begin. The Masons had hired quite a large band, and the first song they began to play was the fast-paced, jazzy arrangement of "Sing, Sing, Sing" by Benny Goodman. With a glint in his eye and a grin on his face, my partner took my hand and began spinning me around like a top as we quickly tapped our feet to the beat.

As the evening progressed, it didn't take long to realize what a wonderful time I was having, and I was surprised to find that most of the men I danced with either didn't notice my accent or didn't care. Everyone was polite and happy and just having a good time, which was rare these days with the war, and I soon began to relax and enjoy myself. Jackson, from the restaurant, was also at the party, and asked me to dance three times; he was about to ask for a fourth when the band began to play another fast-paced song and he backed out.

"I'd better not," he said, running his fingers through his thinning, brown hair. "I have a heart murmur, you know, which is why I couldn't enlist."

"I didn't realize that," I said, stepping off to the sidelines with him to take a break.

As we watched the others dance, Jackson glanced at me and asked, "How is your son doing?"

"He's much better, thank you," I replied, smiling.

He smiled back, reaching up to loosen the black tie that was cinched tightly at his throat. He was in his early thirties with a rather large, crooked nose and dark, squinty eyes, and I noticed for the first time that he had a small scar running along his left temple.

Before we could talk any longer, a young man stepped up and asked me to dance, and I accepted. As he spun me out onto the dance floor, I suddenly realized that I hadn't told Jackson about Davey's illness, and wondered how he had known about it.

By the time ten o'clock rolled around, I was exhausted, but still enjoying myself. I took a break and sat in one of the chairs that lined the walls, reaching down to rub my aching feet.

"You look tired," a familiar voice said, and I looked up to find Zachary smiling down at me. He wore a gray suit with a neatly pressed white shirt, gray vest, and matching tie. I noticed that, even with all the gray, the color of his aqua eyes hadn't changed a bit. He looked very handsome and well put together, with not one hair out of place. "Would you like some punch?" He asked.

"Oh, no, I wouldn't want to bother you," I said, shaking my head.

"It's no bother at all," he assured me, returning seconds later with a glass full of the tangy, red liquid.

Sitting next to me, he asked, "How is Davey?"

"He's much better," I told him as I took a sip of the refreshingly cool drink. "I believe he'll be back to normal by Monday."

"That's good," Zachary said, his eyes trained on all the couples dancing around us. "Are you having a good time tonight?"

"Yes, very much," I replied, tilting my head as I smiled.

Turning to face me, Zachary asked, "Have you seen any more of the man that was following you?"

I took another sip and shook my head. "No," I replied, shivering at the memory. "Perhaps…perhaps it was just my imagination."

"Has anything like that ever happened before?"

I hesitated, thinking the question over. "No," I finally answered, "it hasn't."

"Then it probably wasn't your imagination," Zachary said, his tone serious. "I'm not trying to scare you, but our instincts are often correct. Just keep an eye out and be careful, okay?"

"Okay," I nodded.

"Do you own a gun, by chance?"

"Oh, no," I said, my eyes widening. "I could never shoot anyone."

"No, I suppose not," Zachary stated with a knowing smile. "You're much too gentle and sweet to harm anyone."

I blinked, a bit surprised by the kind words. Just then, a young woman came up to Zachary and quite boldly asked him to dance. With a look of surprise, Zachary nodded and, after excusing himself, followed the woman to the dance floor.

As I sat there quietly watching everyone, I thought about the conversation with Zachary and felt a sense of heaviness settle over me. I hadn't said so to Zachary, but I felt he was possibly right, and found myself wondering who the man was and why he would be following me.

19

THE SHADOW

He stood against the wall, watching as the doctor left Eva to sit alone. She had a thoughtful, worried expression on her face, and he wondered what they'd been talking about. He was too far across the room to read their lips, but by the troubled look in her eyes, it must have been quite a serious conversation.

A young woman bumped against him then, and he moved out of her way with a scowl. He could be pleasant when he wanted, but he was here for one reason only and didn't wish to be distracted. He strolled the perimeter of the room in the direction of the punch table, his eyes trained on Eva, and chuckled under his breath as he thought of his uncanny ability to be a chameleon. He could be charming, pitiful, and hateful all within the span of just a few seconds, and the way he could so easily disguise his voice was second to none. During high school, he'd been told time after time that he should be an actor, and in another life, perhaps he would have been.

He stopped at the refreshment table and poured himself a glass of punch, downing it like a shot of whiskey. He wished the stuff really was spiked with something stronger; he'd been here all evening, and his feet ached from dancing. He wouldn't leave, however, until Eva did.

He watched as another young man asked Eva to dance, and his eyes followed the couple as they joined the others on the dance floor. Within seconds, the look of worry was gone from Eva's face and her cheeks turned pink with enjoyment as her newest dance partner spun her around to the fast-paced song. Her soft blue eyes had come alive and were sparkling like two sapphires, and he couldn't seem to pull his gaze away from her. She really was a beautiful woman, despite the old, outdated clothes she wore, and the fact that she had no idea how beautiful she was just made her even more appealing. He could imagine how she looked at night when she slept, her angelic face bathed in moonlight, and those long eyelashes softly brushing against her cheeks…

Another party-goer brushed past him again, bumping his arm and causing the punch in his glass to slosh onto his fingers. His jaw clenched, he snatched a handkerchief from his pocket and wiped the liquid from his hand. He disliked being around so many people and hoped he could control his temper for the rest of the evening.

20

Eva

M y new dance partner asked me to dance three more times until, exhausted and out of breath, I finally told him I needed to take a break. When I found the closest chair that I could sit in, I collapsed with a sigh and reached down to rub my throbbing feet.

I spotted Savannah pushing her way through the crowd and smiled at her as she came to sit beside me. She'd danced just as much as I had, and during her breaks, she'd helped the organizers hand out refreshments instead of resting. She was like a top that never quit spinning, and I liked her warmth and energy.

"Are you having fun?" She asked, slipping out of her shoes to wiggle her toes.

"Yes, very much," I said, nodding.

"Wonderful! Have you gotten a chance to dance with Leon? He was looking for you earlier."

"No, I haven't," I replied, glancing around the room in search of my neighbor.

With a yawn, Savannah leaned back against the chair and watched as the dozens of couples twirled and skipped to the beat of the music, a small smile tugging at her lips. "You know," she said after a moment, "this reminds me of a dance that The Red Cross held for Valentine's Day on Tybee Island a few years ago."

I turned to look at her, noting the wistful tone in her voice as she spoke. "I'd never learned to dance," she continued, smiling ruefully at me, "so I stayed behind the refreshment table and kept myself occupied. Well, Connor insisted I learn how, and proceeded to drag me out onto the dance floor. I was so embarrassed at first, but looking back now, I only remember how much fun that night was."

Seeing the nostalgic look on Savannah's face that only a sweet memory can bring, I smiled and said, "You must have caught on quickly; I've been watching you tonight, and you're a wonderful dancer."

"No, I didn't catch on quickly at all," she shook her head, laughing. "Connor had to continue teaching me for several weeks after that."

Sighing, her smiled slipped a bit and she said with a small sigh, "Sometimes I really miss those days."

I knew what she meant. Being young and carefree was a memory that one would always hold on to and look back on with fondness and even a bit of yearning. It was a time of fun and gaiety and no worries, and I could clearly remember the warmth of summer days spent swimming in the lake near our house, and hear the ringing of laughter around the tree at Christmas time. Growing older could be bittersweet, but how else would more memories be made? Every second that passed and each day that went by gives one the chance to discover new things, to learn what it is to love fully and deeply, to realize what's truly important in life, and to grow stronger from the mistakes that are made.

"Perhaps when your husband returns, you can make many more special, meaningful memories together," I said, smiling softly at my new friend.

Savannah looked at me then, her eyes filling with tears as she reached out to take my hand. "Thank you for that, Eva," she said, squeezing my fingers. "I may miss the "good old days" sometimes, but more than anything, I want my husband to come home so we can spend the rest of our days together."

We were interrupted just then when a worker asked Savannah to help her with something, and Savannah quickly excused herself and hurried away with the young woman. As I continued to sit and watch the happy, smiling faces around me, I suddenly noticed a familiar figure standing at the punch table by himself. When he turned towards me, I realized it was Kirk, Mr. Fernsby's grandson, and I threw up my hand in a small wave. He stared at me for a moment, his gaze hard, and then finally looked away without making any form of acknowledgment. My cheeks flushing, I dropped my hand back into my lap and sighed.

"May I have this dance?"

Startled, as I didn't realize anyone had approached me, I glanced up to find a man in his early forties with wispy blonde hair standing beside me, his hand outstretched. With a shy nod, I took his hand and followed him out onto the dance floor.

"What is your name?" He asked politely. "I'm Phil Creed."

"My name is Eva," I replied, and as we danced, I couldn't help but stare at the unusual color of his eyes. One might call them blue, but they were so light in shade that they were almost clear.

"It's very nice to meet you," he said with a pleasant smile. His accent wasn't from any of the southern states, but I couldn't tell exactly from where it came. "Thank you for dancing with me," he added. "I'll admit I'm feeling a bit out of my comfort zone."

Tilting my head to one side, I asked, "Why is that?"

Sighing, he glanced down at the floor and said, "My wife used to go to parties and dances with me, but she recently passed away and…" a cloud passed over his face then, and he stopped to clear his throat. Feeling a wave of compassion for my dance partner, as I knew how he felt, I waited until he could continue. Forcing a smile, he looked up at me and said, "Well, I'm just feeling a little lost without her. I wouldn't have come tonight if my coworker hadn't asked me."

"I'm very sorry for your loss," I said gently. "My husband passed away last year."

His eyes widening, Mr. Creed said, "Oh, my, you're much too young to be a widow. I'm so sorry. I'm thankful to have had nearly twenty years with my wife."

The song ended then, and I spotted Leon heading my way. I thanked Mr. Creed for the dance, and he said kindly, "Thank *you* for your kindness."

"There you are," Leon said, smiling brightly as he stepped around Mr. Creed, "I've been trying to catch you alone all night."

"Why is that?" I asked as Mr. Creed turned and walked away.

"So I could actually have a turn to dance with you," he winked.

Smiling, I accepted his hand and allowed him to pull me into his arms as another song began to play, and I tilted my head back to look up at my handsome neighbor. He'd taken off his suit coat and rolled up the sleeves of his green shirt, the color bringing out the green flecks in his eyes, and his tie was pulled loose and hanging to one side. The song was a slow one, and it didn't take long to discover what a wonderful dancer he was. "Where is your date?" I asked after a moment.

"She went to powder her nose or something," he said, shrugging. "You look beautiful, by the way. I didn't realize you were coming tonight."

"Thank you. Your sister-in-law invited me," I replied, explaining how we'd met at the hospital earlier that week. "She's so nice; I like her very much."

"Yeah, she's great," Leon said, clearing his throat, and I immediately sensed that there was something I didn't know about him and Savannah. When he saw the question in my eyes, he sighed and said, "I fancied myself in love with her about a year ago and, like an idiot, told her so. Needless to say, it didn't go well."

My eyes widening at his statement, I said with sincerity, "I'm very sorry. Her marrying your brother must have been very hard."

"I thought at first that it would be, but after doing a bit of intense, self-examination, I realized I didn't feel as deeply for her as I thought. I can now sincerely say that I'm happy for she and Connor; they're really great together."

"Good, I'm glad," I replied, smiling. "And now you're happy with Lucy?"

Leon blinked, as if caught off guard by the question. "Oh, I wouldn't say that Lucy and I are "together"; we're just good friends. I've known her for ages." He grew quiet for a moment, and I could tell that he was deep in

103

thought about something. Finally, he said, "You know, I'm beginning to wonder if I'll ever find the right woman. I have this idea of what love is or what it should feel like, and I've never truly found it for myself. Oh, I thought I had a time or two, but looking back I now know that it wasn't real."

"What do you think true love should feel like?" I asked curiously.

Leon thought about my question for a moment, and with a faraway look in his eyes, he said softly, "It should have the passion of a thunderstorm, the sweetness of honey, the depth of an ocean, and the honesty of a child. The one you love should make you feel whole and complete, like you don't belong anywhere on this earth but with them." He looked at me then and smiled sheepishly. "I'm a hopeless romantic at heart, and I think I may be searching for something that doesn't exist…at least, not for me, anyway. If you don't mind my asking, how did it feel with your husband?"

I tilted my head to the side, thinking over the question carefully. "It was a feeling of warmth and safety and…belonging," I finally said softly. "Wherever he was, that's where I wanted to be. When I came to America, I didn't fit in and I always felt like a misfit, but with Paul I finally found a home and someone I could trust and lean on."

Leon studied me for a moment, the look in his hazel eyes unreadable. "What about passion?" He finally asked. "Did your heart feel like a runaway train when he was near, or is that something only in fairytales?"

I was a bit taken aback by the question, but before I could answer, the song was over and Lucy had made her way back to Leon's side. She was very tiny and petite, and the dress she wore was stunning and obviously quite expensive. She wore a diamond bracelet with matching earrings, and when she came to stand beside Leon, she raised a thin, manicured brow in my direction. When Leon introduced us, I smiled shyly at her and said that it was nice to make her acquaintance.

"Do you mind if I have my date back now?" She asked, cutting straight to the point.

I blinked, surprised by her abruptness. She stared at me with the same cocked brow, her gaze cool, and I noticed Leon was momentarily distracted by a friend and wasn't paying any attention. I always tried to see the best in people, and as I nodded and stepped back, I told myself that she probably hadn't intended to be so rude.

"By the way, honey," she said, leaning closer and lowering her voice, "that dress it terribly out of style."

She took Leon's arm and pulled him away then, leaving me to stand there in utter humiliation. Wishing that I could find somewhere to hide, I went to sit by myself in the corner, fighting the tears that burned my eyes. I could see now why Savannah didn't like Lucy, and after being the recipient of such harsh, hateful words, I was beginning to wish that I hadn't even come tonight.

The music started playing again, and I closed my eyes, grateful for the distraction as I soaked in the slow, beautiful melody. This was one of my favorite songs, and I couldn't stop the words from flowing softly past my lips as the verse started. I hadn't, however, realized anyone was close enough to hear me when, suddenly, someone called out, "Hey, Henry, wait a minute!"

The music stopped and everyone, including myself, turned in surprise to look at the man who stood before me. Grinning, he took my arm and pulled me to my feet, calling loudly to the band, "This beauty can sing it better than y'all can." He then turned back to me and said, "Go show 'em how it's done, sweetheart. I heard you singing just now, and it was gorgeous."

My eyes widening, I felt the blood leave my face and immediately shook my head. "Oh, no, I couldn't," I said pleadingly.

"Oh, come on," he insisted as he began leading me through the crowd. "They'll love you."

Before I knew it, I was standing before the microphone with everyone's eyes on me. My heart was pounding so fiercely in my chest that I thought for a moment I might be sick. I simply couldn't bring myself to sing in front of all these people, I just couldn't! I'd suffered from severe stage fright since I was a child, and after fainting once from overwrought nerves during a ballet recital, my parents never made me perform in front of people again.

The music started playing then, and before I could flee from the stage, I caught Savannah's eye; she smiled encouragingly at me and gave me a thumbs up, her black eyes sparkling with excitement. She'd been so kind to bring me here tonight and introduce me to everyone that I realized I couldn't embarrass her by running off.

Taking a deep breath, I closed my eyes, praying that I wouldn't faint as I let the music flow over me for a moment. I forced myself to pretend that I was all alone in an open field full of wildflowers, and when the chords to the verse started, I opened my mouth and softly began to sing.

"Oh, Danny boy, the pipes, the pipes are calling," I sang, my voice trembling a bit at first. "From glen to glen, and down the mountain side."

I'd always loved this song. No one knew if it came from a lover's or parent's point of view, but I'd always felt that it was the lonely, sad cry of a woman bidding farewell to her one and only true love. When I reached the chorus, my eyes slid open, and I found my gaze drawn to a certain man standing amongst the crowd. He stared back at me with a smile of admiration on his handsome face, and I wasn't certain if it was the music or the lyrics or something else entirely, but suddenly I felt something stir deep inside of me. We continued to gaze at one another, as if our eyes were locked together somehow, and I found myself growing warm and a bit breathless.

The song ended then, breaking the spell, and there was a loud thundering

105

of applause. I blushed profusely and smiled, thanking everyone with a small curtsy before I quickly left the stage and hurried to Savannah's side.

"You were amazing!" She cried, grabbing my hand. "You sing like an angel, Eva."

I was trembling all over, my face as red as a tomato as everyone came by to compliment me. I dipped my head and thanked them all, grateful that Savannah remained at my side for the rest of the evening.

That night after Savannah dropped me off at my house, Leon's question suddenly flitted back through my mind. Did Paul and I have the kind of passion that Leon had described? We'd loved each other very much and I felt lost without him, but I wasn't certain if one would have called our relationship a passionate one. I was comfortable with him, yes, but for the life of me I couldn't remember my heart ever feeling like a "runaway train", and that bothered me. Perhaps, though, it was like Leon said and that sort of thing only existed in fairytales.

As I slowly ambled up the driveway, I began to think of how I'd felt while I was singing. I wasn't certain if I'd simply gotten caught up in the lyrics or if the attraction I'd felt was real, but I didn't believe I was ready to travel down that road again just yet. I had been married and widowed and suffered the pain of losing a spouse, and it was too soon to develop an attraction to someone new. Besides, I had no way of knowing if he felt the same way, and so I convinced myself to just forget the whole thing.

When I finally made it to the door and walked inside, I failed to notice the shadowy figure standing alone on the sidewalk beneath the weeping willow, his steady gaze watching my every move.

21

Vivian

It was a Thursday evening, and I had to work late in the kitchen. By the time I stepped out the back door to leave, the sun had gone down and darkness had spread its heavy, umbrous blanket. The moon was full, but the grounds were covered in shadows, and I pulled my sweater tightly around my shoulders, shivering as a cool breeze whistled and moaned along the side of the building like a ghost searching for its lost love. As the moon slipped in and out of the clouds, shadows of trees and branches moved along the wall like puppets with reaching hands and grasping fingers, and I found myself feeling a bit uneasy.

Suddenly, a different sound made its way through the wind's whispers and the rustling of leaves, and I hesitated, peering uncertainly through the darkness.

"Maisie?" I called out, thinking that perhaps she'd been waiting outside the kitchen and wanted to walk back to our building with me. There was, however, no answer, and I wondered if perhaps it had been the wind after all.

The back door opened just then, and Mrs. Dobson stepped out to toss a bag of trash into the nearby can.

"You'd better get going, Vivian, or you're liable to get into trouble," she warned when she saw me standing there.

"Yes, ma'am," I nodded.

I walked around the back way, deciding to take the shortcut. There was a small path that ran behind all the buildings and, if I hurried, I might be able to get back before the night shift attendant took over; she was irritable and didn't like me, and I knew she would kick up a fuss if I got back too late.

As I walked, leaves crunched beneath my feet and the breeze ruffled fallen tendrils around my face. The path was narrow and lined with a thick forest on one side and buildings on the other, and I had to squint in order to discern where to walk. As I couldn't see very well, my ears magnified every sound; the distant hooting of an owl, the sound of pine cones falling in the forest, the rustling of leaves and branches as if something other than the wind walked amongst them. I took a deep breath, wondering what it was about a dark, windy night that always put me on edge.

Suddenly, I heard it again. The same noise I'd heard outside of the kitchen. It sounded like the deep, heavy breaths one takes in their sleep, and I paused, listening intently. I then turned and peered down the path, my eyes taking in the dark abyss which drifted out behind me. I couldn't see a thing, and was about to continue on my way again when I heard the crunching of dead, dry leaves. With a catch of my breath, I realized the shadow I'd thought was part of the trees was actually a large, hooded man…and he was coming right towards me.

I couldn't see his face, but there was something very sinister about the calm and quiet way he steadily approached me. With my heart in my throat, I turned and ran as fast as I possibly could, and like a gift from above, the moon moved from beneath a cloud and illuminated the path before me in a soft, shadowy light. The heavy breathing and snapping of twigs grew louder, and I knew the man was chasing me as the sounds drew closer and closer. I needed to scream, to call out for help, but all of my energy was focused on getting away, and I couldn't seem to find enough breath in my burning lungs to force out anything above a whimper.

I could see the back light of my building just up ahead, and I pushed myself to go faster. ***Keep going…you're almost there…just a few more yards***. I could hear him panting as he drew nearer, the sounds growing louder with each passing second, and I was too afraid to look over my shoulder for fear I would trip and fall. Suddenly, the back door to my building opened, and a figure stepped outside to take a smoke; I could see the smoldering of a cigarette in their hand.

Grasping the opportunity, I took a quick, deep breath and yelled, "Help!", my voice too breathless to carry much volume.

The young attendant somehow heard my cry and spun to face me, and I could hear the man behind me skid to a stop. Without looking back, I continued running until I made it to my building. Once there, I turned back to point out the man to the attendant, but he was gone. The attendant called several night guards and commanded them to search for an intruder or a patient on the loose, but they found no one.

Much to my dismay, the night-watch attendant, Mrs. Dash, had already arrived. When I told her what happened, she accused me of lying, of trying to cover up for being so late. She was a cruel woman in her mid-forties, with graying brown hair and hard, brown eyes; I'd seen her slap Ruby on many occasions simply for not moving out of her way fast enough. I stood in obedient silence as I listened to her rant, all the while trembling on the inside over what had almost happened. No matter what she said, someone had been after me, and I decided to never use the back way again.

That night, I lay awake as our building came alive with screams, shouts, cries, and moans. Although I'd grown accustomed to such sounds, it was much worse tonight, and I would later come to learn that it was because of the full moon. It made some patients nervous, some emotional, and others more violent and paranoid than they already were. I finally covered my head with my pillow, trying to shut out the sounds.

The next morning, I arrived in the kitchen a few minutes before seven. As soon as I stepped through the door, I could hear the buzz of excited chatter emanating throughout the room, and as I pushed my way to Alice's side, I heard whispered comments like "she didn't even see it coming" and "no one knows why he did it".

"What's going on?" I asked Alice as I tied an apron around my waist.

"You haven't heard?" She asked incredulously. When I shook my head "no", she said, "One of those new, young nurses got her skull bashed in late last night; they found her body this morning. After doing a bit of investigating, they found a bloody axe handle under one of the male patient's beds. He said the full moon made him do it."

I felt the blood drain from my face as I stared at Alice, wide-eyed. "What will they do to him?" I wanted to know, wondering if it was the same man that had been after me last night.

"They called the sheriff and I guess there'll be a hearing or something, but I don't think they quite know what to do yet."

That night, everyone had just settled into their beds when there was a sudden, loud commotion which came from outside. We all jumped up and, ignoring the shouted commands of our night attendant to stay put, gathered at the windows, some patients pushing others roughly out of the way to see what was going on.

There, across the lawn, lights pierced the darkness as shadowy figures forced their way past the gates and onto the hospital property. At least fifty men, some carrying rifles and others axes, pushed past the guards and marched towards our building. There were shouts and whistles and warnings to stop, but the ignored commands soon faded away as fear of the mob and their rifles took control.

Maisie and I opened our window so that we could better hear what was going on, and I winced in pain when Ruby pressed closer and stepped on my bare foot. Ignoring the discomfort, I pressed my face against the metal bars, squinting as I strained to see through the darkness of the night.

The men were drawing closer, the lanterns they carried rocking back and forth in their hands like the beams from a lighthouse, and in the glow of the lantern lights, I could see the men's faces. Their jaws were set, their eyes glittered fiercely, and by the determined, almost savage expression on each of their faces, I knew they were out for blood.

They all moved as one, giant shadow across the lawn, their steps in perfect sync as if they were soldiers marching to war, and I held my breath, waiting to see if they would stop at our building or continue on. When they suddenly turned to the right and began moving away, I realized where they were going and that was to Building M3, where the murderer was.

We could hear shouts off in the distance, and the excited chatter in our room died down as we all strained to listen. We couldn't make out much, but it wasn't long before we saw them again. They were quieter this time and less hurried as they made their journey back across the lawn. Their faces were still set in stone, but the fierceness in their eyes had dwindled out like a dying fire. They didn't speak or make any sound as they made their way back out through the gates, and as their silhouettes faded off into the darkness of the night, I wondered just what they'd done.

A young guard scurried past our building just then, stopping to glance up at us when one woman called out and asked what happened.

"They killed him," he said in a breathless voice. "The townsmen killed him."

Eva

It was almost eleven o'clock, and the breakfast crowd was finally dwindling down. I was helping Cook slice vegetables for the afternoon meal when Mr. Parker entered the kitchen with a slightly familiar man by his side. I stopped what I was doing to study the man, trying to remember from where I knew him. When he suddenly looked directly at me, I blinked in surprise; it was Mr. Creed, from the dance.

"Everyone," Mr. Parker said, clearing his throat to gain our attention, "this is Mr. Creed. Someone reported smelling gas while they were eating their breakfast this morning, so he's here to look at all the gas lines. Please, be courteous and stay out of his way."

As I turned around to get back to work, I heard one of the dishwasher's murmur, "I ain't smelled no gas."

"Some people always have to complain about something," someone behind me replied with a sigh.

"Well, they can't complain about the cooking, so I guess they had to go looking for something else," Cook grunted, eyeing Mr. Creed.

Minding my own business, I'd just placed a handful of chopped celery into a large bowl when a figure stepped up beside me.

"Well, hello there, Eva."

Turning to look into the unusually translucent colored eyes, I smiled and said, "Hello, Mr. Creed. I didn't realize you worked for the gas company."

"Yes, I've worked there for years," he replied with a friendly smile. "I also didn't realize that you worked here at the restaurant. I've eaten here a few times and always enjoyed it, so I must give my compliments to the chef."

"She's not the only one that does the cooking," Cook interrupted,

110

cocking an eyebrow at the two of us, "and she needs to be helping me chop vegetables right now instead of standing around gabbing with an old friend."

His brow furrowing at her rude comment, Mr. Creed turned his icy gaze on Cook and stared at her for a moment in silence. Finally, with a tight smile and quick nod, he turned back to me and said warmly, "I'd better get to work. It was nice seeing you again, Eva."

I nodded, my cheeks flushing at Cook's glare, and I hurriedly got back to work. As Mr. Creed walked into one of the side rooms, a couple of the workers raised an eyebrow at me and said, "Looks like Eva here has a friend."

"He's a bit old for her, though, ain't he?" another said.

My eyes widening at their cruel jokes, I did my best to ignore the snickers and comments, breathing a sigh of relief when Mr. Parker chose that moment to step back into the kitchen and check on things. When he came around, everyone immediately toed the line and became quiet and contrite. He stopped and spoke to me, as he always did, and my heart warmed at his kindness.

Mr. Creed didn't stay long, and once he was gone, everyone had forgotten about my "friend" and left me alone. After that, the day passed quickly and easily. Cook allowed me to try my own recipe for the first time for the evening meal, and I received raving reviews from the patrons for my Schnitzel and mashed potatoes with Black Forest Cake for dessert. As I didn't want the dish to be associated with a German name, however, I simply called it "breaded, pan-fried pork and chocolate cake with cherries", and no one knew the difference. Both recipes were from my grandmother, and a very popular dish in my country; I could still see us standing at the counter in Oma's small kitchen as she showed me how to pound the meat into thin pieces before we fried them, and I could smell the amazing aroma that filled the house as the cake was baking. I was only seven when she died and cherished the few memories I had of her.

When I got home that evening, I noticed Davey was in an unusually grumpy mood. As we all ate supper together, he didn't want to eat his food and kept swinging his feet and kicking the bottom of the table, even after I asked him to stop. After supper, he went into the living room to play, and I asked Nana and Mutter what was wrong.

"He's been in a contrary mood all day," Nana replied, shrugging. "Perhaps he didn't sleep well last night."

"He also wouldn't take his nap this afternoon," Mutter spoke up, "so he's probably just tired."

I couldn't help but smile as I helped gather the dishes to wash up. Neither of them wished for him to get into trouble, and they were both making as many excuses for him as they could.

Once the dishes were done, I called out to Davey that it was time for bed and asked him to put his toys away. When I stepped into the living room a few moments later, he'd made no attempt to clean up and was still playing with his toy soldiers.

Thinking that perhaps he hadn't heard me, I said, "Davey, put your toys away and let's go brush your teeth."

"No," he stated stubbornly. "I still playing."

"Put them away, honey, it's time for bed," I said patiently.

When he simply ignored me and continued playing, I tried, "If you don't put your toys away, you won't get a bedtime story tonight."

Frowning, Davey turned his back to me and sat on the floor, making no effort to do as he was told. With a sigh, I walked across the room and picked him up. When he started to fuss, I sat on the sofa with him in my lap and looked him in the eye as I said, "You're always such a good boy, Davey, so why won't you do as I ask? Is something wrong?"

His eyes filling with tears, Davey looked down at his hands and said, "I broke our pictures."

Brow furrowing, I asked, "What do you mean, sweetie?"

In a downtrodden voice, Davey replied, "I was lookin' at our pictures and broke them."

Uncertain of what he meant, I asked Davey to show me. Taking my hand, he led me into his room and opened the bottom drawer of his dresser. When I looked inside, I saw that he'd apparently been looking through the family picture album and dropped it. In an attempt to hide his blunder, he'd shoved the loose photos and torn pages under his clothes inside the drawer.

"I sorry, Mommy," he said, his lower lip trembling.

"Oh, honey, it's alright," I said, picking him up as he began to cry. He loved those pictures and knew how important they were, and when he thought they were ruined, he'd felt guilty and tried to hide them.

Touching his chin so he would look at me, I said gently, "Don't cry, Davey. The picture album isn't broken, and you can even help Mommy fix it, okay?"

Nodding, Davey wrapped his little arms around my neck and said, "I wuv you, Mommy."

I smiled, relieved to know that the problem had been solved. It wasn't always easy being a single mother, but I would be eternally grateful for this precious little boy God had blessed me with.

22

Vivian

April 1944

I stepped into a large, dark room and heard the door slam shut behind me, the lock sliding into place with a loud *click*. I couldn't see a thing; there were no windows and no lights, but I could feel the presence of another living being in the room with me. I stood trembling in the darkness as I listened to the swooshing sound of footsteps walking all around me; first to the left, and then to the right. I jerked my head in each direction, but still couldn't see through the thick, black darkness. Suddenly, laughter rang out and bounced along the walls, the sound sending chills up and down my spine. The footsteps drew closer, and I waited, my heart pounding with fear.

Just then, something clicked next to my ear, and I jerked, the flame from a lighter illuminating a twisted, ugly face only inches from my own. I tried to scream but found that I couldn't, and suddenly realized I wore a straight jacket and could not defend myself.

"Vivian, what have you done?"

Turning, I saw Howard standing in the doorway, his face filled with disgust. I felt an odd sensation of heat then and glanced around in confusion to see my house engulfed in flames. The sound of my baby screaming rang in my ears, and I tried to wave at Howard to go inside and help him, but the straight jacket kept me from moving my arms.

Then, through the smoke, I saw Maisie running towards me, only to trip and fall. She began to have a seizure and I tried to get to her, but large, gnarly hands began reaching out from the shadows to wrap around me, halting my steps and choking the life out of me. I fought and tried desperately to get away from it all, my breathing becoming labored as my heart rate steadily accelerated.

Just before my heart burst, it all started to fade away, and I began to wake up. Something in my brain, however, stopped my ascent back into total consciousness, and I lay there in a motionless trance, my eyes only able to open a crack. *Wake up*, I screamed inwardly as I tried to force my eyes to open fully or my hand to move, but there was no use.

I was experiencing sleep paralysis, something I'd only ever encountered once in my entire life. I was awake, but I wasn't. My mind told me I should be able to open my eyes and move around, but my body was still asleep. It was a horrific, terrifying experience; I couldn't move, couldn't speak, and I was beginning to feel like I couldn't breathe. My heart rate was flying out of control once again as I fought with everything in me to wake up, and in my mind, I begged for someone to help me.

Suddenly, I felt two hands grab me by the shoulders and shake me, and in the blurred confusion of my mind, my eyes popped open and I let out a bloodcurdling scream. The overhead lights switched on almost immediately and patients began crowding around my bed, question in their eyes.

I was covered in sweat and shaking all over. The only coherent thought in my mind was that I wanted something to drink, but could not say so when a loud, commanding voice overrode all the murmurs and said, "What is going on here?"

I looked up to find the night attendant, Mrs. Dash, standing over me, hands on her hips as she glared down at me.

"I…I had a bad dream," I said, my throat dry and voice raspy. "I was trying to wake up, but couldn't. I'm sorry."

Maisie was sitting beside me and reached out to take my hand. "You were making a terrible noise, like you couldn't breathe," she said softly. She then looked at the attendant and said, "She only screamed because I shook her too hard and scared her. It's my fault."

I started to deny it, but Mrs. Dash interrupted me and, her eyes narrowing, said, "You're the one that burned your house down in your sleep, aren't you? I'll be having a talk with Doctor Hagan about this tomorrow. I've heard you moaning and muttering in your sleep before, but apparently you're getting worse and the last thing we need around here is a crazy patient trying to burn the place down." Before I could attempt to defend myself, she spun on her heel and ordered everyone to get back into their beds immediately.

Maisie patted me on the hand and I laid back against the backboard, my body drained. As soon as the lights were turned off, I gave in to the tears that had been threatening to spill over, my shoulders shaking in silent sobs. I'd known that it would eventually happen, I just didn't know when. I'd dreaded it, prayed that it could somehow be avoided, but knew that I wouldn't be able to keep it up forever.

Somehow, during the last two months, I'd managed to stay just enough on the edge of sleep that I hadn't had a nightmare bad enough to cause me to act out. Even after I was nearly attacked by the man who murdered that nurse, or when I witnessed Anthony's horrible death, I'd stayed awake most of the night. When I would sleep harder and start to mumble, Maisie had always managed to wake me up somehow without the attendant noticing.

Tonight, however, it all changed.

It had been a long week, and I was exhausted when I went to bed. The work load had been considerably more than usual, and it seemed that everyone in the kitchen had tried to be as difficult as possible; a fight between two of the female patients had even broken out once, leading to their dismissal and more work for the rest of us. When I had finally collapsed into bed, my head was throbbing and my feet ached. All I'd wanted was to relax, and before I could jerk myself awake, I fell into a deep sleep.

I forced myself to stay awake for the rest of the night; I was too frightened of possibly going through the same thing again. I dreaded having to see the doctor and hoped he wouldn't try anything experimental on me, as I knew that some doctors here did.

The next day, I was called into Dr. Hagan's office.

"I was asked to not try any form of treatment or put you on medication," he said, "but after what happened last night, I think it would be a good idea to put you on a mild sedative. It will calm your mind and nerves and help you sleep."

I was so tired and drained that I simply sat and stared at him in silence for a moment. Finally, I asked in a monotone voice, "Do I have a choice?"

"I'm afraid not," Dr. Hagan replied, smiling tightly. "I'll give the nurse instructions on what to give you every evening."

I left his office feeling defeated. What would the sedative do to me? I hoped it would be mild, like the doctor said, and wouldn't affect me much, but I suspected otherwise.

I was walking across the lawn when a middle-aged attendant carrying a large load of laundry called out to me. "Can you help me, dear?" She asked, beads of sweat on her forehead. "I need to take this upstairs, but I just don't think I can make it up those steps."

"Yes, ma'am," I said, scooping the heavy load from her arms.

I followed her inside and up the stairs of what I would soon learn was the children's building. Once upstairs, we walked through the ward and my eyes were drawn to the sights around me. The room was filled with children of all ages, male and female. Some were locked in small, barred cribs with a cover on top, the eyes behind the bars watching me as I went by like curious, caged animals, while others sat quietly in the corner by themselves. The faces were void of typical child-like smiles and laughter, and the room was mostly quiet except for the occasional screech or cry. My stomach jolted at the smell of excrement and dirty bodies, and my heart squeezed at how thin most of the children were. Where were their parents? How could a mother or father send their child off to a place like this? Most of these children would never know the meaning of love or family, or even the soft, kind touch of someone that cared. The only thing they knew was a cold and empty life void of happiness, love, and freedom.

I couldn't get out of there soon enough, and once outside, I leaned against the brick wall and cried.

Two weeks later, I was leaving the kitchen early, my energy completely depleted. The sedative helped me to sleep at night, but I always felt like Frankenstein's monster the following morning; I was bleary-eyed and could barely put one foot in front of the other, and finally Mrs. Dobson told me to come to work in the afternoons.

"You're going to chop off a finger if you keep coming in the morning," she'd said.

I hated not being at my full capacity, at no longer feeling normal, and I missed working in the kitchen all day instead of going back to bed after breakfast.

"Can't you get those night terrors under control so you can get back to normal?" Alice asked me after my talk with Mrs. Dobson. "I hate seeing you this way; it's not right."

"Don't you know she ain't normal, Alice?" One patient cackled out. "She's as crazy as the rest of us."

Feeling tired and defeated, I simply shrugged at Alice and left, not bothering to defend myself. I felt that the life was being drained right out of me, and I didn't know how to stop it.

A bit later, I was on my way to do laundry when I heard someone calling my name, and I turned to see Maisie hurrying towards me.

"Vivian, you're not going to believe this," she cried, grabbing both my hands. "Mother has talked Father into letting me go home for my sister's wedding! He's here for me now and I have to go pack my things, but I had to find you first. Oh, Vivian, I just know they're going to let me stay home for good!"

My eyes wide, I immediately pulled my friend into a hug, joy over her good news flooding over me. "That is wonderful, Maisie! I'm so happy for you."

When I pulled back, Maisie's eyes were filled with tears and she said softly, "I wish you were coming with me."

My heart dropped, as I hadn't even realized I was being left behind, but I forced a bright smile and said, "Oh, don't you worry about me. I'm sure I'll be out of here in no time."

"I hope so," she said. "I'll write to you; promise you'll write back?"

I nodded. "I promise. Now, go on before they think you decided to stay!"

"Alright," she said. Her face filled with tenderness, she added in a choked voice, "This is an odd place to find friends, but I'm so thankful to have met you; you've made my life here these last few months so much more bearable. Take care of yourself, my friend. I'll be praying for you."

116

"You, too," I said, fighting the tears that pricked my eyes as I watched her walk away. I was thrilled for Maisie, but losing the only person I'd truly come to trust and care about in this place was devastating. Would I ever know what it felt like to be in her shoes? Would I ever really get out of this place, or be forced to stay here forever?

I turned to continue on my way, my shoulders stooped as if they carried the weight of the world. I went back to my ward and pulled out the letters from home, trying to gather strength and encouragement from the words.

One week later, Maisie wrote to tell me she'd made it home safely and that her family seemed to be glad to have her back. *They've never understood my condition*, she wrote, *but when I told them the doctors hadn't even treated me yet, they said there was no point in my returning. So, it looks like I may be home for good!* She then asked how I was doing, and in my return letter, I said that I was fine, although I knew I wasn't.

The days crept by agonizingly slow. Zachary hadn't been able to visit, and the letters I received from home were like lifelines. I continued to push myself day in and day out, but often wondered if I'd end up like the ghostly silhouettes who stared down at me when I passed the solitary confinement building; lonely, lifeless, and empty.

It was a perfectly normal Monday afternoon when I was told that I had a long-distance phone call. Surprised, I hurried to the building with the telephone and told the operator I was ready. Seconds later, I heard Savannah's voice on the other line.

"I have something to tell you, Vivian," she said, and my stomach sank at the heavy tone in her voice.

"What is it?" I asked, resting my hand on the wall for support. "What's happened?"

Sighing, Savannah said, "Your parents were leaving church yesterday morning when a drunken truck driver veered into their lane and hit them head on. Your father is in bad shape, but I believe he will be okay. Your mother…oh, Vivian, she didn't make it; she passed away just a few hours ago. I'm so sorry."

It felt as if the entire world was caving in around me. The room began to spin as I slowly sank to the floor, the receiver clutched between my hands. I could hear Savannah calling my name, but her voice sounded so far away, and I wondered if I could possibly be dreaming. My mother was dead? How could I not have known? Why hadn't I felt the pain of something very important, very special, slip away from me? Instead, I'd been going about my day as if everything back home was still the way it should be.

I curled up into a ball on the cold, hard floor and cried deep, wrenching sobs. Mother had died, and I wasn't even able to say goodbye, and knowing that I'd never see her again was more than I could bear. The pain in my chest was so real and strong that I couldn't think straight, and when one of the male nurses carried me to my bed and gave me a sedative, I lay there shivering and shaking for the rest of the day and night as tears continuously soaked my hair and pillow.

The next morning, I woke with a pounding head and blurred vision. I walked around the ward, refusing to work in the kitchen, and sat in front of a window for hours, staring out sightlessly. I was in so much pain that it was almost as if my entire body had shut down, refusing to go any further. What would I do without my mother? How could I keep going with the knowledge that she was no longer at home, waiting for me? I felt empty and broken, and wished that I would suddenly wake up and realize this was all just a crazy, horrible dream.

Sometime around twilight that evening, my eyes were drawn towards the garden, as if a small voice was calling to me, and a thought began to form in the back of my muddled brain. During one of my last visits to gather vegetables for the kitchen, I'd noticed a mound of loose stones at the bottom of the garden wall. It was hard to see, as several rose bushes grew wildly about, and the thorns on the bushes would cut me to pieces, but I had to try. I didn't care what they did to me afterwards, but I had to be at my mother's funeral. It was time to get out of this place and maybe, just maybe, they wouldn't force me to come back.

Once nighttime arrived, I had it all planned out. The nurse gave me my medicine, but I only pretended to take it. The night attendant kept a cup of coffee on her desk and when she wasn't looking, I poured the sedative into her cup.

I lay as still as possible in my bed, listening to the soft snores and moans of the other patients. When it finally seemed that everyone was asleep, including the night attendant, I slowly sat up and crawled out of bed. I'd left my clothes on under my nightgown and quickly pulled the garment over my head, leaving it draped across my pillow like a limp, white ghost. Carefully, my shoes in one hand, I tiptoed through the ward, barely breathing as I passed the attendant. She snorted softly when I stepped by and I stopped, my heart catching in my chest.

The room was mostly dark as I went on, the lamp from the attendant's desk casting an eerie glow about the room. I finally made it to the door and, holding my breath, I opened it only wide enough to slip through. Once out in the corridor, I blinked as I tried to adjust my eyes to the total darkness. As I began walking down the hall, my socks brushing softly against the cold tile, I wondered if I would truly be free once I escaped, or if this place would always own a small part of me. ***Don't think about that now***, I told myself.

After what seemed like an eternity, I realized with a sigh of relief that I was almost there and could see the sliver of light under the door from the stairwell drawing closer. Just a few more steps and…

Suddenly, the door behind me squeaked open. "Oh, Vivian," a shrill, childlike voice sang out, echoing loudly off the bare walls. "Where are you going, Vivian?"

I stopped, knowing I'd been caught. Shoulders stooped, I turned in defeat just as the overhead lights flipped on. Ruby stood in the open doorway, a smile on her face as if we'd been playing a game of hide-and-seek and she'd found me. The attendant, who was blowing her whistle loudly, pushed past her and marched towards me on unsteady feet, grasping hold of my arm in a painful grip.

"W-what do you t-think you're doing?" She asked, her words slurred from the sedative as two more attendants from the other wards hurried in. "Y-you drugged me, didn't you?"

Rearing back, she slapped me hard across the face, and before I could catch myself, I slapped her back. She stumbled, and the other two attendants immediately grabbed me by the arms and jerked me away. As they dragged me down the hall, I began to sob uncontrollably, my emotions and overwrought nerves getting the best of me.

I was thrown into a solitary room meant only for the dangerous and out-of-control patients with the words, "You'll be taken to the superintendent's office tomorrow," bouncing off the walls just before the door slammed shut and the lock clicked into place.

I curled up on the lone mattress that rested on the floor and cried, my hopes of escape and attending my mother's funeral gone with the echoed slamming of the door.

23

Eva

When Jackson called to tell me the news about Mr. Parker and his wife, my eyes widened in disbelief and I began to cry, my heart breaking for the man who had been so kind to me. I knew that when he woke up and was alert enough to understand, it would devastate him to learn about his wife.

"The restaurant is going to be closed until he gets better," Jackson said, his tone heavy. "If, that is, he gets better."

That night, I said a prayer for Mr. Parker, and made a note to send some flowers to his hospital room. I hated to think of him being all alone and wondered about his daughter, if she would come to see him and attend her mother's funeral. I knew little about her, as everyone kept their lips sealed in that particular subject, but it seemed that she'd moved away after her baby died and hadn't been back since. I'd gotten the feeling there was more to it than that, but didn't want to ask questions.

Saturday evening, I received a phone call from Savannah Danes. She invited us to join her family on a picnic lunch the following afternoon, and after consulting Nana and Mutter, I told her we'd love to come. Mutter was nervous, as she was very shy when meeting strangers and self-conscious of her accent, but I assured her she would love Savannah.

The next afternoon, we piled into Leon's car and headed towards Forsyth Park, excited about a day out. I hadn't met the rest of Savannah's family and, like Mutter, I was nervous, but hoped that they would be as kind and inviting as both Savannah and Leon.

As we drove towards the park, I gazed out the window at the beautiful city in which I lived. The azaleas were in full bloom, their colors ranging from brilliant pinks to a soft, delicate white. It was a sign that all of Savannah waited for when the weather started to warm up, an indication that spring had arrived and was making a grand and glorious entrance. Unfortunately, the beautiful blooms didn't last long, but I'd concluded that their short display of captivating color and charm made us appreciate them all the more.

When we arrived at the park, Savannah and her family were already there. Leon helped us unload the picnic basket and quilt we'd brought along, and we hurried over to join the group where they sat under the shade of an oak tree.

Savannah jumped up and, after giving me a quick hug, introduced everyone. Her mother-in-law, Mrs. Emma, and her Aunt Debra kindly asked Nana and Mutter to sit by them, and Savannah's uncle offered to help me spread our quilt. As we all sat down to eat, I noticed with a sigh of relief that Mutter seemed immediately to relax at the kindness of the two older ladies.

The meal, which consisted of chicken salad sandwiches, potato salad, deviled eggs, and homemade pickles, was delicious. The five of us women discussed recipes and the latest fashions, while Leon and Savannah's uncle talked about the war, and after we were through eating, the two men asked Davey if he'd like to play a game of kickball. His eyes lighting up, Davey nodded exuberantly and jumped to his feet, dancing around in excitement as he waited for Leon to retrieve the ball from his trunk.

"He is adorable," Savannah said to me as she watched Davey skipping along beside Leon and her uncle. "I hope that Connor and I will be blessed with children someday."

"I'm sure you will," I replied, smiling. Looking back at Davey, I said, "I hope he isn't bothering them; he gets so excited when other men are around."

Her expression sober, Savannah turned to me and said in a soft, compassionate tone, "Raising him without your husband must be very hard."

Swallowing over the sudden lump in my throat, I nodded in agreement. "Yes, it has been hard, but I'm so thankful for Davey. He is the most precious of gifts."

While the men played ball, we cheered them on and chatted amongst ourselves. I smiled and waved when Davey, with Leon's help, successfully kicked the ball, excitement on his face when he turned to see if I was watching. I was glad that he was enjoying himself so much, and that the men were being so kind and patient with him.

Savannah's aunt, who seemed to be a very friendly, boisterous sort of person, rattled on with Nana about the people they knew and the schools they'd attended growing up. Mutter and Mrs. Emma, I noticed, seemed also to be getting along quite well as they talked about the early loss of their husbands and how hard it had been. It thrilled me to see Mutter smiling and acting so comfortable around people she barely knew, and thought that Savannah's family was just as kind and wonderful as she was.

Suddenly realizing I'd left my purse in the car, I told the others that I'd be right back and hurried across the grass towards the small parking area. As I opened the passenger side door and grabbed my purse, I noticed a figure approaching out of the corner of my eye. Turning, I blinked in surprise when I saw who it was.

"Jackson," I said as I closed the car door behind me, a little surprised at bumping into my coworker.

"Hello, Eva," he said with a smile, his eyes taking in the rather simple dress I was wearing. "You look nice."

I thanked him, glancing toward the others when I heard Davey cry out in delight.

"That's your son?"

I looked back at Jackson, and he must have seen the look of question in my eyes because he shrugged and said, "He looks just like you."

"Oh, yes, I suppose he does," I replied with a small smile.

"I've missed seeing you at the restaurant since it closed," he stated, disappointment in his voice.

I blinked, uncertain of what to say. Shuffling my feet awkwardly, I said, "Yes, well, I've certainly missed being there."

When he simply stood there looking at me in silence, I cleared my throat and asked, "Do you come here often?"

"Sometimes," he nodded. "When I need some fresh air and space."

I heard Davey call out for me just then and told Jackson I should get back. Waving goodbye, I hurried away, and when I reached the others, I glanced back to see that he was still standing there, watching me.

"Mommy, you see me play?"

Turning my attention back to Davey, I gave him a hug and said, "Yes, honey, you did so good."

The men had returned, panting and tired, and I soon forgot about Jackson as I watched them fill their cups with tea and eat more of the chocolate cake Nana had made.

"Now I need to play ball again," Leon said, patting his belly after finishing an enormous slice of cake.

"Let's go for a walk," Savannah suggested, and we all agreed.

We'd strolled around the city for nearly twenty minutes, enjoying the beautiful day as the birds sang and a cool breeze blew gently along the streets, when Leon said, "Mrs. Hamilton, have y'all told Eva about the ghosts we have here in Savannah?"

Chuckling, Nana shook her head "no" while Mrs. Debra, Savannah's aunt, tsked and said, "Leon, don't be ridiculous."

His eyes twinkling, Leon looked at me and said, "See that building over there?"

Moving my gaze in the direction which he pointed, I nodded, my eyes taking in the three-story building with interest. The roof was mostly flat and the bottom floor all brick, while the upper two floors were wood. I turned to look back at Leon, my eyes alight with interest.

"That's the 1790 Inn and Restaurant," Leon said. "Legend has it that in the early 1800s, a young woman who was betrothed to an older man fell madly in love with a visiting sailor who promised to marry her. When the sailor left, however, and she realized he wouldn't return for her, she was so brokenhearted that she threw herself from the window in room 204 and died instantly." Lowering his voice dramatically, Leon stepped closer and said, "To this very day, people say they can hear her crying at night as she walks up and down in front of the window in that very room, waiting for her love to return."

"That is absurd," Mrs. Debra spoke up, sighing.

"But deliciously thrilling, don't you think, Aunt Deb?" Savannah asked, her eyes twinkling as she grabbed her aunt's arm and squeezed it.

"Absolutely not," Mrs. Debra sniffed, pulling her arm away. "I don't believe in such nonsense."

Laughing, Leon winked at me and whispered, "She's just no fun."

Smiling, I took Davey's hand, and we walked back to the park. Before we turned the corner, however, I looked over my shoulder at the inn and wondered if the story of the brokenhearted girl jumping from the second-story window really was true.

When we arrived back home, I was tired but happy to have had such a pleasant and enjoyable day. Everyone had been so kind and inviting, and it was nice that we were finally making some friends here. Mrs. Emma and Mrs. Debra had even invited Mutter and Nana to come over soon so they could learn how to make apple strudel. I'd often felt guilty over the fact that Nana had lost so many friends because of my German roots and was grateful that Savannah's family was attempting to befriend her and Mutter.

Leon helped Nana and I carry the picnic basket and quilt inside while Mutter pulled a sleeping Davey from the back seat of the car. I'd just stepped onto the porch when I noticed a single white rose lying in front of the door. My brow furrowing, I picked it up and studied it, wondering where it had come from.

"It seems that you have a secret admirer," Leon said as he peeked over my shoulder.

"I can't imagine who it could be," I murmured.

"I'm sure that a beautiful lady such as yourself must have plenty of admirers," Leon stated, winking at me.

My cheeks flushing, I shook my head and took the rose into the kitchen to find a vase. Leon followed me and leaned against the counter, a twinkle in his eye as he watched me.

"So, are you going to tell me who the lucky fellow is?" He asked, raising his eyebrows.

I was never the coy type, but I knew he was teasing me, and so I cleared my throat and said nonchalantly, "His name is Edgar."

Leon blinked in surprise, and I hid my smile as I leaned under the counter in search of a vase. "Edgar, who?" He wanted to know.

I paused, trying to think of a last name. "Edgar...Shufflebottom."

I heard Leon choke down a laugh, and when I turned to look at him with raised eyebrows, he said, "That's…an unusual last name."

"It's Scottish," I replied in a serious tone.

Sniffing, Leon crossed his arms and slowly nodded his head. "So, the two of you are pretty serious, huh?"

I could tell that he was uncertain as whether or not to believe me, so I sighed dramatically and said, "Oh, I don't know. Can you imagine going through life as Eva Shufflebottom?"

I pronounced the name with a thick Scottish accent, and Leon burst into laughter.

"You had me going there for a minute," he chuckled, his eyes sparkling with admiration. "I didn't realize you had such a mischievous side."

"It stays hidden most of the time," I replied, laughing along with him.

Still in search of a vase, I opened the cabinet above the sink and finally found one sitting towards the back behind some candles and a box of matches. I stood on my tippy toes and stretched out my arm, but with my short, 5'2" frame, I could barely reach the matches, let alone the vase.

"Here, let me help you with that," Leon said, hurrying to my side.

His body was warm against mine as he reached over my head and grabbed the vase. I tried to slide over a bit, but the ice box had me blocked in, and I caught a whiff of the woodsy aftershave Leon was wearing as he leaned around me. He lowered the vase from the cabinet and handed it to me, our fingers brushing when I reached to take it. Leon made no attempt to release the vase, and feeling a bit awkward, I glanced up to find that he was staring at me with an unreadable expression in his eyes. We stood only inches apart, the silence in the room louder than anything we could say, and I suddenly grew a bit flustered.

I finally cleared my throat and stepped back, my cheeks flushing as I thanked him for his help.

"Anytime, Mrs. Shufflebottom," he replied, his voice warm as he smiled at me.

Later that night, I went into the kitchen in search of a midnight snack, and my eyes fell upon the white rose sitting in the middle of the table. I couldn't help but wonder once again who it was from and found myself smiling as my thoughts traveled to Leon. He brought out a side in me that no one else ever had, and I was quickly coming to realize what a special person he was. He rarely saw it for himself, but his easygoing, light-hearted manner brightened up not only my life but also the lives of others he encountered. I enjoyed teasing with him, and he never failed to make me laugh, and I was growing more and more grateful to have found such a wonderful friend.

I fixed myself a small sandwich and took it back to my room, the white rose completely forgotten.

The next day, I ran down to the market to pick up some canned tomatoes for a soup Nana and Mutter were making. I was in such a hurry that I wasn't paying any attention to the thick, dark clouds forming in the sky. By the time I stepped foot inside the market, I could hear thunder rumbling in the distance, and it wasn't long before rain began tapping against the windowpanes. The lights flickered, and I could hear the wind picking up as it howled around the building.

Since I hadn't thought to bring an umbrella and would have to walk over three blocks in the pouring rain, I moaned with frustration as I paid for the tomatoes, my eyes glued to the windows as I watched buckets of rain pour from the sky.

"It's supposed to be like this for the rest of the day," the cashier told me as he bagged the tomatoes. "I don't have a car, or I'd offer to drive you home."

With a sigh, I thanked him and tucked the bag under my arm as I headed out into the torrential downpour. The rain was cold and heavy, and I shivered as I hurried along the streets towards home. Dense, billowy clouds covered the sky, making the day seem much darker than it was, and thunder rumbled sporadically, shaking the ground beneath my feet. I'd walked a little over a block when I noticed a car approaching slowly from behind, its headlights illuminating thick sheets of rain that fell against a dim, shadowy backdrop. The car gradually pulled up beside me and stopped, the breaks squealing slightly. I paused uncertainly, not recognizing the vehicle, and wiped the rain from my eyes as the window slowly rolled down.

"Come on, get in," a voice called, and I realized with shock that it was Kirk, Mr. Fernsby's grandson.

Hesitating for a brief moment, I hurried around the car and got in, my clothes dripping all over the leather seats. "I-I really appreciate this," I said, shivering from the cold. When I realized what a mess I was making, I looked at him apologetically and added, "I'm getting water all in your car, though, a-are you sure it's okay?"

"Look, I know you're German, but my grandfather would have my hide if he knew I intentionally let you walk home in this kind of weather," he snapped.

Not saying another word, I sat back in the seat and wrapped my arms around my waist, watching as the wipers scrubbing frantically back and forth across the windshield. Thunder rumbled loudly once again just as a flash of lightning illuminated the sky, and I flinched; I'd never liked storms, they'd terrified me since I was a little girl.

With a sigh, Kirk reached into the back seat and handed me a coat. "Put this on or you'll catch your death."

I took the coat and gratefully wrapped it around my shoulders, a bit confused by Kirk's actions. He acted as if he despised me, and yet he'd felt the need to drive me home and even give me his coat. I thought his behavior to be quite strange, but was thankful for his act of chivalry.

"You don't talk much, do you?" He suddenly asked, and I glanced at him in surprise.

"I'm sorry," I replied softly, brushing a wet strand of hair from my face. Clearing my throat, I said, "I've...uh...read about the work you all do down at the shipyards building Liberty Ships for the war. What is your job?"

"I'm a welder," was his short reply.

Chewing my bottom lip, I said, "I heard that it only takes about three months to complete a ship. It all sounds very exciting, especially getting to do something so important for the war effort."

Glancing over at me, Kirk raised an eyebrow and asked, "You'd rather we build ships for the Germans, though, wouldn't you?"

My eyes widening, I clamped my mouth shut and glanced out of the window, relieved to see that we were almost to my house. Kirk pulled up by the curb and stopped, and I took the coat off and handed it back to him.

"Thank you," I mumbled.

I reached for the door handle, sucking in a quick breath when Kirk grabbed my arm and stopped me. Turning to look at him warily, I waited with dread to hear what else he had to say.

"You're welcome," he said, his expression hard to read. "If we talk again, I'll try to refrain from making any more derogatory remarks about you or your heritage."

Uncertain if he was serious or being sarcastic, I nodded and said softly, "I would appreciate that."

He released my arm, and I quickly jumped from the car and hurried inside, grateful that the rain was subsiding. As I changed from my wet clothes and took a quick, hot shower, I puzzled over the encounter with Kirk. What a strange man he was, and I couldn't help but wonder how he treated his grandfather. Mr. Fernsby was such a kind old gentleman I hoped Kirk wasn't taking advantage of him in any way.

24

THE SHADOW

He sat at a local hamburger joint, his half-eaten burger resting on the counter before him as thought after thought ran through his mind. Everything with Eva was going according to plan, but he was trying to figure out a way to get into her house without arousing any suspicions. It would need to be during the day when she was at work, or else she would recognize him, and he'd have to play his cards just right for her mother and grandmother to allow him entrance.

With a smile, he took a long gulp of his cold Coca Cola, wiping his upper lip as he sat the glass back down with a *clunk*. There was no reason to worry about it; he knew he'd figure out something, and there wasn't any hurry. He had all the time in the world.

A woman sitting at a booth behind him suddenly began making a ruckus, and he glanced over his shoulder at her in annoyance. She was crying and arguing with the man sitting next to her, and it quickly became obvious that the man was ending the relationship. They continued to argue until finally, her companion slapped his hand on the table and stormed from the diner, leaving her to lean against the table and sob broken-heartedly.

After a few moments, the owner went over and asked if there was anything he could do to help, and she stated she had no way of getting home.

"I can take you once we close in a couple of hours," the man said, glancing at his watch.

The woman started crying again, and the owner looked around until his eyes landed on the man sitting at the counter. "Sir," he said, "could you possibly drive this lady home?"

Sighing, the man nodded and tossed the money for his burger onto the counter as he climbed from the stool and grabbed his coat. The owner helped the woman from her seat and thanked the man for his help, clapping him gratefully on the back.

The night was dark and the parking lot empty as the two walked outside. The woman was still crying and sniffling into her handkerchief, and the man clenched his jaw in irritation as he opened the car door for her; just like his father, he couldn't stand any type of weakness. After climbing into the driver's seat, he asked for her address, cranked the car, and pulled from the dimly lit parking lot.

As they drove out of town, the woman finally calmed down and in a soft, soulful voice, she began telling him what happened. He hadn't asked, nor did he care to know, but he remained silent as she rambled.

"He promised to leave his wife and marry me, but now he's changed his mind," she said, leaning against the headrest with a sigh. "Can you believe it? I don't know what I'm going to do now. I'm all alone in the world, and I don't have anyone to turn to."

Glancing over at her, he raised his eyebrows and asked, "You don't have anyone?"

"No," she shook her head, tears welling up in her eyes once again. "My father ran off when I was a kid, and my mother died last year."

After a moment of silence, he said, "Why don't you close your eyes and get some rest? We still have several miles left to go."

Nodding, the girl closed her eyes, and it wasn't long before she started to breathe heavily. He glanced over at her, taking in the fullness of her lips and long, slender neck. His fingers tightening around the wheel, he moved his gaze to the windows as he quickly took in their surroundings. The city lights had well faded from view, and his headlights pierced the dark, lonely road ahead. After a moment, he caught sight of an old hunting trail and turned the car on to it, slowing so the tires bumping along the ruts wouldn't wake her.

Thick trees arched overhead, their branches cutting any light that the moon may have provided, and he noticed two deer darting across the path just up ahead. When he hit a particularly deep rut, the woman woke with a start, sitting up in her seat to look around.

Her eyes slowly filling with fear, she looked at him and asked, "W-where are we going?"

Reaching across the console, he rubbed her arm and said, "I thought you could use a bit of comfort, so I found a nice, private place for us."

Jerking away, she began desperately clawing at the door handle in an attempt to get out. He stopped, the brakes squealing, and allowed her to jump from the car, chuckling under his breath as he calmly stepped out behind her and watched as she tripped and stumbled back down the path towards the main road. She wouldn't get away, but he enjoyed playing a bit of cat and mouse; it was thrilling, to say the least.

"That's far enough," he finally called out in a singsong voice, flicking on the flashlight he carried and aiming the beam directly at her.

She spun around with a gasp, her eyes wild and chest heaving. "D-don't hurt me," she said, her lips trembling. "Please. Just let me go, and I won't tell anyone."

Rolling his eyes, he said, "Don't be ridiculous."

He drew closer, reaching out to grab her arm when she spun around and attempted to flee once again. He quickly ducked as she began flailing her arms wildly about, and when her fist connected with his jaw and caused him to drop the flashlight, his calm, light-hearted demeanor changed and anger flooded over him. He slapped her across the face and jerked a knife from his pocket, pressing it firmly against her throat. She immediately stilled, and he could feel the pounding of her heart against his forearm, the heat from her breath blowing across his face as she panted.

"You should have just played along, honey," he growled, wrapping his fingers around her neck.

Her screams echoed through the forest, breaking the stillness of the night, but there was no one around to hear the pathetic cries for help. It wasn't long before the sounds faded away, and the night became quiet once again as the girl slumped into a lifeless heap on the forest floor.

25

Vivian

As punishment for trying to escape, drugging the attendant, and slapping her, they sent me to the isolation building. I wasn't allowed any mail, nor was I allowed to shower; the attendants would bring in a small basin of water for me to wash in, and they would also deliver my meals, as I wasn't allowed to leave my room.

No one would tell me if Savannah or anyone from home had tried to call. I was in agony from worrying so much about my father; what would I do if I lost him, too? I couldn't stand to think about it, and all I dreamed of during the few restless hours in which I slept was Mother. I could see her, smell her, and hear her voice, and after I awoke each time, I'd only cry myself back into a fitful sleep yet again.

As the days slowly passed by, I paced back and forth in the small room like a caged animal with nothing to do and nothing with which to occupy my mind. I could hear others crying, moaning, and sometimes screaming, and I would cover my ears to keep the sounds out. When I grew tired of pacing, I'd stand at the window and watch the people down below, yearning to be among them, and once when a little bird lit upon the brick windowsill before me, I began to talk to it, as if it could understand me. When it finally flew away, I cried, feeling as if I'd lost a friend.

Day by day, I felt myself drifting further and further away, as if I were on a broken board or plank that was floating out into an endless black sea. I fought to remain sane and composed, but found myself crying much too often, fighting against sleep for fear of dreaming, and quickly losing weight, as I didn't want to eat. I was lonely, and despair was never far away, and with each moment that passed by, I quickly lost all track of time.

When the lighting was just right, I could see my reflection in the window, and what I saw was just another of the lifeless, ghostly silhouettes who stared out, watching hopelessly as the world passed by. I'd finally joined them, and wondered if perhaps one day, I wouldn't even be able to see my reflection any longer. I was fading away, my will to live and exist as fragile as the white fluff on a dandelion during a windy day, and I fell upon the thin, lumpy mattress and prayed, begging God to please help me.

I couldn't stand much more of this; I was weary and my spirit weak, and I wondered how long it would be before I quit fighting and simply gave up.

On my thirteenth day in isolation, I was surprised when the door to my room squeaked open and the nurse told me to follow her. I stood huddled against the far wall for a moment, afraid of what they would do to me.

"Come on," she snapped impatiently. "Hurry up."

On shaky legs, I slowly walked from my prison cell, glancing back into the lonely, dark hole as I walked away and wondered if they would now start with exploratory treatments or electroshock therapy. They led me to the showers and told me to strip, that I smelled like a skunk. I did so, and even though the water was barely warm, I was thankful to be clean.

I was given an old but clean dress and led outside, where another nurse waited with what appeared to be a bag of my belongings. She handed it to me and said, "It's your lucky day, honey," before she walked off, leaving me to stand there in utter confusion.

Then, I saw a familiar figure walking towards me. It was Zachary, his face tight with concern as he hurried to my side.

"My God, Vivian, what have they done to you?" He asked, and it was the first time I'd ever heard anything akin to anger in his voice. Sighing, he shook his head and said, "Come on, it's all over now. I'm taking you home."

I could hardly believe my ears; I was going home? All I could do was stare at Zachary in shock.

"What…what about Father?" I wanted to know, almost afraid to ask.

"He's going to be alright," Zachary replied, gently taking my arm. "He's been in pretty bad shape, but he's finally coming around."

As Zachary began leading me away from the isolation building, emotion threatened to close my throat completely and I squeezed my eyes shut, taking a deep breath. Father was going to be okay; I told myself to keep holding on to that thought.

When we arrived at Zachary's car, I looked up at him questioningly. "How is this possible?" I asked. "Did they find Howard?"

Zachary hesitated, as if uncertain of whether I could handle the truth. Finally, he sighed and said, "Yes, they did. I'm sorry, Vivian, but Howard is dead. The police think he was murdered."

I was silent most of the drive home, the only exception being when I answered Zachary's questions of: "Are you hungry? Are you comfortable? Do you need anything?" He was being so kind and considerate, but made no attempt to talk any further beyond that; it was as if he knew I needed time to process everything.

Howard was dead; murdered. I was shocked and surprisingly a bit saddened by the news. I knew he wasn't the same man I fell in love with and married over two years ago, but he was still my husband and someone I'd once loved. I wanted to know what happened, but couldn't bring myself to ask just yet.

It was hard to fathom the unexpected turns my life had taken. I'd gone from a wife and mother to a childless, motherless widow on her way home from a mental institution. Would I ever be able to live a normal life again? As we had driven back out through the gates I'd entered only a few months ago, I stared out the side mirror, watching almost in disbelief as the hospital faded from view, and knew that I would forever bear its scar.

I didn't realize I'd fallen asleep until Zachary stopped for gas just outside of Savannah. I rubbed my eyes and got out to stretch my legs a bit, nodding my head when Zachary asked if I wanted a cold Coca Cola to drink.

While I waited, I walked to the edge of the road and looked east, sighing inwardly at the comforting thought that "home" wasn't very far away. It was a strange thought, going home, and it seemed like three years instead of three months since I'd gone away. Everything was such a blur; it felt like I'd been living underwater or in some crazy nightmare. Could it really and truly be over? Maybe this wasn't real; perhaps I was still in that lonely, isolated room, sitting hopelessly against the wall and only dreaming about going home.

Zachary called my name then and when I turned to look at him, I realized with an overwhelming sense of relief that this wasn't a dream; I really was going home.

Once we were back on the road, Zachary cleared his throat and said that there was something he'd like to tell me. My stomach clenching at his tone, I turned to look at him, waiting for him to proceed.

"As I said earlier, your father is going to be alright," he began, "but he suffered a bad head injury in the accident and…well…he can't see, Vivian."

I gasped. "*What*?"

"It may be temporary," he hurriedly explained. "Blindness or blurred vision can be a side effect of a head injury."

"So, you believe it will go away?" I asked hopefully.

"I don't know," Zachary shook his head. "It may or it may not; we'll just have to wait and see." After a moment, he asked, "Would you like me to take you to your parents' house or the hospital?"

Although the dress I wore was clean, it was old and stained, and I asked him to take me to the house.

"I'd like to freshen up first and then I can just walk to the hospital," I said, my eyes moving to stare out of the window as we entered the outskirts of the city. Oh, how I'd missed this place! The beauty and familiarity brought a strange sense of comfort to me, as if the rivers, golden marshlands, and giant oak trees we passed were all calling out a loud and boisterous "welcome home!".

"I'll wait and drive you to the hospital," Zachary said. "It's at least a two-mile walk, and I don't think you're up to that just yet."

I didn't argue with him, as I knew he was right. Turning to look at the man I'd barely known three months ago but who had now become such a good friend, I smiled softly and said, "Thank you so much for everything, Zachary. You have no idea how much your kindness has meant to me."

"It's been my pleasure," he replied, glancing over at me. "You've been through so much, Vivian. I'm sorry I wasn't able to get you out of there sooner."

Ten minutes later, we pulled up in front of my parents' house and I sat quietly for a moment, glued in place as I was confronted with a sudden, unexpected wave of pain. As if watching a movie or slideshow, I could clearly see myself being dragged through the yard just three months ago, kicking and screaming and out of my mind with fear as Savannah rushed after us. I could see the cold, hard looks in the eyes of the orderlies as they pushed me into the back seat of the car, and feel the tightness in my chest and trembling of my body as we drove away. None of it, however, compared to the pain I felt at seeing my parents' house, the place where I'd grown up, and knowing that Mother wouldn't be coming out to greet me.

My heart squeezing tightly in my chest, I clenched my jaw, pushing the pain away with every ounce of strength that I could muster; I felt tears pricking the backs of my eyes, and I didn't want Zachary to see me that way.

"Are you okay?" He asked gently, his aqua eyes filled with concern.

Forcing a tight smile, I nodded my head. "I won't be long," I told him, clearing my throat as I climbed from the car.

I stepped quietly into the house, the door squeaking as it clicked shut behind me. I stood just inside the entranceway and let my eyes drift slowly across the familiar living room, and the first thing I noticed was the quilt lying rumpled up in the corner on Mother's sewing table. I stared at it for a moment, and then slowly walked across the room to touch the fabric gently, my fingers trembling as tears flooded my eyes. The pattern was Grandmother's Flower Garden, my favorite, and it had the makings of one of the most beautiful quilts I'd ever seen. It was trimmed in a pink border with bright and bold flowers of the prettiest, most perfect array of colors dancing in the middle, and every bit was hand stitched.

"I know I'm not the best quilter in the world, but at least you'll know I made it with love."

The words from one of her letters drifted through my mind, and I heard the sound of her voice as clearly as if she were standing right beside me. Mother wanted to give me this quilt when I returned home, and it broke my heart into a million pieces to know that her wish would never come true.

Through blurry, tear-filled eyes, I stared down at the quilt as it rested quietly beneath my fingers, half-finished, so limp and lifeless, like a picture of what once was. If only I'd taken the time to learn how to quilt, I would finish it myself. Why hadn't I ever asked her to teach me?

Stepping away, I wiped my eyes with the back of my hand and glanced around the room, my eyes falling on a pair of Mother's gloves sitting on the foyer table, just waiting for her to slip them on. It was so strange to see all of her things right where she'd left them and know that she would never come back. I noticed her shawl draped across the armrest of the sofa and walked over to pick it up, breathing in her scent as hot tears seeped down my cheeks. How was I to keep going without my mother? Without her comfort and love? All I'd wanted while I was in Martinsville was to come home to my mother and father, to heal and rebuild my life with their love and support, but it seemed that "home" would never be the same. I'd lost my child, my husband, and my dearest friend in the whole world. How was I going to get through this?

Suddenly, a conversation I once had with my mother drifted into the forefront of my thoughts, and I remembered it as clearly as if it were yesterday. I was fifteen or sixteen, and had asked how she'd dealt with the pain of losing two unborn babies before having me.

"Life isn't guaranteed to be all sunshine and roses," she'd said, the yarn and knitting needles in her lap forgotten as we talked, *"and sometimes it's during our darkest hours that we realize how strong we truly are. I didn't think it would ever be possible to get over the pain of losing my two precious babies, but I made it through, and then God gave me a wonderful gift. He blessed me with you."*

I'd smiled at her words, while at the same time tears gathered in my eyes. I'd always wanted siblings, and I wondered how life would have been if Mother hadn't miscarried.

"How did you get through it, though?" I'd asked after a moment.

"One day at a time," was her reply, and I could still see the emotion written on her face as she spoke. *"I forced myself to move forward, even when I didn't want to, and I learned to be thankful for the little things. It wasn't always easy, but looking back now, I can say that I'm stronger for it."* Reaching out, she'd taken my hand and added softly, *"God won't leave us joyless, honey, always remember that. We might not be able to see the sun shining in the midst of the storm, but it's there, waiting to shine again. We just have to be patient and wait for the clouds to pass, because they always do."*

Would the sun ever shine for me again? I couldn't be certain, but I would hold on to the hope that Mother's words brought with all that I had. And even if I never found peace and joy again, I **did** still have my father with me, and I was eternally grateful for that.

Knowing that Zachary was waiting, I put the shawl back and wiped my eyes, sighing heavily. I went into my old bedroom and, after changing my clothes, stared at myself in the mirror for a moment. I was deathly pale and thin, with heavy dark circles under my eyes and colorless lips. I'd put on one of my old dresses, which now hung around my thin frame, and I cinched the belt as tightly as I could at the waist. I combed and pinned back my hair, dabbed on a bit of makeup, and spritzed myself all over with perfume.

Fifteen minutes later, I emerged from the house and hurried to the car.

"You look great," Zachary said as he opened the car door for me.

"Thank you," I replied, forcing a smile. After he'd climbed into the driver's seat, I took a deep breath and stated, "I'd like to know the details of Howard's death."

Zachary nodded, his eyes straight ahead as we drove towards the hospital. "Due to the weather, the corn on your farm was ready to be harvested early, so the government sent workers out to do so," he said. "About two days later, they found Howard's body half-buried in the field; the coroner said he'd been dead for at least a month."

"Why do the police think he was murdered?"

Zachary hesitated a moment before answering. "Because the cause of death was a severe blow to the head," he finally said.

I sat for a moment, trying to process everything Zachary had told me. Howard's murder had to be connected to the men that burned down our house, but who were they and what were their reasons? I decided that once I regained my strength, I would go to the police station and have a chat with Officer Wright. I wanted more details, and I wanted to know what they were doing to find these men.

When we arrived at the hospital, the first person I saw was Savannah. She was standing at the front desk talking to the receptionist, and when she saw me, her eyes flew open wide and the most beautiful smile spread across her face. She rushed over and pulled me into a hug, and we stood there crying on each other's shoulders while everyone around us wondered at the spectacle we were making.

"You're finally home," she said, pulling back to wipe her eyes. She looked at me then, really looked at me, and asked, "How are you, Viv?"

Taking a deep breath, I blew it out and said, "I'm okay. Thank you, Savannah, so much for the letters and packages you sent; you do not know how much it all meant to me."

Savannah nodded, her gaze searching my face as I spoke, and it was as if she could tell simply by looking into my eyes every hardship I'd been through the last three months.

"When I came home from Hawaii," she said, her voice soft, "I didn't think anything would ever feel normal again, but life went on and with each day, I healed a little more. Just take it day by day, Viv, and give yourself time to adjust to the changes life has made. And remember that

I'm here for you if you ever need a shoulder or listening ear."

I hugged her again, hot tears dripping onto her uniform, and in that moment, I was more grateful than ever for her friendship.

A bit later, after I agreed to go over and eat supper with Savannah and her family soon, I followed Zachary upstairs, steeling myself inwardly for the reunion with my father. All I wanted was to fall into his strong arms, let him fuss over me and make me feel better, like when I was a little girl, but I couldn't do that. Father was injured and perhaps blinded permanently, and he'd lost Mother, too. I refused to add more to his burden by rushing into the room a blubbering, sobbing mess, so I dried my eyes, took a deep breath, and marched into the room with my chin up.

As soon as I entered the room, my eyes immediately went to the bed where my father lay. His arm was in a sling, there was a bandage wrapped around his head, and I didn't fail to notice the fading, yellow bruises on his neck and forearms. My heart squeezed in my chest at the sight, and I slowly walked over to his side and gently touched his arm.

"What is it?" My father asked, turning his head towards me.

"It's me, Father," I said, reaching out to take his hand. "I'm home."

Just saying those two words felt so surreal to me. I'd feared for so long that I would be forced to live in that asylum forever that it was hard to believe it was all over.

Tears immediately flooded my father's eyes, and he laid there in silence for a moment, too overcome with emotion to utter any words.

"Are you alright, honey?" He finally asked, his voice choked.

"Yes, I'm just fine," I assured him. "Please, don't worry about me. How are you feeling?"

"I don't know, Vivvy," he said, his voice shaking a bit as the old childhood nickname slipped out. "I'm afraid I won't ever see again, and what…what am I going to do without your mother?"

His voice broke, and I bent over, wrapping my arms around him as we both cried. In that moment, we bonded more than we ever had, and I held him close, feeling overwhelmed with gratitude to still have him with me.

"I'll see about you, Father, don't worry," I whispered, kissing his cheek.

"No," he said, pulling back. "I need you to see about the restaurant."

"But someone will have to see about you," I protested, sitting on the edge of the bed.

"We can hire a nurse." Reaching out, he tried to find my hand, his fingers reaching blindly through the air. I touched my hand to his, and he squeezed it almost desperately. "The restaurant is a part of us, Vivvy, it's a part of your mother," he said, "and I…I don't want to lose it, too."

Fighting to keep more tears at bay, I patted the back of his hand and said reassuringly, "Don't worry, Father, I'll see about the restaurant. I promise."

"Thank you," he said, relaxing his grip.

The next morning, I went to the cemetery, a small bouquet clutched tightly in my hand. I stood before the freshly dug grave, salty tears dripping from my chin like rainwater from an old tin roof.

"Hi, Mother," I whispered, kneeling down to touch the dirt above my mother's final resting place. "I'm sorry I wasn't here to say goodbye. If…if only I could have seen you before you died…"

My words trailed off as broken sobs wracked my body and tears turned the dirt above Mother's grave to mud. All I could think of was the last time we'd seen each other; I was dragged from the house, kicking and screaming, while Mother collapsed inside, unable to watch as her daughter was carried away to a mental institution. Why hadn't I acted more rationally? Why didn't I hug her goodbye and tell her how much I loved her? Mother had died worrying about me, never to know what would become of her only daughter.

I rested the flowers against Mother's headstone and stood to my feet, wiping dirt and pieces of grass from my skirt. I stared at the grave for another long moment until I finally turned and walked back to the car, my head down and shoulders stooped.

Over the next couple of days, I threw myself into getting everything done before Father came home from the hospital. I cleaned the house from top to bottom, found a nurse to stay with Father during the day, and did my best to ignore the fact that I wasn't up to being so busy just yet. I was weak and drained and found it difficult to put one foot in front of the other, but I pushed myself anyway; Father needed me, and I refused to just lie in bed until I felt better. I also knew that if I gave myself time to dwell on everything, I may never be able to pull myself out of bed again.

When I brought Father home, he was very quiet and subdued. I knew he was thinking of Mother, and when I helped him into their bedroom, he asked to be left alone. For the rest of the afternoon, I could hear him crying and it broke my heart. He missed her just as much as I did, and I wondered if we'd ever stop thinking of her when we smelled the familiar scent of honeysuckle, or stop listening for the lyrical sound of her voice coming from the kitchen. Life just wasn't the same without her, and I knew that it never would be.

That night, as I lay in my old, comfortable bed, my thoughts spun around in circles. When I was away at the hospital, all I'd wanted was to come home where everything was safe and familiar, and now here I was and everything was drastically different. The pain was almost more than I could take, and I needed something more to take my mind off of it all. Before I drifted off to sleep, I decided to reopen the restaurant as soon as possible.

He stood across the street from her parents' house, the light of the moon reflecting off the windows. He'd heard she was back home and had come to see for himself; she was skinnier than he remembered, but it was her, nonetheless.

He watched as the lights in the house turned off one by one and considered going in through one of the windows, but finally decided against it. If she screamed, he'd have to deal with both her and her father and possibly even the neighbors, and he wasn't in the mood for cops. Besides, there were a couple of things he needed to do first, so he'd just have to wait until the timing was better to have his little visit with Vivian McCombs.

26

ASHER

Asher stepped from the hut, his pockets filled with dirt and sand taken from the tunnel. He glanced slowly around, spotting no one as he walked through the prison camp, and tried to act as nonchalant as possible. They'd been secretly digging the tunnel for over three months, and one method for disposing of the sand was to fill the men's pockets so they could scatter it sporadically on the ground throughout the day.

Asher walked around the edge of the building and put his hands into the deep pockets of his pants, feeling the sand between his fingers. Grabbing a handful, he eased his hands out and began dropping little bits of it at a time along the ground. As he did so, he failed to notice the guard walking quietly up behind him. Before he even knew anyone was there, a large hand grasped him around the back of the neck and spun him around, slamming him against the nearby brick building.

The guard kept one hand at Asher's throat while he searched his pockets with the other, his eyes narrowing when he discovered the sand.

"Where did this come from?" He growled, his accent thick and heavy as he held up a fistful of sand in front of Asher's face.

"I was going to build a sand castle," was Asher's casual response.

His jaw clenching in anger, the guard squeezed his fingers tighter around Asher's neck. "Where is it?"

Asher raised his eyebrows in question, and the guard spat, "The tunnel! Where is it?"

"I don't know what you're talking about," Asher whispered, barely able to speak from the pressure on his throat.

His face growing red, the guard slammed Asher's head against the wall with as much force as he could muster, standing there to watch as Asher slid slowly to the ground, stars floating before his eyes. With a sneer, the guard said, "Maybe next time you'll think twice before being a Schlauberger."

The guard stalked off, leaving Asher to pull himself to his feet and stumble towards the bunkhouse. He could hear his heartbeat pounding in his ears like the beating of a drum, and he felt sick to his stomach as razor sharp pains shot through his head. He barely made it through the door of the bunkhouse before he fell to his knees, and one man quickly rushed to his side and helped him to his bed.

"Should I take you to the doctor?" The man asked, his voice filled with concern.

"No," Asher shook his head as he eased himself back against his pillow. "I'll be fine."

Later that night, Asher told his buddies what happened. "They know we're digging, they just don't know where," he said, keeping his voice low. He'd developed a nice sized goose egg on the back of his head, but the nausea had passed and the pounding in his ears was subsiding.

"The tunnel is almost finished," Watson murmured from his bunk above Ethan's. "As soon as it's done, we'd better scram before they find the entrance."

It had been a long and tedious job, but it kept the men occupied. Not only had the tunnel been constructed with fortified walls, but they also built a pump to keep enough oxygen flowing for the lamps to stay lit and the workers to breathe. Nearly one hundred men were planning to escape when the time came, and for Asher, that day couldn't come soon enough.

27

Eva

W hen I received the phone call that the restaurant would soon reopen, I was beyond relieved. I'd enjoyed the time off spent at home, but we were getting low on money and I'd considered looking for a part-time job if there were any available. Thankfully, I wouldn't have to go through the process of job hunting again.

On my way to work the first day back, I walked with a spring in my step; I was so happy that the restaurant was reopening that I couldn't wait to get there. I'd just crossed the street and was standing in front of Mr. Fernsby's house when I realized my shoe had come untied. Squatting down, I quickly retied it and stood back up. I was about to continue on my way when something caught my eye and, glancing at my elderly neighbor's house, I blinked in surprise when I realized Kirk stood at the window, watching me. I threw up my hand to wave, but he didn't wave back. His gaze was steady and intense, and his body didn't move an inch; he simply stood there like a dark shadow as he stared. Shaking off the feeling of unease that pricked my spine, I hurried along my way, wondering why he wasn't at work.

When I arrived at the restaurant, there were murmurs and a lot of whispering among the employees. Throughout the day, I tried to ask what was going on but no one would tell me, and I couldn't ask Jackson because he hadn't come in to work today. Finally, as Cook and I were making the sauce for a new chicken recipe, she begrudgingly told me what everyone was so stirred up about.

"Mrs. McCombs, the boss's daughter, is back from the loony bin and has taken over the restaurant while Mr. Parker recuperates."

"The loony bin?" I asked, unfamiliar with the term.

"An asylum, honey, the place where they keep crazy people," she said with a snicker.

I felt my eyes widen and turned to look at her. "Mr. Parker's daughter is crazy?"

"I guess so," she shrugged. "They accused her of setting the fire that burned down her house and killed her baby. Couldn't prove it, but her husband sent her away all the same."

My brow furrowed as I thought over what Cook had said. "But I thought you two used to work together before she got married?"

"Yeah, well, she hasn't always been crazy," Cook stated. "I guess she had some sort of breakdown or something."

One dishwasher overheard us talking, and with a smirk, he said, "Yeah, and maybe she developed a dislike for Germans in that hospital, Eva. You may be looking for a new job soon."

My cheeks flushing, I got back to work and didn't say another word, but for the rest of the day I thought about Mrs. McCombs and what everyone was saying. I hadn't met her yet, and I wondered if she wouldn't be as kind and generous as her father. The more I thought about it, the more worried I became; maybe the others were right, and I'd soon be out of a job.

As if she'd read my mind, I got a message later that evening from the receptionist that Mrs. McCombs wished to see me in her office. I hurriedly took off my apron and smoothed down my hair, ignoring the snickers and comments from the others as I walked from the kitchen. Would this be it? Was she going to fire me?

When I reached the office door, I stopped and took a deep breath. My hand shook as I raised my arm and lightly knocked. At the words "come in", I opened the door and slowly stepped inside.

Behind the desk sat a tall, striking young woman. She looked to be in her mid-twenties, around my age, and had shoulder-length, dark hair that was rolled back on the sides, while the rest hung in soft curls around her shoulders. She was pale and very thin, with dark circles that rimmed bright, piercing green eyes, but I still thought her to be quite breathtaking.

"You must be Eva," she greeted me in a serious, professional tone. Motioning towards the chair in front of her desk, she said, "Please, have a seat."

I sat down, my hands clenched nervously in my lap. "It…it's nice to meet you, Mrs. McCombs," I said quietly, feeling very intimidated by my new boss.

"Please, call me Vivian," she said, her eyes cast downward as she flipped through some papers. "You're from Germany, is that correct?"

"Yes, ma'am," I replied, my heart sinking.

When Vivian didn't respond, I found the silence too much to bear and heard myself blurt out, "Please let me continue working here, Mrs. McCombs. I need this job very much."

Vivian looked up at me in surprise, the papers forgotten. She opened her mouth to say something, only to close it back again. I felt my ears burn at the forwardness of my speech and looked down, unable to meet her direct gaze any longer.

After a moment, Vivian asked coolly, "Are you certain that you care to work for someone who's fresh out of the 'loony bin'?"

When I looked up and my eyes widened in dismay, she sniffed and said,

"Yes, I know what everyone is saying. I was on my way to the kitchen earlier when I overheard the lovely little conversation everyone was having about me."

The blood draining from my face, I said in a trembling voice, "It was my fault, Mrs. McCombs. I…I only wished to know a bit about you, but I never meant for the conversation to go in such a negative, unkind direction. I'm very sorry that it did."

I couldn't tell by the look on Vivian's face if she was angry or about to cry, but she quickly pulled herself together and, sitting up straighter, said, "It's quite alright, really. I don't care what they think, anyway. I know, however, that you aren't to blame, and I had no intention of firing you. I simply wanted to introduce myself and get to know you a bit better. Father tells me you have a little boy?"

I sat back, feeling so relieved that my whole body seemed to deflate against the back of the chair like a balloon, and I smiled timidly at Vivian. "Yes, ma'am, his name is Davey; he's three."

"I'm sure he's adorable," she said, and I thought I saw a flash of pain in her eyes.

I hesitated for a brief moment, taking a deep breath before I gently said, "Your father told me about your son. I'm so sorry; I can't imagine losing a child."

"I believe it's the worst thing that could ever happen to anyone," she replied, her voice clipped.

The conversation ended shortly thereafter, and I returned to the kitchen to finish cleaning up. More remarks were made about my time being "limited", but I ignored them. All I could think about was Vivian and everything she'd been through. Although she hadn't admitted it, the words of the restaurant employees had hurt her; I could see it in her eyes. I knew how it felt to be talked about and looked down upon, and hoped that I could be of some help to her. And maybe, just maybe, we could even become friends.

Vivian

After Eva left my office, I sat at the desk and rubbed my temples, feeling a bit emotional. Eva's kind words had touched me, and I could clearly see what Father meant in his letter when he said she had a big heart. I'd noticed she attempted to cover her German accent; one would immediately know, however, just by looking at her that she wasn't from around here. I'd never seen such light blonde hair in all my life, and with her alabaster skin and soft, blue eyes, she looked almost like a porcelain doll. She was very pretty, and her quiet, kind way just made her appear even more beautiful. Although I hadn't intended such, I'd been short with her and now regretted it. I hadn't, however, been prepared for the reception I'd received that day and had struggled ever since. Perhaps I would apologize tomorrow when I saw her.

Sighing, I stood up and moved to stand by the window, pulling the curtain back to gaze out onto the street as I watched the people pass by. In the south, manners were a huge part of our heritage, and I watched as the men tipped their hats to the ladies, some even taking their elbows to help them cross the street. Cars stopped at the intersection and patiently waited their turn, never blowing their horns or yelling out of the window. I wondered, however, where those ingrained niceties had disappeared to when it came to the hateful comments I'd overheard today.

"She's back from the loony bin...that's where they send the crazy people...perhaps she had a breakdown."

The words from my father's employees, some of whom I'd known for years, kept running over and over through my brain. I hadn't even considered the fact that people would truly think I was crazy, but I'd felt it at the hospital all week when I visited Father, and even at the market yesterday; the stares and tight smiles from those I'd recognized and spoken to, how everyone would turn and go the other way when they saw me. I'd expected my acquaintances to greet me cheerfully and welcome me home, but instead they'd kept their distance and made excuses to leave as soon as they could. I'd even noticed that the restaurant was unusually crowded that morning and hadn't realized why until now; they'd all come to see the "crazy woman", to stare and whisper like I was some circus sideshow. I hadn't wanted to admit to myself the reason behind all of this behavior, but now I was forced to and it hurt; badly.

Turning to sit back in my chair, I took a deep breath and let it out slowly. I felt so tired and drained, and it was only my first day back at work. How would I survive the rest of the week?

Just then, I heard the bells from St. John's Cathedral ring and glanced at my watch. It was six o'clock, and I'd promised Savannah that I would eat supper with them at six-thirty. I'd asked Father to go with me, but he'd declined, so I arranged to have his nurse stay with him until I got back. I hurriedly gathered up my things and rushed out to my car, making it to Emma Danes' house with five minutes to spare.

I knocked on the front door, and Raymond Coleman immediately opened it. Savannah's uncle was a large man, but very quiet and one of the kindest, most gentle souls I'd ever met. Smiling, he pulled me into a hug and patted me on the back.

"It's good to see you, Vivian," he said, his voice rumbling against my ear as he spoke.

Pulling away, I smiled up at him and said, "Thank you, Mr. Ray, it's good to see you, too."

"Savannah is in the kitchen, and just between us, I think she could use some help," he told me, his soft eyes twinkling.

Laughing, I hurried through the house and found Savannah pulling a somewhat burned loaf of bread from the oven.

"Oh, Viv, look at what I've done," she huffed with frustration. "This is what I get for trying to cook for a restaurant owner."

"It will be fine," I assured her, chuckling. "We'll just slather lots of butter and jelly on top."

"You'd think by now I would have learned how to cook," Savannah muttered, picking up a platter full of baked chicken. "After this, Mama Emma and Aunt Deb won't ever let me cook again; let's just hope the main course is edible."

"Where *are* your aunt and Mrs. Emma?"

"Since they do all the cooking on Sundays, I insisted on doing it tonight," she replied, "so they're next door baking a pan of brownies for dessert because Aunt Deb is craving chocolate and, according to her, she makes the best brownies in town."

Shaking her head, Savannah shot me a knowing look, and I couldn't help but laugh. Savannah's aunt was very outspoken and opinionated, yet one couldn't help but love her.

I helped her carry the food into the dining room and had just placed a bowl of creamed corn on the table when the front door opened and Leon stepped inside, followed by his mother and Mrs. Debra

His eyes lighting up when he saw me, Leon rushed over and scooped me up into a bear hug. "Viv, it's wonderful to see you!" He cried. Setting me back on my feet, he pulled away and quickly surveyed me. Turning to look at the others, he gestured towards me and said, "Doesn't she look great?"

"She certainly does," Mrs. Emma agreed with a smile as she came over to hug me.

"Still a charmer, I see," I told Leon, shaking my head playfully at him.

"Perhaps, but at least I'm an honest one," he winked.

Leon pulled out a chair for me at the table, and we all sat down. After saying grace, we quickly dug in to the food, and I asked everyone to fill me in on everything I'd missed since being away. Mrs. Debra shared the latest gossip from her sewing circle, Savannah talked of the last few letters she'd received from Connor, and Leon told me about his job promotion and the house he'd bought.

"I'm actually living next to Eva Beckett, one of your Father's employees," he said.

"I met her this afternoon," I told him. "She seems very nice."

At the mention of Eva and the restaurant, I felt a pang in my chest as I once again recalled the conversation I'd overhead in the kitchen. I quickly pushed it aside, however, as I was determined to enjoy myself tonight and didn't wish to put a damper on the mood.

After supper, we went into the living room for a game of charades. Savannah and I were on a team, Mrs. Debra and Emma were on another, and Mr. Ray and Leon teamed up. I'd always been very competitive, and I was on the edge of my seat with anticipation as we waited for our turn.

Mrs. Debra went first, her bright green eyes sparkling with excitement. Leon looked at his watch, said "go!", and she ran around the room, flapping her arms and bobbing her head up and down.

"Bird?" Mrs. Emma guessed. "Chicken…rooster…duck?"

Sighing, Mrs. Debra stopped and shook her head. She stood still for a moment, thinking, and when she bent over slightly and began shaking her rear, Savannah and I burst into giggles.

"Peacock!" Mrs. Emma cried.

"Yes, for goodness' sake," Mrs. Debra exclaimed as she re-joined Mrs. Emma on the sofa. "I don't know why I always get such ridiculous words."

Still laughing, I got up and went to stand before the fireplace, drawing my word from the hat on the hearth. When Leon gave me the signal, I cupped my hand around my mouth and pretended to whisper.

"Secret?" Savannah immediately guessed.

"Yes!" I cried, clapping my hands with excitement.

"Now why didn't I get such an easy word?" Mrs. Debra sighed.

We continued to play in this fashion, with Savannah and me fighting for the lead against the other two ladies. We'd all been such close friends for so many years that it seemed we could almost read each other's minds.

"I feel that we're somehow at a disadvantage here," Leon said to Mr. Ray in a teasing tone of voice. "Why aren't you guessing my cues as good as they are?"

"I could ask you the same question," Mr. Ray replied with a chuckle.

It was Leon's turn next, and he took his place before the mantle. The word was "shotgun", and when Leon made the motion of holding and firing a gun with his hands, he also made the corresponding sounds with his mouth. Mr. Ray immediately guessed the word, and the four of us ladies cried, "You cheated, Leon, that doesn't count!"

"Look, we've got to get points somehow," Leon laughed, dodging me as I reached out to slap his arm.

"Have a little mercy on us poor fellas," Mr. Ray said, his shoulders shaking as he laughed at the expression on his wife's face.

Regardless of the men and their cheating, Savannah and I won the game, and it was nearly ten o'clock when I hugged everyone goodbye and thanked them for such a wonderful evening.

"Even if the bread was burned?" Savannah teased as she walked me to the front door.

"Was it?" I asked innocently, and we both laughed.

Leon walked me out to my car, and we stopped for a moment to talk.

"I'm so glad you're home, Viv," he said, reaching out to touch my arm. "I'm just sorry that you've had to go through so much."

"Thank you, Leon," I said with a smile. "Tonight helped…a lot."

"We'll have to do it more often then," he replied. "You'll just have to promise that you and Savannah won't beat us at Charades so bad next time."

Grinning, I said tartly, "I'm afraid I can't make any promises."

As I drove home, I realized with a sigh of relief that I was feeling better. Most of the people in the city may gossip and think me crazy, but knowing that I had the support of my closest friends filled me with gratitude.

28

THE SHADOW

He walked up the narrow driveway, softly rehearsing the speech he would make under his breath. Eva was at work and wouldn't be home, but he still wore a disguise, just in case. He walked up the porch steps and knocked on the front door, waiting patiently until it was opened by a middle-aged carbon copy of Eva.

"Good day, madam," he said, a smile on his face as he tipped his hat. "I have here one of the newest rug sweepers on the market. It's very well priced, lightweight, and does its job better than any of its competitors. If you wouldn't mind sparing just a moment of your time, I'd like to step inside and demonstrate its quick and powerful cleaning abilities."

He paused, waiting with bated breath as Eva's mother hesitantly considered his request.

"I don't know," she said uncertainly, "my grandson is napping and I don't wish to wake him."

"I promise to be as quiet as a mouse," he said, lowering the tone of his voice as proof of his promise.

Finally, Eva's mother nodded and stepped out of the doorway, motioning for him to come inside. He hurried by, quickly taking in his surroundings as he attempted to conceal a victorious smile; he'd been trying to figure out a way to get inside for weeks.

The house was small, very clean, and apparently run only by women, as there was no sign of male occupancy. He also noticed several areas in need of repair, such as a broken shelf on the bookcase, a few cracked floorboards, and a door which hung crooked on its hinges.

As he followed Eva's mother into the living room, he carefully took inventory of everything around him. There were many photographs lining the walls and placed along the top of the mantle, one of which was of Eva and her late husband. He stared at it for a moment, clenching his jaw at the look of happiness on Eva's face as she leaned against the handsome man beside her.

Forcing himself to look away and keep a neutral expression, his eyes then fell upon several odd little statues sitting on the coffee table. He'd never seen anything like them before and thought them to be quite strange.

What do they represent? He wondered. He heard someone moving about in the kitchen then and assumed it to be Eva's grandmother; he'd seen her outside watering the rose bushes many times.

"Okay, here we go," he finally said, dropping a few pieces of straw onto the living room floor. "This won't take long."

He quickly demonstrated the wonderful abilities of the rug sweeper, his eyes continuing to dart all around the room. The straw was gone, and he turned to smile triumphantly at the quiet little German woman behind him.

"There, now what do you think?" He asked, sweeping his hand out dramatically as he gave her a price.

"I...I really don't think we can afford it. I'm very sorry," she said apologetically.

Pursing his lips as if disappointed, he nodded his head and said, "I perfectly understand."

She turned to show him out, and he wracked his brain for an excuse to stay and poke around a bit more.

"Uh," he cleared his throat, "would you mind terribly if I asked for something to drink? It's awfully hot outside for a salesman."

"Oh, of course," she nodded, and he followed her into the kitchen.

Eva's grandmother turned to look at them questioningly, and as Eva's mother explained, he slowly surveyed the kitchen. An ice box sat in the corner, a small table with four chairs rested to his left, and he spotted what appeared to be a small wooden train sitting on the floor. The back door was open, revealing a tiny backyard through the screened door and a full load of laundry hanging from a clothesline that fluttered gently in the breeze.

Eva's mother handed him a glass of sweet tea and he sipped it slowly, eyeing the two women for a moment before he stated, "Your husbands are fortunate men; this is the best sweet tea I've ever had."

"Oh, my husband and father-in-law are both dead," Eva's mother said softly.

"Is that so?" He asked, eyes wide. "How sad. You said that you have a grandson?"

"Yes, he's three," she nodded.

"And quite spoiled," Eva's grandmother spoke up, smiling. "I'm afraid my granddaughter has her hands full trying to keep him in line with the two of us doting on him so."

"What about her husband?" He asked casually. "Doesn't he object to all of the spoiling?"

"He's gone, too, I'm afraid," Eva's grandmother said with a sigh.

"I'm sorry," he replied. "I'm sure you're all doing a fine job of raising the boy."

With his glass empty and no other excuse to stay, he picked up the rug sweeper, thanked them for the tea, and left. He hadn't been able to investigate the rest of the house, but had a pretty good idea of its layout

149

now.

The sweeper thrown carelessly over his shoulder, he walked back down the driveway and smiled, feeling quite pleased with his performance. He'd be back tonight, only he wouldn't be invited in this time.

Eva

I gently kissed Davey goodnight, the sound of his deep breaths a sure sign that he was finally asleep. I'd read him a bedtime story and sung two lullabies before his eyes ultimately fluttered closed, and I yawned quietly as I tiptoed from the room, exhausted after the long day.

After taking a quick bath, I fell into bed and was asleep almost as soon as my head hit the pillow. Two hours later, just before midnight, I awoke out of a deep sleep, my mind foggy as I looked around the dark room in confusion. The clock at my bedside ticked loudly, and I could hear the crickets and frogs chirping just outside of my window. Rubbing my eyes, I sat up in bed, wondering what had awakened me.

Thinking that perhaps Davey had cried out in his sleep, I climbed out of bed and put on my robe, tiptoeing out into the hallway in my bare feet. The house was quiet as I listened, and when I didn't hear any sound coming from Davey's bedroom, I shrugged and turned to step back into my room.

Suddenly, a floorboard creaked just down the hall, and I paused. The house would creak and groan sometimes, and Nana would always say it was just "settling", but there was something different this time. I could feel it. Squinting, I peered through the darkness, unable to see a thing in the pitch-black abyss, but I had the instinctive feeling that someone was there, and felt the skin on my arms stand on end.

"Eva."

A whispered voice, barely audible, drifted through the darkness, and I caught my breath, my pulse quickening.

"M-Mutter? Is that you?" I asked softly, my voice trembling.

There was no answer. The floor creaked again, and I pushed myself back against the wall, heart pounding. Could someone possibly be in the house, or was I imagining things? The hallway was so dark it was blinding, and I told myself to feel along the wall for the light switch, but was too afraid of what else I might find with my fingers. I stood there, frozen in place as I waited, listening.

"Eva."

The voice was much closer this time, and I felt a whiff of warm breath blow across the side of my face just as a large hand coiled tightly around my wrist.

I jerked back and screamed, my voice filled with terror as it echoed off the walls, and I desperately tried to pull my arm away, white-hot fear shooting through my veins like an electric current. The fact that I couldn't see who or what had a hold of me was just as terrifying as the cold hand that gripped my wrist, and I continued trying to jerk away like a wild bear caught in a trap, my head striking the wall behind me with a loud *thud*.

Suddenly, I saw the light under Mutter and Nana's door flip on. The hand released mine, and I heard a slight growl emanate from the back of the man's throat as he brushed past me and hurried through the house and out the front door.

"Eva, honey, what happened?"

The hall light clicked on, illuminating my shaken form huddled against the wall like a frightened animal. My mother and grandmother rushed to my side, their eyes filled with worry.

"C-call the police," I said in a choked whisper. Nana rushed to the phone, and I glanced wildly down the hall, my heart pounding. "Davey," I said in a panicked voice. "Mutter, ch-check on him. Please."

Mutter ran to Davey's room and emerged shortly after, carrying my son in her arms. He was awake and gazing around in confusion, and I held out trembling arms to him, tears coming to my eyes as I sank to the floor and cradled him against my chest.

The police arrived, and I hurriedly told them what happened, my voice shaking as I spoke. Nana took Davey into the living room and sat with him in the rocking chair, humming under her breath as he drifted back off to sleep.

"Did you see the man's face?" Officer Sallow asked, taking notes.

"No," I replied. "B-but he knew my name."

"Did you recognize his voice?"

I shook my head, my body beginning to tremble again as the sound of his voice when he whispered my name rang through my mind.

Wrapping my arms around my waist, I asked in a weak voice, "What…what do you think he wanted?"

"I don't know, but would it be alright if I helped you search the house?" He asked, stuffing the notepad back into his shirt pocket. "I want to make certain that nothing was stolen."

Nodding, I led the officer throughout the house, my legs trembling and skin clammy. I felt weak and drained, as if I'd been very ill with a fever, and I wondered how I'd ever be able to sleep peacefully again after this.

When we went into Davey's room, I noticed the officer's forehead wrinkle, and when I followed the direction of his troubled gaze, my eyes widened at what I saw. There, lying beside my son's bed, was an open pocket knife.

Picking up the knife, the officer looked questioningly at me and asked, "How old did you say your son is?"

151

"He's almost four," I replied, my eyes glued to the knife.

"And you allow him to have a pocket knife?" He asked disapprovingly. "Mrs. Beckett, I know it's none of my business, but your son is much too young to have such a thing."

Blinking, I looked at Officer Sallow in confusion and said, "That's not Davey's knife; I've never seen it before."

His eyes narrowing, Officer Sallow asked, "Then where did it come from?"

"I do not know…" I paused, the color leaving my face. Eyes wide with fear, I looked at Officer Sallow and asked, "Do you think the intruder intended to harm my son and…and was interrupted when he heard me open my bedroom door?"

"Why would someone break into your home intending to do harm to your son?" He asked skeptically.

I shook my head, feeling sick to my stomach. "I don't know," I whispered.

"Mrs. Beckett, are you sure you weren't dreaming?" Officer Sallow asked suspiciously.

My eyes widening, I said, "I'm positive that I wasn't dreaming."

Nodding, Officer Sallow sighed and said, "Alright, well, it doesn't look like anything was stolen, so there's nothing more I can do. Call us if you should remember anything else."

After the police were gone, I locked up the house as tightly as possible, making certain that every window was secure as well. When I put Davey back to bed, I noticed that Officer Sallow had left the knife behind, and I knew he hadn't believed me when I said that it didn't belong to Davey.

I picked up the knife and took it into my room, studying it closely. It was the cheap five-and-dime type and appeared to be brand new, and I placed it in the drawer of my bedside table, shivering. Why had the intruder been in my son's room, and why had he left the knife behind?

After retrieving one of Davey's little baseball bats, I went back to his room and sat in the chair next to his bed, where I stayed for the rest of the night.

29

Vivian

A few days later, I finally went out to the police station to discuss the details of my husband's death with Officer Wright; I hadn't had time to make the visit yet, and I was tired of putting it off. I wasn't, however, in the frame of mind to have a serious conversation with anyone, as the last several days hadn't gone well at all. Father had decided he didn't want me to stay with him at night, and we'd ended up in a heated discussion over the matter this morning.

"I can't just leave you here by yourself at night, Father," I'd told him, exasperated.

"You certainly can," he'd insisted stubbornly. "I don't need my daughter to babysit me, especially when you're trying to work and can't get any sleep at night with me bumping around. I can see shadows and a bit of light, so there's no need to worry about me. You can move in to the apartment above the restaurant."

After a bit more arguing, I could see that he wouldn't back down, so I finally gave in. I hated to leave him there alone and would worry myself sick about him, but it was his house and I would obey his wishes.

To make the morning even worse, I was forced to fire an employee for being rude and insolent. I could still see the man's face when I asked him why he wouldn't do as Cook told him.

"Because she's being too bossy and I won't have any woman telling me what to do," he'd declared, his neck growing red. He was in his fifties, and I'd heard others complain about how hard he was to work with.

"Well, I'm sorry, but I'm afraid you'll have to do what she asks because that's part of your job," I told him as gently as possible. I'd been taught to respect my elders, and it was often difficult to assert my authority over someone so much older than me.

"I guess you expect me to take orders from *you*, too?" He'd guffawed. "A young slip of a girl who's fresh out of the crazy house?"

That had been the last straw; I gave him the money he'd earned for the week and told him not to come back. I then left the kitchen, my head held high, and went into my office and cried.

When I arrived at the police station, I was taken to Officer Wright's small corner office, and I didn't miss the look of surprise on his face when he saw me. I stood silently in the doorway, waiting for him to speak as thoughts of the last time I saw him ran through my mind.

"Mrs. McCombs," he said, clearing his throat. "Please, come in and have a seat."

I sat in the chair opposite his desk and stated, "I came to ask if you've any news on Howard's death."

"No, I'm afraid not," he said, shaking his head. He began clearing the clutter from his desk, a lock of dirty blonde hair falling over his forehead and giving him a slightly boyish appearance. I hadn't particularly noticed before, but he didn't appear to be much older than me. "All we know is that he was murdered, but we don't know why or by whom. Do you have any idea who could be responsible?"

"No, I don't, but I'm afraid that you can't blame *me* for this crime because I wasn't here," I said, the words slipping from my mouth before I could stop them.

Officer Wright blinked, his cheeks flushing red. "I don't believe I was the one who accused you before," he stated in a clipped tone.

Sighing, I said, "You're right, I'm sorry." Clearing my throat, I asked, "Have you been able to find out anything of the men I told you about? They could be the ones that killed Howard."

"As I told you before, there were no signs of anyone else being on your property that night, Mrs. McCombs, so I'm afraid we had no way of finding those men."

By the slightly annoyed tone in his voice, I could tell that he still didn't believe I'd ever seen those men, and I felt myself growing frustrated.

"Well, perhaps that's why you haven't solved Howard's murder," I said with a sniff. "Maybe you should hire a better forensics team so y'all could actually solve the crimes that are being committed around here."

"It wouldn't matter if we had the very best forensics team," he replied coolly, his jaw clenched, "because you simply can't find something that was never there."

I opened my mouth to snap back at him, only to clamp it shut again. With pursed lips, I stood and began to walk from the room, stopping only when Officer Wright sighed and called my name.

When I turned back to look at him with a raised eyebrow, he said, "I apologize. I shouldn't have said that. I'm not the enemy, Mrs. McCombs, and I'd appreciate it if you'd trust me enough to let me do my job. We'll find your husband's murderer, I promise."

"Thank you," was all I said before walking from the room.

When I got back into my car, I sat there for a moment, feeling upset and disconcerted with myself. While I'd always been outspoken, I was never rude or impolite and found myself growing edgier and more short-tempered every day.

Deciding to take a break, I drove down to the library, checked out a book, and walked over to Columbia Square. As Savannah is known for its many beautiful squares, I had several to choose from, but Columbia Square was my favorite, with its picturesque little fountain and beautiful, surrounding homes. I sat on one of the park benches, the thick branches of live oaks shading me from the sun, and read my book, the trickling of the water in the fountain and the chirping of birds instantly soothing my tense nerves.

By the time I arrived back at the restaurant later that evening, everyone was leaving for the day, and I waved goodbye to all of them and went into my office. I hadn't planned on staying long, but soon got caught up in some paperwork and before I knew it, the clock was striking eight.

I was just gathering up the mound of papers so I could quit for the night when I heard a creak out in the hallway. Stopping, I listened intently, but all that reached my ears was silence. With a sigh, I shrugged my shoulders and quickly locked the papers up in the safe. As my back was towards the door, I didn't notice when it slowly opened and someone quietly stepped inside, and he was behind me before I even realized anyone was there. One hand snaked quickly around my mouth while the other wrapped around my arms, and I froze in place, terror causing my heart to beat overtime.

"We meet again," a voice said against my ear, and I felt the blood drain from my face. I'd recognize that voice anywhere; it was the same one from that horrible night almost four months ago. I began to squirm, but he tightened his hold on me and said, "I killed your dearly beloved husband, sweetheart, and I won't hesitate to kill you, too. All you have to do is tell me where the money is, and I'll leave. Now, I'm going to move my hand from your mouth, but if you even so much as raise your voice, I'll break your neck."

He slowly moved his hand away, and I took a deep breath, trying to calm myself. "W-what money are you referring to?" I finally asked, my voice strained.

"The five thousand dollars Howard stole from me," the man snapped, the stubble on his face scratching my cheek. "He said you knew where it was and I want it now."

Bewildered, I shook my head and said, "I'm sorry, but I don't have any idea what you're talking about."

"Don't play games with me," he growled, his arms tightening painfully around mine. "I want my money, and if you don't give it to me, I'll just travel on down to your father's house and…"

"I can't tell you something that I don't know," I cried, desperately trying to think of a way to get out of this. "Look, why don't you let me go through the few personal items that were found in the remains of the fire, and I'll see if I can find something that might give me a clue where this money is?"

155

He hesitated, and I held my breath, waiting for him to wrap his fingers around my neck any second and start squeezing. Finally, he said, "I'll give you four days. When you find the money, put it in a briefcase and sit it in Forsyth Park beside one of the light poles. We'll be following you, so don't try any tricks, and if you go to the police, I'll kill your father and force you to watch."

With those words, he let me go and was gone before I could even turn around. I let out the breath I was holding and leaned against the safe, my legs weak and stomach churning. I hadn't any idea where this supposed money was. What would I do if I couldn't figure it out within the next four days?

30

Eva

As soon as I walked into the restaurant the next morning, I received the message that Vivian wished to see me in her office. Wondering what she wanted, I hurried back and knocked lightly on the door. When I heard the words "come in", I walked inside to find Vivian seated behind her desk. Her normally neat and tidy appearance was a bit disheveled, and I noticed she looked even more pale than usual.

"Eva, I need you to do something for me," she said. "I've been in contact with a new produce supplier in Bloomingdale, and he called this morning to tell me he has a load of beans, cabbage, and potatoes ready for inspection. If we like the way his produce looks, he'll deliver from now on, but someone has to go inspect everything first before I agree to work with him. Normally I would go, but something has…well, come up and I can't go. Cook has to stay here, and you're the only other person around that knows the quality of fruits and vegetables well enough to do the inspection. Will you do it? You'll need to take the truck, of course, to bring the load back if you like how everything looks."

I stared at Vivian wide-eyed as she rambled, her words rushed and almost breathless as she opened every drawer in her desk and looked inside as if searching for something.

"I…I don't know how to drive," I finally spoke up.

Vivian blinked and stopped everything she was doing to look at me. "Oh, well, that is a problem," she said, sighing.

There was a knock at the door just then, and we were both surprised when Leon poked his head in.

"Good morning, ladies," he smiled at us both. "It's my day off and since I was driving by, I thought I'd stop in and see how you're doing, Viv. How's your father, by the way?"

"He's much better, but I'm afraid his eyesight is still the same," she replied. A light suddenly lit in her eyes, and she said, "Leon, would you do me a huge favor?"

"Of course," he nodded, and before I knew it, we were both seated in the restaurant's truck, bumping along down the road with instructions on everything we were to do.

"I didn't realize when I stopped in for a visit that Viv would put me to work," Leon said, grinning over at me.

"You were very kind to have agreed," I replied, gazing out the window as we drove from the city. The only time I'd ever been very far outside of Savannah was when we'd first arrived from Germany, and I was interested in seeing more of the farmlands I'd heard so much about.

"It was the least I could do; she's been through a lot lately."

I turned in my seat to look back at Leon and, hesitating slightly, asked, "Will you tell me a bit more about her situation? I've heard bits and pieces, but I honestly know little about it. Why exactly was she sent to a mental hospital? Cook told me a bit, but it didn't make much sense."

Sighing, Leon said, "From what Savannah told me, Viv walks in her sleep, and her husband accused her of doing so the night someone set fire to their house and killed their baby. Viv, however, claims that there were three men who are responsible, one of which held her captive while the others set the fire."

"How awful," I breathed, eyes wide. "Her husband nor the police believed her?"

"There apparently wasn't any evidence that supported Viv's story," Leon replied, shrugging his broad shoulders. "Since Howard was killed, I think he was involved somehow, but it seems the police are stumped."

"Poor Vivian," I stated softly, shaking my head.

"Their farm is down that road," Leon said, pointing out a long, dirt road coming up on our right. "She was able to pay off most of Howard's debts after the corn was harvested, and the insurance covered the loss of the house, so she's asked the bank to find a buyer."

"She's been through so much," I said, sighing. "Did she seem a little…I don't know…odd today?"

"What do you mean?"

"She just seemed distracted and a little upset when she called me into her office," I replied, shrugging slightly. "She kept digging through her desk drawers and said that something important had come up or she would be the one going to Bloomingdale today. Do you think everything is okay?"

"Hmm, I don't know," Leon replied thoughtfully. "She's always been very energetic and a bit high-strung, but it seems like something was bothering her. Perhaps I should ask Savannah to talk to her."

After about an hour of driving, we arrived at the farm. The owner, Mr. Bringer, was very pleasant and patient as I examined everything carefully and was pleased when I told him how wonderful it all looked. He was such a nice man that it relieved me to give him the good news; I would have felt terrible if I had to turn his produce down.

"I'll have my boys load everything into the back of your truck," he said, shaking my hand.

158

With Leon's help, they loaded the truck in less than twenty minutes, and we were just about to leave when Mr. Bringer asked if we'd like to take an early lunch with him and his wife. Surprised at the kind offer, I glanced at Leon for confirmation before I admitted shyly that I was, in fact, quite hungry and would love to stay. Mrs. Bringer was very gracious and pleased to have the company, and by the time Leon and I left, our stomachs were full and it was well past noon.

We'd been on the road for about twenty minutes when the truck suddenly began to make a sputtering sound. I held on to my seat as the vehicle stalled and jerked, the breaks squealing in protest, until we finally came to a dead stop on the side of the road. Leon tried getting it to crank again, but it refused to go any further.

"Well, this is just great," Leon muttered as he climbed from the truck and lifted the hood. After a moment, he returned to say, "I think I could fix it if I had some tools. Vivian's farm isn't far from here, so I think I'll walk on over and see if I can find what I need in her barn."

"Wait for me," I said, quickly climbing from the truck to follow him.

"Are you sure you want to come along?" He asked, looking at me in surprise. "It's about a mile there and back."

"Oh, I don't mind," I said, hurrying to catch up with him. "I don't want to stay out here on this long, lonely road all by myself."

"Scaredy-cat," Leon laughed.

We walked along the side of the road, green farmlands stretching out as far as the eye could see. To our left, cows grazed peacefully in a large, fenced-in pasture, their tails flicking off pesky flies that buzzed around their backs, and I spotted two calves frolicking playfully in the sun. I then noticed that just beyond the cow pasture was an enormous field dotted with what appeared to be white snowballs, and when I asked Leon what it was, he said it was cotton.

After a moment, Leon glanced over at me and said, "Tell me more about your husband. What was he like?"

Tucking a strand of hair behind my ear, I thought the question over for a moment and said, "Charming, handsome, and very stubborn when he wanted to be. He came from a wealthy family in Connecticut, and when his parents forbade him to marry me, he quit the family business but still worked in the shipping industry, which kept him out of the war."

"Interesting," Leon said, kicking a rock with the toe of his shoe. "So, how did his parents react after y'all were married?"

"They disowned him, and he never spoke to them again," I replied, sighing. "I've tried to contact them a few times, but they won't answer; I still feel so guilty for causing their severance."

"You shouldn't feel guilty, Eva," Leon said gently. "They should have honored their son's choice and accepted his decision." He glanced over at me then and smiled warmly, adding, "I feel sorry for them; they've missed out on having a wonderful daughter-in-law."

Blushing, I ducked my head and said, "Thank you, that's very kind of you to say."

"So, I know that you're a splendid cook and you sing like an angel," Leon said, changing the subject, "but is there anything else that I don't know about?"

"I daydream."

The words popped out of my mouth so fast that I blinked, my cheeks flushing with embarrassment.

Leon looked over at me in surprise, his eyebrows raised. "Okay, that's not what I expected you to say," he laughed. "What do you daydream about?"

"Oh, it's silly," I shook my head, glancing down at my feet.

"I doubt that," Leon persisted. "Tell me. Please?"

It took me a moment to answer, as I didn't quite know how to put it into words. "Well, I daydream about a world with no tears or pain," I said slowly, "where everyone is happy and no one goes hungry...but I suppose most people dream of those things."

"What else?" Leon asked. "I know there's got to be more."

"Well..." I hesitated, feeling a bit foolish, "sometimes I dream songs into existence. I'll hear an unknown melody in my head and often put words with it. It's almost like I have my own, personal music box that I carry with me."

I can't believe I just told him that, I immediately thought, feeling embarrassed. Glancing at Leon uncertainly, I asked, "Is...is that strange?"

Shaking his head, Leon said, "Not at all. In fact, why don't you sing one of those songs for me now?"

I blinked, surprised at the request. "Oh, I couldn't do that," I said, my ears burning.

"Why not?" Leon asked. Opening his arms wide, he gestured at our surroundings and said, "There's no one here but us and the cows, and I've already heard you sing. Please? The cows are dying to hear one of your songs."

My lips twitching at his foolishness, I said, "I don't know if I could think of one right now."

"Are you stalling?"

Sighing, I shook my head and said, "Alright, I'll try."

Hoping that I didn't look as foolish as I felt, I closed my eyes, trying to concentrate as I listened to the chirping of the birds and the tinkling of cowbells. It all seemed to speak to me and, after a moment, I slowly began to hum, the music flowing past my lips like a gentle breeze. The tune was soft and sweet, like the wind as it whispered through the tall grass, and I soon forgot my fears and uncertainties as the magic of the melody swept over me. I felt Leon wrap one arm around my waist while his hand took

160

mine, and we danced right there in the middle of the road. My eyes remained closed as I continued to hum, and it almost felt as if we were floating among the clouds.

Suddenly, the sound of an approaching vehicle brought us back to earth, and we immediately pulled apart and stepped back as an old pickup breezed by. Leon tried waving the driver down to ask for help, but the man simply blew his horn as he passed and I covered my mouth in mirth.

When Leon realized I was laughing, he said, "You won't think it's so funny when you have blisters on your feet tonight."

I couldn't help but giggle when he reached out to pinch my waist playfully, and as I dodged his fingers, I said, "I can't imagine what he must think of us, dancing in the middle of the road like that."

"Probably that we're a couple of gypsies or something," Leon chuckled.

My hair blew over my face then and Leon reached out to gently brush it aside, smiling softly down at me as he said, "You know, you're an unusual woman, Eva Beckett. I don't believe I've ever met anyone quite like you. Thank you for the song; the cows and I loved it."

With a smile, I stepped back and said, "I'm not entirely certain of how much the cows enjoyed it, but thank you." Glancing at my wristwatch, I added, "We'd better hurry. At the rate we're going, it'll be midnight by the time we get back to town."

When we finally arrived at Vivian's farm, I stopped and gazed around the property, sadness sweeping over me at the sight of the burned, charred ruins of what used to be their home. How horrible it must have been for Vivian to witness such a thing!

"I'll check the barn," Leon said, and I followed him to the large wooden structure.

We stepped inside, stopping in our tracks at the sight before us. It appeared that someone had been looking for something, as several sections of the dirt floor had been dug up, and boards all along the walls were busted and removed. Crates were overturned, a trunk in the corner stood open with rope and tackle hanging partly out, and several bags of chicken feed had been torn open and apparently dug through.

"What on earth has happened here?" I breathed, eyes wide.

"I don't know, but I don't like the way this looks," Leon said, his voice low. "When we get back to town, I'm going to call the sheriff."

He went over to the trunk, pulled out a couple of tools, and crammed them into his back pocket. We were turning to go back outside when, suddenly, we heard voices coming from the other side of the barn door. Leon grabbed my arm and pulled me into a dark corner, motioning for me to be quiet.

"It can't be here," a man said, and I heard the barn door creak as it opened. Shadows bounced along the walls and I held my breath, pushing myself further into the corner. "She's got to have it; that's the only plausible explanation."

"I'm telling you, she didn't act like she knew anything about it," another, more gruff voice spoke out.

"Well, I'm tired," a third man stated in a whiny tone. "Let's come back tomorrow. There can't be many more places to look, anyway."

"This farm is huge, you idiot," the second, gruff voice stated. "It could be buried anywhere."

What could be buried anywhere? I wondered, fighting the urge to squirm. I glanced up at Leon and, noting the intense look on his face, knew that we were both thinking the same thing; it could be very dangerous if these men discovered us.

Finally, after a bit more arguing, the men left, and both Leon and I sighed with relief. After waiting in our hiding place a bit longer, Leon took my hand and said softly, "Come on, let's get out of here."

Once we were away from the farm and back out on the road, I asked, "Who were those men, and what do you think they were looking for?"

Running his fingers through his hair, Leon sighed and shrugged his shoulders. "I have no idea, but they were definitely up to no good, and I intend to speak with both the police and Vivian about this."

31

Vivian

Early the next morning, I received a phone call from Officer Wright requesting that I come down to the station. Curious by what it was all about, I quickly dressed, pinned my hair up, and hurried out to my car. When I arrived at the station, I was surprised to find that Leon was there as well.

"I hate that you had to come down here on a Sunday morning," Leon said apologetically. "I would have done this yesterday evening, but it was too late by the time Eva and I got back."

"Done what?" I asked, following him into Officer Wright's office. "What's going on?"

Once inside the office, Leon closed the door and quickly explained what he and Eva had witnessed the day before at my farm. "I called Officer Wright yesterday evening, and he immediately sent some men to your farm to check things out," Leon said.

"My men went inside the barn and saw what Leon had described," Officer Wright stated, leaning back in his chair. I met his direct gaze head-on, refusing to allow the memory of our last visit to cause me any discomfort. "After searching the farm, they stumbled upon three men camping out on the back side of your property. We've been looking for these men for months; the head guy, Mack, runs a gambling ring, and apparently business hasn't been going well lately. We have them in custody now; do you wish to press charges for trespassing?"

Gambling? Is that what Howard was involved in? I wondered.

"Only for trespassing?" I asked, clearing my throat. "Why not also for damage to personal property?"

"Because neither Leon nor Mrs. Beckett saw their faces," he replied. "You can't arrest someone simply because their voices sound the same." Leaning forward to rest his elbows on the desk, Officer Wright asked, "Do you have any idea what they were looking for in your barn?"

"Perhaps…" I hesitated, deciding to avoid the question. "Perhaps they're the ones that killed Howard."

"They could be," he said, nodding. "Unfortunately, we have no way of proving that."

163

"Do you think Howard was involved in gambling, Viv?" Leon asked in surprise.

"I...I don't know," I replied, wrapping my arms around my waist. Glancing back at Officer Wright, I said, "I'd like to see them."

His brow furrowing, Officer Wright asked, "What for?"

I hesitated, uncertain of how to answer. I wanted to see them, to hear their voices and determine whether these were the same men who had burned down my house and were now after the money Howard had supposedly stolen from them. Should I tell Officer Wright about the man who'd broken into my office and threatened me? *Why should I?* I thought. *He didn't believe me the first time, so why would he believe me now?*

After a moment, I finally shrugged and said, "I'd just like to see the men who were trespassing on my property."

I followed Officer Wright into a dark room with a very bright light shining against the opposite wall. They led the three men out, their backs against the wall, and I squirmed as they faced my direction, although I knew they couldn't see me. Officer Wright asked them a few questions, and my blood went cold when the man on the far left spoke out. His gruff, low voice sent chills of recognition down my spine, and I subconsciously took a step back. His eyes were dark and beady, his hair black and slicked straight back, and there was a long, deep scar on his cheek.

Shivering, I nodded to Officer Wright, and the men were taken from the room.

"Will they be sent to prison?" I asked once they were gone.

"Yes, for at least a couple of years," Officer Wright replied.

"Then yes, I'd like to press charges."

When we left, Leon walked me to my car, his face filled with concern. "I hope those three men really are the ones responsible for Howard's murder," he said. "I don't like the thought of a bunch of murderers running around loose."

"Neither do I," I replied. "I'm just glad they didn't find you and Eva yesterday; if they really are the killers, I'd hate to think of what they would have done if they'd found y'all."

"Me, too," Leon said, opening my car door for me. "See you at church in a bit?"

"Yes," I nodded, smiling.

As I returned to Father's house, my thoughts were stuck on the three men back at the police station. I'd searched and searched for any clue as to where Howard may have hidden that money, and was growing more and more fearful every day as I wondered what I would do and how I would get out of this mess if I couldn't find it. I was so thankful that it had been taken care of for me, and since those men were going to prison, I wouldn't have to worry about it anymore.

Once back at home, I quickly changed into proper church attire, and after making certain that Father would be alright by himself, drove to the large, brick building where I'd attended services my whole life. As soon as I walked inside, however, I realized this was my first time back since arriving home, and I immediately felt the weight of stares boring down upon me. The people I passed nodded and spoke but made a point to keep their distance; I'd known most of them my whole life, didn't they know me well enough to realize I wasn't truly crazy? Tamping down the hurt, I straightened my shoulders, lifted my chin, and pushed through the crowd, giving my own cool nods of greeting as I passed.

Upon entering the sanctuary, I saw Savannah sitting with her family on the far right-hand side. She turned and, when her gaze landed on me, her face broke into a smile and she waved for me to come sit with her. Father's eyesight had improved a bit, but he hadn't left the house for anything other than doctor's appointments, and I was grateful to have someone to sit with.

"I'm so glad you came this morning," Savannah said, reaching out to hug me. Her voice low, she added, "Leon was just telling us about those men trespassing on your property. Do you think it's the same men that set fire to your house and killed Howard?"

"Yes, I do," I nodded, also keeping my voice down. I hadn't told her about my visit from Mack and didn't plan to now; they were going to prison, and I saw no need to upset her. "I listened to their voices, and I certainly believe they're the same men that set the fire."

"Did you tell the police?" She asked, her eyes wide.

"No, there was no need," I replied, sighing. "They didn't believe me in the first place, but Officer Wright also made the remark that you can't arrest someone simply because their voice sounds the same."

"Well, well, well, look who's back," a snide, high-pitched voice sounded to my left.

Both Savannah and I turned to find Lucy Michaels standing there with a smirk on her face.

"Hi, Lucy," I said, forcing a smile. "I've actually been home for a couple of weeks now."

"I see," she said, flipping a lock of hair over her shoulder. "I didn't know if you'd ever be allowed to come back."

I felt Savannah stiffen beside me, and I quickly said, "Thank you for the kind welcome, Lucy. It's good to be home."

With a sniff, Lucy brushed past us to go sit by Leon, and I leaned closer to Savannah and asked, "Since when did she attend church here?"

"About two months ago when she, once again, set her cap for Leon," Savannah replied, rolling her eyes.

"He might as well give in and marry her," Savannah's aunt whispered with a chuckle, apparently overhearing our conversation.

"He'd better not," Savannah stated emphatically. "I don't think the two of us could ever coexist as sisters-in-law."

"I don't think Lucy coexists well with anyone," I snickered, remembering the time the restaurant had catered her high-class, snobbish birthday party. One of our workers hadn't shown up, and we'd been short-staffed; we later learned the girl had been murdered by a serial killer right outside in the woods. Savannah came to help me, and after Lucy snapped at me in front of everyone in the kitchen and said that she wouldn't be using our services in the future, Connor and Savannah and a few others "busted up" her party by doing a dance-off. I could still remember the exact shade of red Lucy's face had been as she'd angrily watched from the sidelines, and I couldn't help but smile at the memory.

After church, I told everyone goodbye and was walking to my car when I overheard two women talking. They didn't see me, and I stopped to listen when I heard my name mentioned, feeling only slightly guilty for eavesdropping.

"That Vivian McCombs certainly walked in with her head held high this morning," one woman said. "I would have thought she'd be too embarrassed after spending time in a mental hospital."

"Maybe she just doesn't know any better, bless her heart," the other said, sighing.

"It seems that she and her husband must have had serious marriage problems," the first spoke again, lowering her tone. "Do you think that's what drove her insane?"

"It's possible, I suppose," the second replied. "Do you think she really set fire to her own home in her sleep?"

They continued talking, but I didn't want to hear any more. Turning on my heel, I all but ran to my car, my cheeks burning with humiliation. If two ladies I'd known my whole life were spreading such lies about me, what must everyone else in town be saying behind my back?

By the time I made it across the parking lot and opened the driver's door, my hands were shaking and hot tears splashed onto my dress. I was shocked, embarrassed, and angry at what I'd just overheard. It was bad enough that regular, random folks around town thought ill of me, but the people I'd known and gone to church with my whole life? To say that it hurt was an understatement.

I drove home, surprised to see Zachary's car parked in the driveway. I quickly dried my face and hurried inside, concerned that Father might be sick. Upon entering the living room, however, I found he and Zachary sitting on the sofa, chatting comfortably.

Zachary stood to his feet when I entered, a smile on his face. "Vivian, it's good to see you. Your Father called and invited me over for dinner this afternoon," he said, the smile slowly slipping as he apparently realized I'd been crying.

"That was nice," I said, forcing myself to sound cheerful as I wondered why Father hadn't bothered to mention we would have a guest for dinner.

"It's good to see you, too."

I quickly changed clothes, threw on an apron, and began preparing lunch. I'd left a chicken baking in the oven on low all morning, so within the hour the food was ready and the house smelled heavenly.

We all sat down to eat, and Zachary had barely taken two bites when he looked at me and said in a sincere tone, "This is amazing. I can certainly see why you're in the restaurant business."

"Thank you very much," I replied, forcing myself to sound friendly and agreeable. After the morning I had, I didn't feel up to making conversation, and both Zachary and Father seemed to sense my mood. I didn't, however, want to be an inhospitable hostess.

After dinner, I announced I had some packing to do and excused myself. When Zachary asked why I was packing, I explained I was moving into the restaurant apartment soon.

"Vivvy, why don't you get Zachary here to help you?" Father spoke up. "That way, you could get moved in today."

Blinking, I glanced at Zachary, feeling a little embarrassed that Father had so readily offered his services.

"Oh, Father, I'm sure that Zachary doesn't care to spend his day off helping me…"

"On the contrary," Zachary interrupted, smiling pleasantly. "I'd love to help."

The apartment was furnished with a bed and nothing more, so Zachary helped me load up the vanity, chest of drawers, chairs, end tables, and lamps from my old bedroom into the back of the restaurant's truck.

"I really appreciate this," I told him as we climbed into the truck and drove towards the restaurant.

"It's my pleasure." Glancing over at me, Zachary studied me for a moment before asking, "Is everything alright, Vivian?"

"I would have thought she'd be too embarrassed after spending time in a mental hospital."

At his question, the harsh, hurtful words suddenly ran through my mind again, and I winced. I didn't, however, want to talk about it, nor did I want Zachary's pity. I knew he was my friend, and I appreciated everything he'd done for me, but my pride wouldn't let me tell him what I'd overheard; it was just too humiliating.

Feeling that I should tell him **something**, as he could apparently sense the mood I was in, I explained about my visit to the police station that morning.

Once I was finished, Zachary said, "In case there are more men hanging around your farm, I don't think you should ever go out there by yourself."

"I've already spoken to the bank about selling the farm," I told him, "so I have no reason to go out there alone."

Zachary nodded, satisfied with my answer. "Do you think you'll miss living on the farm?" He asked after a moment.

I paused, giving his question some thought. "I loved the house," I finally said, smiling softly as I pictured it in my mind. "It was so old and full of history, and Howard did a really great job fixing it up. We didn't even live there for two years, but there are so many memories lying amongst the ashes." I stopped and sighed, my eyes not seeing the road ahead but the very ashes I'd just spoken of, and my heart squeezed a bit.

I could feel Zachary's eyes boring into me, and I cleared my throat, throwing a small smile in his direction. "I planted roses around the porch," I continued, trying to keep my voice light, "just like Mother's roses in her backyard, and I enjoyed tending my garden. Country living is a different way of life; it's peaceful and serene, but running a farm is also a lot of hard work. I think I'll miss it a bit, but to be honest, I never enjoyed living so far away from everyone and everything, especially when Howard started leaving the baby and me alone so much at night."

Nodding, Zachary asked, "Do you think he was involved with those men somehow?"

"It certainly seems that way," I replied.

I pulled up to the back of the restaurant and parked, grateful to have arrived, as I didn't wish for the conversation to continue any longer. Zachary was very perceptive, and I was afraid if we talked more of Howard and those men, he would end up somehow digging it out of me that one of them had paid me a visit, and I didn't want anyone to know about that.

As we began carrying everything inside, Zachary asked, "How do you feel about moving in here?"

"I'm worried about Father," I replied, shaking my head, "but he won't have it any other way."

"Is that where your stubborn streak comes from?" Zachary grunted as we lugged the heavy chest of drawers up the creaky old stairs.

Out of breath, I raised my eyebrows and asked, "What…what makes you think I have a stubborn streak?"

"Oh, it's just a feeling I have," Zachary grinned, his eyes twinkling.

Pursing my lips, I ignored his statement as I sat my end of the chest on the floor at the top of the landing and flipped the overhead lights on.

"I'm glad I already got this place cleaned up," I stated as we shoved the piece of furniture into the bedroom. "It was a dusty mess full of cobwebs before."

It took nearly an hour to get everything moved from the truck and into the apartment, and once we were finished, I was exhausted. As we walked back down the stairs to leave, my heel suddenly slid off the end of the last step and, with a shriek, I began flailing through the air in a wild attempt to catch myself. Just before I hit the floor, Zachary spun around and grabbed me around the waist, quickly pulling me against his chest as he steadied me.

"Are you alright?" He asked, his piercing blue eyes filled with concern.

"I…yes, I think so," I stammered, feeling embarrassed as I quickly stepped back and laughed sheepishly. "Thanks for catching me; that was almost a bad one."

"I've got your back, Vivian," he said, smiling gently. "I hope you know that."

Blinking, as I didn't fail to miss the meaning behind his words, I nodded slowly and said, "I do, Zachary. Thank you."

Once we were in the car driving back to Father's house, Zachary said, "Tell me your middle name."

I turned to look at him in surprise. "That's a random request," I stated matter-of-factly.

"I know," he laughed, "but I'd like to know what it is."

My brow furrowing, I said, "I don't want to tell you."

"Why not?" He asked, raising his eyebrows questioningly.

"Because…well…it's quite unusual and a bit embarrassing."

"I won't tell a soul," he promised, a grin pulling at his lips.

Sighing, I rolled my eyes and said, "Fine, if you're going to be so pushy about it." I stopped, glancing over at him with the hope that he would give in, but he simply stared back with wide, blinking eyes and an innocent smile. Pursing my lips, I hurriedly said, "My mother read somewhere that Oriana was the nickname of Queen Elizabeth the first, but Father refused to let her name me that. So, they compromised, and it became my middle name. There, are you satisfied?"

"Very," he replied, his eyes twinkling.

We'd arrived back at Father's house and I pulled into the driveway, parked, and climbed out. I was just about to walk up the front porch steps when Zachary said, "If I remember correctly, Oriana means 'sunrise'. I believe I'll start calling you Sunny from now on."

"I'd really prefer that you didn't," I stated in a no-nonsense tone; he was teasing me, and I knew it.

"You don't like it?" He asked, pretending to be hurt. "How about Ori then, or even Oreo? Those are my favorite cookies."

Shaking my head, I took off one of my gloves and swatted him with it, unable to stop the laugh that passed my lips as he attempted to dodge me.

Zachary reached out and quickly grabbed my hand, locking it tightly between his. "You know, by the way your face lights up when you laugh, I really do think that 'sunshine' is quite fitting," he said, smiling. "You should laugh more often, Vivian Oriana, it's very becoming."

"You're incorrigible, Doctor Holt," I stated with a sniff, pulling my hand away. "You should be ashamed for teasing me so."

"I probably should be," he replied, grinning, "but the laugh was worth it."

Shaking my head, I asked if he'd like to come inside for a cup of coffee, but he declined, stating that he'd taken up enough of our day. I thanked him for all of his help, and after he'd gone and I walked inside, Father announced that he wished to speak with me.

"Vivvy, I'm going to just come right out and say it," he said. He was sitting in his favorite chair in the living room, his eyes pointing in my general direction, and I sat on the sofa across from him and waited. "I want to sign the restaurant over to you. If, that is, you still want it."

I stared at him in shock, my mouth hanging open slightly. I'd known my entire life that this moment would come, but I hadn't expected it to arrive quite so soon.

"Are…are you sure you're ready for that?" I finally asked.

"Yes," he said with a sigh, nodding. "I wish…I wish I'd done this when your mother was still with us so she and I could have spent more time together, but I'm ready to retire. Even with my eyesight continuing to improve, things will never be the same and I don't want to keep holding on to something that's already slipped through my hands. It's yours, honey, it always has been, and I think you're ready to run things fully from now on."

I could hardly believe my ears. The restaurant was mine now! But what would Father do with himself, sitting in this house all alone day in and day out? I rose from my seat and went to his side, leaning down to kiss him on the cheek.

"Thank you, Father, for entrusting me with your baby," I said gently. "I know how much that restaurant means to you, and if you ever want to come back, the door is always open."

Reaching up to pat my hand, he said in a soft voice, "You're an amazing young woman, Vivvy girl, and I'm proud to be your father."

Blinking, I couldn't say anything for a moment, as an overwhelming flood of emotion swept over me. With tears in my eyes, I leaned over and pressed my cheek against his, whispering, "Thank you for telling me that. I love you so much."

After a little while, Father went outside to sit in the sun for a spell, and I stood at the back window watching him. He'd softened and mellowed so much over the last few months, and I knew he hadn't any idea of how much I'd needed to hear the words he'd spoken to me just now. They'd given me strength and solace, and the fact that he was willing to turn the restaurant over to me after everything that had happened was like a priceless gift.

32

THE SHADOW

He ambled along the sidewalk, glancing left and right to make certain no one else was around. Stopping at the tree in front of the house, he peered around the thick trunk and watched as the small, towheaded boy played with his hand full of marbles. The little tyke jabbered to himself as if he hadn't a care in the world, his ash blonde hair glistening in the afternoon sun like corn silk.

After a moment, he stepped from behind the tree and smiled as the startled little boy looked up to find that a strange man had appeared seemingly out of nowhere.

"Hello there," he greeted with a friendly wave. "You must be Davey."

"Who you?" The little boy asked suspiciously.

"I'm a friend," he said, squatting down to be eye level with Davey. "Is your mama home?"

"No," Davey shook his head. "Mama workin'."

"She works a lot, doesn't she?"

Davey nodded, his eyes cast downward as he tossed one marble at another. Reaching into his suit coat, the man pulled a sucker from his pocket and held it up. "Would you like to have a sucker, Davey?" He asked.

His eyes lighting up, Davey nodded exuberantly and took the offered sucker, immediately popping the piece of candy into his mouth.

"Davey, does your mama have a boyfriend?" The man asked casually.

"What that?" Davey asked, his forehead scrunching in confusion.

"A man that she likes," he explained, glancing around to make certain that they were still alone. "Someone who brings her gifts and makes her smile."

"No," Davey replied, frowning. Then, his face lighting up, he added, "But I make her smile."

"I'm sure you do," he said, chuckling. Glancing up at the river birch tree he'd been standing beneath, he pointed to the eastern bluebird's nest that was high in the branches and said, "Davey, did you know that if you look inside of a bird's nest like that one up there, you'll be able to fly?"

His eyes widening, Davey gazed up into the tree, completely awestruck at the idea. "Really?" He asked.

"That's right." Slapping his knees, he stood back up and said, "Well, I've got to be going. Take care of yourself, Davey, and maybe keep this little visit of ours a secret, okay?"

The man turned and walked away, not bothering to look back. He knew that all little boys wanted to fly and, being naturally curious, Davey wouldn't be able to resist trying. Eva would be upset, but she'd get over it.

Eva

When I received the phone call that Davey had fallen from a tree and hit his head, I nearly collapsed. My legs shaking, I ran to Vivian's office and begged her to drive me home.

"Of course," she immediately agreed when I told her what happened, and after grabbing her purse, we hurried from the restaurant and jumped into her car.

Five minutes later, I rushed into the house, my stomach clenching anxiously when I saw my baby lying on the sofa with an elderly doctor leaning over him. His head lay in Nana's lap, and when Mutter saw me, she jumped from the rocking chair and hurried to my side.

"I am s-so sorry, Eva," Mutter said, tears streaming down her cheeks. "He's never climbed trees before, and I nearly had a heart attack when...when I s-saw him lying on the ground, so limp and h-helpless."

"Is...is he okay?" I asked in a choked voice, my legs rooted in place as I stood at the entrance to the living room and stared.

The doctor turned to look at me and said, "He's got a pretty nasty bump on his head, but I think he'll be alright. He's very lucky, Mrs. Beckett; he could have broken his neck."

The blood leaving my face, I went over to sit at Davey's feet, tears flooding my eyes when I saw the lump on his forehead. He was awake and watching everything the doctor did, and I breathed a prayer of thanks that it hadn't been worse.

"Keep your eye on him for the next twenty-four hours," the doctor instructed me later as I walked him out. "If he complains of a bad headache or starts to vomit, take him to the hospital immediately."

"Yes, sir," I said, nodding.

Before he walked out the door, the doctor turned to look at me and said, "You really shouldn't let him climb trees, Mrs. Beckett."

"I-I don't...I mean, he never has before," I stammered, the look of disapproval in his eyes unnerving.

Vivian told me to take the rest of the day off and stay home with Davey, and I was very grateful. After she was gone, I sat next to Davey and, gently running my fingers through his hair, I asked, "Honey, why did you climb that tree? You know Mommy doesn't want you doing things like that."

"I wanted to fly like the man said," Davey replied, cradling his teddy bear against his chest.

My brow furrowing, I asked, "What man?"

"I dunno him," Davey replied, shrugging.

I began listing all the men he could be referring to: Leon, any of our close neighbors, the milkman, the mailman, but Davey continued to shake his head.

Finally, he sighed heavily and said, "No, Mommy, him was hiding behind the tree."

"You mean...you've never seen him before?"

Davey shook his head "no" and I grew concerned, immediately thinking of the man who had broken into our home and left the pocket knife by Davey's bedside.

"What did you two talk about, Davey?" I asked, trying to act nonchalant; if Davey suspected I was upset, he'd clam up and refuse to say another word.

"'Bout you," he replied, yawning. "Him was nice...him gave me a sucker."

Unable to get anything else out of him, I kissed Davey on the cheek and told him to get some rest. I went out to the backyard where Nana and Mutter were hanging clothes on the clothesline, and immediately told them what Davey had said.

"I didn't see anyone out there, and you know that Davey never wanders away from the yard," Nana said, her forehead wrinkling. With a heavy sigh, she took my hand and said, "I feel so terrible about this; he could have been killed."

"It's not your fault," I said, tears choking my throat. Both Nana and Mutter felt guilty because they were supposed to be watching Davey, and I felt guilty for not even being here at all when it happened. Clearing my throat, I said, "You don't suppose it was the same man that broke into our home, do you?"

"Perhaps not...maybe it was just another of his imaginary friends?" Mutter spoke up in a hopeful tone.

"Perhaps," I said softly, not entirely convinced.

Wrapping my arms around my waist, I shivered as the memory of the intruder floated through my mind once again. If it was the same man, why was he apparently after my son?

173

JUNE 1944

"Under the command of General Eisenhower, Allied naval forces supported by strong air forces began landing Allied armies this morning on the northern coast of France."

"Men and women of the United States, this is a momentous hour in world history. This is the invasion of Hitler's Europe."

"The first news flashes do not say, but a large proportion of this assault is believed to be in the hands of American men. They are making the attack side-by-side with the British Tommies who were bombed and blasted out of Europe at Dunkirk. Now, at this hour, they are bombing and blasting their way back again. This is the European front once again being established in fire and blood, not only by the Americans and British but by many Allies in the fight against Axis aggression."

All of America was tuned in as reports of "the invasion" in France kept rolling in over the airwaves. Everyone anxiously awaited more news, each hoping and praying for reports of a victory. Newscasters told of the horrible battle and many deaths, and President Roosevelt called on the nation to continue praying in the coming days.

"Many people have urged that I call the Nation into a single day of special prayer," he stated during a radio address. *"But because the road is long, and the desire is great, I ask that our people devote themselves in a continuance of prayer."*

Churches held special services for people to come together and pray, and as the days passed, the invasion was continually on my mind. I went to the services, prayed by my bed every night, and all throughout each day, I thought and prayed for the many brave men who were fighting so hard and sacrificing their lives to win this war.

When I mentioned to my coworkers that I'd attended many of the prayer services, I hadn't realized how they would react until it was too late.

"Which side were you praying for?" One waitress spat, a sneer on her face.

"For the Germans, no doubt," Cook said with a sniff. "They *are* her people, after all."

"I don't like to think of *anyone* being hurt or getting killed, whether it be Germans or Americans," I said quietly, my voice trembling a bit, "but I don't stand for the evil path Hitler has led my country down; I want the Allies to win this war just as much as you do."

They all stared at me for a moment, no one saying a word until one of the dishwasher's took a step toward me and said in a low, menacing tone, "My brother was killed by your people, Eva, so don't bother telling me who or what you stand for. You're a German either way and you don't belong here, so why don't you just shut your mouth before I really get annoyed."

Suddenly, Jackson stepped forward and grasped hold of the man's arm, his face red as he hissed, "Leave her alone!"

The other dishwasher spun around to face him, his eyes blazing, and I feared that a fight was brewing. As I watched the two men, my heart pounding, I realized I'd never seen Jackson so angry before, and I felt a wave of guilt over it being my fault.

"That's enough," a sharp voice suddenly spoke out.

We all turned to see Vivian standing in the doorway, her green eyes flashing as she glared at the dishwasher. "If I hear one more hateful comment come from this kitchen, I'm going to fire every one of you. Now get back to work."

I stood still and silent, as if my feet were glued to the floor, and I had to force myself not to burst into tears as everyone around me slowly did as they were told. *They all hate me*, I thought, feeling miserable.

The red fading from his face and neck, Jackson smiled at me before he returned to his station, and I finally forced myself to turn around and get back to work, my ears burning as I chopped a stalk of celery with trembling fingers.

"Eva," Vivian called to me. "Come into my office, please."

Grateful for the chance to escape, I hurried from the kitchen and followed Vivian back into her office. As soon as we stepped through the door, Vivian grabbed her hat and said, "Come on, let's go for a walk. I think we could both use a break."

Once we were out on the street, she turned to me and asked, "Are you alright?"

A single tear slipping down my cheek, I nodded and whispered, "Yes, thank you."

"What they said was uncalled for," she stated, sighing. "It seems like people think they have a free card these days to be just as rude and unkind as they please."

I knew she wasn't simply referring to my incident, but also to all the insensitive things that had been said to her lately, as well.

"Yes, I don't understand it," I said, glancing down at my feet. "Thank you for putting a stop to it just now."

We walked along Broughton Street for a bit, chatting and looking in store windows. Until now, I hadn't gotten much of a chance to get to know Vivian, but I quickly found her to be quite warm and friendly.

"I believe today is Savannah's day off," she said suddenly, her eyes brightening. "Let's find a phone booth and ask her to meet us here and drive us all to Leopold's."

"Don't I need to get back to work?" I asked uncertainly.

"It's not quite noon yet, so let's just take some time off; we can go back in an hour or so," she replied, waving a hand.

Within twenty minutes, we were seated in a booth at Leopold's Ice Cream, chatting with Savannah and sipping on chocolate malts. I'd never had such a delicious malt in my life, and I wanted to taste each and every ice cream flavor the parlor offered. I'd learned from one of the soda jerks that Leopold's was founded by three brothers from Greece in 1919, and had quickly become one of the city's favorite places to visit for frozen delights.

"I am so worried about Connor," Savannah was saying, her voice heavy. "I'm sure he and his men are involved in the invasion, and I can't stop thinking that I may never see him again."

Her eyes were rimmed with dark circles, and I could tell that she'd been worrying herself sick. Reaching out, I took her hand and squeezed it gently as Vivian said encouragingly, "I'm sure he'll be just fine, Savannah. This isn't his first rodeo; he knows what he's doing."

"I just hope this war will end soon," I said softly.

"So do I," Savannah nodded, blinking back tears. Clearing her throat, she pasted on a smile and said, "Enough about me and my worries. How are the two of you doing?"

As we sat and talked for over an hour, I began to feel such a kinship with these two women. Other than my family and Paul, I hadn't had a true friend since I was a young girl in school, and it felt so nice to have women my age to talk to and laugh with. Savannah was open and kind and a good listener, and Vivian was warm and energetic. I had the feeling, however, that Vivian was doing her best to pretend that she was perfectly alright when, in fact, she wasn't. As I was the quietest of the group, I would often sit back and observe while the others talked, and I noticed a look of wariness in Vivian's eyes that I sensed hadn't been there a few months ago. When someone would brush past our booth or speak loudly, her whole body would tense, almost as if she were preparing herself for something bad to happen. I wondered if her time spent in the asylum had caused this, and felt my heart go out to my new friend.

At ten minutes past two, Vivian looked at her watch and gasped. "Goodness, Eva, we'd better get back to the restaurant!"

"I'll drive y'all," Savannah said as we all slid from the booth and walked outside.

We were just about to get into her car when someone called Savannah's name. Turning, I saw a young African-American woman hurrying our way, a gigantic smile on her face.

"Lizzie!" Savannah squealed, pulling the girl into a hug. She then turned to Vivian and me, and said, "Eva, this is Lizzie, a very dear friend of mine; she used to work for my aunt and uncle. Vivian, you remember Lizzie, don't you?"

"Of course," Vivian said, smiling warmly at Savannah's pretty, young friend. "How are you, Lizzie?"

"Well, I'm expecting a baby in about seven months, so Samuel and I are over the moon," she replied, beaming, her voice soft and a bit husky.

"Oh, Lizzie, that's wonderful news!" Savannah cried. "Come by my house soon, okay? It sounds like we need to have a nice, long visit."

"I'll do that," Lizzie nodded.

We waved goodbye to Savannah's friend, and once we were on our way back to the restaurant, Savannah explained what had happened to Lizzie's first fiancé, Joseph, a few years before.

"Three women were bludgeoned to death by an ax at a local boarding house, and Joseph was accused of committing the gruesome murders. Lizzie was so determined to uncover the truth and clear Joseph's name that she and I were both nearly killed," Savannah said, chuckling slightly. "I was worried that she'd never get over him, but I'm so glad that she found Samuel."

"That certainly was a scary time with a serial killer on the loose," Vivian spoke up, shivering slightly. Turning to look at me from the passenger's seat, she said, "The actual killer began murdering women that reminded him of his ex-lover, one of which was a worker at our very own restaurant. He then set his sights on Savannah, and her family finally convinced her to leave for a few months. It really was terrifying."

My eyes wide, I asked, "Was he ever caught?"

"He was killed a couple of months after I returned home," Savannah replied, proceeding to relay all the details. I sat in the back seat and listened with my mouth agape, hardly able to believe that it was all true. Just thinking of a serial killer stalking our streets was scary enough, but knowing that my friend had barely escaped with her life was utterly horrifying.

When I got back to the restaurant, I heard a couple of comments about taking off work for so long and being the boss's favorite, but I was grateful when they said nothing more. I didn't like conflict and hated being the center of attention, whether the attention was good or bad.

As I was leaving work later that evening, Jackson walked me out and asked if I was okay.

"Yes, I'm fine now," I said, smiling kindly at him. "Thank you so much for taking up for me."

"You're welcome," he said, adding in a passionate tone, "I think I could have broken that guy's neck if Mrs. Vivian hadn't interfered."

Blinking, I said, "Oh…well…I'm certainly glad you didn't."

"I'd do anything for you, Eva," he said earnestly, stepping closer. "I hope you know that."

Feeling a little uncomfortable, I stepped back, trying to put some space between us. "I-I appreciate that, Jackson," I stammered. When he stepped towards me again, I said hurriedly, "Well, I'd better get home; my family will wonder where I am. Good night, Jackson."

I turned and hurried away, and after I'd crossed the street, I glanced over my shoulder to find that Jackson was still standing there, watching me.

33

ASHER

After months of hard work and planning, of back breaking labor and tense, overwrought nerves, the moment they'd all been waiting for had finally arrived.

It was time to escape.

Asher and the other men gathered everything they would need and waited on pins and needles until after midnight, when they were certain that everyone was asleep. Then, one by one, they slipped quietly from the bunkhouse, their footsteps soft and soundless as they slipped through the camp toward the hut where the tunnel entrance was hidden. They'd waited for the darkest night of the month, and their plan had worked beautifully; the camp was smothered in a thick, black coat of darkness.

Tick tock, tick tock.

Asher could hear the ticking of a clock pounding loudly in his head, but the only timepiece around was the small, black leather watch at his wrist. He was so tense and on edge that it seemed as if every sound was magnified, and when the door to the washroom squeaked on its hinges, he caught his breath and froze, waiting for the spotlights to flash as Nazi guards came running.

The man behind Asher thumped him lightly on the shoulder, and Asher continued his trek into the large wooden building, breathing a sigh of relief. *Relax, Beckett*, he told himself. *This isn't your first mission.*

The last two years had been the toughest that Asher had ever endured. Growing up in one of the wealthiest families in Connecticut, he was used to getting what he wanted, and when he wanted it. He was the fun-loving "ladies" man, quick to spend a dollar, and always ready to have a good time, but when he joined the military, everything changed. His wealth and name no longer mattered, and he was forced to learn what it was to start at rock bottom and work your way up. The war had opened his eyes to so many things, and forced hardships upon him he'd never had to face before. He'd been taught the value of hard work and brotherhood, of freedom and unity, and he'd quickly learned that life isn't always easy or fair, especially when he was captured and sent to the POW camp. He only hoped that escape and freedom really was only a few hundred feet away.

"You're up next," Ethan whispered from behind, and Asher shook his thoughts away, telling himself to focus on the task at hand.

Each man was given a full minute in the tunnel before the next one would enter, and when Asher stepped up to the trap door, Watson slapped him on the back and whispered, "I'll be the last one in, but don't wait for me if something happens; get out while you can."

Asher squeezed his buddy's arm, saluted to both Watson and Ethan, and climbed head first through the small trapdoor. Thankfully, the tunnel was equipped with electric lighting, or else the men might have been overcome with a bought of claustrophobia in this sandy, underground grave that ran thirty feet beneath the surface.

Taking a deep breath, Asher slithered along on his belly like a snake, the air thick and musty, and the two square feet of crawl space tight and cramped. The tunnel was three hundred feet long, and Asher counted each foot under his breath as he crawled. He'd just made it to the halfway point when a faint, whining sound reached his ears and he paused to listen. The sound grew louder and the ground suddenly began to shake, causing Asher's heart to kick into overdrive. He was too far underground to know what was happening, and he'd just begun to crawl again, this time much faster, when the tunnel was plunged into total darkness.

34

Vivian

I had been back home for two months and some days my time spent at the asylum felt like a distant dream, while others it still felt like a painful wound that was open and bleeding. I would catch myself waiting tensely for a sharp command or wild scream, and often at night I would lie awake too afraid to go to sleep and face the dreams that often awaited me. I couldn't talk about it, as no one but Maisie understood. We'd written to each other faithfully since our release, and as I'd just received a letter from her that morning, I sat down and wrote one in return, pouring out my feelings to her. ***Will I ever feel normal again?*** I wrote, knowing that she'd understand.

After mailing the letter, I went back to the restaurant and began cleaning out my office like a madwoman. I had too many thoughts swirling around in my head after writing about Martinsville, and I didn't want to sit still and think them through. I'd just heard the clock strike eight when I stopped to look at the mess I'd made. Papers and boxes were strewn all over the room, and I wasn't even close to being finished.

How long has it been since Father went through all of this mess and cleaned everything out? I thought, sighing. He'd moved all of his belongings out after retiring, and I now realized it was up to me to clean the place up and get rid of all the old, unnecessary papers and files.

I decided that while I was cleaning, I would also do a little rearranging and began to shove one of the filing cabinets into another corner. When I turned to the empty space I'd just cleared, I noticed a loose board where the cabinet had been sitting. Sinking to my knees, I reached down and wiggled the board, my eyes widening when it suddenly pulled loose and I realized something was hidden in the space beneath. I quickly slipped my fingers inside and pulled out a rectangular metal box.

Pushing myself to my feet, I hurried to my desk and pried the box open with a letter opener. When my eyes fell upon the contents of the box, I felt the blood drain from my face and I gasped. Stacks of one hundred dollar bills filled the container, and I knew even without counting it that this was the five thousand dollars Mack claimed Howard had stolen from him.

My legs giving out, I sank into my chair, unable to believe what I was seeing. Not only had Howard been involved in gambling, which I now realized was what happened to all of our money, but he'd also stolen five thousand dollars and hidden it in my father's office? How could he have done such a thing?

Anger coursing through my veins, I stood up and slammed the metal box shut. All along, I'd been married to a man that was a complete stranger, someone who had lied to me, betrayed me, and cared only for himself. Through all the anger and confusion, I knew one thing for certain; I'd die before I married and trusted another man again.

I picked the box up and put it back into its hiding place, quickly shoving the filing cabinet back to its original spot. I then paced about the room, wondering what to do with the money. I could turn it over to the police, but what if they tried to say I was involved somehow in its theft? I didn't trust the police, not anymore, but I knew I'd have to do *something*.

I stopped pacing then, a sudden thought crossing my mind. Howard had used our hard-earned money to satisfy his gambling habits, so wasn't this five thousand dollars basically mine? I could keep it, pay off the remainder of Howard's debts, and forever wipe him from my memory.

No, I told myself, *you can't do that. This money is illegal, and it's not yours!*

Sighing, I sat back down, suddenly feeling exhausted. After a moment of deliberation, I finally decided to go to bed and think about it later. It wasn't, after all, something I had to figure out right now; I could give it a few days and go from there.

Nodding my head in satisfaction, I pushed myself back up, turned off all the lights, and went to bed.

35

ASHER

Ethan's whispered voice drifted up from behind as he explained that a sudden and unexpected air raid had caused the camp's electricity to shut off, and now all the men would be forced to crawl through the tunnel in complete darkness.

Sighing, Asher pressed on, eager to reach the end of this black hole. He couldn't help but wonder, however, if freedom really waited on the other side, or if the men would all be caught and killed, or brought back to the camp. Was it foolish to believe that they could make it to the border safely? He hoped not. Hope was all that they had to hold on to, and Asher refused to let go.

One hundred and fifty feet…one seventy-five….he continued counting under his breath, getting closer with each second. Even with the air pump to assist with ventilation, it was still hard to breathe, and the tunnel seemed endless. He could hear Ethan crawling behind him, the rustling of their feet, knees, and elbows echoing in the darkness as they dug into the sand.

Suddenly, the tunnel came alive and began to creak and groan, as if speaking to the men held captive within its walls. Asher stopped, his heart accelerating as the sounds grew louder and sand and dust fell on the back of his neck. With a sinking stomach, he realized the tunnel was about to collapse.

He began to crawl faster, the thought of being buried alive propelling him forward, but he'd barely made it ten feet when part of the tunnel just ahead caved in, halting his journey to freedom with a shuddering crash. He stopped and covered his head; the dust burning his eyes and making him cough, and once it was over, he crept forward until his hand found the solid wall of sand and wood that blocked his path.

"What happened?" Ethan whispered from behind.

"The tunnel collapsed," Asher said. "Send word back to let them know what's happened."

The wait was long and grueling. The men were finally able to pass candles, picks, and other tools up to Asher to repair his end, while a man on the other side crawled back in to help. Asher had assisted in the digging and construction of the tunnel over the last few months, but he found the work to be much harder tonight. The heat from the candle, the added stress and pressure, it was all causing him to sweat profusely, and he continuously shook wet, salty droplets out of his eyes.

The internal clock was ticking again, and Asher glanced at his wrist watch, squinting in the dimness to read what it said. Valuable time was passing, time that they desperately needed to get every man through the tunnel and on their way to safety before daylight, and Asher did his best to work as quickly as possible.

It took a little over an hour, but the tunnel was finally repaired. Asher waited until the man in front of him crawled back out, backwards, and then blew his candle out. He could see the smoke drifting up through the darkness, and he blinked a few times, trying to readjust his eyes to the change in lighting.

After a moment, Ethan thumped his foot and said, "Let's get out of here," and Asher began moving forward once again.

Two hundred and twenty-five feet...two fifty...he was almost there. It had been hours since he'd eaten or had anything to drink, and Asher was exhausted, but he pushed himself to go faster. The sooner he was out, the sooner they could all get through the tunnel and be gone before daybreak.

With a breath of relief, Asher finally reached the end. Giving the rope a quick tug, the trap door slid open, and Asher climbed out and stepped aside, waiting for Ethan. The night was peaceful and quiet while crickets chirped in the distance, and as Asher's eyes adjusted to his surroundings, he realized with a feeling of dread that the tunnel hadn't extended all the way to the tree line like they'd planned. Instead, it stopped several feet from the trees, and one of the guard towers stood in clear view to his right. As soon as the sun started to come up, they'd be spotted if they weren't gone.

Ethan emerged from the tunnel and quickly wiped the sand from his skin and clothes before following Asher across the grass and into the trees where the other men waited. Asher was grateful finally to have clean, cool air to breathe, but now that the tunnel crawl was behind him, he found himself filled with nervous energy. It seemed to take longer than a minute for each man to exit the tunnel, and the moments crept by agonizingly slowly.

Finally, at nearly four o'clock, Watson stepped from the tunnel, and it was all the men could do to keep silent and not call out a loud, resounding cheer. They waited as Watson closed the trapdoor and covered it up, and as he turned to make his way toward the tree line, a beam from the guard house suddenly landed on his face and he froze.

They'd been caught.

Shouts and whistles immediately pierced the still, quiet night, and every man broke into a dead run. Asher and Ethan waited for Watson to join them, and the three took off through the forest, their feet crunching over leaves and fallen branches. Asher could hear the yells of the guards as they pursued after them, and when guns began to fire, he pushed his burning legs to go faster.

The flight through the forest seemed never ending as the men dodged trees, leaped over logs, and pushed through thick, brambly bushes. Low-hanging branches continually slapped Asher's face until he felt blood trickling down his cheeks, but he paid it no attention; the only thought that reigned prevalent in his mind was "keep going, and don't get caught."

Over half of the men broke off and went to the left, while Asher and his two buddies decided at the last minute to go right. They knew the guards would expect them to head left toward the nearest train depot, and they didn't want to take the risk of getting caught at the station.

Just up ahead, Asher finally saw a break in the trees. There was a river not far beyond that tree line, and if they could only make it before the guards caught them, they planned to swim downriver.

He could hear the shouts getting louder, and realized with a sinking stomach that a few of the guards had broken off and followed them. Suddenly, Watson tripped and crashed to the ground, and Asher and Ethan skidded to a stop to hoist him quickly back up on his feet.

"My ankle is broken," he said, his voice filled with pain. "You two go on; I'll stay here and surrender."

"No," Asher shook his head, clenching Watson's arm. "You can make it; we'll help you."

His eyes flashing, Watson shoved him back and hissed, "Don't be a fool, Beckett. Get out of here. Now!"

The sound of running feet and crunching branches was drawing closer and, guilt ripping at his chest, Asher turned with Ethan and the two ran, leaving their friend behind. They'd just passed through the break in the trees when they heard Watson call out in surrender, and then the deafening sound of gunshots ripped through the air. Asher and Ethan stopped, their chests heaving as they listened, but Watson no longer called out and they knew their friend was dead.

His jaw clenched, Asher shook his head and continued to run, ignoring the stabbing pain in his heart. If not for Watson, none of this would have ever been possible, and it wasn't fair that he'd been killed while everyone else escaped. He should have stayed behind and helped him, even if it meant they both were killed. At least Watson wouldn't have died alone.

Asher could hear the sound of rushing water and knew they were nearing the river. As he and Ethan continued to run, the burning cramps in Asher's legs were excruciating, but he still pressed on. Ethan panted next to him, sweat dripping from his forehead, and Asher knew he was just as exhausted. Could they make it?

Seconds later, they stood at the edge of the river, staring down through the darkness at the water that rushed by about twenty feet below. They were both excellent swimmers, but it was too dark to tell where they would land if they jumped. Slowly and meticulously, they made their way down the rocky slope, their hearts beating double-time when they heard the sound of approaching footsteps overhead. They both froze and pressed themselves against the ground, hoping that the guards wouldn't see them.

After a moment, it seemed the guards had moved on, and the two men continued their trek towards the water. They'd just made it to the river's edge when, suddenly, a flashlight clicked on and the beam landed directly on Asher. Ethan immediately dove into the water, but before Asher could follow, a gunshot pierced the air and it felt as if a hot, searing knife sliced right through his shoulder.

"Come on!" He heard Ethan yell, but it was like his feet were frozen in place as he swayed back and forth, the pain in his shoulder almost unbearable.

He could hear the guards sliding down the slope towards him and, the world spinning, Asher turned and fell into the cold water, striking his head on a rock. Stars danced before his eyes as everything around him faded from view, and he slowly began sinking beneath the water's surface as the river swept him away.

36

Vivian

efore I could decide about the money, a black shadow crept silently into town. It was something unseen and deadly, something that could steal into one's home without ever being detected.

After receiving the good news that Connor was safe after the invasion at Normandy, Savannah had asked me to come over to her house on Friday night to celebrate. Early Thursday morning, she called to cancel.

"At the beginning of the week, we had a few patients, mostly children, come in with a fever, headache, and sore throat," she said, her voice heavy. "Now we've got people coming in left and right. Vivian, we think it's polio."

I couldn't believe my ears. Polio was something everyone had feared since the epidemic of 1916. I'd seen a few people here and there in wheelchairs or wearing leg braces, and our own President was a victim of the dreadful disease, but our city had never suffered a major outbreak. It was, however, something that stayed in the back of all our minds; a constant worry and feeling of unease, especially during the hot summer months.

"Is there anything I can do to help?" I asked, my fingers tightening around the telephone. "I caught polio one summer in Atlanta when I was a teenager, so it's less likely that I'll catch it again."

"Call everyone you can and ask them to stay at home," she said. "The mayor is going to release a statement on the radio tonight. If we need you to come to the hospital and help, would you be willing?"

"Of course," I replied, nodding my head although she couldn't see me.

After we hung up, I closed the restaurant for the foreseeable future, and did just as Savannah asked. I called everyone I could think of, and that evening, I listened with the rest of the city as our mayor delivered the somber news. Somehow, the virus was brought to us and already spreading like wildfire. Father's eyesight was much better, and he was in Atlanta visiting his sister when I called to tell him the news; I was grateful when he decided to stay until all of this was over.

Three days later, Savannah called to ask if I would come to the hospital and help.

"We're doing all we can," she said, and I could hear the exhaustion in her voice, "but it's getting difficult to keep up."

I agreed, and as soon as I arrived, I was immediately put to work. I checked temperatures, fed warm broth to the patients that could keep it down, administered sponge baths, and washed linens. I was shocked at how full the hospital already was, and prayed that many more people wouldn't have to be brought in. As I tended to the coughing, feverish patients that lined the hospital's ward, I wondered who would be hit the hardest, and who would go home with a clean bill of health.

What a strange disease this polio was. It was difficult to predict who would walk away with just a headache and who would never walk again. It didn't leave everyone it touched with paralysis or death, but those it did touch were filled with terror as they wondered whether they would be among the unlucky five to ten percent. When I contracted the disease in Atlanta, I wasn't sick enough to go to the hospital, but I'd heard many horror stories of people dying from suffocation because the muscles in their chest became paralyzed and they could no longer breathe on their own. I wasn't allowed into the area where the Drinker tanks, or "the iron lungs", were kept, but I'd seen pictures of the contraption which encloses a person's body from the neck down within a tube-like machine and "breathes" for them. So far, Savannah told me that only three children needed the machines, and I prayed that there wouldn't be any more, and also that their paralysis would only be temporary. I thought it must be very hard, especially for children, to have to endure such a thing, and how horrible for those who had to live the rest of their lives that way. It was like they were trapped or imprisoned, not only within their own bodies but also within the long metal canister that constantly wheezed and sighed, forcing their lungs to expand and deflate.

When I arrived, Savannah warned me the patients could get a little testy, which was understandable, but something I hadn't counted on was the prejudice that the few adult patients showed towards me. They didn't want a "crazy murderer" tending to them, and after a while, I could no longer deal with the rude, insolent comments.

"Would you prefer that I just leave you here to starve or wallow in your own excrement?" I snapped at a man who was being particularly disagreeable. "Because the hospital is over-crowded and I'm sorry to say it, sir, but beggars can't be choosers. You'll either have to deal with my offensive presence, or not be tended to at all."

The man stared up at me, open-mouthed, and I suddenly realized that the other patients in the ward had heard my declaration, as well.

So be it, I thought, squaring my shoulders. *It is, after all, better to kill two birds with one stone.*

Thankfully after that, most everyone seemed to accept my presence, and nothing further was said. I tried to work with the children as much as I could, doing everything possible to make them comfortable. They were such precious little things, and so pitiful the way they cried for their mothers. I'd read of how the health workers in New York during the 1916 epidemic would physically remove children from their homes and even from playgrounds if there was a suspicion that they were infected, sending them away to be isolated in sanitariums. I couldn't imagine being taken away from my parents at such a young age; it had to be devastating, to say the least.

By the time Monday morning arrived, I realized I'd been on my feet for nearly forty-eight hours. I must have born the cloak of exhaustion very openly, because Zachary stopped me and politely suggested that I go home.

"You're exhausted, Vivian," he said, his eyes filled with concern. "Go home and get some rest before you collapse."

"What about you, Doctor?" I asked with a half-smile. "And all the nurses who have been here longer than I have? If anyone needs to go home and rest, it's all of you."

His lips pursed, Zachary shook his head and said, "There's that stubborn streak again."

"I'm no more stubborn than you are," I shot back, cocking an eyebrow at him.

"Well, at least get something to eat," he stated, chuckling.

Just then, the door to the waiting room opened, and I saw Eva sitting in one of the chairs. She'd obviously been crying, and Davey lay cuddled up in her lap.

"Oh, no," I breathed, reaching out to clutch Zachary's arm. "Do you think Davey is sick?"

His face immediately turning sober, Zachary rushed out into the waiting room, with me following closely behind. Eva looked up and saw us coming, her eyes filled with fear. "He's running a fever, Doctor," she said when we reached her side, her accent much more prominent than usual, "and I don't think it's his tonsils this time."

I watched as Zachary laid the back of his hand on Davey's forehead, a grave, solemn look in his eyes. He then took the boy from Eva's arms and told her to follow him to a room. Eva reached out and took my hand as I walked back with them, her fingers clutching mine tightly.

Savannah saw us walking down the hall and hurried our way, her eyes filled with concern.

"Savannah, help me get Davey settled into a bed," Zachary told her, his normally calm, congenial tone clipped and to the point.

We went into one of the larger wards where beds were lined up side by side with a small divider between each one. Some beds held still, silent patients, while others were filled with the miserable sounds of coughing and feverish moans. Savannah directed Zachary to an empty bed where he

188

gently lay the little boy and hooked him to an IV, barking orders to Savannah on which medications Davey would need. After they were finished, I retrieved a chair for Eva, and she slowly sank onto its surface, her eyes never leaving her son.

"I'm afraid you can't stay with him, Eva," Zachary told her gently. "I'm sorry, but you'll have to go home."

"No," she softly gasped, looking up at Zachary with a desperate, pleading expression. "I can't leave him here all alone."

"Savannah and I will be here, Eva," I said softly, reaching out to touch her shoulder.

Taking a deep breath, Eva said to Zachary, "I've already been exposed, and I can stay and help, just like Vivian. I'll work and do whatever you need me to do, just please don't make me leave him."

Zachary hesitated, skeptically eyeing the woman before him who was usually so quiet and timid, but now fighting to be with her child. I knew the parents weren't normally allowed to stay, but the hospital needed all the help they could get, and he finally gave in with a sigh.

"Alright," he said, raising a hand as he continued with a warning, "but you'll have to control your emotions with Davey; we can't allow hysterical parents to stay and cause problems for our nurses."

"You won't even know I'm here," Eva promised, and I believed her; she seemed to have the magical ability to melt into the background and do what needed to be done without ever being seen or heard.

With a nod, Zachary turned and left the room. I was a bit surprised at his gruffness, but realized that he had more on his mind than being polite. He, along with the other doctors and nurses, hadn't left the hospital in almost a week, and I knew he was exhausted and worried about his patients.

Turning to Eva, I took her hand and said, "Come with me, and I'll show you what to do. And try not to worry about Davey; he's in excellent hands."

Taking a deep breath, Eva took one last glance at her son and nodded, turning to follow me. She did everything I asked and worked tirelessly, never once complaining or asking to take a break, and later that night when I walked past Davey's bed, I found her sitting beside him, crying and praying. I stood there for a moment, listening to her desperate pleas, and felt tears pricking my own eyes as I thought about Howard Junior. As a mother, I knew how these parents felt as they worried and prayed for their children, and I suddenly felt a searing, cutting pain at the loss of my child.

Needing a distraction, I noticed a little girl a few beds down from Davey that was moaning and rubbing her head. Hurrying to her side, I leaned over and asked, "What's wrong, sweetie? Does your head hurt?"

Her fevered eyes opened and she looked up at me, tears sliding down her rosy red cheeks. "Yes, ma'am," she nodded, her lower lip trembling pitifully.

After checking her chart, I gave her a bit of medicine to help with the pain, and then sat next to her as I gently began massaging her head. She was a tiny little thing, only five or six years old, with blonde pigtails and large, soulful brown eyes.

"When can I see my mommy?" She asked, her voice soft and very weak.

My heart caught at the fear I heard in her voice, and I desperately wished that the mothers could be with their children. I remembered how it felt to be young and sick, and the only person in the whole world that could make me feel better was my mother. There was something about a mother's presence and touch that let you know everything was going to be alright, and these children needed that comfort and reassurance nearly as much as they needed fluids and medication, if not more so.

I suddenly felt a longing so deep and strong for my own mother that I had to stop and close my eyes for a moment, trying to endure the pain as it rushed over me. No matter what happened, no matter how hurt I was or how hard I cried, she'd somehow always known how to make me feel better. When I was little and cried over a scraped knee, she'd kiss it and the pain would magically disappear. Even when I got older and had my heart broken over Timmy in the eighth grade, she took me out for a "girl's day", and by the time we got back home, my tears had somehow turned to smiles. I knew exactly how these children felt, and my heart broke for them.

Realizing the little girl was waiting for an answer, I forced my eyes open and cleared my throat, smiling softly. "I'm sure you'll be able to see your mommy soon, honey."

She watched me for a moment as I continued to rub her head, and finally asked, "Will you sing to me?"

Blinking in surprise, I nodded and began to sing the first lullaby that came to my mind. "Sleep my child and peace attend thee, all through the night. Guardian angels God will send thee, all through the night."

As I sang, my voice low and soft, I gently ran my fingers through her hair and watched as her eyes began to grow heavy and flutter closed. I continued with the song, even after she was asleep, remembering all the times I sang it to Howard Junior. Every night before I put him in his crib, I would hum this song and he would stare up at me with sleepy eyes that looked so much like my own, and I would lean down and kiss his little cheek..

I laid my head over on the bed and began to cry, unable to stand it any longer. Needing to be alone, I pushed myself to my feet and hurried from the room, past all the beds filled with frightened little children, and headed toward the stairwell. I was almost there when I heard someone call my name, but I didn't stop or turn around. Instead, I hurried on and pushed through the door, allowing myself to fall to my knees as I began to cry deep, heart-wrenching sobs.

The door behind me opened, and I felt a strong pair of hands take me by the arms and pull me towards a warm, broad chest. After a few moments, the steady, rhythmic heartbeat against my ear calmed me and the sobs slowly faded away, leaving my body exhausted and limp.

"Here," a deep voice rumbled against my ear, and I pulled back to accept the handkerchief that was being offered.

Blowing my nose, I looked up into Zachary's face, which was very close to my own, and immediately moved back. I attempted to stand, but my legs were very weak and trembling, and I gratefully accepted Zachary's hand as he helped me up.

"Are you alright?" He asked, watching me closely. "Did something happen?"

"I'm fine." I sniffed, glancing down at my feet as I explained, "I just know how these parents feel worrying about their children, and I began thinking of Mother and Howard Junior, and I just…I don't know…started feeling a little overwhelmed."

"You never really got the chance to grieve properly for them, did you?" Zachary asked gently.

My eyes began welling up with tears again, and I shook my head. "No, I didn't," I whispered, clenching my jaw as images of Martinsville ran through my mind. Glancing up, I added angrily, "And it's all *Howard's* fault. I still don't understand how he could have done such a thing to me."

Zachary said nothing for a moment; he simply stood there and studied me with those piercing blue eyes of his. I began to feel self-conscious and wrapped my arms around my waist, glancing away to avoid his probing gaze.

"Neither do I," he finally said, his tone low. Clearing his throat, he reached out, took my arm, and said, "Come with me."

Blinking in surprise, I allowed Zachary to lead me from the stairwell and down the hall to his office. He closed the door behind us and said, "You've pushed yourself enough, Vivian, and I must insist that you get some rest. As I don't think you should drive right now, I want you to lie down on my sofa. I often take naps on it myself, and it's very comfortable."

"Oh, I don't think I should.. "

Raising his hand, Zachary interrupted my protest. "Most of the nurses, including Savannah, have gone home to rest for a while, so I want you to do the same. If I see you outside of this room in less than four hours, I'll take you home myself and tie you to your bed."

Before I could stop myself, I stated saucily, "I don't think that would be very appropriate, Doctor."

I had to force myself to keep a straight face when Zachary's eyes widened and his cheeks flooded with color. Much to my surprise, however, he cleared his throat and, taking a step closer to me, said in a low voice, "Perhaps not, but that still wouldn't stop me."

My eyes narrowing, I said, "I don't like to be told what to do."

"I know," he replied, his lips twitching, "but in this instance, I think you should, for once, do as you're told before you collapse and we're forced to see about you along with the others."

Lips pursed, I sighed and said, "Fine, I'll lie down and rest. Are you satisfied?"

"Quite," he replied, grinning. He turned to leave then, throwing over his shoulder as he walked from the room, "There's a pillow and blanket in the closet. Sweet dreams, Mrs. McCombs."

Shaking my head, I couldn't help but chuckle as I retrieved the things from the closet and settled down on the sofa. I admit I was a bit surprised by Zachary's stubbornness, as I hadn't realized he could be so hard-headed. I knew he was right, however, about my needing to rest; I'd pushed myself extremely hard the last few days and had broken down because of it.

I was embarrassed by the scene I must have made, sprawled out on the floor and sobbing like a child. But that was yet another area in which Zachary was correct; I hadn't been able to grieve properly for Howard Junior. Everything had happened so fast after his death, and when I was thrown into the asylum, I'd been forced to focus on simply trying to survive. Once back at home, I was assailed by yet more pain over Mother's death, and with running the restaurant and worrying about Father, I still hadn't had time to process everything that had happened.

This Polio epidemic, however, had changed everything, and now that I was confronted with other parents who were going through a similar trial to my own, I was forced to face my own pain, and it hadn't been pleasant. I knew, though, that dealing with my baby's death and grieving for him was something I needed to quit hiding from, and as I drifted off to sleep, I allowed more tears to seep from my eyes, hoping to find healing for my hurting, broken heart.

37

Eva

I had never been more frightened in my whole life. Seeing your child lying so still and helpless in a hospital bed is a mother's worst nightmare, and I kept wondering how he'd contracted the disease. Had I brought it home to him? Had he gotten it at church? Whatever the cause, I blamed myself for not protecting him. I was his mother, the only parent he had, and I'd failed to keep him safe.

I stayed at the hospital for three days, refusing to leave. I worked and did whatever the nurses and staff asked of me, stopping to look in on Davey as often as I could. He slept a lot, his fever was still too high, and when he was awake, he would cry in pain and ask for me. I would sit by him for a few moments during those times and sing to him, his little cheeks flushed with fever as he held on to my hand. Two children in the same ward as Davey died, and it appeared one other would be forced to grow up in a wheelchair. Fervent prayers for my sweet boy never ceased to pass from my lips, and I held on desperately to the hope that he would get through this.

I called Mutter and Nana every morning and evening to keep them posted, as I knew they were frantic with worry, and Leon called the hospital several times to ask about Davey's condition.

"I'm praying for him," he said each time. "Take care of yourself, okay? You've got to be exhausted."

He was right; I was beyond exhausted, but I wasn't the only one. I didn't know how the doctors and nurses kept going. Vivian was still helping, and I was grateful that she and Savannah were there. Although we were all too busy to do any socializing, it was nice to have my friends nearby; their presence alone gave me strength.

On the third night, I sat next to Davey's bed, trying to convince him to eat. His throat hurt and all he wanted was tea or juice, but I finally convinced him to take a little soup. It thrilled me that he could still swallow, as losing that ability was a sure sign of upcoming paralysis. He'd just finished eating when the curtain moved and Zachary stepped in.

"How is he?" He asked softly, dark circles lining his eyes.

"His fever seems to have come down a bit," I said, my voice filled with hope.

Zachary came over and checked Davey's vitals. "Yes, his fever does seem better," he said after a moment. "We'll know more in a couple of hours if it continues going down or if it spikes up again." Smiling at Davey, he asked, "Can you talk to me, Davey, and show me where it hurts?"

"My head," Davey said, his eyes weary and voice weak, "and my legs and arms."

I saw the look of worry in Zachary's eyes, and my stomach clenched. I knew those were all dangerous signs and wondered how much longer my little boy could keep fighting before the paralysis struck.

"Keep eating and drinking, even when you don't want to," Zachary told him, gently touching Davey's arm. "I'm sure you'll feel better in no time."

Nodding, Davey's eyes drifted closed, and it wasn't long before he was asleep. My eyes filling with tears, I looked up at Zachary and whispered, "What if he doesn't get better?"

Zachary sat on the end of the bed, his face solemn as he studied me. "Don't think that way, Eva," he finally said. "Davey is a tough little guy, and I feel certain he's going to pull through. Don't give up hope."

Sighing, I reached up to rub the back of my neck, trying to work out the stiffness. My head was pounding, and I suddenly wondered how I would make it through another sleepless night. I would, however, do whatever it took to stay by my son's side.

"Would you like to join me downstairs for my fifth cup of coffee?" Zachary asked, rubbing his eyes. "I feel like the stuff is replacing the blood in my veins, but it certainly comes in handy on these long, hard days."

Smiling, I nodded and stood to my feet. Before I could step forward, however, the room suddenly began to spin, and I would have fallen if Zachary hadn't caught me by the arm.

"Are you alright?" He asked with concern.

"Y-yes, I'm fine," I nodded, blinking as I tried to clear my head.

His expression stating that he wasn't convinced, Zachary reached up and rested his hand on my forehead. His eyes widening, he asked, "Eva, how long have you been running a fever?"

"I...I don't know," I replied, shaking my head. "I hadn't really noticed."

"Come with me," he said.

I followed him into an exam room and sat on the table, feeling more weak and tired by the moment, and it was all I could do not to rest my head against Zachary's chest as he examined me.

Finally, he stepped back and, with a grave expression, said, "You have polio, Eva."

194

I was taken to a spare room, given some medication, and put to bed. My head pounded like the beating of a drum and my joints ached painfully, but all I could think of was Davey. Was he awake and calling for me? What would happen to him if I died?

My fever spiked in the night and refused to come down. I lay in the hospital bed, shivering and aching all over while I faded in and out of delirium. I kept asking for Mutter, as all I wanted was her cool, comforting hand on my brow, but she'd never had polio, and it would be too dangerous for her to be exposed again.

The next few days were a blur. The fever wouldn't subside, and in my half-conscious state, I could hear Savannah and Zachary talking in muted tones.

"We've got to get her fever down," I heard Savannah say, and it seemed as if her voice was a million miles away. I could feel the gentle touch of her fingers along my forehead, but couldn't seem to open my eyes or move my lips.

"I've done everything I know to do," Zachary replied, his tone heavy. "I fear that if it doesn't break soon, the nerves will be too badly damaged."

I continued fading in and out incoherently, my thoughts and dreams blurring together into one ever-changing image. I saw Davey running away from me, his blonde hair bouncing in the sunlight, and I tried to chase after him, but my feet were heavy and wouldn't move.

"Wait, Davey!" I called desperately as he faded further and further away. "Wait for Mommy."

"Men and women of the United States, this is a momentous hour in world history. This is the invasion of Hitler's Europe."

The radio announcement from "the invasion" suddenly burst through my mind as visions of soldiers storming the beaches of Normandy flashed before my eyes. I heard the whistle of bullets and watched as men fell, one by one, to their deaths onto the wet sand. The ground beneath my feet shook while the whir of airplane engines sounded overhead. It was like I was there, standing at a distance and watching helplessly, and I began to cry, the trail of hot tears stinging my cheeks.

Then, just like Dorothy in The Wizard of Oz, I clicked my heels and was transported back to Germany, my beautiful homeland. I could see the breathtaking mountains and green grass of spring, with wildflowers growing in the meadow. I could hear Oma, my grandmother, speaking in her native tongue as she called to me, and I felt her arms pull me close to her breast as she softly sang a lullaby. She'd died when I was seven, but I could still hear her voice and smell the scent of honeysuckle on her skin and clothes.

I closed my eyes, soaking in the feeling of comfort and security I felt in her arms, and when I opened them again, everything changed. Oma was

195

gone, and a thick, heavy mist had come over me. I rubbed my eyes and blinked, feeling lost and confused. I wanted desperately to see light and trees and feel the heat of the sun on my skin, but the fog surrounded me like a cold, empty tomb.

Then, there was Paul, walking toward me through the dense, white mist, his eyes warm as he smiled and reached out his hand to me. I moved to step towards him but hesitated, feeling afraid and uncertain.

"Come on, Eva," he beckoned. "Come with me."

"No," I shook my head. "Davey…I have to stay with Davey."

Suddenly, through the fog, I heard another voice calling to me. It was a deep, familiar voice, but one that I couldn't quite recognize in my state of delirium. Gradually, I felt myself draw away from Paul and began turning towards the voice, Paul's face slowly fading from view.

"Eva," I heard the voice say. "Don't go, Eva. Please don't go."

Someone took my hand and kissed it and I felt myself relax, the images fading from view as I finally drifted off into a peaceful, dreamless sleep.

The fever took its toll on my body, but I slowly came around after a few days. The first person I saw upon waking was Savannah, and I immediately attempted to ask about Davey, my words slurred and jumbled.

"He's doing much better," she assured me, smiling as she checked my vitals. "He's been eating and even walked a few steps for us this morning."

A feeling of overwhelming relief swept over me at the good news, and I closed my eyes and drifted back off to sleep, tears of gratitude sliding softly down my cheeks.

Once I was more alert, Zachary came in and checked my breathing and muscle strength. After overhearing his and Savannah's conversation, I was terrified of not being able to walk again, and had been wiggling my toes as much as I could. My legs seemed very weak, however, and I was quickly growing concerned.

"You'll feel very tired and lethargic for a couple of weeks," he told me as he listened to my lungs, "but I expect you to make a full recovery."

Circling around to stand at my feet, he took one foot in his hand and moved it around, then lifted my leg and bent it. He then told me to move my foot, wiggle my toes, and push against his hand with my heel. Once he was finished, I held my breath, waiting to hear what he had to say.

His face a bit grave, he picked up my foot again and said, "Let me try one last thing…"

Suddenly, he tickled the bottom of my foot and I squealed, pulling my foot away as quickly as I could. Laughing, he said, "The nerves and muscles in your legs are fine, Eva; you'll be running around after Davey in no time."

196

"That's wonderful," I replied, sighing with relief. "And Davey is doing well?"

"He's doing great," Zachary nodded. "You both were very fortunate."

I almost couldn't believe just how fortunate we really were. So many people were dealing with the terrible aftereffects of polio, and I knew that Davey and I had both received a miracle, something for which I was very grateful.

"I'm glad that you both are on the mend," Zachary added with a warm smile.

After begging to see Davey, Vivian brought him to me the next day, and the look of pure delight on his face when he saw me was all the medicine I needed. His eyes brightened and when he reached his chubby little arms out to me, I pulled him against my chest and rocked him, singing the same sweet lullaby my Oma once sang to me. As we sat there, holding on to one another, I began to cry. My tears were of both joy and sadness, for although I was grateful for our healing, I also mourned all the lives that had been lost during this epidemic. When polio came and went, it always took something precious with it.

A week later, Davey and I were well enough to go home. Leon had been kind enough to offer to drive us home, and as he pulled up in front of the hospital, I couldn't stop smiling when Nana and Mutter jumped from the back seat, both of their arms outstretched as they covered us in hugs and kisses.

"I was so worried," Mutter cried, tears sliding down her cheeks as she cupped my face between her hands.

"I know," I whispered, my throat tight as I pulled her into a hug. I'd missed her so much and yearned for her presence throughout mine and Davey's sickness, but knowing that both she and Nana were safe had given me comfort. "I'm so glad to be going home," I told them.

"Look at you two, the absolute picture of health!" Leon cried, grinning as he walked around the car to pull me into a hug. I hugged him tightly in return, his words muffled as he said into my hair, "It's so good to see you."

Turning to Davey, Leon picked him up and exclaimed, "Just look at you, young man! You've grown at least a foot since I last saw you."

Davey giggled, his cheeks turning pink with pleasure as he wrapped his arms around Leon's neck. We all climbed into the car then, and as we drove home, I gazed out the window and sighed, joy at finally being able to leave the hospital sweeping over me and bringing tears to my eyes. Everything looked so fresh and beautiful, and I smiled and waved at everyone we passed.

When we got home and walked inside, I soaked in our surroundings. Mutter and Nana must have scrubbed the house from top to bottom, as everything seemed to sparkle, and it surprised me to find a bouquet of flowers sitting on the foyer table.

"One of your friends left them on the front porch," Mutter said, handing me a folded piece of paper. "We didn't see who it was, but this note was under the vase."

I opened the note and read: *Eva, I hope you get better soon. -Jackson*

Smiling at his thoughtfulness, I folded the note and placed it in my pocket, leaning over to smell the mixture of wildflowers he'd obviously picked himself.

"Is this the same Edgar Shufflebottom that left the white rose?" Leon asked, grinning mischievously.

"I don't know," I replied, chuckling. "I never asked him."

I noticed a wonderful aroma drifting from the kitchen then, and Leon led me through the house, his hand at my elbow.

"Pecan pralines," Nana said with a wink when we entered the kitchen. "Your favorite. You can have as many as you want after you've rested for a bit."

Without complaining, both Davey and I headed to bed. We were still weak and very drained, but I knew it wouldn't be long before we were both back to normal.

"I sleep with you, Mommy?"

I held Davey's hand as we walked towards his room, and when I stopped to look at him in surprise at the request, I saw the look of apprehension in his eyes and my heart squeezed. Ever since I became sick and we were separated in the hospital, Davey had been extra clingy when he was near me, and I knew he was afraid of being left alone again.

"Yes, sweetie, you can sleep with me," I said, smiling gently.

As we climbed into bed and Davey curled up next to me, my eyes once again filled with tears and I pulled my son closer, thanking God for sparing both of our lives. How would I feel at this very moment if something had happened to him? I could have been like the other parents who'd lost their children during the epidemic, or Davey could have been sent home in a wheelchair or leg braces like so many others. I was overwhelmed with a sense of gratitude, and I kissed him gently on his forehead as he slept, tears of thanks sliding down my cheeks and dripping into his hair.

After a few moments, I was beginning to relax when a snippet of memory suddenly floated through my brain. Something had happened while I was sick and in the hospital, something I'd forgotten about until now. I'd been dreaming and fading in and out of consciousness, and somewhere in the midst of it all, I'd thought I heard a voice and even felt someone kiss my hand. Had it been it real, or simply another hallucination? Whatever it was, it felt very real and warm and…something else.

You must have just dreamed it, I convinced myself, finally drifting off to sleep.

38

THE SHADOW

He watched as they helped Eva and Davey inside, and from where he stood, it looked as if they were both still very weak. Ever since the polio outbreak, the entire city had basically shut down and everything changed. When Eva took Davey to the hospital, he'd expected her to come back home, and when she didn't, he did a bit of investigating and discovered that she, too, was sick. He wasn't supposed to care, but it hadn't taken long to realize that he missed seeing her, and he was glad she was finally back home.

It was now time to continue on with his plan, and as he turned and began walking down the street, a small, malicious smile curled his lips. He thought it was so funny that no one had a clue what he was up to, and the body of the young, brokenhearted woman he'd killed had yet to be found; he doubted that it ever would be. Having so much control was thrilling, and he felt as if nothing or no one could ever stop him. It was like he was a ghost, or a thin, vaporous shadow that couldn't be caught or trapped, and he could do as he pleased when he pleased. It was powerful, this feeling, and he liked it; a lot.

The next part of the plan with Eva would take place very soon, and he couldn't wait to play it out all the way to the end.

39

Vivian

Within two months, the epidemic was finally coming to an end. In the middle of it all, however, I feared it never would, as it seemed they brought in more and more sick people every day. The hospital had grown overcrowded, events were canceled, many businesses shut down, and crowds were avoided. I'd left the restaurant closed, and my father was still with my aunt in Atlanta. I continued to work in the hospital and help as much as I could, and by the time September arrived, I was exhausted, both physically and mentally. Out of the several hundred who'd grown ill, five children and two adults had died, and two more were left paralyzed. One might say those numbers were better than the statistics in other cities who had suffered polio epidemics, but I believe the families and people who were affected the most would disagree.

Now that the epidemic was nearly over, I, along with the other volunteers, decided it was time to go home; the hospital was back to normal occupancy, and our help was no longer needed. I told everyone goodbye before I left, stopping on my way out to pay a quick visit to the little girl I had sung to who was now learning to walk in leg braces. I hugged her goodbye and wished her luck, my eyes filling with tears as I left the building. It had been a long, hard couple of months, and I wasn't certain I'd ever forget the suffering I'd seen.

As I drove home, I pondered the fragility and uncertainty of life. Only a short while ago, families were whole and happy, none of them knowing what lay just around the corner. I thought of my own life, of losing my child and mother, and the betrayal and death of my husband, and wondered if perhaps it was best not to even have a family. Why love someone, why get close to them and give them your heart when you haven't any idea when they could be taken away from you? It was just too risky.

I reopened The Park Bench, and the city gradually got back to normal. I hadn't even considered how much of an affect being closed for two months would have on the restaurant, but when I started going over the books, I realized we were going to be in serious trouble if we didn't start making money soon.

The load of the restaurant and pressure that went along with it was now totally on me, and I was feeling it greatly. I kept thinking about the money hidden in the office; how convenient would it be simply to take a little here and there to pay the bills? I couldn't bring myself to do it, though, nor could I tell the police of its discovery. To use a phrase from my mother, I was "caught between the rock and the hard place", and I didn't know what to do.

After one particularly long day at work, I turned in early and immediately fell into a deep sleep. Sometime around midnight, I suddenly awoke, my body tense and ears listening intently. I'd heard something…hadn't I? Or was it simply another one of my dreams?

There it was again, the creaking of the stairs that led up to my apartment. I quickly got out of bed and put on my robe, my hands shaking as I reached out to turn on the lamp. In my haste, I knocked it over, and it shattered loudly to the floor. Unable to move for fear of stepping on broken glass, I stood in the darkness and waited, trembling. I could hear the footsteps drawing closer, and I reached down to fumble about for a piece of glass to use as a weapon. I heard my bedroom door slowly open, and a flashlight suddenly clicked on, shining directly into my eyes.

"Hello, love."

I'd recognize that voice anywhere, and I felt chills grip the back of my spine like a cold, steely hand. I clutched the piece of glass between my fingers, waiting for him to make any sudden moves.

"W-what are you doing here?" I whispered.

"Didn't they tell you?" He asked, stepping closer until we were only a few inches apart, his shoes crunching the glass beneath his feet. "I broke out of prison."

I stared at Mack, unable to believe my eyes. Surely, I was dreaming. Was it possible that my worst nightmare was, in fact, living and breathing and standing right in front of me?

"What do you want?" I asked, trying to stop myself from shaking so badly; I didn't want him to know how frightened I was.

"We both know why I'm here," he said, his eyes hard. "Now why don't you just make this easy and tell me where the money is so I can be on my way?"

I hesitated, consciously weighing my options. Should I just hand the money over and possibly end up dead, or did I dare try to make some sort of deal?

"I'm waiting," he barked, but I didn't flinch.

Instead, I drew myself up to my full height and said, "Why should I tell you where it is? That money is just as much mine as it is yours."

Mack blinked in surprise, and then, his eyes narrowing suspiciously, he asked, "How do you figure?"

"By becoming involved with you, Howard gambled away most of our savings," I stated, keeping my tone even, "so basically, that money belongs to me."

Mack threw back his head and laughed, the sound echoing loudly off the walls. When I simply stood in silence, staring at him, his laughter died down and a hard look replaced the mirth. Stepping closer, he growled, "I don't know who you think you're kidding, but I'm not here to play games. Give me the money or I'll…"

"You'll what?" I interrupted. "My father is out of town and won't be back for weeks, so you can't threaten to do him any harm."

"Your father may be out of town, but you happen to be standing right here in front of me," he said, a smirk pulling at his lips as he scanned me from head to toe. "I can think of several fun things we could do together, and afterwards, I'll tie you up and burn this place down around your ears."

Cringing on the inside, I fought to maintain control of my reaction to his words. "How do you know you wouldn't be burning the money up with me?" I asked with a cool smirk of my own.

His jaw clenched, he said with a snarl, "You're just about to make me mad, girly."

"Then let's negotiate."

Mack hesitated, his eyes narrowing once again. "What did you have in mind?"

"There's five thousand dollars, and I want half."

"Half!" Mack guffawed. "You'll have to do better than that."

I'd expected him to say as much, which is why I'd started the bidding so high. "Alright, fine," I said, "I'll settle for one thousand dollars and no less."

Mack stood deathly still, his piercing black eyes studying me as he considered the offer. Suddenly, he sprang forward, wrapping his hand around my neck as he shoved me roughly against the wall. The broken glass on the floor slashed painfully at my feet, and I fought back the yelp of agony that leaped into my throat.

"I'm not playing your little games anymore," he hissed, his breath hot against my face. "Tell me where the money is *now* or I'll start cutting off tiny little pieces of your body until there's nothing left to cut."

As he spoke, I slowly crept my hand towards his upper thigh, trying my best to keep a grip on myself when all I wanted to do was give in and beg him to leave. I refused, however, to be intimidated by this man. I knew if I told him where the money was, he'd kill me and disappear forever, and I had a plan in the back of my mind that, if executed correctly, could work to my benefit…if only I could pull it off.

"If you don't release me at once and back away, I'm going to slice your leg wide open," I spoke slowly, resting my weapon against his leg with just enough pressure to get the point across. "In case you didn't know, there's an artery just beneath this razor sharp piece of glass that I'm holding, and if it's cut, you'll bleed to death in minutes."

Mack let me go, our gazes never wavering from each other as he slowly moved away. "You're crazy," he said, the look in his eyes letting me know he was beginning to take me seriously.

"You seem to forget that, thanks to you, I spent three months in a mental hospital; nothing scares me anymore," I stated evenly. "I've lost my child, husband, and mother, and I have nothing else to lose. Now, will you agree to the deal that I've offered, or would you prefer I keep it all to myself?"

"Okay, have it your way," he said slowly. "Give me my share now, and I'll be on my way."

"No," I shook my head, "Meet me at midnight in Bonaventure Cemetery two nights from now at the Theus grave."

His brow furrowing suspiciously, he asked, "Why?"

"I have my reasons," I stated evenly. "If you want your money, you'll have to do this my way."

Mack hesitated once more, his expression uncertain. "Alright," he finally said, "but I'll be watching you, and if I see anything suspicious, I'll do just as I threatened earlier. With or without the money."

He was gone then, his shadowy figure disappearing once again out into the hallway, and I hurried across the room to close and lock my door, my entire body shaking like a reed in the wind. I couldn't believe he'd agreed to my plan, but now that he had, I needed to figure out what to do next. He said he'd be watching me, and I knew he would hold true to his word; I'd have to be very careful and plan every little detail with caution and precision. The next two days would be brutal, but I *had* to do this. I didn't have any other choice.

The next day, I was in my office when Zachary paid me an unexpected visit. I normally would have been pleased to see him, but ever since Mack's reappearance, I'd been locked in my office and avoiding everyone as much as possible. I was tired and nervous and not in the mood to see anyone, and it must have been obvious, because as soon as he stepped into the room, Zachary's penetrating gaze seemed to see right through my fake smile.

"Is everything alright?" He immediately asked, and I had to force myself not to sigh.

"Of course, why wouldn't it be?" I asked innocently.

"Because Savannah said you didn't act right when she called yesterday, and when I spoke to Eva just now, she said you've been locked in this office all day."

"Eva is still weak from her illness and shouldn't even be here, and Savannah just caught me at a busy time," I replied, shrugging.

He stood there studying me in silence, and I struggled not to fidget.

"Okay, just checking," he finally replied with a smile. "I thought I'd come by and ask if you'd like to go to dinner with me tonight?"

I blinked, caught totally off guard by the invitation. "I…uh…I can't," I stammered awkwardly.

"Why not?" He asked, walking casually across the room to lean against my desk.

"Because I'm busy," I stated.

"You're telling me you're too busy to go out on a Friday evening?"

"I have loads of paperwork to get caught up on," I said with a sniff.

"So, you're just going to work through supper and not eat anything?"

"I live in a restaurant, Zachary; I can get food whenever I want," I replied drolly.

"That's true," he nodded thoughtfully, suddenly turning on his heel to march out of my office without another word.

Surprised at the sudden exit, I shook my head and got back to work. Twenty minutes later, Zachary returned with a tray full of food.

"If you refuse to go out to eat with me, then I'll just have to bring the food to you," he stated triumphantly as he placed the tray on my desk before me.

With raised brows, I couldn't help but laugh. "You don't give up easily, do you?" I asked.

"No, ma'am, I don't," he replied with a grin.

Shaking my head, I cleared off my desk and made room as Zachary sat out the napkins and silverware, my stomach rumbling loudly as I eyed the bowl of steaming hot shrimp and grits, freshly cut side salad, and a slice of coconut cream pie.

"Cook certainly did a fine job with tonight's menu," I said appreciatively as I took a bite of the deliciously creamy shrimp and grits.

"Eva said to tell you she saved that piece of pie just for you."

"She's the best," I replied, smiling. "She knows it's one of my favorites."

After a few comfortable, silent moments of enjoying our meal, Zachary asked, "Are you happy to be back at the restaurant now that the epidemic is over, or do you miss your tireless volunteer work at the hospital?"

"Hmm, let me see," I said, tapping my chin. "Do I miss standing on my feet all day, cleaning bedpans, and washing an endless supply of linens, or would I prefer to be here sitting in my cool, comfortable office?"

"I see what you mean," he replied, chuckling.

With a smile, I said, "I don't know how y'all do it constantly. My respect for doctors and nurses rose significantly after my time working at the hospital."

"It's a sort of calling, I think," Zachary said, the ice in his glass rattling as he took a sip of his sweet tea. "You love running this place, don't you?"

I nodded exuberantly. "Oh, yes. I grew up working alongside my parents in the kitchen; I even ran it by myself for nearly two years before we hired Cook. I love the hustle and bustle of running a business and hearing the chatter of patrons enjoying their meal. Keeping busy is like food for my soul," I said, adding with a wink, "Pun intended. You know I like to keep busy, though, which is why you arranged for me to work in the kitchen at Martinsville, isn't it?"

"You figured that out, huh?" He smiled, his eyes twinkling. Nodding, he said, "Yes, I knew you needed something to do or else you would just waste away. How was it, working in the kitchen there?"

"Well, the kitchen is one of the largest I've ever seen, but what surprised me the most was the fact that they allowed Alice Layne to work there."

"The woman accused of poisoning her husband?" Zachary asked, his eyes widening in surprise.

"Yes," I nodded. "She was very nice, though. She even took up for me a few times when some of the other patients wanted to fight."

Zachary poked around his plate for a moment with his fork, his expression thoughtful. "Did they ever hurt you, Vivian?"

"No…" I paused, some of the darker memories playing over in my mind. "It was a pretty terrible experience for me, for anyone, to deal with mentally," I said after a moment, "but I think your influence helped a great deal in how I was treated, and I am very grateful for that. I did, however, see many patients that were abused needlessly." I thought of Anthony then and felt a lump form in my throat. Glancing down at my hands, I said softly, "I'm just glad I was able to get out of there."

"Me, too," he replied. As if sensing the need for a lighter topic, he cleared his throat and said, "Tell me something silly that annoyed you when you worked there in the kitchen."

"Hmm," I said, giving it some thought. "One thing that drove me crazy was that they refused to give anyone the choice between ketchup and mustard; they always just mixed the two together."

"So the poor souls, such as myself, that hate mustard had to either suffer through it or eat their hotdogs dry?"

"Precisely," I nodded, and we both laughed.

Once we were down to the dessert, I offered half of my pie to Zachary. "I really can't eat it all," I told him when he protested.

"Well, if you insist," he said with a grin, proceeding to eat his half of the pie in two bites.

"What made you decide to become a doctor?" I asked as I nibbled on my half.

"That is a long story," Zachary replied, leaning back in his chair as he laced his fingers across his stomach. "When I was young, I fell off the porch at my home and broke my leg so severely that the doctors didn't think I'd ever be able to walk again. One man, a Doctor Steele, was able to set it as good as anyone possibly could and later introduced me to physical therapy. You may have noticed that I still have a limp, but if not for him, I would most likely be in a wheelchair today. When I got older, I decided I wanted to be like Doctor Steele; someone who not only helped people, but who went above and beyond to make their quality of life the best possible."

"He sounds like a wonderful man," I noted, pushing my now empty plate away. "Just like you."

"Flattery, my dear, will get you everywhere," Zachary stated, wiggling his eyebrows, and I laughed.

The church bells began to ring then, and Zachary stood up and started gathering the dirty dishes. "Well, thank you for joining me for such a lovely dinner. I'll let you get back to all of that work you spoke about," he said, winking at me.

Smiling, I stood up to help him and, before I could stop myself, let out a yelp of pain. The cuts on my feet were very swollen and painful and when I stepped wrong, it felt like needles pricking my skin. I leaned back against the desk, my faced tight from the pain.

"What's wrong?" Zachary asked, hurrying to my side.

"Oh, I just stepped on some broken glass last night," I replied, waving the incident off nonchalantly.

"Let me have a look," he said, and before I could protest, he wrapped his hands around my waist and hoisted me up onto the desk.

Knowing there was no need to downplay the matter, I took off my shoes and stockings and showed him the bottoms of my feet.

"Do you have a first aid kit?" He asked, and I pointed to the top shelf of the bookcase. After retrieving the small red and white box, Zachary opened it and gently cleaned my feet with some alcohol. I winced and forced myself not to jerk my feet away as he then applied a bit of ointment, followed by a layer of gauze.

"That should help, but you need to stay off of your feet as much as possible for the next few days," Zachary said as he returned the first aid kit to its shelf.

"I'll try," I replied, slowly easing my feet back into my shoes.

Zachary reached out to help me from the desk, and when his fingers found the bruise on my arm left by Mack, I sucked in my breath and quickly pulled my arm away.

His brow furrowing, Zachary jerked my sleeve up before I could stop him, his eyes widening when he saw the finger shaped bruises on my upper arm.

"Vivian, where did you get these bruises?" He demanded, his eyes flashing.

"Don't worry about it," I stated, moving away from him.

"So there really is something going on, just like Eva and Savannah said. Why won't you tell me who did this to you?" He wanted to know, hands on his hips.

"I can't tell you," I replied, turning my back to him as my mind whirled. Oh, why had I allowed him to stay so long this evening? I'd been avoiding everyone for this very reason!

I heard Zachary come up behind me and felt him grab my hand, spinning me around to face him. "Whatever is going on, please let me help," he said, his eyes beseeching mine. "You can trust me, Vivian."

I stood there silently for a moment, struggling inwardly; I knew I couldn't tell him, or Mack might kill us both.

Finally, I pulled my hand away and said, "I can't tell you, Zachary, I'm sorry." I went over to my desk then and withdrew a letter from the top drawer, holding it out for Zachary to take. "You can, however, deliver this letter for me tomorrow morning. Will you do that? And please don't say anything to anyone."

Zachary took the letter, frowning when he read the recipient's name. Looking back up at me, he sighed and said, "I don't like not knowing what this is all about, but I'll do it with no more questions asked."

I thanked him and, after gathering up the tray of dirty dishes, Zachary left without another word. I knew he was upset, and I didn't blame him, but I couldn't tell him about Mack, or my little plan for the following night. It was just too dangerous.

40

Eva

It was Saturday and Vivian had, for unknown reasons, given everyone the day off. It thrilled me to be home with my family, but I was also secretly glad to have some time to rest, as I still hadn't totally regained my strength back yet. It was almost noon, and I was sitting on the front porch, watching Davey ride his tricycle up and down in front of the house, when Zachary pulled up with a quick toot of his horn.

Waving, I walked out to the yard to see him, smiling as he climbed from his car. "To what do we owe the pleasure of this visit?" I asked, blocking the sun with my hand.

"I was out this way and thought I'd stop by to see how you and Davey are doing," he replied, taking off his hat. "You looked a little pale when I saw you yesterday. You're not pushing yourself too much, are you?"

"Oh, I'm fine, just a little tired," I assured him. "Davey seems to be as energetic as always."

Seeing the doctor, Davey jumped from his bike and ran to Zachary's side as fast as his chubby little legs could carry him. "Hi!" He said, smiling up at our visitor.

Zachary kneeled down and talked with Davey for a moment, asking how he felt and even rubbing his throat and neck "just to check".

"What happened there?" Zachary asked, pointing at the bandage on Davey's knee.

"I felled off my bike," Davey said with a heavy, serious sigh. "It tripped, so I felled off 'n hurt my leg."

"Goodness, you shouldn't have such a clumsy tricycle," Zachary replied, his lips twitching. Reaching out to ruffle Davey's hair, Zachary stood back up and said to me, "I saw Vivian yesterday and I feel like something is going on. Have you spoken to her today?"

"No," I shook my head, watching as Davey ran back to his tricycle. "Do you think she's okay?"

"I don't know," Zachary replied, sighing. "I'm concerned about her."

He seemed to want to say more, but hesitated, as if uncertain whether he should proceed with what was on his mind. Before he could say anything else, Nana popped her head outside and announced that lunch was ready.

"Would you like to stay and eat with us?" I asked Zachary, beckoning to Davey to come inside.

Zachary readily agreed and followed me into the house. I introduced him to Nana and Mutter, and he greeted them with such warmth that it seemed as if he'd known them for years. Mutter smiled at him, ducking her head in her typical, shy way as Nana ushered him into the kitchen.

We'd just sat down to eat when there was a knock at the front door. I went to open it, surprised to find Leon on the other side.

"Eva," he said, his smile not concealing the look of worry I saw in his eyes. "Can I talk to you for a moment?"

"Of course," I said, nodding my head. "Please, come inside."

We went into the living room and sat down, the clock on the mantle ticking loudly as I waited for Leon to tell me what was wrong.

"I overhead my manager talking on the phone a little while ago," he said, jumping right into it. "I don't know who he was speaking with, but they were discussing the fact that you're behind on your mortgage payment. Eva, I'm afraid that Mr. Manson is considering calling in your loan."

My eyes widening, I said, "I am running a bit behind this month since I wasn't able to work until this week, but surely he'll let me catch up next month...won't he?"

"I don't know," he stated with a sigh. "I plan on speaking with him about it later, but wanted to come by and ask if you're able to even pay half of this month's payment?"

"I got paid yesterday," I said, going over to my purse to withdraw the cash Vivian had given me. "It will only cover about a third of my payment, though. Do you think it will pacify him?"

"I hope so," Leon said, taking the money. "Will this leave you with enough money to get by?"

"We'll be alright," I said, although I hadn't any idea of how we'd be able to buy groceries for the next week. I didn't want us to be forced from our home, though, so we'd just have to make do.

As I walked him out, I asked, "Who do you think your manager was on the phone with?"

Leon sighed and shook his head. "I have no idea," he said, rubbing the back of his neck. "It's a little strange, if you ask me. Who would call him wanting to know if you'd made your payment?"

"I don't have the faintest idea," I replied softly, thinking of all the strange things that had happened over the last few months. The man whom I'd thought was following me home, the white rose by the front door, the intruder into our house and pocket knife he'd left behind, and Davey stating that he'd talked with a strange man just before he fell from the tree. Was it all connected somehow? But why would anyone be interested in knowing if I'd made the payment on my mortgage? It just didn't make sense.

After Leon left, I went back into the kitchen and sat down, telling everyone about Leon's news.

"That's very strange," Zachary stated, his brow furrowed.

"Yes, it is," I agreed as I took a bite of Nana's fried chicken, my mind whirling. Davey kicked the underside of the table, and I asked him to stop, gently patting his knee with my fingers.

"Do you think someone is interested in buying the house?" Nana asked.

"I suppose that could be it," I replied, shrugging. "Let's just hope the bank won't call in our loan."

After lunch, we were all sitting around the table drinking coffee and eating leftover chocolate cake when Zachary suddenly said, "One of my doctor friends is celebrating his birthday this weekend. Since you're all obviously such marvelous cooks, would y'all be interested in baking a birthday cake for a small party the hospital is throwing him on Monday? I'll provide the ingredients, of course, and pay for the service."

All three of us stared at him in surprise. "Why not get a cake from the bakery on Broughton?" Nana asked him.

"Because their cakes don't touch this one," he replied with a grin as he pointed to the half-eaten slice on his plate. "Plus, I've waited until the last minute, and I'm sure they wouldn't accept an order this late."

They all turned to look at me questioningly, and I hesitated, contemplating Zachary's request. He knew I'd given Leon all the cash I had, and I suspected that he'd concocted this little plan because he knew we would need money for the upcoming week; I even wondered if the doctor friend he spoke of really was having a birthday.

After a moment of deliberation, I decided to accept the kind gift he was offering. I didn't like the thought of accepting charity, but since he was asking us to work for it, it wasn't exactly charity, was it?

"Alright," I agreed, touched at such a kind gesture, "I'll give you a list of everything we'll need."

That evening, Leon came back to our house bearing more news. We were all in the kitchen baking the cake for Zachary, and Leon sat at the table with a glass of tea as he spoke.

"Mr. Manson wouldn't tell me who he was speaking with on the phone," Leon said, tapping his fingers absently on the table, "but he said the money you sent today would tide you over until next month."

"Oh, that's wonderful," I said with a sigh. I slapped my palms together in relief and a cloud of flour flew up around my face, causing me to sneeze loudly.

"Don't get overly excited just yet," Leon said, chuckling. "He wanted me to tell you that if you are late again next month, he can't promise that he won't call the loan in then."

"I won't be late again," I quickly assured him.

"Why are y'all baking at this hour?" Leon suddenly wanted to know as he glanced at his wristwatch.

"Zachary asked us to bake a cake for a friend's birthday party," I told him as I stirred the batter.

Out of the corner of my eye, I saw Leon frown. "I didn't realize y'all had gone into the cake baking business," he stated drolly.

"We haven't," Nana spoke up. "I think the sweet Doctor came up with this idea just so we would be able to buy groceries for next week."

"How nice of him," Leon muttered.

"Yes, he's a very nice man," I said with a smile, swiping a bit of the chocolate icing that Mutter was making.

After we put the cake in the oven, Leon announced he was tired and stood up, bidding us all a good night. Taking off my apron, I wiped my hands and walked him out.

"So, that sure was nice of Zachary, wasn't it?" Leon asked as we walked towards the front door.

"Yes, it was," I agreed, wondering why he'd brought it up again.

Leon stuffed his hands into his pockets, not saying anything for a moment. Finally, he asked, "I noticed his car was here earlier and I assume he ate lunch with y'all. Are the two of you seeing each other?"

I was reaching out to open the front door but stopped, my hand hanging in mid-air as I looked up at Leon in surprise. "No," I replied, shaking my head. "We're just friends."

"I see," he said, studying me. After a moment, he cleared his throat and, reaching out to retrieve his hat from the hall tree, bid me a good night.

After he was gone, I stood in the foyer for a moment, wondering why he'd asked such a thing. Did he think Zachary was interested in me? With a sigh, I shrugged my shoulders and headed back to the kitchen to help clean up.

The next day, I took Davey to a nearby park, as I thought the fresh air and sunshine would do us both some good. It was a warm, beautiful day, and as I gently pushed Davey on the swing set, his gleeful, innocent laughter filled the air and I couldn't help but laugh along with him.

"Seesaw, Mommy, seesaw," he said after a bit, and I helped him down from the swing and watched as he ran to the seesaw to play with another child.

I sat on a nearby bench, smiling as the two children immediately became the best of friends, and failed to notice the man standing beneath the trees watching me. He moved closer, his steps light and quiet, and was by my side before I realized anyone was even there.

"Hello, Eva."

With a small gasp, I turned to find Mr. Creed standing at the end of the bench, a small dog at his side. He wore a gray suit that only enhanced the translucent color of his eyes, and his thin blonde hair glinted in the sunlight.

"Mr. Creed, what a surprise," I stammered, feeling a bit flustered. I hadn't seen him in months and wondered how he'd even recognized me; I'd lost quite a bit of weight during my illness, and was still very pale.

"How are you?" He asked, tossing a tennis ball for his dog to chase after.

"I'm doing well, thank you," I replied. "How are you?"

Smiling, he sat beside me and said, "I'm doing better, thank you. I've learned to cope with the loss of my wife, but it's still difficult going on without them, isn't it?"

My heart going out to him, I nodded my head and said, "Yes, it is." Glancing at his furry, tail-wagging companion, I commented, "I see that you have some company now, though. He's very cute."

"He's my neighbor's dog," Mr. Creed replied, tossing the ball once again. "I offer to take him to the park now and then, but I've been thinking of getting a dog of my own. It would definitely give me a bit of company."

"I agree," I said, reaching down the pet the little dog when he brought the ball back.

Turning to look at me, Mr. Creed noticed the locket around my neck and said, "That's a very pretty locket."

I placed my fingers around the silver, heart-shaped pendant and smiled. "My father gave it to me," I said, taking the necklace off for Mr. Creed to see. "There's a photograph of he and my mother inside."

"How nice," he said, taking the locket from my extended hand. He opened it and looked inside, his smile warm as he commented, "What a lovely couple."

He handed the locket back to me, and I said, "Thank you. I miss my father very much; he passed away a few years ago."

"Oh, I am so sorry to hear that," he said, his eyes filling with sympathy. "How has your mother held up after losing her husband?"

"She's done the best she can," I replied, watching Davey as he played with his new friend. "It hasn't been easy, but at least we have each other."

"Yes, be very thankful for that," Mr. Creed said with a small sigh. "It's hard dealing with both grief and loneliness."

"Don't you have anyone, Mr. Creed?" I asked softly.

Shaking his head, Mr. Creed patted the dog and said, "No, my wife and I were never blessed with a family."

My heart clenching, I didn't say anything for a moment. How hard it must be to lose your spouse and have no one else around to comfort you. I couldn't imagine how I would have ever survived if I hadn't had the love and support of my family when Paul died, and I suddenly felt more grateful than ever for Nana, Mutter, and Davey.

Clearing my throat, I said, "Perhaps you could join us at church one Sunday, and then eat lunch with us afterward. We would love to have you."

I could tell he was touched by the invitation, and with a warm smile, Mr. Creed nodded and said, "I would love that. Thank you, Eva, for your kindness."

Before I could reply, Davey cried out and I jerked my gaze in his direction, gasping when I realized he'd fallen from the seesaw. I jumped up and ran to his side, but by the time I'd gotten within three feet of him, he stood up and began dusting himself off.

"Are you alright, honey?" I asked with concern.

"I fine," he nodded, climbing back onto the seesaw.

Sighing, I turned to walk back to the bench, realizing with surprise that Mr. Creed and the dog were gone. I looked around, but he was nowhere to be seen, and I hoped I hadn't upset or offended him somehow.

41

Vivian

It was ten minutes 'til midnight when I parked at the Bonaventure Cemetery gate. Slowly, quietly, I climbed from my car, clicking on the small flashlight I held in one hand. In the other, I carried the bag full of money, and in my pocket was a small gun. I was fully prepared, or so I hoped.

As I slowly made my way through the gate, I took a deep breath, trying to calm my taut nerves. The moon was bright, and there was a dense, heavy mist rising from the ground like the thick haze of ghostly breath. A slight breeze stirred the tree branches overhead, and through the shadows, giant oaks towered above like goblins in the night, their limbs reaching out long, gnarly fingers draped with silvery strands of moss. There was no one about, or so it seemed, and I noticed that not even the crickets chirped. The night was hot and humid, but I fought off a chill of foreboding as I quietly walked across the entrance.

Leaves and twigs crunched beneath my shoes as I slowly walked across the grass toward Theus, the famous grave of the Confederate soldier and his wife. There, just ahead, the statue of the woman sitting atop the grave could be seen glistening in the moonlight, her chin resting thoughtfully against her fingers. I moved closer until I stood before the large stone monument, and in the glow of my flashlight, it seemed that the blank eyes opened wider and stared right at me, as if warning me to run while I still had the chance.

As I waited, I glanced slowly around the old cemetery, many of the monuments and gravestones worn and growing brown with age. The grounds used to be part of a plantation before the city bought the property, and in the daylight the cemetery was beautiful and very garden-like, with its trees, flowers, azalea bushes, and pathways. At night, however, the trees cast about many an eerie shadow, and the breeze that rustled softly through the leaves made it seem almost as if the lifelike statues were whispering to one another.

An owl suddenly hooted from one of the overhead branches and I flinched, glancing around uncertainly. The feeling of apprehension that had clung to my senses all day now threatened to suffocate me. Was I crazy for being here? Mack was a criminal, a murderer, and I'd agreed to meet him in the largest cemetery in Savannah at midnight.

Suddenly, I heard the sound of footsteps and turned, my eyes narrowing as I searched the darkness. There, beneath the mossy shadows, I saw the figure of a man walking slowly toward me and I caught my breath, my whole body tensing. As he drew closer, I could hear the church bells ring, announcing that the time was at hand; it was midnight.

"I was wondering if you'd have the nerve to show up."

The all too familiar voice sent chills up my spine and I took a step back, suddenly beginning to doubt myself. I reached inside of my pocket and touched the gun for reassurance, hoping I wouldn't have to use it.

"Of course I came," I stated, my voice shaky. "I said I would, didn't I?"

He kept walking until we stood only a few feet apart, and the way the moonlight glinted off his hard, black eyes made me wonder why I'd ever decided to do this.

"I ain't here to chitchat," he said, reaching out his hand. "Just give me the money and I'll be on my way."

"I have just one question first," I said, swallowing.

"What's that?" He asked, his eyes narrowing.

"Did you truly not know about my baby when you set fire to my house?"

Mack hesitated, and I held my breath. "*I* didn't set that fire, remember?" He finally replied, smirking.

"No, but you held me back while your two friends set it," I stated evenly.

Mack eyed me for a moment, his gaze as black as his soul. Finally, much to my surprise, he started laughing. "What is it you want from me, Mrs. McCombs?" He asked, snickering. "A confession? Well, you ain't a priest or a policeman, so I don't owe you anything."

He reached out again to snatch the bag from my hand, only to stop when the moon glinted off the gun I now pointed directly at him.

"Yes," I said, my voice low, "I *do* want a confession. You won't get your money without it."

Mack's jaw began to clench and unclench as he eyed the gun, and I could tell he was getting angry.

"Okay, fine," he growled. "No, we didn't know about the baby. Satisfied? If I could go back, though, I wouldn't change a thing; I'd *still* hold you back while my friends burned your house to the ground."

I stood there, shaking all over. The gun was clenched so tightly against my palm that my fingers ached, but still I didn't lower it. At the sound of his words, all I wanted to do was pull the trigger; if not for this man and his friends, my baby would still be alive.

Suddenly, a spotlight broke the darkness and shone on Mack's face like a beam from the sun itself. With a gasp, Mack leaped towards me, his hands reaching for the gun. I screamed and dove backwards, falling against the statue so hard that it knocked the breath from my lungs. I dropped the gun and heard it land somewhere in the grass nearby.

"We've got you surrounded, Mack," a voice called. "Come out with your hands up."

With a crazed look in his eyes, Mack looked at me and hissed, "You set me up!"

Grabbing me by the arm, Mack yanked the bag of money from my hand and turned to run in the opposite direction of the spotlight, his figure quickly melting in among the shadows. Several gunshots rang out with more shouts to stop and give himself up, and then I saw a young police officer take off in hot pursuit of Mack.

I stayed where I was, leaning against Theus's grave as I tried to catch my breath. Within seconds, Officer Wright was beside me, shining his flashlight in my face.

"I was beginning to think you didn't come," I said breathlessly, shading my eyes.

"I almost didn't," he stated, his jaw clenched. "What sort of crazy idea was this? When Dr. Holt gave me your note, I thought you needed to be back in Martinsville. Why didn't you come down to the station yourself or phone me?"

"Because Mack said he was watching me," I told him, sighing. "And I didn't want to call because he'd broken into my apartment once before and I was afraid he'd hear me make the phone call."

"Well, you took a mighty big risk coming out here tonight."

"Why wasn't I informed of his escape from prison?" I demanded, pushing off the statue to stand to my full height, which barely reached his shoulders.

"Why wasn't I informed you found the money he was looking for?" Officer Wright shot back, an eyebrow shooting upwards.

"Because I didn't trust you," I replied, sniffing. Glancing around, I asked, "Where are your other men? He might not have gotten away if you'd brought more than one."

"I didn't bring more men because *I* didn't trust *you*," he said with a sigh. "I thought you were just imagining things again."

My jaw clenched, I shook my head in annoyance. "Well, I hope you heard his confession and can now believe me when I say that Mack and his two friends are the ones responsible for burning down my house and killing my child."

"Yes," he replied, nodding. "I heard him. I'm sorry, Mrs. McCombs, for not believing you before."

"So am I," I snapped. "Perhaps I wouldn't have been sent to a mental hospital if you had."

I spun on my heel to stomp away, but stopped when Officer Wright reached out and grabbed my arm. I turned to glare at him, my temper deflating a bit at the look of guilt in his eyes.

"I truly am sorry," he said again, his voice soft.

Taking a deep breath, I sighed and, forcing a slight smile, said, "Thank you, Officer Wright. What's done is done. I would, however, appreciate it if you quenched any false rumors you may hear about me in the future."

"I'll do that," he said. "And don't worry about Mack; I'm sure we'll catch him. If we don't, though, I doubt he'll be back since he has the money now."

I hoped he was right, but what Officer Wright didn't know was that I'd kept one thousand dollars of Mack's money. Mack had agreed to it, but since I'd double-crossed him, would he come back for his revenge? *No*, I thought, *he'd be crazy to come back*.

As Officer Wright walked me to my car, he suddenly said, "I know that you and I got off on the wrong foot, but I'd really like for us to be friends. Would you mind if we started over, Mrs. McCombs?"

I glanced up at him, surprised. *With everything he's done, why should I accept his offer of friendship?* I thought, frowning. Before I could say what was on my mind, though, I stopped and checked myself. It was all over now; Howard was dead, Mack was gone, and Officer Wright knew the truth. So, why not let bygones be bygones?

"No, Officer Wright, I wouldn't mind," I finally said, a bit surprised at the feeling of peace those six little words brought to me. I remember Mother used to say, *"Forgiveness isn't always easy, but when you refuse to forgive, you're only punishing yourself,"* and I realized now more than ever just how true that was.

"Good," he said, smiling down at me, his deep-set, dark blue eyes glinting in the moonlight. "And please, call me Gabe."

"Only if you'll call me Vivian," I replied, stopping when we reached my car.

"Alright, Vivian," he nodded, opening the door for me. Before I climbed in, he added, "And please don't come up with any more crazy, life-threatening plans, alright?"

"I'm afraid I can't make any promises, Officer," I stated saucily, waving goodbye as I climbed into the driver's seat and drove away.

The next morning at church, Savannah asked me over to her aunt and uncle's house to eat dinner with them. My father was still out of town, so the invitation was very welcome.

"I miss seeing you at the hospital every day," she told me, linking her arm through mine as we walked to our cars.

"I've missed you, too," I said, squeezing her hand.

I drove to Mr. and Mrs. Coleman's house, the smell of baked ham and butter beans wafting from the kitchen when I walked inside. Everyone was already there and the sound of chatter and laughter immediately filled my ears, bringing a smile to my face. These people had always been so kind to me, and never failed to make me feel like a part of their family.

"There she is," Leon announced when I walked into the dining room, a half-eaten biscuit in his hand.

"Did you save any for the rest of us?" I asked, pointing to the biscuit.

"You know very well that Savannah's aunt would have my hide if I didn't," he replied, winking.

Chuckling, I stepped aside as Mrs. Coleman and Mrs. Emma brought the food in from the kitchen.

"Aunt Deb, this smells amazing," Savannah said with a smile as she took her seat.

"Well, Emma made the sweet potato soufflé, and her scrumptiously delicious apple pie is for dessert," Mrs. Coleman said over her shoulder as she pushed past her quiet husband to hurry back into the kitchen for the butter dish.

"Mom makes the best apple pie," Leon said, winking at his mother as he sat down beside me.

"I'll be sure to save room," I told him.

After saying grace, we all quickly dug in to the delicious meal, the only sound in the room that of forks and knives clinking against plates. I was buttering my second biscuit when Mrs. Emma leaned around Leon and asked me how I was doing. Realizing that everyone would most likely find out eventually, I told them what happened the night before. Once I was finished, they'd all stopped eating and were staring at me in shock.

Leon was the first to scold me. "Good grief, Viv, you could have been killed," he said, his face pulled into a frown.

"Yes, Leon is right," Savannah quickly joined in. "What on earth were you thinking?"

"I didn't really know what else to do," I responded with a shrug.

"Why didn't you call me?" Leon wanted to know. "I could have helped you."

"I was afraid he might overhear the phone call," I said, sighing. "Besides, I didn't want to put anyone else's life in danger."

"Well, if anything like this happens again, *please* get in touch with us somehow," Leon said. "We don't want anything to happen to you."

"No, we don't," Savannah stated. Reaching across the table, she took my hand and, giving it a squeeze, added, "But I'm glad you're alright. Maybe now you can stop worrying about everything that's happened and move forward."

I nodded, squeezing her hand in return. As everyone got back to their meal, the conversation moved on to the war, but I wasn't listening. Perhaps Savannah was right; maybe it was time I started trying to let go of the past.

After dinner, I thanked Mr. and Mrs. Coleman for having me and walked outside with Savannah and Leon. I waved goodbye to Mrs. Emma as she walked next door to her house, and hugged Savannah before she climbed into her car.

"Let's do something soon," she said through the open window, waving as she drove away.

I turned to find Leon leaning against my car, his feet crossed at the ankles. His suit coat was draped across one shoulder, and a stray piece of hair had come loose from the pomade he always wore and blew across his forehead.

"Tell me, Mr. Danes, how is life going for you?" I asked, walking over to stand beside him.

"Well," he said, sighing heavily, "I'm still not a millionaire."

I laughed, shaking my head. "But you are still full of jokes, I see."

"Come on, I've grown up a bit, haven't I?"

"Yes, you have," I nodded, smiling. "We all have, and I'll admit sometimes I miss those old, carefree days we used to take for granted."

"Remember the dance Mother held at her house for Christmas a few years back?" Leon asked, tilting his head. "Before Pearl Harbor…before everything changed."

"Yes, that was a marvelous party," I recalled, sighing. "I danced until I wore blisters on my feet, and then I danced some more."

Leon laughed, his hazel eyes twinkling down at me. "If I recall, you're quite a good dancer."

"And if *I* recall, so are you," I replied.

"Well, whenever there's another party, I'm laying claim to your first dance."

With a nod, I reached out and shook his hand. "Agreed," I said, smiling.

As I drove back to my apartment, I yawned, suddenly feeling exhausted. Between my late night and busy afternoon, I felt as if I could sleep for a week. Thoughts of Mack flitted through my mind then, and I wondered if the police had caught him. Surely he wouldn't be able to run forever, but I decided not to worry about it either way. No matter where he was, I knew he would never come back here, and it was time I stopped dwelling on it. I needed to forget Mack, the money, and even Howard, and move on with my life.

42

Eva

Sunday afternoon when Zachary came over to pick up the cake, I had it neatly packaged in a box with a bow on top.

"I hope your friend likes it," I said with a smile.

"Oh, I know he will," Zachary replied as he handed me the money. "I'm going to have a hard time not cutting myself a slice tonight. Thank your mother and grandmother for me when they get back from the market, okay?"

Nodding, I told him I would and said goodbye, noticing from where I stood in the doorway that Leon was just getting home. He waved to us both, and Zachary tooted his horn as he drove away.

Having heard the doorbell ring, Davey woke up from his nap and came to stand beside me in the open doorway, rubbing his eyes. He still wore his pajamas and his hair was standing on end. Reaching down, I did my best to smooth it.

"Mr. Leon," Davey called suddenly, waving his hand when he spotted our neighbor. "I needs help."

Glancing at Davey in surprise, I asked, "With what?"

Ignoring my question, Davey ran out to meet Leon as he walked our way, and I couldn't help but notice how nice Leon looked in his Sunday clothes.

"What do you need help with, bud?" Leon asked him.

"Fixin' my train," Davey replied. "It's broke."

"Well, we can't have any broken trains," Leon stated, placing his hand on Davey's shoulder as they walked up to the house. "Let's see if we can fix it."

"You don't have to do that," I said to Leon when they reached the porch. "I may can fix it…"

"No, Mommy, I want Mr. Leon to fix it," Davey spoke up.

"Davey, I was speaking to Mr. Leon," I scolded my son gently. "It's rude to interrupt."

"But you broke my truck," he stated stubbornly.

"How did you do that?" Leon asked me, obviously trying to hold back a smile.

Cheeks flushing, I cleared my throat and said, "Well, it broke when he dropped it, so I glued it back together."

"And?" Leon raised his eyebrows.

Shuffling my feet, I said, "And....well...I didn't realize the glue was dripping, so when I sat the truck down, it stuck to the table. By the time I got it unstuck, the bottom was torn off. So, now I have the bottom half of a toy truck glued to the kitchen table."

Unable to control himself, Leon burst into laughter and, although a little embarrassed, I couldn't help but join him.

"In that case, I'll look at the train *and* the table," Leon finally said, still snickering as he walked inside.

While Leon and Davey worked on the train, I fixed them both something to drink. I grabbed a bit of ice from the icebox, plunked the pieces into two glasses, and had just filled them sweet tea when I heard the doorbell ring. Wondering who it could be, I handed Leon and Davey their drinks and hurried to the front door.

When I opened the door, I was surprised to find three strangers standing on the other side; a man and woman in their mid-fifties, and another man who appeared to be in his forties. They were all very well dressed, and I thought that the older couple looked vaguely familiar.

"Can I help you?" I asked.

"Are you Eva Beckett?" The older man asked while the woman, whom I suspected was his wife, looked me up and down with a snobbish expression.

"Yes," I replied, nodding hesitantly.

"Mrs. Beckett," the younger man stepped in and said, "this is Mr. and Mrs. Beckett, your late husband's parents. May we come in?"

Blinking, I stood there silently for a moment, my mouth hanging open in complete shock. If the tiniest of breezes had blown just then, I believe it would have easily knocked me over. Paul's parents were here? I simply couldn't believe it.

"Well?" Mrs. Beckett snapped, cocking a well-groomed eyebrow.

"Uh, y-yes...yes, of course," I stammered, quickly stepping aside to allow them entry.

The three brushed by me, and I caught the scent of a very expensive perfume wafting from my mother-in-law's clothes. I showed them into the living room, my hands shaking as I asked them to sit down. They turned their noses up at the old furniture but sat without a word on the soft, creaky sofa, and my mind whirled as I wondered why they'd come for a visit after all this time.

"Would you like something to drink?" I asked, my hands clenched nervously in front of me.

"No," Mr. Beckett said, shaking his head. "I'd like to get right down to business. Oliver, would you like to take it from here?"

Nodding his head, "Oliver" sat up straighter and said, "Mrs. Beckett, after a thorough investigation, it's been decided that it would be in the best interest of your son, David, if he were to live with his grandparents in Connecticut. As their lawyer, I can say that all legalities would be taken care of, and you would be given an adequate sum of money on which to live the rest of your life."

I stared at Mr. Oliver, wondering if perhaps I'd somehow misunderstood, and slowly moved my eyes over to focus on my in-laws. "You...you wish to take Davey away from me?" I asked hoarsely, my voice filled with confusion and disbelief.

Looking slightly uncomfortable, Mr. Beckett shifted in his seat while his wife held my gaze, her face set in stone. "Yes," she replied coolly. "David would have a much better life with us than living here with you in...in *this* dump."

Hurt by her words, I drew back and said softly, "Paul bought this house for our family."

"Paul apparently wasn't in his right mind or he never would have married some poor little immigrant girl and moved south, of all places," Mrs. Beckett snapped, her eyes flashing, and the way she spat out the word "south" made it seem like a dirty word. "He could have had any girl he wanted and lived in the most glamorous of houses anywhere in the country, but he willingly chose to live in this place? I refuse to believe it! What did you do, brainwash him?"

Just then, I heard footsteps coming down the hall and turned, as if in a daze, to see Leon and Davey standing in the doorway.

"Is everything alright?" Leon asked with concern, his gaze on me. He had, no doubt, heard the strain in our voices all the way from the kitchen, and now could see how pale and shaken I was.

I opened my mouth to tell him what was going on when Mrs. Beckett sniffed and said, "You've already forgotten about our son and moved on, I see."

My eyes widening at her words, I felt my cheeks flush with embarrassment.

"Dear, not in front of the boy," Mr. Beckett said softly, reaching over to squeeze her hand. Beckoning to Davey, he said, "Come here, David, and say hello to your grandparents."

Sensing the tension in the room, Davey shook his head and stepped behind Leon, his hand clutching Leon's pants leg.

"Davey, go to your room, please," I told him gently, and he obeyed without protest.

Pursing his lips, Mr. Beckett turned back to me and said, "We'd like to take David with us as soon as possible."

"You...you can't have my son," I heard myself say.

His jaw clenched, Mr. Beckett looked at Mr. Oliver and nodded.

"In that case," Mr. Oliver said, "we will be forced to take the matter to court. We've gathered enough information in the last few months to deem you an unfit mother and have David taken away from you. Trust me, Mrs. Beckett, when I say that any judge will see it our way."

"Eva is a wonderful mother," Leon spoke up, coming to stand beside me, "and there are many people who will testify to that fact, including myself."

"We have quite a bit of evidence that says otherwise," Mr. Beckett snapped.

"Evidence?" I asked, my brow furrowing. "What do you mean?"

"We hired a private detective that spent some time here observing the situation," Mr. Beckett stated. "We know that you barely make enough money to pay the bills and keep a roof over David's head, and after already losing one job, you now have to work six days a week to get by. We also learned that David was nearly killed when he fell from a tree a few months ago, and that he recently contracted polio and came very close to dying. It sounds to me you're so busy working that you cannot be the kind of mother David needs; we had enough evidence to prove this months ago, and would have come sooner if not for the epidemic."

It felt as if they had completely knocked the wind from my lungs, and I stared at them in shock. They'd sent someone to *spy* on me? It was all beginning to make sense now; the strange man that followed me home that cold night in March, Davey's "friend" he'd told me about after he fell from the tree, the phone call to the bank about my mortgage payment, and possibly even the intruder who'd left the pocket knife behind. This was all the workings of my in-laws, these two people seated before me that hated me so much they would take my son away from me.

"I'll...I'll hire a lawyer," I said, my tone breathless and shaky.

"My dear, lawyers cost money, and we know you don't have any," Mr. Beckett stated with a smirk, and I felt that he could see right through me. He knew I was frightened and intimidated, which gave them even more of an upper hand. If Leon hadn't been there to support me, I don't know what I would have done.

"I know a lawyer who is one of the best in Savannah," Leon stated, his jaw clenching. "He's a good friend of mine, and I'm sure he'll do whatever he can to help Eva."

Mr. Beckett glared at Leon for a moment, obviously fighting to control his temper. After a moment, he took his wife's hand and they both stood to their feet. Looking at me, his gaze cold and hard, he said, "If this is the direction you choose to take, then so be it. But mark my words, young lady, you'll lose this case and you won't ever see David again, nor will you get a cent of the money we offered you. And just so you know, that private detective will still be watching you and reporting back to us."

His speech left me chilled and shaken and I took a step back, wrapping my arms protectively around my waist. Without another word, the three marched from the room and out of my house, slamming the front door behind them. I stood like a wooden statue, my back straight and tense until I heard the sound of their footsteps fading away, and then I slowly deflated. Leon took my arm and led me over to the sofa where I collapsed and, burying my face in my hands, began to sob uncontrollably.

Leon sat beside me and gently pulled me into his arms. "Don't worry, Eva," he said, "no judge is going to take a child away from its mother. I'll talk to my lawyer friend tomorrow and see what he says."

He let me cry for a bit and, after a moment, patted me on the back and said, "Come on now, pull yourself together. Davey needs you; he's upset and knows that something is wrong."

Taking a deep breath, I slowly nodded my head and, accepting the handkerchief Leon offered me, wiped my eyes. My head pounded and I felt sick to my stomach, but I knew Leon was right; my son needed me.

"Thank you, Leon," I said, forcing a small, brave smile. "I'm so glad you were here. Please, let me know what your friend says as soon as possible."

"I will," he nodded, leaning over to kiss me lightly on the forehead. "It's going to be okay, I just know it."

I hoped he was right, but the hard, heavy lump of fear in the pit of my stomach made me wonder if he could be wrong.

43

Vivian

When I greeted everyone as they came in to work the next morning, I immediately noticed Eva's red, swollen eyes and knew that something was wrong.

"Can I talk to you?" She asked me in a low voice.

Nodding, I led her into my office and had barely closed the door when she burst into tears and told me everything. I stood there, my eyes widening in disbelief as she relayed her story. By the time she'd finished, I was utterly and completely flabbergasted.

"I can't believe the nerve of those people!" I exclaimed. "How can they be so cruel?"

"I don't know," Eva replied, sniffling. "Leon is going to talk to a lawyer friend of his, but I'm so worried. What will I do if they take my son away from me?"

My mind whirling, I glanced over at the safe that stood in the corner, a thought tickling in the back of my mind. I needed most of Mack's money to pay the restaurant's bills, but Eva was my friend and she needed help. I knew how it felt to lose a child and wouldn't wish that kind of pain on my worst enemy, let alone a close friend. Without a second thought, I made a decision and hurried to open the safe.

"Here," I said, handing Eva a handful of the cash. "You'll need money if Leon's friend charges his full fee."

Eva's eyes were wide as she stared in shock at the bundle of money in her hands. Shaking her head, she looked up at me and said, "I...I can't accept this."

"Yes, you can," I insisted, pushing her hand away when she attempted to give the money back. "Please, Eva, I want you to have it. I lost my child and I don't want you to suffer the same fate."

Her eyes once again filling with tears, Eva threw her arms around me and whispered, "Thank you, Vivian, you do not know what this means to me." Pulling back to wipe her eyes, she added, "I'll pay you back some day, I promise."

"There's no need for that," I said with a smile, patting her on the back. "If you don't think you can work today, it's fine; I don't want you to be so distracted that you chop off a finger or something."

"No, I'll be fine," she replied, shaking her head. "Can I leave my purse in here, though? I don't want to just lay it anywhere with all of that money inside."

Eva handed me her purse and headed to the kitchen, her back stiff as she tried to maintain control of her emotions. I'd just locked the purse in the safe and sat down at my desk when there was a knock on my door.

"Come in," I called.

The door opened and Zachary stepped inside. Pleasantly surprised at seeing him, I was on the verge of saying so when I noticed the unusually stormy look on his face.

"Is everything alright?" I asked hesitantly.

"No, it's not," he stated as he walked towards me. He held a newspaper in his hand and, waving it in the air, asked, "What on earth were you thinking?"

"Uh…I'm a little confused…"

Opening the paper, Zachary slapped it down in front of me and pointed at the headline, which boldly read: **POLICE IN SEARCH OF ESCAPED PRISONER**. I then glanced below and saw my name written in the story. It said, "Vivian McCombs assisted the police in the attempt to catch the man responsible for setting fire to her home last February."

"Wow, I didn't realize this would be in the newspaper," I muttered.

"So, this is what was going on Friday that you wouldn't tell me about?" Zachary wanted to know. "You were planning to trap a man, a dangerous convict, in the middle of the night?"

"Well…yes, but there's a little more to it than that," I stated defensively, not caring for the accusatory tone in his voice.

Leaning over, Zachary placed his hands on my desk and asked, "*Why* didn't you tell me? Good grief, Vivian, you could have been killed!"

"But I wasn't, so it's fine," I said, shrugging my shoulders. I'd never seen him so riled, and I didn't like the way he'd stormed into my office to rant at me over something that had nothing to do with him.

His jaw clenched, Zachary stood back up and said evenly, "I don't know why I'm surprised that you didn't ask for my help. You don't think you ever need anyone's help, do you?"

My temper flaring, I snapped, "I really don't see that it's any of your business."

When a look of hurt flashed through his eyes, I immediately regretted my harsh words.

"Alright then, fine," he stated, spinning on his heel to leave the same way in which he'd come. He'd just made it to the door when someone knocked loudly from the other side, and I moaned with frustration.

"Come in," I called out, adding under my breath, "I'm going to have to get a "Do Not Disturb" sign."

The door opened and Officer Wright stepped inside, glancing at Zachary in surprise as he brushed past him. *Apparently, the good doctor has a hidden temper that matches his hair*, I thought, feeling a bit of guilt over our argument. I probably would have gone after him and apologized if Gabe hadn't shown up.

"You've read the news, I see," Gabe stated, nodding at the newspaper that was still lying on my desk. He wore his uniform and had taken off his hat, his hair a bit mussed on the top.

"Yes," I said, nodding. "You didn't waste any time in clearing my name, did you?"

Gabe laughed as he sat across from me, and I noticed how handsome he looked when he smiled. "I figured the newspaper would be the fastest way of doing so," he replied. "I hope you don't mind."

"Not at all," I assured him. "Thank you, Gabe."

Glancing around the office, Gabe said, "You've really got a nice place. I've eaten here a few times, and the food is delicious."

"Thanks," I replied, leaning back in my chair. "My father has always been the brains of the operation, but he had an accident a few months ago, so I took over."

"He must be the one you get your drive from," he stated, grinning slightly.

"He is," I nodded, laughing. "Well, anyway, I know you didn't come by to talk about the restaurant or my father. Is there any news on Mack?"

"It looks like he's given us the slip," Gabe sighed. "I'm sorry, Vivian. We've sent his wanted poster to police stations all around the country, so I'm sure it's just a matter of time before someone spots him; he can't hide forever."

"I hope not," I muttered, disappointed that my plan hadn't worked.

After Gabe left, I thought again of Zachary and wondered if I should call him. I picked up the phone once, only to put it back down again. He had no right to act the way he did, and if anyone needed to apologize, it was him.

Eva

I saw Zachary leave the restaurant, and by the look on his face, I knew that something had happened between him and Vivian. When I asked her about it later, however, she simply waved her hand and said, "Oh, don't worry about that, you've got enough on your plate right now."

She was right, of course. All during work, I kept thinking about Davey and worrying about what could happen. What would I do if Paul's parents took him away from me? And if they did, would they even let me see him anymore? Mr. Beckett had said they wouldn't, but surely they wouldn't forbid a child from ever seeing his mother.

As I chopped carrots for a soup Cook and I were making, Jackson sidled up beside me and asked, "Is everything alright?"

Sighing, I told him what happened and, his eyes widening, he said, "How awful! I'm so sorry, Eva. Is there anything I can do?"

I shook my head, trying to hold back the tears; I didn't want Cook to get us both into trouble. "No, thank you," I said softly.

He reached out and touched my arm then, and I stopped chopping to look at him. He was, once again, standing too close for comfort, and when his fingers squeezed my arm a bit too tightly, I tried to pull away but he wouldn't let me. His gaze fervent, he said in a low tone, "Eva, I wish…I wish that…"

"Jackson, why aren't you washing dishes?" Cook's loud voice interrupted, and Jackson immediately let go of my arm, his cheeks flushing.

"I was talking to Eva," he snapped, and I blinked in surprise; Jackson rarely talked back to Cook.

Raising her eyebrows, Cook glared at him and said, "Talk to her on your own time and get back to work."

His jaw clenching, Jackson jerked around and went back to his station without another word. I felt a little sorry for him, as it was humiliating to get into trouble at work, and wondered what it was he'd wished to tell me.

On my way home from work, Kirk and Mr. Fernsby drove by and offered me a ride. Thankful for the chance to get off my feet, I readily agreed and slid into the back seat.

"Are there any updates on your son?" Mr. Fernsby asked, turning in his seat to look at me. "Do you think that your in-laws will really take him from you?" Seeing the look of surprise on my face, he added, "One of the neighbors told me what happened."

I knew Leon had told no one and wondered how the other neighbors had found out. Too tired to give it much thought, I said, "They're taking me to court, but I hope a lawyer friend of Leon's will be able to help me."

"Have you ever thought that it just might be for the best?" Kirk suddenly spoke up, looking at me in the rearview mirror.

Blinking, I asked, "What makes you say that?"

With a shrug, Kirk said in a cool, matter-of-fact tone, "Your in-laws are wealthy and could give your son a much better life than you could ever provide."

"Kirk, don't be ridiculous," Mr. Fernsby scolded his grandson, and I felt tears welling up in my eyes.

"How could a life without his mother be better for him?" I whispered, wrapping my arms around my waist.

Kirk pulled up in front of my house and I got out of the car, feeling lower and more drained than when I'd stepped in. Mr. Fernsby told me goodbye, his faded brown eyes filled with concern, and before I could shut the door, Kirk said, "Better do your best to enjoy the time you have left with your son."

I stood on the curb and watched them drive away, wondering why Kirk always seemed to want to punish me. As I turned and walked up the driveway, however, I wondered if he was simply trying to prepare me for the worst. After all, he could be right; I may not have much time left to spend with Davey.

Taking a deep breath, I pasted on a smile and went inside, not wishing for my family to know how upset I was. I'd just gotten out of the shower when Leon came over, and making certain that Davey was still in his room playing, I ushered him into the kitchen where the four of us could talk privately. We all sat around the table with a cup of coffee, nervous and anxious to hear what Leon had to say.

"I have good news," Leon said, pouring a bit of sugar into his coffee. "I talked to my friend, and he said that he'll take the case. His fee is quite high, but I'm sure…"

"I can pay him," I interrupted. "Vivian…well, she gave me an advance of sorts."

Leon looked at me in surprise, but didn't ask any questions. "He said he thinks you have a good chance of winning," he continued, "but your in-laws are very wealthy and carry a lot of influence. I trust him, though, Eva; I wasn't kidding when I said he's the best."

Taking a deep breath, I considered everything Leon had said. "When does he think we'll have to go to court?" I asked.

"Probably sometime in November."

"I can't believe Paul's parents are doing this," Nana spoke up, her tone heavy as she reached up to rub her eyes.

Ever since I'd told her and Mutter the news, they'd both been completely beside themselves, and I hated to see the toll it was already taking on them.

"Just do everything by the book until this is over," Leon said, looking at me. "Keep working, pay your bills on time, and just stay under the radar as much as possible; especially since the detective is still trailing you. I wish we knew who he was."

"So do I," I agreed, shivering slightly at the thought of someone following me, watching my every move.

We talked a bit more, going over details and backup plans, and when Leon stood up to leave, I realized how lucky we were to know him.

"Thank you for all of your help, Leon," I told him as we walked outside. "I don't know what we would do without you. How can we ever repay you?"

"You're quite welcome," he said, smiling warmly. Reaching up to touch my chin, he said, "Just keep that pretty chin up; that's all the payment I'll need."

As I tucked Davey into bed that night and sang him a lullaby, I fought back the tears that threatened to choke me. What would I do without this sweet, precious angel to sing to and cuddle each night? I knew I worked a lot and wasn't able to be with him as much as I'd like, but I made a point to give him my time every evening when I got home from work and all day on Sundays. Nana and Mutter were also just as important to him as I was, and I wondered what would happen if we were all taken away from him and he was forced to live with two cold, heartless strangers?

He was asleep now, his ash blonde hair falling onto the pillow and surrounding his face like a halo, and I leaned down and kissed his chubby cheek, listening for a moment to his slow, steady breaths as he slept. Sighing softly, I stood and walked from the room, glancing back at him once again before turning off the light. I went into my room then and kneeled by my bed, praying well into the night and begging God to please grant us favor.

44

Vivian

It was mid-October when I received a call from the bank with the news that they'd finally found a buyer for the farm. I went down to the office and signed the papers, feeling relieved finally to have it over with, while also feeling a bit dismal. The farm was the last tie I had to Howard and my baby, and now it was gone, too.

Halloween was coming up, and the city had decided to celebrate this year. All festivities had been canceled the last couple of years because of the war, but the mayor thought it would be a good idea to hold a parade and bazaar, with local vendors donating half of their profits to the war effort. I decided to do a booth for the restaurant and would sell baked goods along with some cookbooks full of "rationing recipes" one could use during the sugar shortage. By the time the weekend arrived, I was exhausted from all the planning and baking, but excited for the event. Father had arrived back home and offered to help me; his stay in Atlanta had done him a great deal of good, and I gladly accepted his offer of help, happy to have him home.

The day of the celebration arrived bright and sunny. The parade was to start at six o'clock and would end at the bazaar at Forsyth Park. Father and I worked all afternoon setting up the booth, and we had just finished when I saw Savannah hurrying my way.

"Vivian, aren't you coming to watch the parade?" She asked as she tied a purple scarf around her neck. She also wore two large, golden hoop earrings and a full purple skirt. "We'd better hurry if we want to get there before it starts."

"Oh, I don't know…" I said, glancing uncertainly at Father.

"Go ahead," he said, smiling and waving at Savannah.

"Come on," she said, grabbing my hand. "By the way, Scarlett O'hara, you look amazing!"

I'd worn a full length white dress with green flowers, a green sash, and a wide-brimmed hat with a green bow. I wasn't wearing a petticoat and my dress looked a little different from the one Vivien Leigh wore in Gone with the Wind, but with my dark hair and green eyes, it wasn't hard to imagine who I was dressed as.

"Thank you," I replied, smiling. "And you make a fabulous gypsy. I love the hoop earrings!"

Giggling like girls, we crossed the street and hurried through the crowd until we found Leon and Mrs. Emma waiting at the parade starting point.

"Where are your aunt and uncle?" I asked Savannah, out of breath from the walk.

"Aunt Deb said she didn't care to see a 'silly little parade', but she'll be at the bazaar later," Savannah replied, grinning as she rolled her eyes.

Shaking my head, I playfully elbowed Leon as I stood on my tiptoes to see over the woman's hat in front of me. When he elbowed me back, I almost toppled over, and he quickly caught my arm with a laugh.

"Do excuse me, Miss Scah-lett," Leon said, bowing dramatically from the waist.

My eyes twinkling, I surveyed his costume and asked, "Are you supposed to be a prince?"

"Yes, I am," he replied, holding up his hand as he added, "and I know what you're going to say."

"What's that?"

"That I was a prince before I put the costume on," he replied with a grin, wiggling his eyebrows.

Snickering, I glanced around and asked, "Where is Eva? I thought she told me she was coming."

"She should be here soon," he replied, looking around in search of her. "She's been so upset the last several weeks that I didn't think she would come, but she told me this morning before I left for work that she'd changed her mind."

"I spoke with her yesterday and told her it would be good for both she and Davey; I even talked her into making him a last-minute costume for the contest," I told him.

"There she is," Leon stated, waving his hand.

I turned to find Eva and Davey walking towards us, hand in hand. Davey was dressed like a firefighter in a long, black and yellow overcoat with rubber boots and a red fireman's hat, and I exclaimed, "Oh, Eva, how did you make such a wonderful costume in such a short amount of time? He looks adorable!"

"Nana and Mutter did most of the work," she replied, smiling fondly at her son. "I don't know what I'd do without them. I didn't have time to make myself a costume, so I found some old clothes of Mutter's and tried to dress like a flapper..." she paused, glancing around uncertainly before asking, "Is it too much?"

We all quickly assured her she made a great flapper, and Eva smiled with relief, tugging self-consciously at the bell-shaped hat that fit her head snugly and hung low over her forehead. She wore a loose fitting dress with ruffles, a long strand of pearls, and bright red lipstick. She did, indeed,

232

look stunning.

"Hey, if you're a fireman, buddy, where's your Dalmatian?" Leon asked Davey, tapping the top of his miniature fireman's hat.

Tilting his head up and nearly losing said hat, Davey tried to ask what a Dalmatian was but got his words so tangled that he finally stopped and, brow furrowed, said with a dramatic sigh, "I dunno what that is."

Laughing, Leon picked Davey up and sat him on his shoulders. "It's a big white dog with black spots that firemen have," he told him.

His eyes brightening, Davey looked over at Eva and asked excitedly, "Mommy, can we get one?"

Before Eva could answer, the parade started and we were all immediately distracted by the music, clowns, cars filled with various characters in costume, and marching soldiers. The sight of the soldiers, both young and old, from the current war and the first world war, brought tears to my eyes. Each of the men bore scars, both internal and external, and I wondered if this war would ever end; sometimes I truly thought it wouldn't. Glancing over, I saw that Savannah was crying as well, and I reached out to take her hand, giving it a gentle squeeze. She'd seen the war firsthand in Hawaii, and I knew she was also thinking of Connor.

As I continued to watch the parade, my eyes fell upon a familiar face across the street, and I did a double-take. Zachary was standing among the crowd dressed as what appeared to be a lumberjack, and as I'd never seen him dressed in anything but a suit or scrubs, I stared at him in surprise. He wore a long sleeve, blue plaid flannel shirt tucked into a pair of dark brown pants with matching suspenders, and I couldn't help but notice that, for a doctor, his shoulders looked very broad. I suddenly realized that he wasn't alone, but was apparently with the young lady standing next to him. She was tall and blonde and kept smiling up at Zachary, and I wondered who she was.

Just then, Zachary turned his head and looked directly at me, and I quickly glanced away, feeling embarrassed at being caught staring. I hadn't seen him since our last meeting, and wondered if he was still angry with me. I suppose what I did with Mack *had* been rather foolish, but it was all over now and there was nothing I could do about it.

The parade was almost over, and I told everyone that I'd see them shortly at the bazaar. With thoughts of Mack still lingering in the back of my mind, I felt uneasy as I headed back towards the park and wished I'd asked Leon to walk with me. Nearly everyone in the crowd wore some sort of costume, and the faces of ghosts, goblins, and witches in the growing twilight were making me feel a bit unsettled. I hurried my footsteps, anxious to get back to the safety of my booth as soon as possible.

I'd just made it to the edge of the crowd when someone grabbed me roughly by the arm and yanked me back. Gasping, I spun around to find a gigantic man dressed all in black looming over me, his icy fingers still wrapped tightly around my arm. He wore the costume of a skeleton, and his white mask with the evil smile and black, hollowed out eyes staring sightlessly back at me sent chills down my spine.

My heart in my throat, I was on the verge of screaming when he said, "Be careful, ma'am, you almost stepped out in front of a car."

Blinking as realization set in, I gave a quick, shaky laugh and a "thank you" before hurrying away. ***Pull yourself together, Viv, or you'll end up back in Martinsville***, I told myself.

Once back at the booth with my father, I felt my nerves begin to calm. Pretty soon, everyone from the parade started streaming in to the bazaar and our booth was quickly bombarded with laughing, chattering customers, one of which was Mrs. Fitzgerald, one of the ladies I'd overhead talking about me in the parking lot after church.

"How are you, Mrs. Fitzgerald?" I asked politely, forcing a smile.

"Don't you dare ask about me with everything you've been through, bless your heart," she said, reaching out to grasp my hand. "I read all about it in the newspaper the other day and, goodness gracious, you must have been scared out of your mind! I only wish the police had caught that dreadful man. Tell me, dear, how much are these brownies?"

She was rattling on so that I was having a hard time keeping up. "Brownies?" I asked, blinking. "Oh, they're twenty-five cents a piece. How is your daughter, Mrs. Fitzgerald?"

"She's fabulous, just fabulous," Mrs. Fitzgerald gushed, beaming. "In fact, she and her husband are celebrating their ten year wedding anniversary next weekend, and I was wondering if you'd be interested in catering the party?"

So, the article was already working its magic. It looked like I would owe Gabe another "thank you".

"I'd love to, Mrs. Fitzgerald," I said, graciously accepting the offer.

As if reading my mind, Gabe appeared at my booth right after Mrs. Fitzgerald had left. He was wearing his uniform, and I tapped my chin mischievously and said, "Hmm, let me guess…you're a police officer?"

"Very clever," he replied, chuckling. "I'm on duty tonight because, as I'm sure you're well aware, Halloween is when all the pranksters and vandals decide to come out of hiding."

"Well, I hope you still get to have a bit of fun," I said, giving him the bag of chocolate chip cookies he was eyeing for free. "I know these aren't stale doughnuts and I'm afraid that I don't have any coffee, but I hope you'll still enjoy them."

"I suppose they'll just have to do," he said with a sigh, his eyes twinkling. "Thank you, Vivian. You look stunning, by the way."

Surprised by the compliment, I didn't have a chance to respond as the next person in line leaned in to ask me a question. Gabe moved on to chat with my father, and after a while, I once again caught sight of Zachary and his friend. There was a young man with them this time, and when the woman grabbed both men by the arms and dragged them to my table, I almost laughed at the look of dread on Zachary's face. At that moment, I thought he'd rather be in the morgue than walking toward me.

"Your desserts look absolutely delicious!" The girl cried, flashing a perfect white smile. Turning to bat her eyes at Zachary, she asked, "Don't you think so, Zach?"

"Yes, delicious," he replied softly, nodding politely at me. His reddish-brown hair was parted on one side and hung loose with no pomade, and the deep blue of his shirt brought out the normally hidden, darker flecks in his aqua eyes.

"Aren't you going to introduce me to your friends, *Zach*?" I asked sweetly, knowing he didn't wish to talk to me any more than he had to.

"I didn't realize you two knew each other," the girl said, reaching out to shake my hand. "I'm Violet, and this is my beau, Jeremiah."

My eyebrows shot up of their own accord, but I quickly played it off and said I was pleased to meet them. *If he's her beau, the poor fellow*, I thought to myself, watching as Violet continued to flirt blatantly with Zachary.

"I'll take a piece of this blueberry cake," Zachary stated. He handed me a quarter, spoke to my father, and walked off with the cake without another word, leaving his two companions to stare after him in surprise.

Pursing my lips, I watched him go with some irritation. He was apparently still upset with me, but did he really have the right to act so distant and cool? I nearly went after him to give him a piece of something other than cake, but got sidetracked by another customer.

It didn't take long for the booth to sell out, and after we'd packed everything into the back of the restaurant's truck, I offered to drive Father home.

"It's not a far walk," he said. His eyesight was much improved, something for which I was very grateful, and I didn't protest at his wanting to walk. He'd made it clear that he didn't wish for me to coddle him, and I quickly kissed him on the cheek and told him to have a good night, thanking him for his help.

I then went back to the main event to walk around and find my friends. They'd all stopped by my booth earlier to buy something, and when I heard the announcement for the best costume contest, I hurried in that direction in search of Eva.

When I found her, I nearly turned and headed in the opposite direction, but Leon saw me and waved me over. Sighing, I walked up to stand by Eva's side, forcing a smile at her other companion.

"We meet again," I stated drolly.

"It would seem so," was Zachary's curt reply.

Savannah was there, as well, and she shot me a look as if to ask, "What

235

was that about?"

Rolling my eyes, I shrugged as we all turned to watch Davey line up with the other children, his fireman's hat tilting precariously to one side. My heart warmed as I watched him, his blue eyes bright as he wiggled with excitement, and we all gave a loud cheer when he came in third place. With a cry of joy, Davey ran from the stage to proudly show us his ribbon, tripping along the way over a small hole in the grass.

Afterwards, we made our way through more of the booths, each filled with unique gifts and items that ranged from paintings to flowers to knitted scarves. I bought a scarf, a pair of handmade earrings, and an antique pocket watch for Father; it looked just like the one he used to have, and I knew he would love the gift. Savannah told us she was going in search of her aunt and uncle, and I hugged her bye as the rest of us continued through the park.

When we finally reached the glorious, lit up fountain which rested on the north end of the park, I stopped for a moment and just took it all in. The large pathway that led up to the fountain had been sectioned off for dancing, and an archway with a sign that read "$.15 per couple" rested at the entrance. I heard someone call Zachary's name and watched as he walked toward one of his co-workers, stating he'd catch up to us later, and I felt a bit of disappointment over his sudden departure.

Turning, I gazed back at the scene before me, soaking in the peaceful, breathtaking beauty like a sponge. The huge, gloriously white fountain, which was first erected in 1858, stood majestically at the end of the wide, oak draped pathway with soft, misty arcs of water spraying in all directions. Lamp posts and benches lined each side of the path, and with the music playing and couples dancing, it felt almost like a scene out of a fairytale.

"Dance, mommy, dance!" Davey cried, clapping his hands, and with a smile, Eva picked him up and began to dance with him.

"I seem to remember telling you I had a claim on your next dance," Leon spoke up to my left, smiling at me.

"I believe you're right," I replied, tossing my hat into the nearby grass as I took his offered hand.

Leon dropped the money into the jar with a *clink*, and we joined the others beneath the mossy tree branches and swayed to the slow, soft music. The moon was bright, millions of stars twinkled overhead, and a gentle breeze blew the loose tendrils around my face. The lamps that lined the walkway made Leon's eyes glitter, and when he pulled me closer, I glanced over his shoulder and saw Zachary standing along the sidelines watching us, his gaze never leaving mine until Leon spun me around.

"I was right," Leon said when the song ended, "you *are* an excellent dancer."

Smiling, I followed him back out through the archway, not failing to notice that Zachary was still there. When the music started back up, he put some money into the jar and, much to my surprise, walked over and asked me to dance. After a slight hesitation, I accepted his outstretched hand and let him lead me back onto the dance floor.

The silence between us was thick and heavy, and I struggled with what to say. Should I apologize? Tell him I was sorry for not confiding in him when he asked what was wrong that Friday night? Zachary, however, spoke first.

"I've been acting badly, haven't I?" He asked, his voice low.

I looked up at him in surprise, his eyes as piercing as ever. "Yes, quite," I replied slowly.

"I'm sorry," he said, his face somber, "I had no right to treat you that way."

"No, you didn't," I sniffed. When Zachary cocked an eyebrow at me, I sighed and said, "Perhaps what I did *was* a bit foolish."

Zachary raised both eyebrows. "A bit?"

"Alright, a lot," I admitted.

"Yes, it was," he replied, nodding, "but it still wasn't my place to act the way I did. I just...I was worried about your safety, and a little hurt that you didn't trust me enough to ask for my help. I thought we were better friends than that."

"We are, Zachary," I said, "but I told Mack I wouldn't involve anyone, and I was too afraid to confide in you. I did, however, take a risk and ask you to deliver that note to Officer Wright. Thank you for doing that, by the way."

"You're welcome. Just promise me one thing, will you?"

"What's that?" I asked, tilting my head.

"Promise me you'll do nothing that crazy again," Zachary said, his eyes serious as he studied me.

"Oh, I don't know..." I paused mischievously, a grin slowly spreading over my face when Zachary moaned with frustration. "Okay, I promise."

"Good," he said, a warm smile pulling at his lips as he drew me closer. "Has anyone told you tonight that you're even prettier than Vivien Leigh?"

His breath tickled the hair around my forehead, and the way the light flickered in his eyes made me feel warm all over. Pulling back a bit, I shook my head and said, "No, you're the only one willing to lie to me."

Zachary laughed, his straight, white teeth flashing against the five o'clock shadow he'd chosen not to shave. "I'm serious. Of the two, you're by far the prettier Vivian."

"She spells hers differently, so it doesn't count," I quipped, winking at him. "But thank you."

When the song ended and we walked away, I suddenly realized how much I'd missed Zachary the last couple of weeks.

45

Eva

Holding my son close, I breathed in his familiar scent as we danced beneath the moonlight, his soft hair tickling my nose. I could remember my father dancing with me in the same way when I was a little girl, and I suddenly felt tears prick the backs of my eyes. If only he were here now, he would know exactly how to fix this mess, but it was up to me and I didn't know what to do. I felt worried and stressed, and very much afraid.

As if sensing the depth of my emotions, Davey wrapped his arms tighter around my neck, his little fireman's hat bumping against my ear. I closed my eyes and sighed, soaking in the feeling of holding my precious little boy so close. Surely the judge wouldn't take him away from me; surely no one could be that cruel.

The music ended then and I shook my head, forcing the negative, burdensome thoughts from my mind. Kissing Davey on the cheek, I placed him back on his feet and the two of us wondered off, hand in hand, to do a bit of exploring. I watched as Davey's eyes sparkled with excitement over the thrill and intrigue of the bazaar, and I could hardly keep up with him when he dragged me over to the petting zoo to see the goats, ponies, and rabbits.

A bit later, we'd just finished watching a puppet show when Davey pointed to a nearby clown handing out cotton candy and cried, "Mommy, candy!"

"Alright, you can have one, but then we've got to go home," I said, laughing as he ran up to the clown and politely asked for the candy. It was nearly nine o'clock and way past Davey's bedtime. Leon was going to take us home, and I glanced around in search of him, wondering if he was still dancing.

"Come on," I told Davey, taking his hand, "let's go look for Mr. Leon."

We were just turning to head back in the fountain's direction when someone in the crowd caught my eye and I stopped. Through the laughing, chattering people, there stood a man wearing a black robe with a pointed hood. He carried a large stick, wore a fake white beard that hung to his waist, and I immediately recognized the costume as being that of Knecht Ruprecht, a character from German folklore. According to legend, he was the "dark helper" of Saint Nicholas, and would abduct and punish naughty children.

The hood was pulled low and I couldn't make out the man's face, but I sensed he was looking directly at me; I could somehow feel his eyes boring into mine. The crowd moved all around him, but he stood completely still, and I suddenly realized that something about him seemed oddly familiar. I couldn't, however, put my finger on exactly what it was.

Feeling a bit unsettled, I pulled Davey closer and said, "Let's go see if Mr. Leon is still dancing."

As we made our way back across the grass, I glanced over my shoulder and realized with a quick intake of breath that the man appeared to be following us. His head was angled downward, the hood casting a dark shadow across his face, and there was something so ominous and almost evil in the slow, methodical way in which he moved towards us that I felt a stab of fear shoot down my spine.

Clutching Davey's hand tighter, I quickened my steps, the smiles all around us suddenly more like malevolent sneers, and the laughter like that of loud, barking crows. The sounds of music and chattering seemed amplified somehow and blended together to ring piercingly in my ears. One person bumped into me, and then another, their apologies falling on deaf ears as I tried to push my way through. I glanced back again and saw that he was drawing closer. Should I scream? Was I overreacting? I knew that few people in America had ever even heard of Knecht Ruprecht, so how odd was it that someone had chosen that particular costume and seemed to be following me?

"There you are!"

A hand grabbed my arm, and I gasped. Spinning around, heart in my throat, my panic slowly turned to relief when I realized it was Leon.

When he saw my expression, Leon immediately asked, "What's wrong?"

"That man," I whispered breathlessly, trying to keep my voice low so Davey couldn't hear me. "He's following us."

"What man?" Leon asked, glancing around.

"I-I don't know," I said, feeling flustered as I tried to explain. "He's wearing the costume of Knecht Ruprecht."

"*Who?*"

Turning around to point him out, my hand just drifted aimlessly as I pointed to the crowd full of people. Knecht Ruprecht, however, was not among them.

"I don't know," I said, dropping my hand with a sigh. "It appears he's gone."

Wrapping my arms around my waist, I shivered, my eyes still searching the crowd. I hadn't imagined it, I knew that much, but perhaps he hadn't been following me after all.

"Do you think it's the same man that's been bothering you the last few months?" Leon asked with concern.

"I don't know." I shook my head.

"Come on, let's get out of here," Leon said, reaching out to take my arm.

On the way home, Davey fell asleep in my arms and I covered a yawn as well. I couldn't, however, get that man out of my mind, and wondered if it was the private detective my in-laws had hired. I felt my stomach sink and began to wish that I'd just stayed home tonight.

"He seemed to have a lot of fun at the bazaar," Leon said, interrupting my thoughts as he nodded his head at Davey with a fond smile. "I'm glad y'all came."

"We had a wonderful time," I replied, gently running a finger down my son's cheek as I tried to clear my thoughts. After a moment, I sighed and said, "He'll be four on Thursday, you know, and all I can think about is what if it's the last birthday I'll ever be able to celebrate with him?"

Leon reached out and took my hand, giving it a squeeze. "Don't think that way," he said.

We pulled up in front of my house, and I waited until Leon came around to open the door for me.

"Do you want me to carry him inside?" He asked when we reached the front door.

"No," I shook my head, "I've got him. Thank you for bringing us home."

I went inside and put Davey to bed, not bothering to change his clothes. Afterward, I went into the living room with Nana and Mutter and told them of the fun we had that night, trying to act as positive as I could.

"Davey even won third place for his costume," I told them. "I wish you both could have been there."

"Oh, you know how my rheumatism bothers me at night," Nana said with a smile, "but I'm so glad to hear that you both had a good time."

With a yawn, I kissed them both goodnight, took a quick bath, and went to bed. Before turning off my light, however, I double-checked the lock on my window as thoughts of the private detective and Knecht Ruprecht still hung in the back of my mind.

THE SHADOW

He'd made certain to keep his distance as he followed them home, and after the neighbor left and went into his own house, he stepped from the shadows and crossed the street, drawing closer to her bedroom window. The bushes rustled slightly and he winced, making certain to proceed more quietly. The curtains were drawn, but there was just enough of a crack in the middle for him to see inside. He stood there, waiting for her to go to bed; he wanted to watch her sleep.

As he waited, he thought about the bazaar and how much fun it had been to watch Eva squirm when she spotted him in that costume. The look of fear in her eyes as she hurried away from him was exhilarating, and his little disappearing act afterwards was one for the books. He knew she suspected he was the private detective, she just didn't know *who* he was, and he could hardly wait for her to find out. It would be on his own terms, however, and only when he was ready for her to know.

Finally, she opened the bedroom door and stepped inside. She was in her nightgown, and her beautiful, ash blonde hair spilled down over her shoulders. He watched as she rubbed cream onto her face and neck, and then she reached to turn off the light.

Something seemed to stop her, though, and she hesitated, suddenly looking directly at the window. He froze, his heart pounding when she began to walk toward him. Slowly, he sank down amongst the bushes, hoping she couldn't hear his movements. He heard the curtains move along their rod as she jiggled the window, and after a moment her footsteps drifted away and the bedroom light flicked off.

Sighing with relief, he slowly stood back up to watch her sleep, but the crack in the curtains was gone.

46

Eva

Mid-November and the day we were to appear in court arrived much quicker than I'd anticipated. As I got ready to leave, I was a basket of nerves. My hands shook as I pinned my hair up, and I finally just dropped my arms at my sides and stared at my reflection for a moment. What I saw staring back was fear, worry, and anxiety, and I took a deep breath, trying to calm my nerves and make myself believe it was all going to be okay.

Mutter had agreed to stay home with Davey, and just before we left, she took me in her arms and pulled me close. "It's going to be alright, der Schatz," she whispered, her voice tight with emotion. "I'll be praying for you."

Leon drove Nana and me to the courthouse, and just before we walked inside, Nana took my hand and gave it a gentle squeeze. I knew that she and Mutter were just as nervous as I was, and I squeezed her hand in return, fighting the tears that threatened to spill over. Even though Mutter couldn't be with us, I was thankful to have Nana by my side.

When we entered the courtroom, Leon joined Vivian, Savannah, and Zachary, who were all seated in the back. I smiled bravely at them as Nana and I passed by to go sit up front with Mr. Bennington, my lawyer. My in-laws, who sat just to my right, refused to meet my gaze.

The judge entered then, and like the starting of a movie, everything began. It went by quickly and dreadfully slow at the same time, and I fought to remain calm and not fidget. Mr. Bennington called upon all of my friends to act as character witnesses, saving Vivian until last. She winked at me as she walked by and I smiled, hoping that everything would go smoothly.

"Mrs. McCombs," Mr. Bennington asked, "how long has Mrs. Beckett worked at your restaurant, The Park Bench?"

"Since February," she replied, keeping her back straight as she sat at an angle in the wooden chair. "She's an excellent employee."

Mr. Bennington asked her a few more questions and then sat down. Vivian moved to stand, but Mr. Oliver held up his hand and stated that he had a few questions as well.

"Mrs. McCombs," he said, clearing his throat, "you just stated that Mrs. Beckett has worked for you since February, but you weren't here in February, were you?"

The color left Vivian's face as she slowly shook her head and said, "No."

With a slight smirk, Mr. Oliver stepped closer and asked, "Where were you?"

Vivian hesitated and I cringed, hardly able to believe they were doing this to her. Raising her chin, Vivian replied coolly, "I was in the Martinsville State Hospital."

"Isn't that a *mental* hospital?"

"Yes, but I was sent there by mistake…"

"Of course you were," Mr. Oliver interrupted in a sarcastic tone. Spinning around to return to his seat, he said dismissively over his shoulder, "No further questions."

I could have cried at the look of anger and humiliation on Vivian's face. She had just started to get over the past and now, because of me, it was being thrown in her face all over again. As she walked down from the witness stand, I glanced over at my smug in-laws and wanted to scream at them. How could they do this to my friend? Did they truly hate me so badly?

The bank manager was next to be called upon, and I forced myself not to hang my head in embarrassment as he told the court I'd been late on my mortgage payment twice in the last year.

"She always pays, though," he said quickly, glancing over at me, "even if it is sometimes late."

Officer Sallow, the policeman who came to my house the night it was broken into, was brought to the stand next, and I wondered what sort of testimony he could give. When Mr. Oliver brought up the pocketknife, however, I cringed.

"Mrs. Beckett said the knife didn't belong to the boy," Officer Sallow said, shrugging, "but how else did it get put on his bedside table?"

"Precisely," Mr. Oliver said, nodding his head self-righteously.

Once Officer Sallow took his seat, the doctor that responded to Davey's tree incident was called upon, and I pressed myself against the back of my chair as he told the court of Davey's fall and corresponding head injury, my cheeks red with mortification. They'd said that they would make me look like an unfit mother, and I was beginning to believe them.

Mr. Bennington asked the doctor a few questions, as well, and then I was called to the witness stand. When I heard my name echo throughout the courtroom, I wasn't certain if I could force myself to go up there and speak in front of all those people. Mr. Oliver had already made me look bad; what would he do to me now?

On trembling legs, I went to stand before Mr. Bennington, swore the oath, and sat down, all along praying that I wouldn't faint. Nana smiled encouragingly at me while my in-laws glared with disdain, and I felt so much pressure that I suddenly knew what a boiler must feel like when it was about to explode.

Clearing his throat, Mr. Bennington brought up my marriage first, asking why Paul didn't speak to his parents after we were married.

"They disowned him," I said softly, glancing down at my hands, which were clutched tightly together in my lap. "They didn't approve of me."

"They disinherited their very own son?" Mr. Bennington asked in shock as he looked accusingly over at Mr. and Mrs. Beckett.

"Yes," I nodded. "I wrote them a letter after we were married to try to make amends, but they never answered."

Placing his arm along the railing, Mr. Bennington asked, "Mrs. Beckett, were you and your husband happy?"

I nodded, but before I could utter a word, Mr. Oliver stood and objected. "Your Honor, we have no way of knowing if they truly were happy. We're only going by what Mrs. Beckett says, as Paul isn't here to speak for himself."

The judge agreed and asked Mr. Bennington to move on.

"Mrs. Beckett, what did you do when you realized Davey was sick over the summer?" Mr. Bennington asked.

"I took him to the hospital and stayed with him until he could go home."

"But most of the parents weren't allowed to stay with their children," he stated.

"That's true," I replied, nodding, "but I volunteered to work at the hospital, so they agreed to let me stay."

Smiling warmly at me, Mr. Bennington said, "So, you stayed and worked very long and hard hours just so you could be near your son?"

"Yes," I said, fighting the tears that sprung to my eyes. "I knew he would be frightened if I wasn't there, and I just couldn't leave him. He's my whole world."

Nodding, Mr. Bennington stated he had no further questions, and as Mr. Oliver stood and sauntered towards me, I braced myself.

"Mrs. Beckett," he began, "when did you move here from Germany?"

"In 1939," I replied, hating the way my voice shook.

"And you'd only been here a short while when you met Paul?"

"That's right," I nodded.

"So to make a long story short, you were in a new country, lonely, and immediately attached yourself to a man whom you realized was quite wealthy," Mr. Oliver said with a sniff. "You didn't count on his parents disowning him, though, did you?"

"That's not true!" I gasped, my cheeks flushing red. He was attempting to sully my character by saying I'd only married Paul for his money?

"Your Honor, I object," Mr. Bennington protested. "This has nothing to

244

do with Davey."

"Sustained," the judge said. "Move on, Mr. Oliver."

His lips pursed, Mr. Oliver asked, "You work six days a week, correct?" When I nodded, he continued with, "And your mother and grandmother see about David while you're at work?"

"That's right."

"You don't really have much time to spend with David, do you?"

"I see him before and after work, and all day on Sundays," I stated, trying to keep my tone even. I was getting flustered and could tell that my accent was becoming more and more noticeable.

"I don't know, Mrs. Beckett," Mr. Oliver said, shaking his head. "It seems to me that your grandmother and mother are the ones actually raising your child because you're too busy."

Taking a deep breath, I glanced back at Nana and my friends, trying to draw strength from them. I felt exhausted and a bit swimmy-headed, the result of stress and lack of sleep, but tried my best to hold myself together.

Forcing my gaze back to Mr. Oliver's, I said softly but firmly, "I'm very lucky to have them both to see about Davey while I'm at work, but I'm not too busy for my son."

Mr. Oliver pursed his lips and nodded, going back to his table to retrieve a piece of paper. He quickly read what was written there and, turning back to me, said, "The private investigator hired by Mr. and Mrs. Beckett didn't care to testify in court today, but I have his written statement here, and it says that you have several strange little statues sitting on your coffee table that look a lot like pieces of witchery." Cocking one bushy eyebrow at me, Mr. Oliver asked, "Tell me, Mrs. Beckett, is that what they worship over in Germany? Besides Hitler, of course."

I could feel the blood leave my face and, with a sinking stomach, knew that this was the last nail my coffin needed. It was a bad time to be German, and I felt the disdain in the judge's eyes clear down to my bones.

"Those statues were a gift from my father," I said, my voice shaking and barely above a whisper. "They're simply figures from an old, German fairytale."

"An old, **German** fairytale," Mr. Oliver repeated slowly, his eyes glinting as he looked knowingly up at the judge. Bringing his gaze back to me, he smirked and said, "If you say so," and with that, spun on his heel and walked back to the table, throwing over his shoulder, "No further questions."

The judge told me to return to my seat, and I slowly pushed myself up, my head spinning wildly. I could barely make it down from the witness stand my legs were trembling so violently, and when I sat next to Mr. Bennington, the pity in his eyes was of no comfort to me. The judge stated that he'd made a decision and I looked up at him and waited, dread creeping slowly through my veins and threatening to suffocate me.

"After reviewing everything said here today and as there is no further evidence," the judge said, his voice echoing loudly in my ears, "I think it would be a good idea to send David home with his grandparents for a trial period. He'll stay with them through Christmas, and we will reconvene here in the New Year to see how he's doing and go from there. Please keep in mind that nothing is set in stone; this situation is temporary, and subject to change when I see you all again next year."

The gavel hit the sound block with the force of a clap of thunder. I felt it reverberate through my very soul, and as I pushed myself to my feet, everything went black and I slowly sank to the floor.

47

Vivian

I stood in the back of the courtroom, my face ashen. Leon and the others rushed to the front to see about Eva while I stayed in the back, my feet rooted to the floor. The judge had granted temporary custody to Eva's in-laws? I couldn't believe it. I saw Leon pick Eva up, and I followed everyone outside as he carried her to his car.

"I want to go home," I heard her mumble pitifully.

I stood on the sidewalk and watched them drive off before quietly slipping away. I didn't want to see or talk to anyone, and I walked for blocks, ignoring the ache in my feet as thought after thought ran through my mind. I'd always been the type that felt things deeply, and would often close myself off from the rest of the world while I processed my feelings. Today was no exception.

Tears welled up in my eyes, and I wiped them away with the back of my hand. I knew how it felt to lose a child, and I hurt so badly for Eva. She'd become such a dear friend, and I'd also grown quite attached to Davey during his time spent in the hospital. I could only imagine how hard it would be for him to be torn away from his mother and sent to live with strangers; he was still just a baby, after all, and wouldn't understand why he could no longer see his mother.

Riding on the heels of my sorrow was also anger. With just a wave of his hand, the judge had taken Eva's only child away from her. Oh, he may have said it was just temporary, but I feared that this was the beginning of the end, a salve on the final cut that was to come. It wasn't fair, nor was it right to have such power over someone else's life, over their future. Eva had lost her father, husband, and now her child; how much more could she take? I couldn't understand how her in-laws could do this to her, and the injustice of it all infuriated and frustrated me.

And last but not least, I was humiliated. Deeply and painfully humiliated.

"Isn't that a mental hospital?"

The words of Mr. Oliver reverberated throughout my brain, and I flinched. He'd reduced my testimony, my word, to absolutely nothing, as if what I said didn't matter in the least. He'd made me feel completely worthless, and I wondered if I would ever live down the stigma of being sent to a mental hospital. Would I ever be considered a whole, complete human being, or simply a weak individual that could never measure up to everyone else? I'd thought all of that was behind me, but I could clearly see that it wasn't and probably never would be, and it hurt.

When I finally made it back to the restaurant, it was nearly closing time. Too tired to do any work, I told everyone to go home early, closed up, and went to my apartment. I took a bath and tried to read a book, but couldn't seem to focus. Finally, I gave up and went to bed, only to toss and turn most of the night as my mind repeated the events of the day over and over in my head.

The next morning, I called Eva to check on her.

"Are you okay?" I asked.

"I'm trying to be strong for Davey's sake," she said, her voice heavy, "but I didn't sleep all night. I walked the floors trying to figure out if there's a way to get out of this. What am I going to do, Vivian? I can't believe this has happened."

"Neither can I," I said with a sigh, my heart aching for her. "Let me know if there's anything I can do, okay?"

"I will," she replied. "Thank you for everything, Vivian, and I'm so sorry for the way Mr. Oliver treated you yesterday."

"Oh, don't worry about that," I told her. "And please, let me know if there's anything I can do."

We hung up and I turned around in my chair to gaze out of the window, feeling tired and utterly drained. Eva was the one going through the most right now, and I should do my best to help support her. Instead, it felt as if I carried the weight of the world on my shoulders, and it was all I could do not to break down and cry. It seemed that, once again, everything had caught up to me and I was forced to face the ugly realities of life.

When Zachary stopped by just before noon, I didn't feel up to seeing anyone, but forced myself to be polite.

"I came by after the trial yesterday to see if you were okay, but you weren't here," he said, hanging his hat on the rack by the door. "Where did you hurry off to?"

"Nowhere, everywhere," I replied, sighing as I rubbed my temples. "I just walked around for a while, trying to sort things out in my head."

"And did you?" He sat down before me, crossing one ankle over his knee.

My eyes suddenly brimming with tears, I glanced down and said, "Not really. I'm honestly so sick of this world, Zachary, and of people being able to trample on whomever they want. I spoke to Eva this morning; she's heartbroken. I don't know how she's going to cope if the judge grants her in-laws full custody of Davey."

"I don't believe he will," Zachary said, his tone confident. "I think he's only doing this to pacify the grandparents, to let them spend some time

248

with their grandson over the holidays. I believe that he'll give Davey back to Eva in January."

I shook my head and said, "I don't agree. I think the next six weeks are simply meant to be a trial period for Davey to adjust to living with his grandparents. When January arrives, they can show how good he's doing, the judge will grant them full custody, and Eva will never see her son again."

Zachary leaned over, placing his elbows onto his knees. He looked down at the floor for a moment, and then softly said, "You know, Vivian, just because your son was taken from you doesn't mean Eva's will be taken from her."

I blinked, caught off guard. I hadn't expected him to bring up my own situation, and it almost felt like he was throwing it in my face somehow. Whatever his intentions, I wasn't in the mood to discuss it or hear his advice on how I should or shouldn't be feeling.

Clearing my throat, I said coolly, "Always the philosopher, aren't you, Zachary?" I stood up then and went over to the filing cabinet to sort through some old files, adding over my shoulder, "I'm sorry, but I've got a lot of work to do and I don't really have time for a visit. Could you perhaps come back another day?"

Zachary said nothing, but I could feel his gaze boring into the back of my neck. After a moment, his chair squeaked as he stood and walked up behind me, and I felt the warm pressure of his hand on my arm.

"You're upset about more than just Eva's situation, aren't you?" He asked gently. "I saw your expression when Mr. Oliver treated you so unfairly yesterday, and as soon as I walked into this room just now, I could tell that you're taking this all very hard. Talk to me, Vivian. Please."

"I don't want to talk," I stated, pulling out of his grasp.

"I think it would make you feel better," he persisted. "I can help, Vivian, if you'll just let me."

Turning around, I looked him in the eye and said in a straightforward tone, "How can you help, Zachary? Do you know how it feels to be stomped on and talked down to? To be made to feel like you're worthless and incompetent? I doubt it, and I don't really care to hear any of your words of wisdom and inspiration right now."

Nodding, Zachary pushed his hands into his pockets and glanced down at his feet. I stood there with my arms crossed, staring at him, and after a moment of silence, he raised his head and said softly, "I'd like to share something with you, if you don't mind? And it's not any of my annoying words of wisdom, I promise."

Sighing, I nodded my head and waited, eyebrows raised in question.

"When I was a boy," he began, "I couldn't run and play like the other children because of my bad leg. The other boys laughed at and taunted me and even busted my lip a few times, and I remember my father telling me it's what's on the inside of a man that counts. When the war came, I hated not being fit enough to serve my country with the others, and I've borne quite a few snide remarks because of it." Zachary stopped and reached out to take my hand, continuing in a gentle voice, "I don't speak of this often and I try to remain positive about life because I don't want it to seem like I'm complaining or asking for pity, but I *do* understand how you feel, Vivian. I know the circumstances may be a bit different, but please don't push me away because you think I've never experienced hardships or been treated unkindly."

As he relayed his story, there was something in the tone of his voice and a look of pain in his eyes that touched a place deep inside of me. Unable to stop the tears, I turned back around, the files a blurry mess before me as I fought to maintain my composure.

"I know what Mr. Oliver did was wrong and humiliating," Zachary said, his breath warm against the back of my neck, "but we can't control what others do or say. What we can control, though, is how we react." Placing his hands on my shoulders, he forced me to turn back around and face him. "You're not worthless or incompetent, Vivian, you're just the opposite, and you shouldn't let the words of hateful, insignificant people hurt you."

He pulled me against his chest then, and I finally allowed the tears to flow. I was a little embarrassed, as it seemed he was always around during my weakest moments, but he'd known that I needed a shoulder to cry on, and I was grateful for his kindness.

As the tears dripped from my chin and onto his shirt, it felt like every burden I'd carried the last twenty-four hours released from my body like a tidal wave. Zachary was right; I shouldn't allow the spiteful actions of others to affect me so badly, because it was only tearing me up inside. I had the love and support of my father and closest friends, and I needed to quit worrying about what everyone else thought of me.

Once the tears had finally subsided, I took a deep, shuddering breath and simply stayed where I was for a moment, enjoying the warmth and comfort of Zachary's arms. He rested his chin lightly on top of my head and I closed my eyes, breathing in his familiar scent.

"Thank you," I whispered, listening to the soft rhythm of his heart as it beat against my ear and soothed my tangled spirit.

"You're quite welcome," he said softly, reaching down to take my hand. He brought it to his lips and gently kissed my knuckles, and I tilted my head back to look at him, our faces only inches apart.

Zachary's bright, aqua eyes were warm and darker than I'd ever seen them, like the color of the ocean when a thunderstorm was rolling in. There was something hidden there within the stormy depths that pulled at me like a magnet, that both fascinated and frightened me, and before I realized what was happening, he leaned closer and touched his lips to mine.

With a quick intake of breath, my eyes drifted closed of their own accord, and I melted against him, the strength and warmth of his body surrounding me like a safe haven. He wrapped his arms firmly around my waist, pulling me tighter against his chest, and as the kiss deepened, I slowly moved my hands up to grip the back of his neck and pull him closer, my fingers sinking into his soft, thick hair. It was as if nothing or no one existed in the entire world but us, and my head spun so wildly that none of the thoughts running through my mind made any sense. All I could think, feel, and breathe was his touch, the beating of his heart against mine, and his lips as they stole the very breath from my lungs.

Suddenly, a car outside blew its horn, and all at once the magic was broken and I came to my senses, pulling away and breaking the kiss like the shattering of glass. I took a quick step back, bumping loudly into the filing cabinet, and my face burned red with embarrassment. Zachary blinked, one hand still resting at my waist as he stared at me with such a penetrating gaze that I finally had to look away.

Needing space, I moved around him and went to stand by my desk, feeling awkward and struggling with what to say. I was trembling all over, and couldn't form one coherent thought within my frazzled mind.

"I...I hope I didn't overstep myself," Zachary finally said, breaking the silence as he eyed me with uncertainty. "I was only trying to comfort you and, well, I suppose I got caught up in the moment."

"Yes, so did I," I replied sheepishly. Biting my lip, I said, "It would probably be best, though, if it didn't happen again. I appreciate your friendship, Zachary, but..."

"I know," he interrupted, and I blinked in surprise. With a soft smile, he nodded and said, "You're not ready for anything else, and I understand that." Stepping closer, he took my hand and, with warmth and sincerity in his eyes, said, "I'll admit that I *do* care about you, Vivian, but I'm happy to just be your friend if that's what you want. You should know, however, that I'm here for you no matter what, so please don't ever push me away. Will you promise me that?"

I slowly nodded my head. "Yes."

"Good," he said, a smile of relief spreading across his face. "Well, I've got to get back to work. Let me know if you hear anything else from Eva?"

I said I would and then he was gone, his presence sweeping from the room like a gust of wind. I stood completely still and stared at the closed door, contemplating everything that just happened. I'd never had a more unusual encounter in my whole life, and I didn't quite know what to make of it. I was attracted to Zachary, that much was proven just now, but he was right when he said I wasn't ready for anything else. Would I ever be? I didn't know, but if Zachary was content to remain friends, then so was I.

48

Eva

Two days later, my in-laws came to get Davey. I had all of his things packed and ready to go, but *I* didn't feel ready at all. I'd done my best to explain to him that Paul's parents were taking him on a vacation and that I would see him after Christmas, but I knew he didn't truly grasp what that meant. I hadn't slept since the trial, and forcing myself to act cheerful and happy was proving to be quite a difficult task when all I wanted to do was cry.

The knock on the front door was short and firm, and I took Davey's hand and walked outside with him. Nana and Mutter were both too upset to see him go and had already said their goodbyes, and I wished that they'd walked out with me. My heart was pounding and I felt sick to my stomach; could I really go through with this?

"Come along, David," his grandmother said, reaching out to take his hand.

"No," Davey said, stepping back with a frown. Looking up at me, he asked, "You coming, Mommy?"

I glanced at them, hoping they'd agree to let me come along, but when all I received were icy stares, I shook my head and said, "No, honey, we talked about this, remember? You're going on a fun trip with your grandparents."

His grandmother took his hand then and pulled him away, and when Davey started to cry and call out to me, it was all I could do not to run after him and beg them not to do this.

"Mommy, I want you!" He cried, struggling to pull his hand away from his grandmother. I could hear the fear and uncertainty in his voice, and I thought my heart would break into a million pieces. He didn't know these people and didn't understand why they were taking him away from me, and I fought the sobs that strangled the back of my throat with everything in me.

"Be a good boy, sweetie," I called to him, my voice breaking as I walked down the driveway after them. "Mommy will see you soon."

My father-in-law forced Davey into the back seat and closed the door, and it felt almost like the closing of a book after it's been read. Everything was done, everything was finished, and the book would be put on the shelf, never to be seen again.

As the car drove away, I walked out into the street and waved until I could no longer see its dusty silhouette. I stood there, unmoving, and clutched Davey's favorite teddy bear in my arms, suddenly realizing that I'd forgotten to give it to him before he left. I don't know how long I stood in that one spot, but when I felt a pair of hands take me by the shoulders and lead me inside, I didn't protest. We'd barely stepped through the door when I collapsed into Mutter's arms, sobs wracking my body with such force I feared I might be hyperventilating.

"Come on," she said, gently leading me into the living room.

We sat on the sofa and she wrapped her arms around me, our tears mingling together as we both cried. I laid my head on her shoulder, and she rocked me gently back and forth, her heart just as broken as mine. After a moment, Nana joined us, and we all sat huddled together, mourning the loss of our sweet little angel that we feared we'd never see again.

I couldn't eat, nor could I sleep. I sat in Davey's little room every night, holding his teddy bear against my chest and crying. How had I allowed this to happen? What had I done wrong? I tried to call my in-laws a few times to ask about Davey, but the only person I ever spoke to was the maid.

"Mr. David is doing just fine," she said each time, her tone clipped and brisk.

She refused to let me speak to him, but when I asked if she'd tell him I loved him, she agreed. I doubted, however, that she ever did.

Everywhere I looked, I saw Davey. His toys were scattered throughout the house, a pair of his shoes were by the back door, and I could hear his laughter constantly echoing off the walls. I couldn't stop crying, and while Nana and Mutter tried to make me feel better, I knew they were hurting, too. The thought that continually ran through my mind was: *What if the judge doesn't give him back to us? What if I never see my son again?*

When the weekend arrived, I could barely put one foot in front of the other. Vivian had insisted I take the week off, and I was grateful for it; I don't think I could have worked if I'd tried. I'd just finished forcing a piece of toast and a glass of orange juice down for breakfast when the doorbell rang, and I walked slowly toward the front door, my hair not fixed and robe hanging loosely around my ankles.

"Good morning," Leon greeted me when I opened the door, and I didn't miss the look of concern in his eyes as he took note of my appearance. "I hope I'm not disturbing you. How...how are you doing?"

"I'm okay," I said, forcing a small, tired smile. "Would you like to come in? There's a fresh pot of coffee on the stove."

"I am actually about to go to Tybee Island," he said, stuffing his hands into the pockets of his pants. "I have to take some papers down there for an elderly client of ours to sign, and I was wondering if you'd like to go with me? My boss said I can take the rest of the day off once the papers are signed."

A bit surprised at the invitation, I hesitated a moment before answering. "I don't know," I finally replied, sighing softly. "I'm not sure that I feel up to it."

"Which is exactly why you need to go," he said, his eyes warm as he reached out to touch my arm. "You need to get out of the house for a while, Eva. It will be good for you. Please?"

I finally gave in to the pleading look in his eyes and told him I would get ready as quickly as possible. I ran a comb through my hair and pinned it back on the sides, slid into a long sleeve, navy blue and white striped dress, and grabbed my purse. It would be cold, especially on the island, so I also grabbed a sweater and scarf on the way out. As I walked from my bedroom, I hoped I would have the energy to at least try to enjoy myself.

We asked Nana and Mutter if they would like to join us, but they both declined and hurriedly packed us a picnic lunch. We took the bus to Tybee, and as we drove, I stared out of the window and watched as the buildings of downtown Savannah faded from view to reveal sparkling rivers, green and gold grassy marshland, and swaying palm trees. The road to the island was long and narrow, and would often become flooded with water during a very high tide, and Leon pointed out the bridge which led to the fort on Cockspur Island as we passed by.

"Union soldiers took Fort Pulaski in 1862," he told me. "Around six hundred soldiers occupied it at one point, and it later became a prisoner of war camp, as well as a destination on the Underground Railroad. If you climb to the top of the fortification, the view is breathtaking."

The bus finally arrived on the island, and we walked to a beautiful, two-story cottage on the water which was canopied by oaks and palm trees. I was offered a glass of sweet tea while I waited on Leon and his client to finish with their business, and twenty minutes later, we were on our way to the beach.

As we walked, Leon told me a bit of the island's history, and I finally commented, "You certainly know a lot about the area. I believe you missed your calling; you should have been a tour guide."

With a chuckle, Leon nodded his head, reaching up to unravel the tie at his neck and unbutton the top two buttons of his shirt. "When I was young, my father often brought us here to go swimming at the beach or crabbing from one of the docks," he said, smiling at the memories. "He was raised on the island until his family moved after a bad hurricane came through when he was fourteen, and he would tell us story after story of the island's history. See the lighthouse just up ahead?"

I looked in the direction in which he was pointing and nodded when I saw the tip of a lighthouse peaking up through the trees.

"The original tower was built in 1736, but it's had to be rebuilt several times since because of bad weather and fire," Leon said. "It's the oldest and tallest lighthouse in Georgia, and there are 178 steps that lead up to the top. My father worked there with the keeper one summer, and he talked of the amazing, breathtaking sunrises he watched come up over the water every morning. He still knew the family when we visited once, so they let him take us up, and it was like standing on top of the world. You can see for miles up there, and it's so peaceful; I felt like an eagle, soaring above the earth as the wind blew softly against my skin. It was amazing."

"It sounds like it," I said, shading my eyes from the sun as we stepped into an opening and the lighthouse came into full view. I could easily believe it was the tallest in Georgia, as the huge, black and white tower seemed to reach for the clouds. A white picket fence surrounded it, and the keeper's cottage stood proudly by its side. I wished the old place could talk and tell of the many ships it helped guide to safety, of the pirates it watched slip quietly through the night, and of the men returning home from war. I could only imagine the stories it could share, and the many changes it had seen coming to the island year after year.

We continued walking until we finally reached the beach, and I immediately took off my shoes and stockings to bury my toes in the sand. The wind blew my hair, and I wrapped my scarf around my head, securing it tightly as I watched seagulls and pelicans flying overhead. The sound of the waves crashing against the shore was soothing and relaxing, and I walked closer, eager to feel the water slap gently across my feet.

"It will be cold," Leon warned, staying back so as not to get wet.

Laughing, I turned to look at him and said, "You forget I'm from Germany; I'm used to the cold."

Leon was right; the water was cold, but I didn't mind. I wiggled my toes in the wet sand, backing up a bit so my dress wouldn't get wet as the tide kept coming in. I spotted a dolphin just up ahead and pointed it out to Leon, smiling over my shoulder at him.

We continued on towards the pier, and it wasn't long before I saw the beautiful, wooden walkway looming up before us as it stretched out into the ocean. We climbed the steps leading up to the covered pavilion and took our picnic basket to a nearby picnic table. I unloaded the basket, which consisted of cold fried chicken, cornbread, deviled eggs, and two slices of apple pie. Leon got us a couple of lemonades from a nearby stand, and we sat down to enjoy the delicious meal.

"So, tell me about your childhood," Leon said as he tore off a piece of chicken from the drumstick he held. "What was it like growing up in Germany?"

"Peaceful, happy," I replied, smiling softly. "We lived with my grandparents along the Danube River in The Black Forest region, and I can remember Papa and Opa, my grandfather, taking me fishing many an afternoon and evening. We would often go swimming during the summer, too, and Mutter and Oma would always have a delicious picnic lunch waiting for us to eat. Oma made the most delicious streuselkuchen, a German crumb cake, you'll ever taste."

"No wonder you don't mind the cold here if you used to swim in the Danube," Leon stated, chuckling. "What is The Black Forest like? I've only ever read about it, but I'd love to see it someday."

"Mystical and mysterious, with little bubbling brooks winding their way throughout the thick, dark trees," I replied, sighing as I closed my eyes and pictured it all. "I used to explore those woods for hours on end, dreaming that I was a fairy who lived amongst the birds, foxes, and deer. Mutter constantly worried that I would get lost, but I always found my way back home somehow. The forest was like a friend to me, and I can still hear the birds singing in the treetops, and the sound the snow makes during the winter as it falls through the leaves."

"It sounds like you miss it."

Opening my eyes, I looked at Leon and smiled, shrugging my shoulders as I nodded. "I do, but I suppose it's natural to miss your childhood home. I'd like to go back for a visit sometime, but if I stayed, I'd miss Savannah even more."

"I'm glad to hear that," he said, smiling warmly at me.

Once we were through eating, we walked down the pier and I shivered a bit as the chilly wind blew against my face. When we reached the end and leaned against the railing, Leon wrapped his arm around my shoulders and pulled me close, and I was grateful for the warmth that radiated from his body. I glanced up at him, studying his profile as his dark hair blew gently in the breeze, and couldn't help but notice how handsome he was. His jaw was square and firm, and I watched as his beautiful hazel eyes stared out over the ocean, the waves reflecting in his gaze. I wondered what he was thinking about, as there was a deep, thoughtful expression on his face.

Before I could offer a penny for his thoughts, we heard a low rumble, and Leon pointed to a group of heavy, dark clouds quickly heading our way. We hurried to the bus depot and had just climbed aboard when the rain started to fall.

As we drove away from the island and I listened to the peaceful sound of the rain slapping against the bus windows, I felt my eyes grow heavy and leaned my head back against the seat.

"Come here," Leon said, putting his arm around me once again. "My shoulder will be more comfortable than that seat."

Smiling gratefully, I laid my head on his shoulder and slowly began to relax.

"Thank you for asking me to join you today," I said softly as my eyes fluttered closed. "I feel a little better than I did before."

Just before I drifted off to sleep, I felt Leon take my hand and gently intertwine his fingers with mine.

49

Eva

The next day, Nana and Mutter went to the market, and I was in the kitchen attempting to distract myself with a bit of baking. It was Sunday, the birds were singing just outside the window, but I was exhausted. I had a wonderful time with Leon, but once again, I hadn't slept the night before and wondered how long one could survive with no sleep. The hour of sleep I'd gotten on the bus ride home had helped, but it wasn't enough.

I was slicing apples for a pie when I heard the screen door creak. Thinking that it was just the wind, I turned my back to the door and went in search of more apples in the icebox. I was so tired and my mind filled with thoughts of Davey that I didn't notice the back door slowly opening as a man stepped inside and crept towards me, his hands reaching out while his steady gaze watched my every move. I'd just reached for the ice box handle when I felt his presence behind me and I froze, my fingers dangling in mid-air as his shadow fell over me. Before I could react, his hand snuck out and wrapped around my mouth, pulling me against his firm chest.

"Hello, Eva," he breathed against my ear, and I began to tremble all over. He held my chin at an angle so I couldn't see his face, and when I tried to jerk away, he quickly wrapped his other arm firmly around both of mine, pinning them to my waist.

"I don't mean to frighten you," he said, "but now that Davey is gone, I've come to take you away."

My eyes widening, I tried to shake my head in protest and he sighed, his breath blowing a strand of hair across my face.

"That's why it has to be done *my* way," he said, his voice distorted and unrecognizable as he whispered, as if he were intentionally trying to keep me from discovering his identity. There was something about the pattern of his speech, however, that was vaguely familiar; I just couldn't put my finger on what it was. "You're coming with me, whether you like it or not."

My mind whirled as he began to drag me roughly across the room, and I tried to struggle, but he was much too strong for me. Who was this man, and what did he intend to do with me? My heart pounding, I suddenly heard the front door open and Mutter call out for me.

"Eva, we're back with the groceries," she said. "We bumped into Zachary at the market and he was kind enough to drive us home."

I heard Zachary's voice in the foyer, and realized that he'd come inside as well.

Halting in his tracks, my captor stood there for a moment, his hand clamped so tightly around my mouth that I could barely breathe. Finally, he whispered, "I have a gun in my pocket. If you make a sound, I'll kill them all."

I nodded and he released me, shoving me forcefully across the kitchen. I slammed into the opposite wall with a loud clatter, barely catching myself as my knee painfully struck the edge of the ice box. The room spinning, I turned around to catch a glimpse of my assailant, but it was too late; the back door had already slammed shut.

My legs were trembling violently, and I slowly crumbled to the floor. Tears burned my eyes and I took a deep breath, trying to calm myself as my chest heaved up and down.

The kitchen door opened just then, and I heard Mutter gasp, "Eva, what's wrong?"

Stepping around her, Zachary hurried to my side and kneeled down to feel my forehead and check my pulse while Nana fixed me a glass of water.

"Your pulse is through the roof," Zachary said, his face tight with concern. "Just stay where you are and sip the water slowly."

After a moment, I calmed down enough to tell them what happened. Zachary immediately called the police, and within fifteen minutes, Officer Wright was knocking on my front door.

"I-I couldn't see his face," I told Officer Wright, my voice trembling as I told him everything that happened. "He kept my head turned away from him."

"Did you recognize his voice?"

I shook my head. "No, I...I don't think so."

Once he'd asked me all the expected questions, Officer Wright placed his notepad back into his shirt pocket and said, "I'll have some of my men keep watch on your house for the next couple of days."

Just then, I heard the front door open and turned around to find Leon poking his head in. When he spotted me, he said, "I noticed the police car outside and wanted to make sure everything was okay."

I asked him to come in and quickly explained what happened. He was so upset when I finished that I feared he'd march right out and hunt the man down himself.

"I don't think you should walk to and from work alone, Mrs. Beckett," Officer Wright told me.

"I totally agree," Leon nodded. "I'll drive her from now on."

"But, Leon, you go into work earlier than I do," I protested weakly, reaching down to rub my throbbing knee.

Chewing his bottom lip, he asked, "You know how to drive, don't you?"

"Yes, Vivian has been teaching me."

"Then you'll drive my car," he stated. "If anyone walks to work from now on, it'll be me."

I started to protest once again, but Zachary spoke up and said, "I think that will be for the best, Eva. We don't want Davey to lose his mother, too."

I finally agreed, feeling guilty for taking Leon's car but realizing that it was the only option right now.

"Call us if anything else happens," Officer Wright stated as I walked him out.

I said that I would, but nothing else happened. For the next two weeks, I drove Leon's car to and from work, made certain the doors to my house were always locked, and kept a knife by my bed at night. Thankfully, the intruder seemed to have disappeared.

My first day back at work, Jackson sidled up beside me and asked how I was doing since Davey's departure.

"I'm trying to be strong, but I miss him terribly," I said, tears gathering in my eyes.

"I'm sorry," he said, sighing heavily. After a brief pause, he added, "I heard that someone broke into your house again."

Glancing at him in surprise, I was about to ask how he knew, but then assumed that Vivian must have mentioned it.

"He hasn't come around since," I said, shivering at the memory of his hand around my mouth and the sound of his spine-chilling whisper. "I hope the police will catch him."

"Any idea who it is?"

I shook my head. "No, unfortunately not."

As silence fell between us, I continued beating the bowl full of egg whites before me, wondering why Jackson was still standing there instead of getting back to work. When he cleared his throat, I glanced up at him questioningly and noticed the look of uncertainty on his face.

"Uh...would you," Jackson began, only to stop and swallow past the obvious lump in his throat. Taking a deep breath, he tried again, "Would you like to go out with me sometime?"

I blinked in surprise, embarrassment flooding over me. I opened my mouth to answer, only to close it again. I had to be careful not to hurt his feelings, as we worked together and it could become very awkward between us.

"While I appreciate the kind invitation," I said gently, "I'm afraid..."

Cook cleared her throat then and gave us a look, and Jackson said in a clipped tone, "You don't have to say any more. I understand."

When he turned to walk away, I put my hand on his arm and said, "Jackson, wait."

Pulling his arm away, he said over his shoulder, "I have to get back to work," and hurried across the room to his station.

Feeling terrible for upsetting him, I fought tears as I returned to my half-beaten eggs. I didn't mind being friends with Jackson, but I got the impression that he wanted more, and I didn't wish to lead him on. For the rest of the day, he kept his distance and wouldn't even look at me, and while I felt miserable about the whole thing, I knew he would get over it eventually.

The next few days passed slowly. I missed Davey and worried about him so much that my energy was totally depleted; it was all I could do to put one foot in front of the other. I cried for him at night and often went into his room just to feel closer to him, wondering what the judge would decide in January. What would I do if Davey could never come back home?

Sunday morning, one week after the invasion into my home, there was a knock at the front door. I was getting ready for church and had just taken the curlers out of my hair, sighing as I glanced around for my robe. I slipped it on and rushed through the house to open the door, my stockings making a *swooshing* sound on the hardwood floor.

When I swung the door open, ready to greet the milkman or perhaps one of my neighbors, I felt the blood drain from my face as my eyes fell upon the man who stood before me.

With a gasp, I put my hand over my mouth and whispered, "Paul!"

The man, whom I believed to be my husband for a shocking, earth-shattering split second, smiled and said, "You always *did* say Paul and I looked enough alike to be twins." Stepping forward, he kissed my cheek and added warmly, "Hello, Eva, it's so good to see you."

I stared at my brother-in-law, the shock of seeing him here and alive racing through my veins like a bolt of lightning. "Asher," I finally spoke in a choked voice, "I...I can't believe it. We thought you were dead."

"So did I a couple of times," he replied with a chuckle. "Well, are you going to invite me in or keep me out in the cold?"

Tears flooding my eyes, I pulled him into a hug and said, "It's good to see you, Asher."

Stepping away, I wiped my eyes and took his coat and hat, ushering him into the living room. Nana and Mutter came in to see who our visitor was, both gasping in surprise when they saw Asher.

"It's good to see you both again," Asher greeted them with a warm smile and kiss upon their cheeks.

We all sat down and, his face turning serious, Asher told us, "I just came from Connecticut; my parents were every bit as shocked to see me as you are." Turning to me, he took my hand and said, "Eva, I'm so sorry about Davey. I can't believe my parents have done this. I tried talking them out of it but they just refused to listen."

My eyes welling up with tears once again, I nodded and said, "Thank you for trying. How is Davey? Is he alright?"

"He's doing fine, but he misses you," he replied. "He kept asking Mother where you were. I can't believe how much he's grown; he looks so much like you."

"Is there anything we can do to get him back?" Nana asked hopefully.

Asher considered the question for a moment, his deep blue eyes somber. "I don't know," he finally replied, his tone heavy. "I'm going to stay in town for a few days, so perhaps we can come up with a solution."

"That would be wonderful," I stated, sighing. "Would you like to join us for breakfast? We haven't eaten yet."

Asher readily agreed and as he followed Nana and Mutter into the kitchen, I ran back to my bedroom and quickly put on the dress I'd hung out for church. It was navy blue with gold buttons going all the way down the front and sported a fur collar; Savannah had been sweet enough to lend it to me a couple of weeks ago, as she knew that all of my winter clothes were growing a bit ragged. I slipped into a pair of navy heels and hurried to the kitchen, leaving my hair unpinned and hanging in soft curls around my shoulders.

As we sat down to eat the breakfast Nana had prepared, I asked Asher where he'd been for the last two years.

"In a German POW camp," he stated, pouring a bit of cream into his coffee. "My plane went down in enemy territory and we had to surrender. Living in a POW camp wasn't the most pleasant of experiences, but thank God several of us were able to escape. We dug a tunnel that took months and a lot of careful planning; there were some days I didn't think we'd ever make it, but we finally did. Unfortunately, some of the men were recaptured and killed. I was one of the lucky ones, but I received a head injury and a shot in the shoulder during the escape, so I now suffer from severe headaches and can no longer raise my left arm above shoulder level."

"How did you manage to still escape with such injuries?" Nana asked, her eyes wide.

"My buddy, Ethan, pulled me out of the river and carried me to the nearest town. I taught him how to speak German, Eva, just like you taught me, and thankfully no one was suspicious enough to call the authorities," Asher explained. "If not for Ethan, I wouldn't be alive." His jaw clenching, he glanced down at his hands and added in a low voice, "Our other friend, however, didn't make it."

"It all must have been so horrible," I said, my heart aching for him. He'd lost weight and his face now bore wrinkles that hadn't been there before. I also noticed a scar on his temple and another on his neck. I couldn't imagine what he'd gone through, but knowing that he was alive was such a wonderful gift. "I wish Paul was here to see you," I added softly.

I saw a wave of pain pass over Asher's face and instantly wished I'd kept silent. "So do I," he said in a tight voice. "I was shocked when Mother and Father told me. I'm so sorry, Eva."

I reached out and squeezed his hand, a wave of compassion filling my eyes with tears. I'd had time to process Paul's death, to deal with the pain and begin healing, but it was all new to Asher and I knew how much he'd loved Paul.

After breakfast, Asher said he was going to get settled in to his hotel and that he'd come back by later that evening for supper. I walked him out and watched him drive away, still hardly able to believe that he was alive.

50

THE SHADOW

He paced back and forth in his room, the floorboards creaking and groaning under his feet. So far, his plan hadn't worked the way he thought it would, and he was growing more and more agitated. Oh, he'd known that Eva would put up a fight, he'd been prepared for that, but his timing had been all wrong and that angered him a great deal. He didn't like failure, not one bit; it caused him to become frustrated very easily.

Don't worry, he told himself, trying to calm down, ***you can try again. She still doesn't know who you are.***

Feeling a bit better, he sat on the edge of his bed and sighed, smiling slightly as he thought of the brilliant way in which he was so easily able to disguise his voice. Keeping his identity a secret had been a marvelous idea, a sort of game that kept him in control, and he intended to continue hiding his identity until the very last possible moment.

Yes, he would try again, and he would keep trying until he got what he wanted.

51

Vivian

There was a chill in the air when Thanksgiving Day arrived and, as I'd decided I wanted to do something a little different this year, I got up early and headed to the kitchen. With everything that had happened over the last several months, I felt the need to celebrate a bit extra this year. So, I decided to hold a Thanksgiving dinner at the restaurant for all of my employees and their families. I'd been able to pay all the bills with Mack's money and wanted to use what was left to show my appreciation for the people who worked for me.

This would be my first time cooking Thanksgiving dinner without my mother, and I was grateful when Eva offered to help me; I was also pleasantly surprised when she arrived with both her mother and grandmother in tow. Lina Hamilton, Eva's mother, was the most graceful, gentle woman I'd ever met; it was clear where Eva had gotten her beauty and shy, timid disposition. Mrs. Hamilton, Eva's grandmother, was a small, gray-haired lady with the typical "old" southern way of not pronouncing her r's when she spoke, and I was instantly impressed by her splendid cooking abilities. The four of us had a wonderful time as we cooked; we talked and laughed, discussed local gossip, and before we knew it, the clock chimed six and it was almost time for everyone to arrive. The three ladies went home to clean up, and I rushed upstairs to take a quick bath, change my clothes, and go get Father.

As the two of us drove back to the restaurant, Father surprised me by reaching over to take my hand.

"Vivvy, I'm so proud of you," he said, his voice a bit choked. "You've had to overcome so many obstacles this year, but still you have managed to get your life back on track. You're doing a marvelous job running the restaurant, you've helped take care of me these last few months, and you've worked so hard today to offer this wonderful and kind gesture of thanks to our employees for Thanksgiving. You're an incredible young woman, honey, and your mother would be just as proud as I am."

My throat tight with emotion, I fought the overwhelming urge to cry as I squeezed his hand in return and whispered, "Thank you, Father. You have no idea how much that means to me."

It was so hard to celebrate holidays without Mother; my heart had ached for her all day. I was, however, thankful to still have my father with me. If he'd been killed in that wreck, too, I don't know how I could have survived.

At seven o'clock sharp, everyone began arriving at the restaurant. We lined the food up on a long table that stretched out along the back wall, and the delicious aroma of turkey, dressing, yams, creamed corn, lady finger peas, pumpkin pie, and pecan pie filled the air.

Eva and her family, along with her visiting brother-in-law, stepped through the door just then and I waved, making my way across the room to them. I was surprised when Eva told me about Asher's visit and immediately decided I didn't like him simply because of his parents.

"He's nothing like them," Eva assured me. "He even tried to convince his parents to send Davey back home to us."

Even though I'd just seen her, I pulled Eva into a quick hug. I knew how hard it was for her to be without Davey on such a special day and I was glad she'd agreed to come tonight, as I knew the distraction would be good for her. She introduced me to Asher and I greeted him with a kind smile, receiving the same in return.

"It's nice to meet you," I said, reaching out to shake his hand.

"It's very nice to meet you, as well," he replied, his blue eyes filled with warmth. He was tall and well dressed, and I could tell simply from his clothes that he came from a wealthy family. His curly blonde hair was cut short on the sides with a slight poof in the front, and his smile was bright and pleasant.

After chatting with everyone for a bit, I went to the front of the room and, after getting everyone's attention, said, "I just wanted to thank you all for your loyalty to my family and to this restaurant. It's been a tough year, but we made it through and I hope we'll be together for many more years to come. Now, let's dig in!"

As everyone lined up and began serving themselves, I stepped back to watch, smiling at the cheerful faces and friendly smiles. I rarely had the opportunity to see the families of my employees, and watching them interact together brought a feeling of warmth to my heart. I missed having that feeling for myself. I missed being a wife and mother, of having others to care about and tend to, and wondered if perhaps some day I'd be ready to have that again.

I was just about to serve myself when I thought I heard the knob on the front door jiggle. Seeing the shadow of a silhouette on the other side of the glass, I went to unlock the door and open it. Much to my surprise, Officer Wright was walking away.

"Gabe," I called out, stopping him. When he turned and came back, I asked, "Is everything alright?"

"Good evening," he said, smiling. "Yes, everything is fine. I just saw the lights on and all the cars parked outside and thought the restaurant might be open. I didn't notice the "closed" sign until after I tried to open the door."

I'd never seen him out of his uniform before and was struck by how nice he looked in regular attire. He wore a navy blue plaid suit coat with a white shirt, navy vest, and solid navy pants. His hair was soft and combed to the side, and I didn't fail to notice how broad his shoulders looked in the suit coat.

"You know, as a police officer, you really should be more observant," I teased, my eyes twinkling.

Laughing, he shrugged sheepishly and said, "You're right. I guess the smell of food and the rumbling in my stomach distracted me."

"Isn't your family having a Thanksgiving meal?"

"My family lives in Macon," he replied. "I guess I could have cooked something for myself, though."

I blinked in surprise; Gabe didn't have any family to be with today? Feeling sorry for him, I immediately said, "Well, in that case, why don't you join us? I'm holding a Thanksgiving dinner for my employees and their families so there's plenty of food." When he protested, I held up my hand and said, "Please, I insist."

"Alright then, thank you," he said, following me back inside.

As we began filling our plates with food, Gabe said, "This looks delicious. The restaurant must be doing really well to afford all of this."

Glancing over at him, I replied, "We're doing alright."

Gabe said nothing else about it, and I led him to the table where my father, Eva, and her family were sitting. After introducing Gabe to Asher, we sat down and began eating.

"This food is amazing," Gabe said within just a few bites. "Did you cook this all by yourself?"

"No. Eva, Mrs. Lina, and Mrs. Hamilton helped me," I replied, winking at the three ladies. Turning back to Gabe, I added with a grin, "We cater, too, you know. The next time the station holds a party, I expect a phone call."

Laughing, Gabe nodded his head approvingly and said, "Don't worry, you'll definitely get one."

Glancing at Asher, my father asked, "So, my boy, you're in the Army?"

Nodding, Asher replied, "Yes, sir. I signed up just after Pearl Harbor."

"Do you plan on making a career out of it?"

"No, sir. I'm attempting to get an honorable discharge due to my headaches and shoulder injury, and then I plan on doing something else."

Father nodded, and my heart pinched as he nearly knocked his glass of tea over. Mrs. Lina, who was sitting beside him, managed to catch it and hand it to him, and I breathed a sigh of relief; his eyesight was better, but still not completely back to normal.

"What do you plan to do?" Father asked after taking a sip of his tea.

Glancing over at Eva, Asher hesitated before saying, "I'm not entirely certain yet."

He, Gabe, and Father continued talking about the war, and leaning around Gabe, I asked Eva, "Have you seen any more of the intruder?"

"No, thank goodness," she replied, shaking her head. "I hope he's gone for good now."

"I hope so, too; it gives me the creeps just thinking about it," I said with a shiver.

Overhearing our conversation, Asher looked at Eva and asked, "What is she talking about? What intruder?"

As Eva quickly explained, I could see the skin on Asher's face and neck slowly growing more and more red by the second. "Do you mean that someone is actually *stalking* you?"

"Well, I wouldn't say he's stalking me…"

"He broke into your home, tried to force you to leave with him, and then threatened to kill your mother and grandmother if you screamed," Asher interrupted, his tone heated. "I'd say he's stalking you."

"I agree, Mrs. Beckett," Gabe spoke up. "Men like that rarely just "disappear". You should definitely keep your guard up in case he comes back."

Eva looked at me then, as if begging me to change the subject, and I cleared my throat and said, "Well, it looks like it's time for dessert. Coffee, anyone?"

Everyone's attention was immediately diverted, and as I stood to gather our plates, Eva mouthed the words "thank you" to me. I nodded and threw a sly wink in her direction as I went to get the coffee. Before long, all the pies were eaten, and everyone was gradually beginning to leave. I was about to clean up when Mrs. Lina, Eva's mother, approached me.

"May I speak to you about something?" She asked.

"Of course," I nodded, and we stepped away from everyone for a bit of privacy.

"I-I hope I'm not overstepping myself, but your father was telling me that you take time out of your busy schedule to clean his house twice a week," she said. Her voice was so soft that I had to lean closer to hear what she was saying, and I found her German accent to be quite charming. "Would you consider allowing me to clean your father's house? I have nothing else to do now that Davey is…" she paused, glancing down as tears gathered in her blue eyes. Clearing her throat, she continued, "Now that Davey is gone, and I would like to help you and your father in any way that I can."

"Oh, Mrs. Lina, how thoughtful of you," I said, reaching out to squeeze her arm. "We'll pay you, of course."

"Oh, no, I don't expect that," she said, shaking her head. "You've become such a dear friend to Eva that I would love to do this for you."

My heart warming, I smiled and said, "That is such a kind offer, but I insist; this will really take a load off my shoulders."

After discussing everything over with Father, I told Eva the news and hugged her goodbye.

"Oh, but I was going to stay and help clean," she said, pulling back.

"You've done more than enough, Eva," I insisted. "Go home and get some rest."

"But you can't possibly clean all of this by yourself…"

"I'll stay and help her, Mrs. Beckett," a voice spoke out from behind.

Glancing over my shoulder at Gabe, I raised my eyebrows in surprise and he said with a chuckle, "Sorry, I wasn't trying to eavesdrop, but you allowed me to stay and eat at a party only intended for your employees, so helping you clean is the least that I can do."

Turning back to Eva, I smiled and said, "See? I've got all the help I need."

"Okay, but at least let us take your father home," she said. "There's room in Asher's car."

After asking Father if that would be okay, I agreed and, thanking them again for everything, we said our goodbyes and I locked up behind them. I then turned to survey the mess that was left behind.

"I'm glad you offered to stay and help clean," I laughingly told Gabe.

After carrying all the dirty dishes into the kitchen, I handed Gabe an apron and we began the long task of washing and drying.

"You know, Vivian," Gabe suddenly said, "what I told Eva about her stalker quite possibly applies to you, as well."

My brow furrowing, I glanced over at Gabe and asked, "What do you mean?"

Tossing the towel over his shoulder, Gabe leaned against the counter as he waited for me to finish washing one of the larger pots. "I mean with Mack," he replied, crossing his arms. "You *did* double-cross him when you sent me that note, and if you kept any of the money you found, that just makes the likelihood of Mack coming back for revenge even greater."

Pausing, I cut my eyes over at Gabe and slowly asked, "What makes you think I kept any of that money?"

Turning to look at me, Gabe raised an eyebrow and asked, "Well, did you?"

"If I said 'yes', would you arrest me?" I asked, raising an eyebrow of my own.

Gabe laughed and shook his head. "No, but you would need to turn it over to the police. That is illegal money."

"I don't think anyone actually knows that," I stated matter-of-factly. "I found it in *my* restaurant. For all I know, it's part of the money Howard took from our savings account."

269

"But Mack said it was stolen from him."

Feeling slightly annoyed, I placed a hand on my hip and turned to face Gabe. "Mack is a criminal," I pointed out. "Why would you take his word for it?"

Blinking, Gabe slowly nodded his head and, after a moment of thoughtful contemplation, he said, "You know what? You're absolutely right. I apologize."

Nodding my head pertly, I turned back to the dishes and began scrubbing with renewed force. When Gabe reached out and touched my arm, I stopped and glanced over at him questioningly.

"Just be careful, okay?" He said, his tone impassioned. "Mack is a dangerous fellow, and even though he may be long gone for now, that doesn't mean he will be forever. Now that you and I have become friends, I care about your well-being."

"I will be careful, I promise," I said, smiling. "I appreciate your concern."

We got back to work, and once we were finished, it was well after midnight. Pressing my hands into the small of my back, I sighed and said, "Wow, I'm exhausted."

"Try doing a stakeout for twelve hours straight," Gabe replied with a chuckle.

"You're telling me that sitting in a car doing nothing is harder work than standing on your feet all day cooking and cleaning?" I asked, raising an eyebrow in doubt.

"You're totally right; my feet are killing me," he agreed, laughing.

"There's some leftover banana pudding from yesterday's dessert if you'd like a midnight snack before you leave," I said, sticking my head into the icebox in search of the dessert.

"That would be marvelous. I'm starving after all of that hard labor you just put me through."

Chuckling, I dipped the pudding into a bowl and handed it to him. "You know, for a cop, you're a bit of a wimp," I stated, my eyes twinkling.

"Only when I stay up past my bedtime," he quipped, winking at me.

I joined him at the table and took a bite of the pudding, closing my eyes as I savored the smooth, creamy flavor. After a moment, I asked, "How is it you became a police officer?"

A strange look passed over his face then and I blinked in surprise, almost wishing I hadn't asked, when suddenly the look was gone and he said with a laugh, "It wasn't for the pay, that's for sure."

Smiling, I asked, "You said that you're from Macon?"

"That's right," he nodded.

"How did you end up here?"

Glancing up at me, Gabe smiled and said, "I'm the police officer, you know. Seems to me *I* should be the one asking all the questions."

"True," I replied, laughing. "Ask away."

"Do you like to dance?"

Blinking, I said, "That's a bit of an unusual question, but yes, I do like to dance. Why?"

"Well, the station holds a Christmas party every year," he said, pushing his now empty bowl away, "and this year we're teaming up with all emergency personnel, which includes the local fire stations and hospital staff. It's going to be a wonderful party with lots of fun. Would you like to go with me?"

He must have seen the look of surprise on my face and when I hesitated, he quickly added, "Just as friends, I promise."

"Uh…well…I suppose that would be alright," I stammered, my cheeks flushing.

"Good, then it's settled," he said, smiling. Slapping the table lightly with his hand, he stood up and, after stretching his back and shoulders, said, "Well, thank you for a lovely evening, Vivian. I'll see you soon, okay?"

Nodding, I walked him out and, thanking him once again for his help, locked the door behind him and went back into the kitchen to wash our bowls. As I finished cleaning up, I thought about Gabe's request and wondered if I should have declined. He'd caught me off guard, but he *did* say it would be just as friends, so why was I worried?

52

Eva

Asher decided to stay in town for a couple of weeks, and I was glad for his company. His charismatic, fun-loving personality hadn't changed a bit, and when I got home from work every evening, he came over to eat supper with us and even helped with a few of the repairs around the house. Having him around was comforting somehow; perhaps because he was a connection to both Paul and Davey, and maybe even because I'd missed him. It was so nice to know he would be back in our lives now.

I introduced him to Leon and was a bit surprised when the two men didn't seem to hit it off. I'd thought they would get along really well since their personalities were so similar, but I'd felt the tension between them immediately upon introduction; Asher even questioned me about our relationship later.

"Are you two courting?" He'd asked.

Surprised, I blinked and said, "No. Why do you ask?"

He hesitated for a moment, eyeing me closely. Finally, a grin spread across his face and he said, "I'm just curious why every single man in Savannah hasn't tried to snatch you up."

Blushing, I laughed and said, "Don't be silly."

On a Sunday afternoon, two weeks after Asher's arrival, he and I were walking around Savannah doing a bit of sightseeing. I'd always loved the old, Victorian style architecture and cobblestone streets; something about it was so magical. After a while, we stopped to get some ice cream and then walked along the sidewalk beneath the oaks, talking as we ate our sweet treats. I was looking up at Asher, listening as he spoke about his experiences in the Army, when someone stepped from a store we were passing and bumped into me. Asher quickly grabbed my arm, steadying me, and I could barely keep from dropping my ice cream.

"You should really watch where you're going."

Blinking in surprise, I looked up into a pair of familiar brown eyes. "K-Kirk," I stammered, taking a step back, "I'm sorry."

"You two know each other?" Asher asked, leaving his hand protectively at my elbow as he eyed Kirk curiously.

"You could say that," Kirk replied with a sniff. "We live down the street from each other." Looking Asher up and down, Kirk's jaw clenched slightly when he noticed Asher's hand at my elbow and he asked bluntly, "Who are you?"

I opened my mouth to make the introductions, but Asher cut me off. "I'm Asher, her brother-in-law," he stated. "And next time, why don't *you* watch where *you're* going?"

With a smirk, Kirk cocked a brow and said drolly, "Who says I wasn't watching this time?"

Before Asher could respond, Kirk turned and walked away, leaving us to stare after him.

"What is his problem?" Asher wanted to know, his brow furrowed with irritation.

"Oh, who knows? Let's just forget about it," I said, forcing a smile; I didn't want Kirk to spoil the pleasant day we were having. Taking a lick of my chocolate cream, I began to walk again, making certain to "watch where I was going" this time.

"Alright," Asher said, following along. Glancing over at me, his eyes crinkled at the edges as he stopped walking and reached up to swipe his thumb along the corner of my mouth. At the look of question on my face, he explained, "You had a bit of ice cream on your lip."

Feeling a bit embarrassed, I dabbed at my mouth and thanked him, laughing sheepishly.

"Do you remember when you and Paul took me crabbing during one of my visits?" Asher asked.

"Oh dear, I was hoping you'd forgotten about that," I replied, a smile pulling at my lips.

Grinning, Asher said, "How could I possibly forget the look on your face when Paul pulled that first crab from the net and dangled it before your eyes? When that thing snapped its claws in the direction of your nose, you jumped back and shrieked so loudly I think you scared the poor thing to death."

My cheeks burning, I shook my head and said, "Can I help it I'd never seen a live crab before? Those little creatures are terrifying!"

Asher threw back his head and laughed, and I couldn't help but join him. After a moment, he looked down at me and said warmly, "It feels good to laugh again. Thank you for that."

We spent the rest of the day together, and Asher even took me out to eat at a fancy restaurant on the river. We laughed and reminisced about all the good times we had during his visits when Paul was still alive, and Asher told me stories of his and Paul's childhood. After we'd finished eating, we walked out onto the dock and watched the sun set over the water. A chilly breeze blew through the marsh and I shivered slightly, wishing I'd brought along a heavier sweater.

"Cold?" Asher asked, wrapping his arm around my shoulders and pulling me close, and I suddenly thought of mine and Leon's trip to Tybee.

We stood there for a while, talking and breathing in the salty fresh air until it was almost dark. Asher had grown quiet, as if deep in thought, and I was about to suggest we head back to the car when he suddenly asked, "Eva, if there was a way to get Davey back, would you do it?"

Glancing at him in surprise, I said, "Of course I would."

"Well…" he hesitated, "I might have a solution."

"What is it?" I asked, eager to hear what he had to say.

After a slight hesitation, Asher cleared his throat and said in a low tone, "We could get married."

I blinked, caught totally off guard, and when I tried to pull away, Asher grabbed my hand and hurriedly said, "I know it sounds crazy, but just hear me out. If you have a husband, someone to provide for you and take care of you and Davey, the judge wouldn't hesitate to give him back to you."

"Your parents would never agree to this, Asher," I interrupted. "It would only make things worse."

"I'm Davey's *uncle*, the brother of the boy's father; my parents wouldn't have a leg to stand on," he insisted. "And if they continue to fight it, I have my own money with which to fight them back. They won't win, Eva, I promise."

"But we can't just get *married*, Asher," I stated, trying to get him to see reason.

"Why not?"

"Because…well, because it wouldn't be right," I stammered, my mind whirling.

"Because I'm Paul's brother?" He wanted to know, his gaze steady.

"Well, yes, that's one reason," I replied. "You and I are like brother and sister; we can't get married."

With a sigh, Asher released my hand and ran his fingers through his hair. After a moment, he looked back at me uncertainly and said, "What if I told you I didn't see you as my sister? That I never saw you in that way?"

My brow furrowing, I asked, "What do you mean?"

Asher stuffed his hands into his pockets and turned around to lean against the dock railing, his eyes warm as he looked down at me and said, "Eva, I fell in love with you the first moment I saw you. I couldn't tell you then because you were my brother's new bride, but that doesn't make it any less true."

I suddenly felt very lightheaded as the blood drained from my face. My mind was so muddled, I could barely make sense of what Asher was saying, and I shook my head.

"I know this is a shock," he said, laying a hand on my arm, "but I never stopped loving you, Eva. During all of those months spent in a prison camp, the only person I thought of was you, and when I came home to discover what my parents had done, I *knew* I had to come to you. Please, Eva, I realize that this is sudden, but at least consider it."

I stared at him, dizzy and feeling a bit like I was standing outside of myself watching all of this unfold. I'd never thought that Asher cared for me in that way, but now that I knew, I could look back and see it all very clearly. The way he visited so often, the look in his eyes when I would catch him watching me, the warm smile, the gentle way in which he'd hold me when we would hug goodbye…it all added up. But what did that *mean*, exactly? That I should marry him? I loved Asher dearly, but not in the romantic sense.

Wrapping my arms around my waist, I walked a few steps away and leaned against the dock railing, my back to Asher as I considered his proposal. He was one of the most warm and kind souls I'd ever met, and I had no doubt he'd treat me like a queen. Was it possible that love would come eventually?

I sighed, not knowing what to do. Was it crazy to marry someone with the expectation of falling in love? Or was all of that simply overrated? When it came to doing the right thing, for my sake and for Davey's, should there even be any hesitation?

Taking a deep breath, I turned around and walked back to Asher's side, my voice trembling a bit as I said, "Alright. I'll marry you."

His eyes lighting up, Asher pulled me into his arms, crushing me tightly against his chest. He kissed me on the forehead and said softly, "You won't regret it, Eva, I promise. We'll get Davey back and have a wonderful life together."

As we walked back to his car, hand in hand, I tried to feel hopeful about this arrangement. Perhaps this *would* work, and perhaps Asher and I would be happy together. Getting Davey back would be the best gift I could ever hope for, and if it meant marrying someone that I wasn't in love with, then so be it. I glanced at Asher's handsome face then, one that looked so much like Paul's, and chewed on my bottom lip thoughtfully, hoping I'd made the right reason.

That night, I sat on my bed discussing the engagement with both Nana and Mutter. I thought I was doing the right thing, but I wanted their opinion all the same.

"It's your decision, honey," Nana said, adjusting the glasses that were slowly sliding down her nose, "but my advice would be to give it a little more time. You two haven't seen each other in over two years."

Mutter had said little, which wasn't unusual, but I didn't fail to notice the look of worry in her eyes. When she saw the question in my gaze, she cleared her throat and said, "You know how much we've always liked Asher, but do you think it's wise to marry him only for Davey? And what about Leon?"

I blinked, caught off guard by the question. "Leon is just a good friend, Mutter," I said, shifting uncomfortably on the bed. "I…I have no reason to think otherwise."

She watched me in silence for a moment, her gaze piercing as she studied me. Finally, she took a deep breath and said softly, "As Nana said, it's your decision, and if you think this is for the best, then do what your heart is telling you to do. I just want you to be happy, Eva."

After we'd all gone to bed and the house was dark and quiet, I laid awake, staring up at the ceiling as thought after thought ran through my mind. Nana said to give it more time, but I didn't *have* much time. If we wanted to ensure the judge give Davey back to us, I'd have to marry Asher before the New Year. It *was* very quick, and although I hadn't seen Asher in two years, could he have really changed so drastically that he was no longer the same man I once knew him to be? I didn't think so.

"What about Leon?"

Mutter's question ran through my mind then, and I felt my breath catch. Leon and I had grown very close over the last few months, but he'd said nothing to make me think he was interested in being more than friends, and I couldn't leave my son's life hanging in the balance simply because Mutter thought she saw something between us.

Turning over onto my side, I told myself that I'd made the right decision and to stop worrying about it. I didn't, however, fall asleep until well after midnight.

Two days later, I arrived home from work to find a yellow 1941 Buick Roadmaster Convertible sitting in my driveway.

"It's all yours," Asher announced, kissing me on the cheek. He then added with a wink, "Perks of being my fiancé."

"Oh, Asher, it's beautiful," I said, my eyes wide. "But don't you think it's a little much? I don't need such a fancy car."

Wrapping his arm around my shoulders, he shook his head and said, "I think it's perfect for you, darling. I've got to leave for a few days to see about some military business, and I wanted to make sure you were taken care of before I left. I'll be back this weekend, and I'll be bringing your engagement ring with me."

Blushing, I shook my head and said, "I don't need an engagement ring; a plain, gold ring when we get married will be enough."

"But…"

Holding up my hand to stop him, I softly pleaded, "Please, Asher."

Sighing, he nodded and said, "Alright, darling, whatever you want."

We talked a bit more and even discussed a few details of when we wanted to get married, and then he left. I watched him drive away, hoping that he wouldn't get another headache soon; he had one for the last two days and had stayed cooped up in his hotel room.

Exhausted after a long day at work, I turned on my heel to go inside, but suddenly realized that Leon would wonder about the new car in my driveway, so I headed over to his house.

I knocked on his front door and waited, feeling a little flustered when I realized there were knots in my stomach. I would, of course, have to tell Leon about the engagement. He would be surprised, I knew that, but I wondered how else he would react. Hopefully, he would be happy for me.

The door opened and a look of pleasure passed over Leon's face when he saw me. "Eva, what a pleasant surprise," he said with a smile. Noticing my solemn expression, his smile faded and he asked in a serious tone, "Is everything okay?"

Nodding, I took a deep breath and said, "I...uh...well, I just wanted to let you know you can have your car back now. Thank you so much for letting me borrow it."

His brow furrowing, Leon glanced over my shoulder and caught sight of the convertible. "Wow," he whistled, his eyes widening, "where did you get that beauty?"

Anxiously twisting my fingers together, I said, "Well...a lot has happened. You know Asher is still in town, right?"

"Yes," he replied, nodding. "Is he the one that bought you the car?"

Clearing my throat, I said, "Yes, but there's a bit more to it than that."

Leaning against the doorframe, Leon crossed his arms and looked at me closely. "Oh?" He asked in a serious tone.

Taking a deep breath, I squared my shoulders and said, "Yes, he...he's asked me to marry him, Leon, and I've accepted."

Leon stared at me, as if not totally comprehending what I'd just said. Slowly, he stood to his full height, his voice filled with disbelief as he asked, "*What*?"

Fidgeting, I crossed my arms and said, "We're getting married. We talked about it and...and we think it's for the best."

"How exactly is it for the best?" He wanted to know. "You haven't seen each other in, what, two or three years?"

"For Davey," I hurriedly explained. "We think that if we get married, the judge will give him back to us."

Leon didn't say anything for a moment; he simply stared at me as if I had grown another head. "You can't be serious," he finally said. "Eva, you can't just marry someone out of convenience. It's ludicrous!"

"It's ludicrous to want to get my son back?" I asked, feeling frustrated as tears began to burn the backs of my eyes. "Leon, Asher is a wonderful man. Once you get to know him, you'll realize what a good decision this is."

"Do you love him?"

I blinked, unprepared for that question. "Uh…well, of course I do. He's my brother-in-law," I stuttered.

"That's not what I mean and you know it," Leon stated, his eyes flickering intensely in the porch light.

I hesitated, struggling with what to say. Finally, I sighed and said softly, "I'm very fond of him. Please, Leon, be happy for me. You've become such a dear friend, and I can't bear to think that you're upset with me."

Stuffing his hands into his pockets, Leon glanced down at his feet, but not before I saw something flash across his face. I couldn't identify the look, but it was something very akin to pain, and I suddenly wanted to cry; I'd hurt him somehow and hated myself for it.

Finally, after a long, heavy moment of silence, Leon glanced back up and said in a monotone voice, "If this is what you want, Eva, then who am I to protest? I want you to be happy, and if this makes you happy, then that's wonderful. Congratulations."

"Leon…" I said, reaching out to him, but he stepped away.

"Look, I've got some stuff to do inside so I'll see you around, okay?" He said, avoiding my gaze.

I handed him the keys to his car and thanked him again, my feet rooted in place as he took the keys and went back inside, closing the door in my face. I didn't know what was wrong with me, but I felt like opening the door and running after him and…what? What would I say? I'd wanted his approval, but it felt as if I'd lost my best friend instead, and it left me feeling cold and empty as a result.

Turning, I slowly walked back to my house, feeling as low as the grasshopper that leaped across my path. A tear slid down my cheek and I sat down on my front porch step, looking up through blurry eyes at the night sky. Why did life have to be so hard, so confusing? Leon had asked if I loved Asher, but wasn't fondness and friendship enough with the hope that love would come later?

My mind was in such turmoil that I failed to notice the shadowy figure creeping slowly and quietly in my direction. Before I knew what was happening, a hand snaked out through the darkness and clamped down on my arm, yanking me up from the step. Gasping, I tried to scream, but his other hand quickly covered my mouth, preventing any sound from passing my lips.

"Hello, Eva," a familiar voice breathed next to my ear and I froze, my heart jumping in my chest. He pulled me into the shadows and said, "If you promise not to scream, I'll move my hand."

I nodded, and he slowly removed his hand from my mouth. Turning to look at him, I peered through the shadows but couldn't make out any discernable features. He wore a black mask and hat which shadowed his entire face, and I fought to remain calm when my eyes fell upon the knife he slowly pulled from his pocket. If I tried to scream, he would kill me before anyone had a chance to help.

Swallowing, I asked, "Who...who are you?"

The mask tilted up around the mouth, and I knew he was smiling; I could almost see the cynical tilt of his lips. "You'll find out when I'm ready and only then," he said in that same, unidentifiable whisper. "Tell me, Eva, is it true that you're engaged?"

I nodded hesitantly, gasping when he suddenly lunged toward me and gripped my arm painfully in his hand.

"You shouldn't have done that," he hissed, and I began to tremble all over, my heart pounding loudly in my ears. Shaking his head, he said, "You won't get married again; I won't allow it."

He turned and began to drag me roughly across the yard, nearly ripping my arm from my shoulder. I could see the silhouette of a car parked in the shadows just up ahead and knew if I didn't do something quickly, he'd force me into the trunk and I would never see my family again. I didn't know who this man was or what exactly he wanted, but I couldn't let him put me into that car; I had to stop him.

I began struggling with every ounce of strength I had, slowing our trek across the damp grass. Breathing hard, he spun around and slapped me hard across the face, my head snapping back from the force. I fell to the ground, the fall nearly knocking the breath from my lungs, and with a growl, he yanked me back onto my feet and pressed the knife against my throat.

This is it, I thought, my chest heaving as tears swam before my eyes. *He's going to kill me.*

Suddenly, my front porch light clicked on, illuminating the yard in a warm, yellow glow, and I heard Mutter calling for me. Relaxing his hold on my arm, the man glanced wildly about and, without giving it a second thought, I kneed him in the groin as hard as I could. With a grunt, he released my arm, and I took off at a dead run toward the house.

"Go back inside!" I cried breathlessly to Mutter, waving my arms as I ran.

I was almost there. The front porch was only a few feet away when he lunged forward and slammed into my back. We landed in a heap on the front porch steps, his hat tumbling off into the grass, and I gasped in pain when my palm struck an exposed nail in the wooden plank. I tried to continue struggling, but the stars that danced before my eyes and the ringing in my ears let me know that my strength was almost gone.

"If you won't cooperate with me, then you'll die," he growled in my ear, and I felt the cool metal of his knife blade press against the back of my neck.

I waited for death to come, the weight of his body too much for me to fight against, when suddenly there was a loud *crack* and the man yelped in pain and jumped away, stumbling backwards.

279

"Come, Eva," Mutter said breathlessly, and I felt her hands grasp my arms and jerk me upward.

We hurried inside, the sound of the man's moans blending in with the slamming of the door as we crossed the threshold. Mutter quickly locked it, and I looked out of the window to watch as my assailant stumbled to his feet, grabbed his hat, and ran to his car. Several neighbors flipped on their lights and looked outside, each wondering at the cause of all the noise.

Nana hurried to my side, her face as white as a sheet. "I called the police," she said, her voice trembling.

I nodded and, looking over at Mutter, asked in a breathless tone, "What did you hit him with?"

"Davey's little baseball bat he always kept by the back door," she said, tears filling her eyes as she reached out to pull me into her arms. "I'm so glad you're alright, mein Schatz."

There was a knock on the front door just then, and we all jumped back in fear. My heart pounding, I tiptoed over to see who it was and breathed a sigh of relief when I realized it was Leon. I opened the door and, before I could think twice, threw myself into his arms.

"Are you alright?" He asked, holding me tight. "What happened?"

Pulling back, I told him everything, my words a shaking, stuttering mess. Once I'd finished, Leon closed his eyes and said, "I am so sorry, Eva. I should have walked over with you. If anything had happened…" he stopped then, his jaw clenching, and my heart warmed at his concern.

"It's not your fault," I assured him, reaching out to squeeze his hand.

Leon held on to my hand, his gaze intense as he looked at me. I hadn't realized until then that Nana and Mutter had gone into the kitchen, leaving us alone, and when Leon opened his mouth to say something, I was sorry when the sound of approaching sirens interrupted.

That night, after the police were gone, I sat up in bed with Davey's baseball bat beside me. I was terrified to go to sleep, and although there was a police officer keeping watch from his car outside, I kept wishing that Leon had offered to stay and sleep on the living room sofa.

I finally drifted off into a fitful sleep, but instead of my dreams being filled with ghoulish visions of my attacker, all I dreamed of was the look on Leon's face when I told him about Asher, and then the way he held me so tightly in his arms after the attack. I knew things wouldn't be the same between us now that Asher was in the picture, and when I awoke the next morning, I felt an odd sense of grief, as if I'd lost something very special.

When I went in to work that morning, I stopped by Vivian's office and told her what happened.

"Who do you think this crazy man is?" She asked, her eyes wide with horror.

"I don't know," I replied, shivering. "Maybe I don't even know him personally."

"You think he's just some random man who's stalking you?"

I hesitated. "Perhaps," I muttered, although I wasn't convinced; something about him was so familiar.

When I went into the kitchen, I was putting on my apron when I noticed a new dishwasher working at Jackson's station.

"Jackson quit yesterday," Cook told me, "so we had to find someone else."

I blinked in surprise. "Why did he quit?"

"I don't know," she replied, shrugging. "He wouldn't say."

I began gathering bowls and ingredients to prepare breakfast, my mind on Jackson. Why had he left so suddenly, and without even saying goodbye? I was very surprised by his sudden departure, and wondered what his reasons were for leaving.

53

THE SHADOW

He slammed his foot down on the gas, causing the car to accelerate at an alarming speed. His hands tightly clutched the wheel and he leaned forward, staring out at the road in fury as everything passed by in a blur. He'd never been so angry before, and his pulse pounded loudly in his ears. Eva was engaged, and she'd managed to escape him once again. Reaching up, he touched the lump on his head where her mother had hit him and winced, clenching his jaw as white-hot fury swept over him once again.

The speedometer climbed higher and higher, and sweat dripped from his forehead. He needed to calm down, to think of an alternate plan, but he couldn't seem to shake the feeling of anger and self-belittlement at being bested once again. All he could see was the sneer on his father's face as he loomed over him, a belt wrapped around his hand and a look of disgust in his eyes. His father despised failure and inadequacy, and so did he.

Just then, his eyes landed on a road sign, and he suddenly realized he was heading north. Blinking, he slowed the car down a bit as an idea began to form in the back of his mind. If Eva wouldn't play it his way, he'd have to change directions and alter the rules, giving her no other choice but to do exactly as he wanted.

Sitting back against the seat, he sighed and began to relax, a victorious laugh bursting past his lips. This was such a brilliant plan, he wondered why he hadn't thought of it before, and he could hardly wait to see it all play out. Eva would be his; he had no doubt about that now.

54

DAVEY

Davey ran down the long hallway, his blonde hair billowing out around his ears as he pushed his chubby legs to go faster. She was calling him, the sound of her voice nearer now than it was before, and with a grin, he skidded to a stop and leaped behind a tall, potted plant.

"David, come here this instant!" She yelled, and he watched as his "nurse" stomped down the hall in search of him.

He covered his mouth, trying not to giggle. Mrs. Miller was a grumpy old woman, and he didn't care for her at all; he did, however, love tormenting the poor soul by running away and hiding where she couldn't find him.

Mrs. Miller hurried past his hiding place and down the stairs, the smell of the peppermint oil she used tickling his nose as it trailed behind her. Once she was gone, Davey tiptoed from his hiding place and ran back down the hall towards the back staircase. Now that he was free of Mrs. Miller for a little while, he planned on doing a bit of exploring.

His grandparents' house was massive, full of rooms, staircases, and winding hallways for a little boy to roam through. He was pretending to be a pirate now, searching through a long, dark cave for lost treasure, when he suddenly found his way into his grandmother's room. Peeking around the door to make certain no one was around, his eyes fell upon a large, sparkling box sitting on the vanity. His eyes wide, Davey bounced into the room, climbed up onto the cushioned chair, and picked up the box. He opened the lid and peered inside, his mouth forming an "O" as he stared at the emeralds, diamonds, and rubies that glittered in the afternoon light.

Davey had just picked up a diamond bracelet, feeling like a real pirate by this time, when the door suddenly opened and his grandmother stepped inside. Startled, Davey dropped the jewelry box and it spilled to the floor with a loud clatter.

"David!" His grandmother gasped, her hand resting against her chest. "What on earth are you doing?"

"I...I just playing pirate," he said, his lower lip trembling as he climbed from the chair.

"You are not supposed to be wandering about by yourself, young man," she scolded, walking towards him. "And just look at the mess you've made of my jewelry!"

Tears welling up in his eyes, Davey looked down at his feet and mumbled, "I sorry, Grandmudder."

Sighing, Mrs. Beckett patted him on the head and said, "Well, there's no need to cry as long as it doesn't happen again. Come now, help me clean up my jewelry and then we'll go find Mrs. Miller."

Nodding, Davey bent over and began clumsily dumping bits and pieces of his grandmother's jewelry back into the box. At home, Nana and Oma had never minded him playing with their things, and he simply couldn't understand why it was different here.

Once the job was done, Mrs. Beckett led Davey back out into the hallway. He reached for her but she ignored his outstretched hand, and with a sigh, he asked, "When I go home?"

Her lips pursed, Mrs. Beckett glanced disapprovingly down at him and said, "This is your new home, David. Don't you like it here?"

"I miss Mommy," he said, reaching out to hold her dress as they walked, "and Nana and Oma and Mr. Leon…"

"That's enough, David," she interrupted, and with a huff, he lowered his head and remained silent.

Mrs. Beckett handed Davey over to his nurse, and after giving him a firm scolding, Mrs. Miller took him back into the nursery to play with his blocks.

Davey didn't understand exactly what it meant to miss someone, but he often longed to feel Oma's sweet, gentle touch when she would pull him into a hug, or kiss the top of his head. He also yearned for Nana's cookies, and to hear her contagious laugh. Even though living in his grandparents' big house could be a bit of an adventure sometimes, he decided he liked his old house much better, where he could run free without getting lost and into trouble.

The person he missed the most, however, was his mother. He often listened for the sound of her voice echoing through the house, especially in the late afternoons when she usually got home from work, but he never heard it. He'd cried himself to sleep many nights, wishing for her to come and sing to him. His grandparents were kind but distant, the house was big and lonely, and Mrs. Miller was too grumpy. As he played with his blocks, he decided right then and there to run away the first chance he got.

That chance arrived sooner than he'd thought. That night, Mrs. Miller put him to bed as usual, and he fell asleep almost immediately. Several hours later, just before the sunrise, something woke him. Rubbing his eyes, Davey sat up in his crib and looked around. The moon shone through the sheer curtains at the windows and bounced along the walls, creating dark, frightening shadows from toys and furniture that sat around the large room.

Suddenly, one of the shadows moved and began coming toward him.

Davey's eyes widened, and he clutched his teddy bear tighter and pulled the cover up to his chin. He wanted to call out, but the last time he did that after having a nightmare, he was scolded for acting like a baby.

"Hello, Davey," the shadow said, stopping at the foot of his crib.

"Don't...don't hurt my teddy," Davey said in a small, trembling voice.

"I'm not going to hurt you *or* your teddy," the shadow said, drawing closer. "I'm here to take you home, Davey. Would you like that?"

Although Davey couldn't see the man's face, he recognized his voice and relaxed a bit.

"You take me home to Mommy?" He asked hopefully, perking up.

"That's right," the shadow nodded. Reaching out two, long arms in Davey's direction, he said, "Let's go, Davey. Just remember to be very, very quiet."

55

Vivian

When Eva told me the news of her and Asher's engagement, I'll admit I was shocked. I liked Asher and thought he seemed like a very nice man, but I knew Eva didn't love him and feared that she was making a mistake. I didn't, however, voice my thoughts. After all, who was I to give marriage advice?

When she came into work Friday morning, I could tell immediately that she'd been crying.

"Has something happened to Davey?" I asked, pulling her into my office.

"No," she replied, shaking her head. "Asher got back last night and said he'd called his parents to tell them of our engagement. They said if we married, they'd see to it that neither of us ever see Davey again."

"Oh, Eva," I sighed heavily. "What are you going to do?"

"Asher said that once we're married, there's no way the judge will keep Davey from us," she replied, reaching up to rub her eyes. "He wants us to get married next Saturday, two days before Christmas."

I blinked in surprise. "That's really quick," I stated, chewing my bottom lip. "Is that what *you* want?"

"I just want my son back," she said, bursting into tears all over again.

Pulling her into a hug, I patted her on the back and did my best to console her. I knew what she was feeling, but what if the judge *didn't* give Davey back? It would be too late for Eva then. I couldn't try to talk her out of it, though. She was a grown woman, and Asher *did* seem like a good man. I couldn't blame her for trying everything she could to get her son back.

"I'm sure this will work." I smiled encouragingly at Eva as she pulled away and blew her nose. An idea struck me then and, my eyes lighting up, I said, "Look, why don't I give you and Asher an engagement party tomorrow night? We'll only invite your closest friends, and it will be my going away gift to you. After all, you'll be quitting the restaurant once you're married."

"Oh, no," Eva said, shaking her head. "You've done enough for me already, Vivian."

"Please let me do it," I pressed, knowing she could use the distraction

286

and a bit of fun. "I'm going to miss having you around here, and you deserve to have a celebration. A marriage is a big deal."

"But I've been married already once before," she continued to protest, "and Asher and I are just going to go down to the courthouse and say our vows; it's not going to be anything big."

"Which is exactly why we need to have a party," I said, hands on my hips, "to make the occasion more momentous."

Eva finally gave in, and I spent the rest of the day planning the party and inviting everyone. I closed the restaurant at two o'clock the following day and Savannah, along with her aunt and mother-in-law, came over and helped with the cooking and decorating. The four of us had so much fun that it felt more like a holiday than work, and by the time six o'clock rolled around, the place looked great. Leon had brought a Christmas tree by, and Mrs. Emma decorated it with ribbons and strands of popcorn while I made the sandwiches, finger foods, punch, cookies, and cake. Savannah decorated the back room we often used for small, private parties with balloons and heart streamers, and when everything was finished, we congratulated each other on a job well done.

Savannah's uncle arrived right on time with Father in tow, along with Asher, Eva, her mother, and grandmother. I'd also invited Zachary, as he and Eva were friends, and when he walked into the room, I suddenly felt a bit self-conscious. I hadn't seen him since the kiss, and as he made his way across the room towards me, I nervously brushed my hair away from my face.

"You ladies did a great job," he said as he openly admired the room. Turning to look back at me, he surveyed my loosely curled hair and long, green dress and said warmly, "You look beautiful."

"Thank you," I replied with a smile.

Mrs. Hamilton, Eva's grandmother, approached Zachary then, and he turned to greet her. I watched them for a moment, no longer feeling nervous as I realized I'd missed Zachary the last few weeks.

Now that the room was filled with all our guests, I walked to the front of the room and, after getting everyone's attention, said, "Thank you all for coming. As everyone knows, we're here to celebrate the upcoming marriage of Eva and Asher." I paused while everyone clapped and cheered, and Asher wrapped his arm around Eva, causing her to blush profusely. "But this is also a 'we're going to miss you' party, as Eva will sadly leave the restaurant next week." Everyone laughingly "booed" then, and I smiled. Looking at Eva, I said in a sincere tone, "Eva, you've become such a dear friend. I wish you and Asher all the happiness in the world because you deserve it." Raising my glass of punch, I said, "To Eva and Asher."

Everyone toasted to the happy couple; everyone, that is, except for Leon. I'd noticed that he'd been unusually quiet and staying in the background, and I made a mental note to find out what was wrong.

We all lined up to fill our plates with the sandwiches and finger foods, and I hadn't realized until I heard his voice that Zachary was behind me.

"What do we know about this Asher fellow?" He asked, glancing around to make certain no one could hear us.

Lowering my voice dramatically, I leaned close and said, "He's Eva's brother-in-law and comes from a very wealthy, snobbish family."

Rolling his eyes, he said dryly, "Is that all you know?"

Smiling, I shrugged and said, "Well, he's very nice, charming, and in the military but planning to get out soon."

"You're not concerned that Eva's marrying him too quickly?"

"Yes, of course I am," I replied, sighing, "but what am I supposed to do about it?"

"Try to talk her out of it?" Zachary responded, cocking an eyebrow at me.

Before we could continue our conversation, Savannah called to me, waving for us to sit beside her. All the older folks were gathered at one table, so the rest of us took our seats at the table next to them. Leon sat quietly and picked at his food for the duration of the meal, while Zachary made polite conversation with Asher. Eva said little, which wasn't unusual, so Savannah and I chatted about our work. Before long, it was time for dessert and I got up to serve the cake.

"Need some help?" Savannah asked, coming to stand beside me at the dessert table.

"Yes, thanks," I replied, handing her a stack of plates.

We'd just served the last slice of cake when Asher stood up and, after opening what appeared to be a bottle of champagne, began pouring everyone a glass.

"I'd like to make a toast to my beautiful fiancé," he said, smiling warmly down at Eva as he held up his glass of bubbling liquid. She blushed and tried to protest, as she hated any form of attention, but he ignored her. "Thank you, Eva," he said warmly as he touched her cheek, "for making me the happiest and luckiest man in the world. To Eva!"

Everyone echoed his words and drank the champagne, some murmuring about how expensive it tasted. I'd never cared for the stuff and put my glass aside, suddenly wondering how "normal" a life Asher would be willing to live after such a wealthy, cushioned upbringing. He'd endured plenty of hardships in the Army, I knew that, but would he really settle down and be happy working at a regular job and living in a small house? If not, I knew Eva wouldn't care to live in a mansion full of servants, nor would she be comfortable rubbing elbows with the upper class, high-society crowds.

Zachary caught my eye then, and by the look on his face, I knew he was thinking the same thing, but I couldn't say anything to Eva. She had to make her own decisions, for herself and for her son, and I would not try to change her mind. It simply wasn't my place.

Leon came up to the table where I was standing to get some punch, his face solemn and gray.

"Leon, are you alright?" I asked, concerned.

"I don't know, Viv, I'm just feeling a little down," he replied, sighing.

He took a sip of his punch and glanced over at Eva, his eyes bearing a look that I'd never seen in all the years I'd known him, and it suddenly dawned on me. Reaching out to rest my hand on his arm, I softly asked, "Leon, why haven't you told her how you feel?"

Startled, Leon looked down at me, his eyes wide and searching. Finally, he let out a heavy breath and said, "I was going to, but then everything happened with Davey and it just didn't seem like the right time."

"When did you begin to have feelings for her?" I wanted to know, making certain to keep my voice down.

"I'm not entirely certain," he replied, running his fingers through his hair. "I felt an attraction immediately upon meeting her..." he paused for a split second, a smile coming to his lips at the memory, "and when I heard her sing for the first time, something stirred deep inside of me. I tried to just shake it all off as nothing, though, and told myself she probably wasn't ready for anything else just yet. I think I knew for sure how I felt, though, when she was so sick with polio and almost died."

I blinked, remembering how he'd shown up at the hospital and insisted he see her. I had thought little of it at the time, as there was so much going on, but I could clearly see him sitting at her side, holding her hand and praying.

"Leon, that was over *four* months ago!" I gasped. "Why have you waited so long?"

"Because I felt like it was too soon," he replied, his tone filled with frustration. "I wanted to wait and be sure, and I also couldn't tell how she felt about me."

"Perhaps if you'd grow up and quit messing around with the likes of Lucy Michaels, you wouldn't be standing here watching Eva get married to another man," I stated, fully annoyed. He and Eva would be perfect together, and I was upset that he'd let her get away because he was too busy running away from his feelings instead of facing them.

"Lucy wouldn't leave me alone," he snapped. "What was I supposed to do?"

"Be a man and tell her you're not interested," I shot back.

His jaw clenching, Leon didn't respond for a moment. We continued to stand there, watching everyone talk and chat, until finally he deflated like a balloon and said, "You're right. I've been searching for that once in a lifetime, "real deal" that my parents had and then when I found it, I was afraid Eva wouldn't feel the same. Now it's too late; I've lost her for good."

Feeling guilty over the harshness of my words, I sighed and said, "I'm sorry, I wasn't trying to be rude." Reaching out to touch his arm, I added, "Tell her how you feel, Leon. It's not too late."

Before he could respond, I heard a knock at the front door and hurried through the restaurant to open it.

"Gabe," I said, surprised when I opened the door. "What are you…"

"Is Eva here?" He interrupted, his tone tense.

Blinking, I nodded and pointed to the back room. "Yes, she's back there."

Gabe rushed by and I hurried after him, wondering what on earth was going on. He went over to Eva's side and asked to speak to her privately. By that time, everyone had quieted down and was watching, each with a curious look on their face.

"What's wrong?" Eva asked when she saw the expression on his face, her voice trembling. "Please, just tell me now."

Glancing around the room, Gabe sighed and said in a heavy voice, "I just received a phone call from the chief of police in Greenwich, Connecticut. Davey was kidnapped early yesterday morning, and they think the kidnapper is heading this way."

56

Eva

The room was spinning out of control. I could hear Asher calling my name, but I couldn't utter a single sound in response. My heart pounded loudly in my ears and I began to sway on my feet. A pair of strong hands grabbed my arms and led me to the nearest chair, and Savannah kneeled at my side and told me to bend over and rest my head between my knees. She and Zachary took my pulse, and I could hear voices all around but couldn't make any sense of the words that were spoken.

Within a few moments, I could breathe normally again and slowly sat up to look at Officer Wright, the solemn expression on his face making me feel sick to my stomach.

"What can we do?" I asked, my voice barely above a whisper. Asher was at my side, and I reached out to clutch his hand.

"The Greenwich police have sent out bulletins with Davey's picture all down the coast," Gabe said. "We suspect the kidnapper is possibly the private detective that Mr. and Mrs. Beckett hired."

Looking at Gabe in confusion, I asked, "But why would he kidnap Davey?"

Hands on his hips, Gabe sighed and said, "He has a reputation for being…unstable. The Greenwich police told me he's got a long record of complaints, many of which were made by the families of young women stating he stalked and harassed them; a couple of them even disappeared."

"Who is this man and why isn't he in jail?" Leon wanted to know.

"We believe that his real name is Bob Simpson, but he seems to have several aliases, as well," Gabe replied. "And the police couldn't arrest him because none of the women he harassed would press charges."

"Why do you think he's headed here?" I asked, my stomach in knots.

"A waitress at a diner in Hardeeville, South Carolina called in and said she served a man with a little boy this afternoon that fits Davey's description. I know that's not much to go on, but it's all we've got."

"But why would he be coming *here*?" Nana asked, her voice trembling.

"It almost sounds like he's bringing Davey home," Asher spoke up.

"He's coming here for a reason, but I doubt it's with good intentions," Gabe stated.

"What does this Simpson fellow look like?" Zachary asked.

"I don't know. We don't have a picture of him on file, and Mr. Beckett said he never saw him; they handled everything over the telephone." Turning back to me, Gabe said, "We're going to do everything we can to find Davey and bring him home safely. I'm going to post one of my men outside of your house all night, and if you hear anything from Simpson, let us know immediately. Alright?"

I nodded, my mind whirling like an out-of-control carousel. Would he hurt Davey? And was this possibly the same man that had tried to kidnap me? None of this made any sense, and my stomach was twisted into so many knots, I felt like a human pretzel.

Gabe turned to leave and Asher said, "Once I get Eva home safely, can I join you in the search for Davey?"

"Yes, meet me at the station in an hour," Gabe nodded, and I watched as Vivian walked him out, her face nearly as ashen as mine.

Asher took us home and when we arrived at the house, there was already an officer parked out front. Asher walked us inside and, kissing me on the forehead, said, "Don't worry, honey. We're going to get Davey back, I promise."

I nodded and told him to please be careful. Once he was gone, I locked the front door and joined Nana and Mutter in the kitchen. Mutter sat at the kitchen table crying softly while Nana busied herself with boiling water for some chamomile tea. Once the tea had steeped, we sat at the table and silently sipped the steaming liquid, each of us lost in our own thoughts and worries.

It was after midnight when I finally convinced Nana and Mutter to go to bed and get some rest. I stayed up, pacing around the living room as I prayed and worried myself sick. It was nearly one o'clock when the telephone suddenly rang and I hurried into the kitchen to answer it, hoping it was Gabe or Asher with good news.

"Hello, Eva," the all too familiar voice breathed on the other end of the line, and I covered my mouth in horror, my eyes growing wide. "Don't scream and don't call for help; just listen. I've got Davey, and I'll kill him unless you do exactly as I say. We'll be at an old, abandoned farmhouse just outside of town, and I want you to come out here now, but you *must* come alone. If I even so much as suspect you've told the police or that you're not alone, I swear I'll kill Davey. Got it?"

"Y-yes," I stammered, my hands shaking.

Mr. Simpson rattled off the directions to the farmhouse, told me to be there in no more than an hour, and hung up. I stood there for a moment, my thoughts whirling as I tried to figure out what to do. He'd said to come alone, so was there any other option? I couldn't risk Davey's life, and if I cooperated, perhaps he'd let Davey go.

I quietly tiptoed to my bedroom and put on a dark, long sleeve dress and covered my hair with a dark scarf. I then wrote a note explaining what happened and left it on the kitchen table. I headed to the front door but stopped, realizing that the police officer outside would insist on following me. *Oh, what can I do?* I thought, the ticking of the Grandfather clock echoing loudly in my ears.

Suddenly, a thought struck me, and I returned to the kitchen and went out the back door. It would be risky, but I didn't have time to think of anything else. Quietly closing the door behind me, I slipped out into the night and climbed the fence that separated our yard from Leon's. I then made my way to Leon's back door and, breathing a sigh of relief when I found it open, I turned the knob and went inside. All the lights were off, and I stood in the dark kitchen for a moment trying to get my bearings. Once my eyes were adjusted, I began to make my way through the house towards the front door, where I knew Leon always left his car keys.

As I stepped out into the living room, my heart stuck in my throat when a floorboard creaked beneath my foot and I stopped. The shadows of lamps, chairs, and various pieces of furniture stood out in the darkness like villains waiting to pounce, and I tried not to let my imagination get the best of me. Taking a deep, calming breath, I continued my trek through the house, hoping that this would work.

Suddenly, another board creaked, but this time from behind. With a gasp, I spun around just as the overhead light clicked on.

"Eva!" Leon cried, his eyes opening wide with shock. He was shirtless and holding a baseball bat in his right hand. "What on earth are you doing?"

Trembling all over, I slumped against a nearby bookcase and sighed, rubbing my head. "Davey's k-kidnapper called me," I said, proceeding to tell Leon everything Mr. Simpson had said in a tight, shaky voice. "I can't go in my car because the officer posted outside would only insist on following me, so I was going to...well...borrow *your* car."

"Eva, are you crazy?" Leon asked, tossing the bat aside. "You can't go out there alone. The man will kill you!"

"He'll kill my son if I don't," I cried, tears of frustration welling up in my eyes. "I've got to do this, Leon. Please don't stop me."

Sighing, Leon ran his fingers through his hair as he considered my words. Finally, he shook his head and said, "Fine, you can take the car..."

"Oh, Leon, thank you," I sighed with relief, pausing when he held up his hand.

"*But* I'm going with you."

My eyes widening, I shook my head. "No, Leon, if he sees you..."

"I'll hide in the back seat," he said, his tone firm. "You're not going by yourself and that's final."

His mind made up, Leon reached above my head and pulled a revolver from the top of the bookcase. He then brushed past me and went into the foyer to get his car keys.

"Let me put on some clothes and I'll be right back," he promised as he hurried to his bedroom.

Less than a minute later, he was back and ready to go. He turned off all the lights, and we tiptoed quietly outside to his car.

"I'll drive until we get close to the farmhouse, and then we can switch places," he whispered, opening the car door for me.

My heart pounded as we backed out of the driveway, and I hoped the officer wouldn't stop us for any reason. I ducked down in my seat as we drove past, breathing a sigh of relief when we made it by and turned onto another street.

The night was dark as we drove, and it seemed to take an eternity to get out of the city. I kept checking my watch, the minutes seeming to tick by faster than they should, and I feared the allotted hour would pass before we could reach Davey. Finally, Leon pulled onto the side of the road, stopped the car, and got into the back seat as I slid over to the driver's side.

Nervously taking the wheel, I pulled back onto the road, the headlights beaming ahead to reveal a dark and desolate area. Five long minutes passed as I drove down the heavily wooded dirt road, and when I rounded the curve, I saw it; just up ahead, a two-story farmhouse rested about fifty yards away. I turned onto the small, overgrown driveway, my heartbeat kicking into overdrive when I saw another unfamiliar car with Connecticut plates parked on the side of the house. I pulled up beside it and stopped, the breaks squealing slightly.

"Don't say anything in case he can see you," Leon said from the floor of the back seat. "Just listen for a moment. I'm going to give you a head start, and then I'll circle around the back and try to get inside. I won't do anything rash, but I will not let you go in by yourself and be at the mercy of that man. Do your best to get a hold of Davey and get away from this Simpson fellow. Everything will be okay, Eva, just try to stay calm."

Taking a deep breath, I climbed from the car and slowly walked around to the front of the house. Most of the windows were broken, the white paint was cracked and peeling, and the shutters hung haphazardly from their hinges, some of them creaking and bumping against the side of the house in the breeze. My shoes crunched the overgrown weeds and dry, dead leaves beneath my feet, and as I climbed the steps leading up to the porch, they groaned like a tired, old man.

As I gingerly pushed the front door open and stepped inside, I wished I'd brought a flashlight. The room was dark and smelled like old wood that had once been wet, and through the shadows I could see bits and pieces of furniture sitting randomly about.

Suddenly, a small light clicked on and I caught my breath. There, just across the room, stood a man wearing the same hat and black mask as before. We both stood completely still, staring at each other, the silence deafening as I held my breath and waited to see what he would do. With slow, methodical movements, the man reached up and removed his face coverings, and I gasped as the light from the flashlight he held illuminated the familiar features before me.

"Mr. Creed," I whispered, his translucent eyes chilling me to the bone.

"Hello, Eva," he said, his voice no longer a strange, choked whisper. "I'm so happy that you could make it."

"*You're* the private detective?" I asked, trying to wrap my mind around everything that was happening.

"That's right," he nodded, a satisfied grin tugging at his lips. "You didn't know it was me, did you?"

"But...but I thought your wife just died, and..."

Mr. Creed burst into laughter and I stopped, staring at him. "That was all a lie," he told me, his eyes glittering triumphantly in the flashlight's glow. "It was all part of the game, Eva, and you fell for it just as I knew you would."

Before I could respond, my eyes suddenly landed on the small, still form lying on a couch behind Mr. Creed, and I realized it was Davey. My heart all but stopping, I rushed towards my son but halted when Mr. Creed stepped between us and held up a hand.

"Not so fast," he said, and I realized he was holding a knife.

I felt the blood leave my face and slowly nodded, only moving my upper body as I attempted to get a better look at Davey. He was lying there so still...too still.

"Don't look so worried, Eva," Mr. Creed said with a chuckle. "He's only asleep. I gave him something that will keep him out for hours."

Looking back at Mr. Creed, I whispered in a choked voice, "Why are you doing this?"

"Because I love you," he stated matter-of-factly.

"But you kidnapped my son," I cried, trying to make him see reason. "If you loved me, you would never have done that."

"*You* made me do it!" He shouted, his face turning red, and I flinched. Slamming the flashlight down on a nearby side table, he began to pace back and forth in front of the couch. "It...it was only just a job at the beginning, but the longer I followed you, the more I grew to love you," he rambled, his words hurried and jumbled. Spinning around to face me, he cried, "If you'd come with me in the first place, Eva, none of this would have happened!"

I stood there in silence, my mind whirling. Mr. Creed glared at me for a moment, his face pulling into a dark, ugly frown as he hissed, "You're just like the others, aren't you? You all hate me and want to turn me over to the police so they can throw me into prison. Well, I'm smarter than that, Eva, much smarter."

He was getting more and more upset, and I fought to think of something to say to calm him down. "That's n-not true," I told him, my voice soft and trembling. "I don't hate you at all, Mr. Creed."

His pale blue eyes hardened, becoming two pools of ice cold water as he asked in a low, deadly tone, "You're not going to marry that other man, are you?"

The question was a test, I knew that, and swallowing past the lump in my throat, I shook my head and said, "No, of course not. What…what is it you want, Mr. Creed? You want me to go away with you?"

Taking a step toward me, he nodded and said, "Yes. That's all I've ever wanted."

Just behind and to the right of Mr. Creed's shoulder was an open doorway, and through the darkness I caught a faint sight of movement. Leon was inching his way through the house, and I had to keep Mr. Creed distracted while somehow getting Davey away from him.

"Alright, I'll go with you only…" I hesitated, praying this would work, "…only if you agree to leave Davey here. We can stop somewhere along the road and call to let my family know where to find him."

Seeing the look of suspicion on Mr. Creed's face, I hurriedly added in a pleading tone, "He would only get in the way if we took him with us. If we're going to be together, I don't want him to tie us down."

His face slowly filling with pleasure, Mr. Creed nodded and said, "What are we waiting for, then? Let's go."

I let him take a few steps toward me before I asked, "May I give him one last hug before we leave?"

When he nodded, I rushed to Davey's side and pulled him into my arms, the slow, steady rhythm of his heartbeat putting my fears to rest. I quickly glanced around the room, trying to judge which door was the most accessible if I had to make a run for it.

Suddenly, the floor creaked just behind us and, raising his knife, Mr. Creed jerked towards the sound but stopped when Leon said in a loud, commanding voice, "Don't move, Creed."

Stepping into the light, Leon pointed his gun at Mr. Creed's head and said, "Drop the knife, slow and easy, and don't make any sudden moves. Eva, go outside and wait for me in the car."

I began walking around Mr. Creed towards the front door, making sure to give him a wide berth as I clutched Davey tightly in my arms.

"You won't get away with this," Mr. Creed murmured in a low voice and, my heart pounding, I quickened my footsteps, the sound my shoes made against the hardwood floor echoing off the walls.

I'd just made it to the front door when I heard Leon say, "Put your hands behind your head and turn around."

I stopped and glanced back, the glow from the flashlight casting both of the men's shadows on the floor and all along the walls. Suddenly, with the speed of lightning, Mr. Creed pulled a gun from his coat pocket and spun around, pointing it directly at Leon. My eyes widened and I screamed, jumping back with Davey clutched tightly in my arms, and two shots were fired simultaneously, the thunderous explosion reverberating through my head like cannon blasts. I stood rooted in place and watched as Leon was thrown back against the wall, a gunshot wound to the upper right side of his chest clearly visible in the dim lighting.

"Eva, run," Leon gasped, reaching up to clutch his chest as he slowly slid down the wall to the floor. "Get...get out of here. Quick!"

Mr. Creed turned toward me then, the look on his face turning my blood to ice. I told myself to run, to do *something*, but my body refused to move a muscle. He raised his gun, pointed it at me, and like a film being played in slow motion, he swayed on his feet and slowly melted to the floor. It was then that I saw a deep, red stream of blood oozing from his neck and watched as his eyes fluttered closed for the last time.

My entire body was shaking so badly that I feared I might drop Davey, but I managed to spin around and stumble the last remaining steps towards the front door, the only thought in my mind that of getting help for Leon. I reached the door, flung it open, and came face to face with a large, looming shadow and a gun pointed at my face.

Screaming, I jumped back and tried to run in the opposite direction, but a hand shot out and grabbed my arm, yanking me backwards.

"Mrs. Beckett, it's alright. Stop struggling!"

With a gasp, I spun around and looked into the man's face, relief flooding over my body when I realized it was Officer Sallow, the policeman that had been stationed outside of my house.

"Thank God!" I cried, tears flooding my eyes as I grabbed his hand and pulled him across the room towards Leon.

"I saw you and your neighbor leave, so I followed you," Officer Sallow explained as he kneeled at Leon's side. "In my attempt to stay a good distance away and drive without my headlights, I lost y'all about ten minutes away from this place. Luckily, I spotted your car parked outside and heard the gunshots."

Officer Sallow checked Leon's pulse, his face grave as he sighed and shook his head. "He's in bad shape, ma'am. If we don't get him to the hospital immediately, he's going to die."

57

Eva

I paced up and down the hospital hall, my mind in a fog as I worried anxiously about both Davey and Leon. The doctor was in with Davey now, checking to make certain he was alright, and Leon was in emergency surgery. I'd called Asher, my family and Leon's family, and they were all on their way. Officer Sallow was out in the waiting room with instructions for me to go with him to the police station as soon as I spoke with Davey's doctor.

My stomach was in knots and I my hands shook with nervous energy. Before rushing Leon into surgery, I'd heard the doctor state that it didn't look good. If Leon died, I would be responsible. How could I ever live the rest of my life in peace knowing that Leon died because of me? He was so dear, so very dear to me...

I stopped pacing and leaned against the wall, burying my face in my hands as I broke down into sobs. Just the thought of losing Leon was almost more than I could bear, and knowing that it was my fault just made it worse.

The door to Davey's room opened just then, and the doctor stepped out. Pulling myself together, I quickly wiped my eyes and waited to hear the news.

"Davey is just fine, Mrs. Beckett," the doctor assured me, and I breathed a sigh of relief. "He was, indeed, given a pretty strong sedative, but not strong enough to be dangerous. His body temperature is a bit low; I think probably because he was sleeping without a blanket in that cold, damp house. He'll sleep for several more hours, and when he wakes up, I'll check him again. There's nothing to worry about, though. He's in great condition."

I thanked the doctor and went in to see Davey for a quick moment before going to the police station. He looked like a little angel lying in the hospital crib, and I leaned over and kissed him gently on the cheek, thanking God for keeping him safe.

When I stepped into the waiting room, Asher immediately rushed to my side and pulled me into his arms.

"I've been so worried," he said, pulling back to study my face. "How is Davey?"

I told him, Nana, and Mutter everything the doctor said, and then asked, "Have you seen any of Leon's family?"

"Yes, they arrived when we did," Nana replied. "They're downstairs in the emergency waiting area."

"Will you two stay here while I go to the police station?" I asked Nana and Mutter. "I don't want to leave Davey here alone."

They assured me that they would, and Asher, Officer Sallow, and I went downstairs. I hesitated at the entrance to the emergency area, wanting to see Leon's family and ask if there were any updates, but afraid to do so. What if the updates weren't good?

"Come on," Asher said, taking my hand, "I'll go with you."

As soon as Savannah saw me, she rushed over and pulled me into a crushing hug.

"I'm so glad you're alright," she said, and I could feel her tears soaking through my blouse. Glancing over her shoulder, I saw the red, splotchy tear stains on Mrs. Emma's face and my stomach clenched.

"Is there any news about Leon?" I asked when Savannah pulled back and wiped her eyes.

She shook her head and my heart sank. "No, he's still in surgery. By some sort of miracle, the bullet went all the way through without hitting anything serious, but I know from experience that he's still very critical. I'll let you know as soon as we hear anything."

As we drove to the station, Asher looked at me and said, "I'm sure he's going to be alright, honey."

"I pray he will be," I replied softly, sick to my stomach with worry.

When we arrived and walked into Gabe's office, my eyes widened when I saw my in-laws sitting across from his desk.

"How is David?" They both asked simultaneously.

I was so shocked at seeing them again that I momentarily could not answer. Were they here to take him back? I felt my pulse quicken at the thought and fought to remain calm. Finally, I replied in a choked voice, "He's going to be fine."

Clearing his throat, Gabe motioned to the two available chairs left and said to Asher and me, "Please, have a seat."

I slowly sank into the chair, clutching Asher's hand so hard that my fingers began to cramp.

"Eva, please start from the beginning and tell me everything that happened," Gabe said.

Taking a deep breath, I began telling the story. I'd just relayed the part of receiving Mr. Creed's phone call me when Mrs. Beckett interrupted and snapped angrily, "Why in heaven's name didn't you call the police?"

Blinking in surprise, I glanced hesitantly over at my mother-in-law just as Gabe held up his hand and said firmly, "I'll ask the questions, Mrs. Beckett. If you interrupt again, I'll have to ask you to leave the room." Turning back to me, he said, "Please continue, Eva."

Trying desperately to block out the hard glares that were directed at me, I forced my eyes to meet Gabe's and continued. As my story progressed, I shook all over, the memories of what happened and the realization of what *could* have happened causing me to feel lightheaded. When I got to the part of the gunshots and Leon slumping to the floor, tears sprang into my eyes and I couldn't finish.

"That's enough, Eva, thank you," Gabe said gently, and Asher squeezed my hand supportively.

"How could you have risked David's life like that?" My mother-in-law asked in a harsh, critical tone. "He could have been killed! Why didn't you call the police? Surely now you can see why we believe you to be an unfit mother."

My ears suddenly began to ring, and I heard Asher say something but couldn't make out his words. Something was coming over me, something I'd never felt before. It was as if every nerve in my body was throbbing as red hot anger coursed over me like a bucket of boiling water, and I slowly stood to my feet and turned to face my in-laws. I was trembling all over and could feel my heart pumping at an alarming rate, and when the words started flowing from my lips, I couldn't stop them.

"How dare you," I hissed, barely able to recognize the sound of my own voice. "How dare you blame me for this when you are the ones that hired that man in the first place. Because of *you*, my son was kidnapped and could have been killed, and a very dear friend is lying in the hospital possibly *dying* as we speak. So, don't sit there with your pompous, high and mighty attitudes when *you* are the ones responsible for *everything* that has happened!"

Asher quickly stood and began pulling at my arm, trying to make me stop, but I pushed his hand away and said firmly, "*No*, Asher, I won't stop. Not until I've finished what I have to say."

A look of surprise passed over his face and, holding up his hands, Asher nodded and stepped away. Turning back to Mr. and Mrs. Beckett, I asked in a choked voice, "Why do you hate me *so* much? Is it because I'm poor, or German? Or because Paul dared to defy you when he married me? Do you have any idea how heartbroken he was when you disowned him?" Tears were streaming down my cheeks by that point, but still I continued. "Please, just stop trying to get revenge. I know you don't care about me, but think of what this is doing to your grandson. And remember this: no matter what you do or how much you hate me, I'll *always* be Davey's mother and your son's widow. You'll never be able to change that."

Unable to bear it any longer, I turned and ran from the room, not stopping until I made it outside. The cold air felt good against my flushed skin as I leaned against one of the police cars, taking several long, deep breaths. I couldn't believe I'd just said all of those things; never in my life had I spoken to anyone in that way, and I couldn't imagine what had come over me. Now that it was over and the adrenaline gone, I was left feeling drained and nauseous, my body trembling as tears continued to seep from my eyes.

The front door opened just then, and I saw Asher step outside and look around for me, concern written all over his face. When his eyes landed on my crumpled silhouette, he immediately hurried to my side.

"Honey, are you alright?" He asked, taking my arm. "I'm so sorry this happened."

I was still crying, and all I could do was nod my head. With a sigh, Asher wrapped his arms around me and I rested against his chest, thankful for the support. As we stood there, however, I was suddenly filled with doubts about our engagement. What I'd said about how hurt Paul was when his parents disowned him was true, so how could I stand by and watch Asher go through the same thing? And I knew that if I married Asher and his parents still got custody of Davey, it would only end up tearing us apart. I feared that perhaps we'd been too hasty in our decision to get married, but there was nothing I could do about it. I'd already promised to marry Asher; I couldn't back out now.

The front door to the station opened again and Gabe called out to us, asking if we'd come back inside. Taking Asher's hand, I followed him and Gabe back into his office. The air in the room was thick and filled with tension, and unable to look at my in-laws, I sat down and stared silently at my feet.

"Eva," Gabe said, eyeing me, "Mr. and Mrs. Beckett have something they wish to say."

Closing my eyes for a brief second, as if to gain a bit of extra strength, I slowly turned in my chair to look at them, awaiting their words with dread.

"Eva..." Mr. Beckett paused and cleared his throat, his eyes barely meeting mine in a surprising show of contriteness. "We've been talking and...well...we realize how wrong we've been. You were right in everything you said, and I want you to know that we're sorry for all the pain we've caused. I wish...I wish we could have said the same to Paul before he died."

Mr. Beckett broke down then and started to cry, and I stared at him and his wife in complete shock. Had he really just apologized, or was I dreaming?

Gabe cleared his throat, and when I looked at him, he picked up a piece of paper and said, "Mr. and Mrs. Beckett have signed this agreement stating that they will no longer attempt to gain custody of Davey. It's over, Eva. You don't have to worry anymore, and you won't have to go back to court."

It felt as if all the oxygen had been sucked from the room. My in-laws stood and left without another word, and after a moment of stunned silence, I leaped to my feet and rushed after them.

"Wait!" I cried, and they stopped but didn't turn around. I stood just behind them, staring at their backs, and said softly, "Thank you. Thank you so much."

Nodding, Mr. Beckett took his wife's hand and they walked outside, the door flapping closed behind them like the ending of a very long and hard chapter.

After signing a few papers for Gabe, Asher and I left the station and headed back to the hospital. We drove in silence, both of us lost in our own thoughts. I felt happy, exhausted, and utterly drained all at once. I wanted to shout for joy over the astounding news of Davey's custody, but was too worried about Leon to do so.

We arrived at the hospital and parked, but before getting out of the car, I reached across the console and took Asher's hand, feeling a bit nervous about the request I was going to make.

"Asher," I began, swallowing past the lump in my throat, "considering what your parents just did, would it be okay if we...waited a bit before getting married? There's no need to rush now, and we could spend some time courting and getting to know one another better."

"You...still **want** to get married, though, right?" He asked, eyeing me uncertainly.

I hesitated, glancing away for a moment before slowly nodding my head. "Yes," I replied in a soft voice. "If you do."

A smile of relief spread across Asher's face, and giving my hand a quick squeeze, he said warmly, "Of course I do."

He jumped from the car then and we walked inside, my stomach in knots as we once again entered the emergency waiting area. I quickly tried to study the faces of Leon's family as we drew nearer, attempting to gauge their expressions in relation to how he was doing. When I didn't see any tears, I began to feel hopeful.

"How is he?" I immediately asked when they saw me.

"He's out of surgery," Mrs. Emma said, a wrinkled handkerchief clutched in her hand. "The doctor said the surgery went well, but that he's still in critical condition. If he makes it through the night, his chances of surviving will improve."

Asher and I went back upstairs to check on Davey, and Nana told us, "He's still sleeping, but the doctor said his body temperature is getting back to normal."

"How did it go at the police station?" Mutter asked, her eyes tired.

When I told them the good news, both of their faces lit up with joy, and they immediately pulled me into a hug.

"Praise the Lord," Nana cried, pulling back to wipe tears from her eyes.

"That is wonderful news," Mutter said, a beautiful smile on her face as she squeezed my hand.

After a while, Asher stated that his head was beginning to hurt. I could see by the look in his eyes that this headache was going to be a bad one, and told him to go to his motel and get some rest. He gave me a quick kiss on the cheek before he left and made me promise to call if I needed him. After he left, I went back downstairs, and for the next three hours, stayed in the waiting room and quietly prayed with Savannah and Mrs. Emma. When the nurse came in around four o'clock and walked toward us, we all held our breath as we waited to hear what she had to say.

"He's coming around," she said, and we all sighed with relief. "He's very weak and seems a bit distraught over something; he keeps mumbling and asking for Eva. The doctor said if she's here, he'd like for her to go in for a quick moment to put Mr. Danes' mind at ease."

Everyone immediately looked at me, and I said to the nurse, "I'm Eva, and of course I'll go."

I followed her through the set of double doors and down the hall. When we arrived at Leon's room, she cautioned me, "He looks pretty bad, but don't let it get to you."

Nodding, I went inside and paused, my heart wrenching at the sight of the bandaged, bloodied form lying so still and helpless in the hospital bed. I rushed to his side and took his hand, gently whispering his name.

Leon's eyes fluttered open, and as he gazed at me in silence, I wondered if he even recognized me. "E-Eva," he finally murmured, attempting to reach out his other hand to me.

"No, no, don't move," I said, leaning over to press his arm gently back onto the bed.

"You're...okay," he whispered, his breath warm against my cheek. "D-Davey?"

My heart warmed at his concern, and I smiled down at him, suddenly feeling an overwhelming urge to cry. There he was, lying in the hospital with a gunshot wound to his chest, and his only worry was of Davey and me.

Gently brushing away the hair that fell across his forehead, I said, "We're both just fine, thanks to you."

His face was rimmed with yellow and black circles, and his skin ghostly pale. When I told him the good news, his eyes lit up and he weakly squeezed my hand, uttering a small sigh of relief.

"Thank God," he murmured.

"Leon," I said, my eyes brimming with tears, "I'm so sorry this happened. It's all my fault and..."

"No, don't," he whispered. "I'm just...glad you and D-Davey are...okay."

He closed his eyes then, and thinking he'd gone back to sleep, I started to

303

pull away but stopped when his hand suddenly tightened around mine.

"Eva," he breathed my name, his voice growing weaker as he attempted to say something else.

"I'm still here, Leon," I said, leaning closer to better hear his words.

Our faces were only inches apart, and when he opened his eyes again, I drew in a quick breath, startled at the intensity I saw in the hazel depths that stared back at me.

"I need…to tell you…something," he said in an almost desperate tone.

"What is it?" I asked.

Releasing my hand, Leon raised his arm and gently stroked the side of my face.

"I…I…," he tried, but his hand dropped back down to the bed as his eyes fluttered closed. I felt a momentary surge of panic at how still and quiet he'd suddenly become, but quickly realized he'd simply gone back to sleep.

The nurse came in and told me it was time to leave, and as I made my way back to the waiting room, I wondered what Leon had been trying to tell me. The way he'd looked at me and touched my face made me wonder if perhaps…

No, he'd simply been out of his head from the surgery and all the medication. There was no reason to think anything else, and I quickly pushed it out of my mind.

Vivian

I awoke to the sound of the telephone ringing downstairs. My eyes blurry, I looked over at my clock, wondering who would call at a little past six in the morning, and immediately thought of Father. Jumping out of bed, I put on my robe and hurried downstairs to answer the phone. It was Savannah, and in a tired voice, she told me about Leon and everything that had happened.

"He made it through the night," she said, "but he's not out of the woods yet. I figured you'd want to know."

"Yes, of course," I replied. "Eva and Davey are alright?"

"They're both perfect," she said. "Eva took Davey home a few minutes ago and asked me to tell you when I called that she's going to bed as soon as she gets home and won't be working today."

Although Savannah couldn't see me, I nodded my head and said, "Thanks, Savannah. Please keep me posted on Leon."

All throughout the day, I thought of Leon and prayed for him and his family. I could only imagine how Mrs. Emma felt; she'd lost her husband, had come close to losing Connor, and now Leon was in critical condition. I called some of my church ladies and arranged to have food taken to Mrs. Emma's house, wishing that I could do more.

I went by the hospital later that day and found Zachary going through some files at the nurse's station. I stepped quietly up to the desk and asked teasingly, "Nurse, where is your uniform?"

Glancing up in surprise, Zachary laughed and said, "Vivian, it's good to see you. Are you here to see Savannah?"

"I just stopped by to ask how Leon is doing," I replied. "Is Savannah or Mrs. Emma here?"

"No, we finally convinced them both to go home and get some rest, but they'll be back soon, I suspect," Zachary stated, closing the files and turning to put them into the nearby filing cabinet. He then stepped from behind the desk and came to stand beside me. "Leon seems to be doing a bit better this evening, but it's still touch and go," he said, leaning against the desk. "He suffered a very serious injury and lost a lot of blood, but the primary concern right now is the risk of infection."

I nodded, sighing heavily. "I hope he'll pull through this," I said softly.

Reaching out, Zachary laid his hand on my arm and said, "He's strong and healthy, so his chances are good. Just keep praying for him."

As Zachary walked me out to my car, he glanced at me and said, "The hospital, fire department, and police department are having a Christmas party this Saturday evening. Would you like to go with me?"

Surprised by the sudden question, my foot slipped on a pebble and Zachary quickly grabbed my arm, steadying me.

"Uh…well…Gabe actually already asked me," I stammered, wondering why I hadn't realized Zachary would be at the party as well.

Raising his eyebrows in surprise, Zachary stuffed his hands into his pockets and asked, "Officer Wright?"

The look on his face made me feel a bit flustered, and I cleared my throat awkwardly. "Yes. Just as friends, though," I hurriedly explained, my cheeks flushing. "We're just going as friends."

"You don't have to explain yourself to me, Vivian," he stated, smiling. "I hope you have a good time with Officer Wright."

He opened the car door for me then and I slid inside, watching in surprise as he walked away. I don't know why, but I hadn't expected him to react so well.

As the days passed, Leon's chances of getting an infection grew slimmer and by the time the weekend arrived, the worst seemed to be over. Savannah told me he would have to remain in the hospital for at least a couple of more weeks, but it seemed he was finally out of the woods. I sent him a large bouquet of flowers and a card, hoping they would cheer him up a bit, as I knew not being able to be home for Christmas would be hard on him.

I received a letter from Maisie, and was excited to discover that she'd gotten a job at the local newspaper working in the circulation department. "*I'm so thrilled at how well I'm doing,*" she wrote. "*I visited a local herbalist and began taking a mixture of herbs that the old lady swears by and, Vivian, I have had no attacks since coming home! After describing how life was at the asylum, though, Father has promised to never send me back, even if I begin having attacks again. It feels so nice to be free to live my life now.*"

She also wrote to say that she'd met a handsome young man, and I smiled at how giddy she sounded. I was happy that she was doing so well, and I immediately wrote a return letter telling her so.

Friday afternoon, I went by to see Father during my lunch break and was surprised to see Lina Hamilton, Eva's mother, sitting on the front porch with him. Even though Davey was back home, she'd asked to continue with the housecleaning, and I'd readily agreed. She did a wonderful job, and I suspected it was nice for her to get out of the house and do something different each week; I also knew that the extra income helped to put food on the table.

"Mrs. Lina, how nice to see you," I greeted her with a warm smile as I climbed the porch steps.

"It's nice to see you, too, Vivian," she replied in her usual soft tone, smiling in return.

"Hello, honey," Father greeted me as I kissed him on the cheek. "I'm afraid I talked poor Lina into sitting with me for a bit before she left; it's such a nice day that I hated to enjoy it all by myself."

"Well, I have enough lunch here for the three of us," I said, motioning to the basket of food I carried on my arm, "so why don't you stay and eat with us, Mrs. Lina?"

After a bit of prodding, Mrs. Lina agreed, and the three of us went inside to eat. As I already knew, Mrs. Lina was very shy, but when I asked her about her homeland and childhood, she opened up almost immediately and began to talk. Father and I sat quietly and listened, the soft lilt of her voice soothing and relaxing as she spoke, and just hearing her speak of Germany made me want to go for a visit some day. I hoped that the war would be over soon; how horrible it must be for Mrs. Lina and Eva to know that their beautiful homeland was in such turmoil.

Once we were through eating, I quickly cleaned up the mess and hurried back off to work. As I was leaving, I heard Father ask Mrs. Lina to sit on the porch with him for a bit longer.

The next evening, I had just finished with the last touches on my hair when I heard a knock on the front door. Grabbing my coat, I hurried downstairs and opened the door, smiling at Gabe.

"Merry Christmas!" I cried, laughing gaily.

"Wow, you certainly look as pretty as a present," Gabe commented, whistling as he looked me up and down appreciatively.

"Thank you," I said, taking his arm as we walked to his car. "You look very nice, as well."

I glimpsed my reflection in one of the restaurant windows and smiled, smoothing my hand down the green velvet dress that I wore. I'd spotted it in the window at Levy's Department Store and hadn't been able to resist buying it, especially when the sales lady said it brought out the color of my eyes. It fell just below my knees, had long sleeves and a high neck, and a black satin sash at the waist.

When we arrived at the Savannah Fire Department, I was blown away by the amount of work everyone had put in to the decorating. The fire trucks had, of course, been removed from the vast area, and several Christmas trees lined the walls, their lights twinkling like little stars in the dim setting. Tables were lined with green cloths, poinsettias, and garland with red berries, and there was even a Santa Claus sitting on a small platform in the corner.

"That's the fire chief," Gabe told me, chuckling. "We convinced him to do it for the kids, but he wasn't too keen on the idea."

I spotted Savannah sitting with a few of her coworkers and smiled, grateful that she'd pulled herself away from the hospital for a few hours; it had been a long week, and she deserved a break. Gabe and I went over to sit with them, and Savannah immediately exclaimed over my dress when she saw me.

"You look gorgeous," she said, smiling.

"So do you," I replied, genuinely in awe at how beautiful my friend was. Her shiny, dark hair was pulled back with her mother's combs, and the red dress she wore brought out the sparkle in her black eyes. I instantly noticed, however, that her smile wasn't as bright as usual, and I knew she was missing Connor.

"How is Leon?" I asked, sitting down at the table beside her.

"He's coming along quite nicely, thank the good Lord," she said, taking a sip of punch. "Mama Emma is with him tonight. I hated to leave them there while I went to a party, but they both insisted."

As she talked, a familiar figure passing across the room caught my eye, and I suddenly realized it was Zachary. On his arm was a very lovely young woman with reddish-blonde hair, a form-fitting black dress, and bright red lipstick.

Savannah noticed I was staring and, with a slight smile, said, "That's Beatrice, one of our nurses. Isn't she lovely? Most of the staff have been trying to set her up with Zachary for weeks."

"They make a nice couple," I murmured, feeling a slight prick of...could it be jealousy? *No*, I told myself, but I wondered why he'd bothered to ask me to the party in the first place if Beatrice was available.

The evening went by at a steady pace, each moment filled with fun and laughter. They served us a delicious meal of barbecued chicken, baked beans, and potato salad, and then all the adults sat back and chatted while the kids visited with Santa. At ten o'clock, the families with children left, and those of us remaining pushed the tables against the wall and prepared to dance. Several of the men had brought along their instruments and quickly formed a band, and before long, the room was filled with the sound of banjos, guitars, juice harps, and fiddles.

"Did this Christmas party just turn into a square dance?" I asked Gabe, laughing as we joined the others in the center of the room.

"Don't tell me you don't know how to square dance," he replied with a grin.

"Oh, I know how," I shot back saucily. "You just concentrate on not tripping."

"Circle up now, y'all!" The caller yelled, and we all quickly formed several circles consisting of four couples. Zachary and his date ended up in our group, and when Zachary smiled and nodded at me, I smiled politely back.

"Alright now, here we go," the caller said, and as the beat started, we all began to clap, waiting for the cues to begin. "Circle left 'til you circle right, listen to my calls or we'll be here all night."

I took Gabe's hand and we, along with the other couples, began circling to the left. Halfway around, the caller told us to change directions and Gabe spun me to the right, my dress twirling out around my calves.

"Hand over hand, right and left grand!"

Hand over hand, we switched partners, making it halfway around the circle until Gabe and I met up again. The sound of laughter, cheers, whistles, and stomping feet filled me with excitement, and I felt giddy all over. The caller told us to cross over and change partners then, and I suddenly found myself paired with Zachary.

"You look beautiful," he said, his blue eyes twinkling as he spun me around.

"So does your date," I replied before I was twirled back into Gabe's arms.

Glancing over my shoulder, I saw Zachary looking at me as he joined hands with Beatrice, a mischievous grin on his face. I knew he suspected I was jealous and stuck my tongue out at him playfully, causing him to laugh. His date glanced in my direction, a slight frown on her face.

The beat picked up and everyone cheered louder. We all twirled and spun to the music, some tripping and bumping into each other as everyone attempted to keep the calls straight. By the time it was over, we were all out of breath but begging for more.

"Y'all, I need a break," the caller said, reaching up to wipe his brow dramatically, and everyone laughed. "Let's have us some slow dancin' for a little while and give me a rest."

The guitarist began to play "White Christmas" then, and the violin soon joined in. Gabe reached out his hand and I took it, allowing him to pull me close.

"You were right," he said, smiling down at me.

Tilting my head, I asked, "About what?"

"You do know how to square dance."

"Yes, I do," I nodded, my eyes twinkling. "And *you* only tripped once."

Gabe laughed. "You saw that, huh?"

"I did, but don't worry," I replied, grinning. "I don't think anyone else noticed."

"Good," he said, sighing with relief, "because I wouldn't want to give the boys at work something else to tease me about."

Once the music ended, Gabe asked if I'd like to go for a walk. I agreed, and after putting on our coats, we stepped out into the cold night air. The fire station stood directly across the street from the Colonial Park Cemetery, and I pointed it out, saying, "Do we dare enter another cemetery after dark?"

"Why not? It can't be as bad as the last time," Gabe stated, chuckling.

The moon shone brightly in a cloudless sky, illuminating the wrought-iron fence that surrounded the cemetery and the giant eagle perched atop the arched entrance. We walked up the steps, and as Gabe pushed open the gate so we could go through, it creaked loudly on its hinges. Lamp posts dotted the little pathway ahead, lighting the way, and we slowly entered the historical landmark, which was originally built in 1750.

"You know, this place is full of history," Gabe said, his breath forming cloudy puffs in the cold, night air. "For example, did you know it served as the city's dueling grounds for nearly one hundred and forty years?"

"I don't believe I've ever heard that before," I replied as I looked around at the graves, many of which were above ground. "I did, however, know that when the yellow fever epidemic came through in 1820, around seven hundred bodies were all buried together in one mass grave."

"Whoa, that's pretty crazy," he said, shivering slightly. "Think they ever come out and haunt the city as a group, or just one at a time?"

Trying to keep a straight face, I sighed and said, "Probably one at a time; I imagine they're tired of each other's company by now."

Gabe laughed, and we continued along the pathway, large branches from the many oak trees casting shadows all along the ground.

"So, what else do they tease you about?" I asked after a moment.

"The boys at work?" When I nodded, he laughed and said, "That question was delayed. Let's see…they tease me about my thick, Macon accent for one thing."

"It is pretty thick," I replied, smiling, "but I happen to like it."

"Did you just pay me a compliment?" Gabe asked, his voice filled with shock.

"Stop it," I said, rolling my eyes. "I've complimented you before; I told you tonight that you looked nice."

"Oh, that was just the polite response everyone gives when they're first given a compliment," he stated matter-of-factly. "I don't believe you've ever voluntarily said something so nice to me."

"You make me sound so rude!" I cried in disbelief.

"Not rude," he said, smiling down at me. "Just a little cautious."

"Well, I'm sure you'll agree that I have good reason to be," I replied, pushing my icy hands into the pockets of my coat.

"Yes," he agreed, nodding. "You certainly do."

"So, are you going home for Christmas?" I asked, changing the subject.

"No," was his short reply.

Glancing up at him curiously, I asked, "Don't you miss your family?"

He didn't answer for a moment, and I wondered why he always seemed so unwilling to talk about his family. Finally, he sighed and said, "I don't come from a very reputable family, Vivian. My father left when I was seven, and my mother is basically an alcoholic. That's why I finally left and came here; I had to get away from it all."

"I'm so sorry, Gabe," I said, my chest tightening. "I didn't realize…"

"Don't worry about it," he interrupted, glancing down at me with a slight smile. "You should feel very lucky, though, to have such a great family."

I nodded my head in agreement, feeling very sorry for Gabe. How hard it must have been to have watched his father walk away, all the while wondering why he didn't love his son enough to stay. I also thought how lonely Gabe must be, spending his holidays alone with no family to share them with. I felt very lucky, indeed, to have had parents who loved me.

After nearly an hour of walking and talking, we made our way back to the fire station. Everyone was still inside dancing, and as Gabe stopped to talk to one of his colleagues, I went over to the refreshment table to get myself a glass of punch. The music stopped and everyone began milling about, talking and chatting, and suddenly someone called out that a couple was spotted standing beneath the mistletoe. Glancing around, my eyes widened when I realized it was Zachary and Beatrice.

"Come on, you've got to kiss her!" The crowed jeered, and I didn't miss the flush of embarrassment that swept up Zachary's neck and onto his cheeks.

Beatrice smiled up at him, batting her eyes, and when Zachary leaned down to kiss her, I turned and moved away from the table, pushing my way through the crowd until I reached Gabe's side. He was finished talking, and I told him I was tired and asked if he'd take me home.

As we drove, Gabe glanced over at me and said, "I had a great time tonight, Vivian. Thanks for going with me."

"I had fun, too," I replied, smiling at him. "Thank you for asking me."

He seemed to want to say more, but hesitated. After a moment, he cleared his throat and said, "I'd like to take you out again sometime. Would you be okay with that?"

I'd had a feeling this was coming, so why didn't I feel more prepared?

"I don't know if I'm ready for that, Gabe," I said softly. "It's been such a hard year."

"I know," he replied, nodding his head, "but you owe it to yourself to move on and start enjoying life again. It wouldn't have to be serious between us; we could just be friends and date sort of casually."

I hesitated, considering his words. Zachary and I had almost this exact conversation just a little over a month ago when he kissed me, and I'd told him I wasn't ready for anything else as well. It seemed, however, that a lot had changed in the last few weeks; Eva had gotten her son back and was engaged, Maisie was moving on with her life, Leon had almost died…perhaps I'd started to realize how precious life was and that no matter how fast you run, it will still catch up to you.

I did, however, feel a bit guilty when I'd told Zachary I wasn't ready. ***Why would he care when he's apparently moved on with someone else?*** I thought to myself.

Taking a deep breath, I looked back over at Gabe and said, "While I'm not ready for anything serious, we can certainly be friends and date casually. I don't, however, want to give you the wrong idea, Gabe. It's been a terribly hard year and I've been hurt very badly. I'd like to take things really slow, and maybe later we can see how we feel about possibly taking things further."

Gabe pulled up in front of the restaurant and put his car in park. Smiling at me, he nodded and said, "I totally understand, and I'm perfectly happy with that arrangement."

He walked me to the front door, kissed me on the cheek, and said goodnight. I watched him drive away, feeling uncertain about my decision. I had a wonderful time tonight, but perhaps I should have told him "no".

"You owe it to yourself to move on and start enjoying life again."

Gabe's words echoed through my mind as I climbed the stairs to my apartment, and I sighed. He was right; I ***did*** owe it to myself. Plus, I had made no commitments; I'd simply told him I was willing to date casually and nothing more.

My mind at ease, I tossed my coat on the bed and twirled my way to the bathroom, humming the song "White Christmas" under my breath.

59

Eva

Christmas came and went, and I made certain to celebrate more than ever this year. Having Davey back was the greatest gift I could ever receive, and watching him open his presents on Christmas morning brought tears of joy to my eyes. I'd never been more thankful for anything in my life, and made myself a promise to do my very best to spend more time with my son. I'd considered asking Vivian if I could start taking off every other Saturday, but wasn't certain that I could afford it.

When Asher came over that afternoon to eat Christmas dinner with us, I found myself feeling more positive about marrying him. Davey was growing up and would soon go to school, and I spent so much time working that I felt I was missing out on his "little boy" years. I still wasn't certain of how things would pan out with my in-laws, but if it all worked out, perhaps marrying Asher was the right thing to do after all. I'd be able to quit work, and it would give both Davey and me the opportunity to live a better, more fulfilling life.

We spent New Year's Day at home, the five of us playing games and making s'mores over a small fire Asher built in the backyard. We sang songs, told stories, and stayed up until midnight to ring in the New Year. As we stood on the front porch, with Davey asleep in my arms, we sang "Auld Lang Syne" and listened to the few fireworks they were shooting off down by the river. After our singing had died out, I thought about the last year; of the difficulty I had finding a job, of Davey being taken from me and then his kidnapping, and I breathed a soft prayer of thanks under my breath for God's helping hand through it all.

After I'd put Davey to bed, Asher asked if he could speak with me privately. I nodded, and we walked outside.

"I spoke with my parents on the telephone yesterday," he said as we slowly walked to his car, "and the conversation went really well. They apologized for the way they've acted and said if we want to get married then we have their blessing."

I turned to stare at him, my eyes widening with shock. "They really said that?" I asked in disbelief.

"Yes," Asher nodded, chuckling. "I almost couldn't believe it either."

We stopped at his car and, running his fingers through his hair, Asher eyed me uncertainly as he said, "I know we agreed to wait and hadn't decided on another wedding date yet, but I feel like we've drawn closer the last few weeks. Now that we have my parents' blessing, I was wondering if you'd consider getting married at the end of next month?"

The carefree, light-hearted feeling I'd had since Christmas vanished into thin air, and I suddenly felt very anxious. Get married next month? That seemed so quick, and yet we'd already be married if Davey hadn't been kidnapped.

I turned my back on him and stepped away, in turmoil over what to do. If I told Asher "no", then he'd leave and my chances of spending more time with Davey and of having a better life would be gone. So, what was holding me back?

Suddenly, Leon's face drifted into my mind and I thought of that night in the hospital and how he'd seemed on the verge of telling me something important. I'd been to visit him twice since then and he hadn't mentioned a word of it, so why did it matter? Why was I thinking of him when I needed to decide about Asher?

Feeling a bit frustrated with myself, I turned back around to look at Asher, considering his handsome face and the love I saw in his eyes. Would I ever feel the same way about him? I couldn't be certain, but knew that it would be foolish to refuse the gift he was offering me.

I walked back to Asher's side, and taking a deep breath, said, "Alright."

Asher blinked, the moon casting shadows on his face. "You'll really marry me next month?" He asked in an uncertain yet hopeful tone.

"Yes," I nodded, smiling softly. "I'll really marry you next month."

A look of relief passed over Asher's face, and with a broad smile, he slowly leaned forward and said, "Happy New Year's, Eva."

I closed my eyes as his lips found mine, and he pulled me close as our breath mingled together in the cold night air.

A few days later, Leon was finally able to come home. Asher had a headache and would be out of commission for a couple of days, and I couldn't help but worry about him during these times. He'd already found a house big enough for the three of us and was in the process of buying it, and I wondered if the added stress had caused the headache.

It was Saturday morning, and I went over to Leon's house to help Savannah and Mrs. Emma decorate for his welcome home party. I'd spoken to Vivian about taking off every other Saturday and she'd readily agreed, stating that it was a wonderful idea.

"You'll be leaving us soon anyway," she'd said sadly, "so I'm glad to

314

have you around for as long as I can."

Mrs. Emma left early to get Leon from the hospital, and they arrived home just a little past noon. As soon as she helped Leon walk inside, we all yelled "surprise!", laughing at the shocked expression on Leon's face.

"I didn't expect this," he said as he sat down and surveyed the balloons and homemade "welcome home" sign we'd strung from the ceiling.

Mutter, Nana, and Davey had come over, as well, and we all sat down and ate the delicious food that was prepared. Leon tried to eat, but only managed to get down about half of what was on his plate. He was still very pale and obviously quite weak; Savannah had said it would take some time for him to get back to normal, and I could see she was right.

We didn't stay long, as it was apparent that Leon needed to get some rest, and after telling him how glad I was that he was home, we said our goodbyes and left.

The next afternoon, Mrs. Emma called and asked if I'd go over and check on Leon.

"I'm not feeling well; I think I'm coming down with a cold or something, but I can't get Leon to answer his telephone and I'm worried about him," she said, her voice filled with concern.

"Of course, I'll go over right now," I told her.

After knocking on Leon's door several times with no answer, I began to feel concerned, too, and after a moment of deliberation, I pushed the door open and went inside. The house was dark and quiet and when I called out, there was no response. Feeling panicked, I rushed through the house to Leon's bedroom, a startled yelp passing my lips when I turned the corner and nearly ran right in to him.

"Eva, are you alright?" He asked, reaching out to steady me. He still wore his night clothes, and his hair was a mess.

"Yes, but are *you*?" I asked, placing a hand on my chest. "Your mother said you wouldn't answer the phone, and when I couldn't get you to the door just now…"

"Sorry about that," he chuckled, reaching up to rub the back of his neck. "Ever since the accident, I've been sleeping like a dead man."

"Well, I'm just glad you're okay," I said with a smile. "Why don't you call your mother and I'll fix you some breakfast?"

"You don't have to ask me twice," Leon readily agreed, his eyes sparkling.

By the time he'd changed clothes, washed his face, and phoned his mother, breakfast was ready. I sat with him and sipped on a cup of coffee while he ate. He seemed to feel a bit better today, and I was thrilled when he finished everything on his plate.

"That was delicious, Eva, thank you," he said appreciatively as I began to clear away the dishes. He stretched his legs out and propped them on the chair beside him, covering a yawn with his hand. "So, has anything new been happening lately?"

I hesitated for a quick second before I said, "Asher is in the process of buying the Watson's house; he's actually using your bank."

Leon said nothing for a moment and I glanced over my shoulder at him, my hands buried in soapy dishwater. He'd removed his feet from the chair and was sitting upright, staring at me.

"I…I thought you two broke off the engagement?" He finally asked.

"No, we just postponed the wedding for a few months," I replied, wondering where he'd heard such a thing.

"I see," was all he said.

Once the dishes were dried and put away, I told Leon to call me if he needed anything. He seemed a bit upset, and I felt a little down as I walked back to my house. I almost considered going back to ask him what was wrong, and maybe even ask what he'd wanted to say that first night in the hospital, but changed my mind. I didn't want to make things any more uncomfortable between us than they already were.

That evening, I'd just put Davey to bed and was about to take a long, hot bath when the doorbell rang. I flipped on the porch light and opened the door, surprised to find Leon standing on the other side.

"Leon, you shouldn't have walked all the way over here," I scolded him gently, motioning for him to come inside. "You're much too weak."

Shaking his head, Leon said, "I'm fine."

He didn't move a muscle; he simply stood there with the strangest look on his face, as if he wanted to say something but didn't quite know how.

"Is everything alright?" I asked uncertainly.

Taking a step back, Leon cleared his throat and asked, "Will you come outside for a moment? There's…something I'd like to discuss with you."

Nodding, I quickly grabbed a sweater from the hall tree and stepped outside, closing the door behind me. The glow from the porch light cast shadows along Leon's face, accentuating the look of distress I saw in his eyes.

"I've been in a turmoil all afternoon trying to decide whether to do this," he said, running his fingers through his hair. "I've never felt quite like this before. I don't want to ruin our friendship…after all, we *are* neighbors…"

He was mumbling to himself, almost as if I wasn't even standing there, and I finally reached out and touched his arm, gaining his attention.

"Leon, what is it?" I asked gently, my brow wrinkling with concern.

He stared at me in silence, and I could see in his eyes that he was fighting a war within himself. Slowly, he reached up and took my hand, his fingers gripping mine tightly.

"There's something I have to say," he said, his voice low and soft. "Do you remember when I told you I've never truly been in love? That I wasn't certain I'd ever find what I'm looking for?"

I nodded, my eyes glued to his. There was such an intensity in the way he held my hand and looked at me as he spoke that I found myself growing strangely breathless.

"That's no longer true, Eva," he said, his throat bobbing up and down as he swallowed. "I *have* fallen in love, so deeply that I can't imagine living my life without…without *you*, Eva."

My eyes widened, and I felt my heart accelerate. Thinking perhaps I'd misunderstood, I softly asked, "Leon, what are you saying?"

"That I love you, Eva," he said earnestly, his warm breath blowing the hair around my face. "I know I should have said something sooner but didn't want to rush you, and then everything happened with Davey and…" he stopped and took a deep breath, closing his eyes for a moment before continuing. "Look, I know the timing is all wrong, but I was so afraid if I didn't tell you now, you would marry Asher and I'd lose you forever."

"Oh, Leon," I whispered, tears coming to my eyes.

He gently pulled me into his arms and held me tightly against his chest. I rested my head against the sound of his heartbeat and cried, my tears soaking through his shirt and onto his skin. I wrapped my arms around his waist and closed my eyes, relishing the way it felt to be held by this man who loved me.

The man whom *I* loved.

I hadn't completely realized it until that moment, but now that I was confronted with the truth, I felt an overwhelming sense of love for him crash over me like a tidal wave. It was as if the two remaining pieces of a puzzle had found each other and were now finally intertwined, completing the puzzle and creating one beautiful picture.

That wasn't, however, the only truth I was confronted with. I'd promised to marry Asher. He'd even begun to buy a house, and I knew he loved me. How could I break both my word *and* his heart?

Pulling away from Leon, I stepped around him and walked to the far side of the porch, looking out at the full moon. Leon followed, and I felt the warmth of his presence close behind me.

"Eva?" He asked, his voice filled with uncertainty.

"I don't know what to do," I whispered, tears choking my words. "I've already promised myself to Asher."

Leon took my arm and gently turned me around to face him, his eyes searching my face. "Do you love me, Eva?" He asked hopefully.

I slowly nodded, my heart feeling as if it would burst. "Yes," I said softly. "Very, very much."

A look of pure joy lit Leon's eyes, and the sweetest smile I'd ever seen swept over his face. He took my hand and kissed it, holding it tightly between both of his like a precious treasure. When I pulled my hand away, he looked at me with confusion.

"Just because I love you, Leon, doesn't mean we can be together," I told him, my heart twisting painfully in my chest.

Leon blinked, his brow furrowing. "Eva, what are you saying?" He asked.

"I gave my word to Asher and…and I cannot break it." Burying my face in my hands, I began crying again.

Leon pulled my hands away from my face, forcing me to look at him. "You mean you'd marry a man you don't love simply because you don't want to break your word? Eva, an engagement isn't binding; you can still get out of it."

"You don't understand," I said, shaking my head. "It is how I was raised. I gave my word to Asher, and I was taught to never break my word for any reason. Getting engaged is taken very seriously where I come from, and I can't just tell Asher I've changed my mind."

"Wouldn't he want that if he knew you loved someone else?" Leon asked, his gaze intense.

"I can't do it, Leon," I whispered. "I'm sorry."

Leon stepped away from me then, and the pain in his eyes broke my heart. Shaking his head, he stuffed his hands into his pockets and said, "Here I've waited my whole life to find you and when I do, you're just beyond my reach. If only I'd told you sooner…"

His words trailing off, he turned and slowly walked away, but not before I saw the tears on his face. It took all the strength I had to watch him go, and once he'd faded into the darkness and was gone, I sank onto my porch and sobbed like a brokenhearted child. After a moment, I heard the front door open behind me with a squeak, and felt the soft touch of my mother's hands rest upon my arm as she sat next to me.

"What happened, der Liebling?" Mutter asked, her voice soft and gentle.

In choked, stuttering words, I told her everything, and without saying a word, she pulled me into her arms and let me cry as she gently stroked my hair.

60

Vivian

I stood in the cemetery, the tiny little grave before me a harsh reminder that it had been one year since the death of my child. The flowers in my hand trembled as I slowly kneeled and placed them beside my son's name, reaching my fingers out to touch the engraved letters gently. I sat there for a long time, just letting the tears flow freely as I thought about the last year and how difficult it had been. In some ways, it felt as if time had paused somewhere along the way and the past year had really been five or ten very long, dark years. So much had happened...so much had changed...

Thunder rumbled in the distance and I stood, softly telling my son "goodbye" as I walked back to my car. I wrapped my arms around my waist, shivering as memories of the fire, the deaths of both my son and mother, and then Martinsville swept over me. I didn't like reliving those horrible memories, but on days like this, it was impossible to avoid them.

When I made it back to the restaurant, it was raining, which I thought to be quite fitting. I'd closed the restaurant for a day of mourning, and when I went inside, it felt silent and lonely. I went to the kitchen to fix myself something to eat when I heard the sound of a car door and then a knock.

When I opened the front door, Zachary was standing there in the rain, holding a bouquet of flowers.

"Hi," he greeted me, smiling.

I quickly ushered him in, and he followed me into the kitchen, where I took the flowers and handed him a towel to dry his wet hair and clothes.

"Thanks," he said, wiping his face. "I forgot my umbrella today."

"What are these for?" I asked as I retrieved a vase for the flowers.

Tossing the towel onto the counter, Zachary looked at me and said, "I knew that today would be hard, so I just wanted you to know I was thinking about you."

My heart warmed at his kindness, and I had to force myself not to start crying again.

"Thank you, Zachary, that was very thoughtful," I told him, smiling softly. Clearing my throat, I said, "I was actually just about to make myself something to eat. Would you like to stay and have lunch with me? It's raining too hard right now anyway to go back out."

"I'd love to stay for lunch," he readily agreed.

As he helped prepare the food, we talked of work and friends and everything in between. It didn't take long for Eva to come up and, once again, Zachary voiced his concerns over her engagement to Asher. It was all I could do not to tell him about Leon, as Eva had talked to me about that in confidence, and I wanted so badly to ask his opinion. Eva was completely heartbroken over what happened and wanted more than anything to be with Leon, but she refused to break her word to Asher and I didn't try to change her mind, even though I thought she was wrong. Both she and Leon were very dear friends, and I felt so terrible for the two of them. How horrible would it be to love someone but feel that you couldn't be with them?

"I wish Eva would give it more time, but Asher is pushing her to get married and she won't tell him no," I said, sighing.

"Well, I'm afraid she's making a mistake," Zachary stated. "He's a nice guy, but they don't know each other well enough."

The food was ready, and we carried our plates over to the small table in the kitchen's corner and sat down to eat.

I'd just taken a bite of my stew when Zachary casually said, "So, I've heard that you and Officer Wright are now seeing each other."

Blinking, I glanced up at him and said, "We've gone out a couple of times but we're not "seeing" each other; we're just friends."

Raising his eyebrows in doubt, Zachary replied, "Is that so? Well, that's where it all starts, you know."

Ignoring his statement, I asked, "What about you and the nurse?"

"Beatrice? Oh, we're just friends," he shrugged innocently, but I knew he was being facetious.

"Well, that's where it all starts, you know," I shot back, and he laughed.

"Vivian McCombs, are you jealous?" He asked, his eyes twinkling.

I cocked an eyebrow. "Are *you* jealous of my seeing so much of Gabe?"

"Yes," he simply stated, his gaze never leaving mine. "I am."

I glanced away, suddenly feeling flustered and a bit uncertain. Clearing my throat, I shrugged and said, "Well, there's no need to be. I…I told him the same thing that I told you; I'm not ready for anything serious. So, we agreed to just be friends for now."

"I see," was all he said, and after a moment of awkward silence, he changed the subject and we got back to our meal.

The rain continued to pour from the sky, the sound of it beating lightly against the windows a bit soothing. I began to relax as Zachary and I chatted, all of my thoughts and memories that had been so real and painful just a couple of hours ago now drifting away like the drops of rain into the Savannah River.

"That was delicious," Zachary said once we'd finished eating.

He helped me put the food away and wash the dishes, and I suddenly wondered why he wasn't at work. When I asked him about it, he simply shrugged and said, "I took the day off. I thought you might need some company."

By the time the kitchen was cleaned, it was nearly four o'clock and Zachary stated it was time he left. I walked him to the door and opened it, gasping when I looked out. The streets were flooded, the water steadily rising, and it didn't look like the rain was going to stop anytime soon.

"It must be high tide," Zachary muttered, rubbing the side of his face.

We went back inside and switched on the radio, trying to find a weather station with any updates. When we finally did, the news wasn't good.

"There are several bands of storms that will sweep through our area within the next twelve hours or so," the meteorologist said. "Be prepared for a lot of rain, which will cause some flooding as it's currently spring tide, and also for the possibility of tornadoes. Everyone, please stay indoors until this is over."

Zachary switched off the radio and sighed. "This is just great," he moaned.

"Well, you can't drive home on flooded streets," I pointed out.

"I can't stay here either," he replied. "We'd be the talk of the town."

"Who would know?" I shrugged. "No one is going to be out in this weather to see your car."

As there was no other logical choice, Zachary finally relented, and we went back into the kitchen for some coffee and cookies. I'd just poured our cups when the telephone rang, and I hurried to answer it. Father was on the other line, his voice worried as he asked how I was doing. I said I was okay, not bothering to mention that Zachary was with me, and then asked if he was alright; I hated to think of him being alone during such a terrible storm.

"I'm fine, honey, don't worry about me," he assured me, and after talking for a few moments more, we hung up.

Zachary and I spent the rest of the evening playing card games and snacking on anything we could find. The rain continued and would get worse at times, only to let up again shortly after. The roads were still flooded by nightfall, and I brought down several blankets and a pillow for Zachary and took them into my office where, thankfully, Father had left his sofa behind.

"Sweet dreams," I told him, grinning as I tossed the pillow at his head.

"You won't be so cheerful when you're forced to marry me because people found out I spent the night here," he stated, raising an eyebrow at me.

"It wouldn't be the first time I was the subject of gossip and I'm sure it won't be the last, so I'm not worried," I replied with a chuckle.

That night, I lay in bed listening to the sound of the rain on the roof and the random rumbles of thunder, wondering how my life would be now if the events of last February had never occurred. Howard had been on a downward path with his gambling habit, and I suspected that we would have eventually lost the farm. Would we have stayed together, or would he have left me? I couldn't know, but thought quite often of what could have been, especially if Howard Junior hadn't died. I was beginning to heal, but knew that I'd never regain the hole left from my baby's death; there would always be a part of me that missed him and longed for his presence.

At a little past eleven, I drifted off into a deep sleep, dreams immediately entering my troubled mind as flashbacks. It had been at least three months since my last nightmare, but my brain refused to be at peace tonight. The images of my home being set on fire were so real that I could clearly see the flames and even feel their searing heat, and the sound of little Howard's cries were so loud and piercing that I thought my heart would burst if I didn't get to him.

Suddenly, Mack's face leered before me, his eyes wild as he lunged forward and coiled his fingers around my neck. I fought against him, but he wouldn't stop, his grasp growing tighter and tighter. My heart pounded so forcefully that I couldn't breathe, and my lungs felt like they were going to explode…

"Vivian."

Someone from very far away called my name and then I felt two strong hands grasp my shoulders and shake me. I fought them at first, as all I could see was Mack's hateful, sneering face, and I knew I was going to die if I didn't get away.

"Vivian, wake up!"

With a gasp, my eyes flew open and I saw Zachary leaning over me, his face only inches from mine. I pushed him away and sat up in bed, my brain foggy and heart racing as I looked around the room in confusion. Zachary had apparently turned on the light, illuminating my bedroom, and as I sat there in a daze, he hurried into the bathroom to get a glass of water.

"Are you alright?" He asked, extending the glass out to me.

I stared at him silently for a moment, making no move to take the glass from his hand. My mind was so muddled that I was having a hard time separating the dream from reality, and I reached up with trembling fingers to tuck my hair behind my ear.

"I…I saw Mack and heard…my baby crying," I said, my voice weak and uncertain as I looked around the room.

"It was a dream, Vivian," Zachary told me gently. "Just a dream."

With a shuddering sigh, I took the glass and sipped the cool water, my nightgown soaked in sweat.

"Will you hand me my robe?" I asked after a moment.

He handed it to me, and after slipping the robe around my shoulders, I attempted to stand. Finding that I was too shaky to walk, Zachary wrapped his arm around my waist and helped me into the bathroom. I sat on the edge of the tub for a moment while he went in search of a new nightgown and I sighed, rubbing my head. It had been a long time since I was tormented by such a bad dream, and I was left tremendously weak and drained.

Zachary returned with the gown then, and smiling slightly, I took it and said, "Thank you. I think I can handle it from here."

His cheeks flushing, Zachary nodded and left the room, closing the door behind him. Once I'd changed, I tied the robe around my waist and walked slowly back out into the bedroom. I'd just stepped over the threshold when a mighty crack of thunder shook the building, and with a start, I stumbled back against the wall.

"I think we should both go downstairs for a while," Zachary said, taking my arm. "It's getting pretty bad out there, and the meteorologist said there was a possibility of tornadoes tonight."

Nodding, I helped him grab the blankets and pillows from my bed and followed him downstairs. The old building creaked and moaned as the wind whipped angrily against its outer walls. The rain was coming down so hard and heavy that it sounded almost like the roar of the ocean, and I flinched as a bolt of lightning lit up the dining room as we made our way into my office.

After dragging the sofa out into the hall where there were no windows, Zachary spread the blankets out for me and said, "Here, you take the sofa."

I flipped on a small, nearby lamp and sank down onto the thick cushions, pulling my knees to my chest. "You can sit up here with me if you like," I said. "I don't think I'll be going back to sleep anytime soon."

Zachary sat down beside me and neither of us barely moved as we listened to the storm blustering loudly outside. Finally, after a long moment, I looked at him and asked softly, "Did I wake you up earlier?"

"No," he shook his head. "I couldn't sleep. I hope it was alright that I went into your bedroom, but I could hear you moaning and crying and I didn't know what else to do. Are you okay?"

I nodded. "Yes," I replied, sighing. "And thank you for waking me; I think my heart might have exploded if you hadn't."

Reaching out, Zachary took my hand and gently squeezed it, rubbing the inside of my palm with his thumb. "You were dreaming of what happened this time last year, weren't you?"

"Yes, I was. It was horrible," I said, closing my eyes with a shudder. "I don't know that I've ever had one quite that bad before." Looking up at him, I added with a soft smile, "I'm glad you were here."

"So am I," he replied, smiling in return. His eyes were warm as he looked at me, and the shadows from the lamp played along the lines of his handsome face, illuminating the strong set of his jaw and fullness of his lips. I suddenly thought of when he kissed me and immediately looked away, my face growing warm.

Like the mighty blast of a cannon, another clap of thunder ripped through the night and I jumped, my heart catching as I glanced fearfully about. It rumbled on and on, the walls shaking from the force of it, and I could hear the wind and rain beating fiercely against the building. I hoped that the old structure wouldn't collapse down on top of us, and I was suddenly very grateful for Zachary's company. Tornadoes rarely touched down in the Savannah area, but as the storm continued to escalate, I feared that tonight may be an exception.

After a tense moment of silence as we both listened to the violence of the storm, Zachary suddenly stated, "I have a question."

When I looked at him and raised my eyebrows questioningly, he said, "Since you've agreed to go out with Officer Wright as a friend, would you be willing to do the same with me?"

"What about Beatrice?" I asked, tilting my head to the side.

A slight smile passing his lips, he replied, "I already told you she and I are just friends."

Pursing my lips for a moment in thought, I finally nodded and said, "Alright then, as long as there's nothing expected beyond going out and enjoying each other's company."

"It's a deal," he said, nodding his head seriously.

We stayed there on the sofa talking until nearly three in the morning when the storm finally began to calm. I was exhausted and yet oddly content as I, once again, bid Zachary a good night and went back to bed. This time, I laid awake thinking of what an eventful day it had turned out to be. I was grateful that Zachary came over; his presence had helped to ease what otherwise would have been a painful, stressful day.

As I rolled onto my side and began drifting back off to sleep, I wondered about him and Beatrice. If what Savannah said was true, everyone was bent on putting the two of them together and when I saw them at the dance, Beatrice had seemed very happy to go along with it. Was Zachary not being completely honest with me about their relationship?

61

Eva

I arrived home from work two days after the storm to find Leon kneeling beside my mother at the steps leading up to my front porch. I feared at first that there had been an accident and leaped from the car, my heart pounding. As I hurried up the driveway, I saw the toolbox sitting just to Leon's left and realized he must have come over to fix the bottom step that had been damaged in the storm.

"Hello, honey," Mutter said when she saw me.

Leon glanced over his shoulder and my heart gave a sudden jolt when our eyes met. I'd, of course, seen him many times since the night he told me he loved me, but I hadn't actually spoken to him. Asher and I were to be married in less than two weeks, and I had tried my best to put Leon out of my mind and act normal around Asher. He seemed, however, to still sense that something was wrong, because once he'd arrived back in town, he asked more than once if everything was alright. I kept assuring him it was, but feared he didn't believe me.

"Hi," I said, attempting to act normal as I drew nearer and smiled at the both of them. "Leon, it's so nice of you to fix that for us."

"I saw your mother trip on it just now and came right over," he replied, reaching to dig through his toolbox for something. "Y'all should have already asked me to fix it."

"Mutter, are you alright?" I asked, touching her arm in concern.

"I'm fine," she assured me, waving her hand in the air. Grunting, she pushed herself up and, with a sheepish smile, said, "My back, however, is feeling a bit stiff. Will you take my place, honey, and help Leon?"

"Of course," I nodded, watching as she walked inside. Glancing down at Leon, I took a deep breath and kneeled beside him. "What can I do?"

"Hold the end of that board there," he replied, not quite meeting my gaze as he straightened the new plank and began nailing it in place.

I held the board steady, trying my best to think of something else and not dwell on the fact that Leon and I were so close, our arms kept touching. He was dressed in casual clothes, his hair was soft and hung over his forehead, and I took a deep breath, breathing in the familiar, woodsy scent that seemed to radiate from his skin and clothes.

"How…how have you been?" I asked, breaking the silence.

"I've been okay," he replied, a nail hanging from the corner of his mouth. After a moment, he stopped what he was doing and turned to look at me. "Eva," he said, taking the nail from between his teeth, "I've decided to go to Atlanta for a while."

My eyes widening, I asked, "What do you mean?"

Glancing down at the hammer he held, he shrugged and said, "Our bank has a branch up there, and I think the change will do me good."

"So…you're going to move up there?"

"For a while, yes," he nodded, reaching out to dig through the toolbox once more. "I'm going to sell my house here, and if I decide to move back to Savannah later, I'll just buy another one somewhere else."

I stared at Leon's profile, his face slowly beginning to blur as my eyes filled with tears. "I hope you're not leaving because of me," I whispered.

Leon stopped what he was doing, his jaw clenched and gaze pointed downward as he sat there silently, not moving. When he didn't answer, I reached out and gingerly touched his arm, saying, "Can't we still be friends, Leon?"

Pulling his arm away, he turned to look at me and shook his head. "No, I'm afraid we can't," he said, and I drew back slightly at the intensity in his gaze. "Look, I know it seems like I'm running away, but I just can't stay here and watch you marry someone else and pretend like everything is alright. I *love* you, Eva, I'll always love you. Do you understand that? Even if I meet someone else some day, it won't be the same; you'll always have my heart, and I'll regret losing you until the day I die. Just…" he stopped and shook his head, sighing heavily as he looked away once again and said in a choked voice, "just please try to understand."

I stared at him in silence, my eyes wide. Never in my life had anyone spoken so passionately to me. I'd been able to read every emotion in Leon's eyes; pain, love, anguish, sincerity. He'd been honest and told me exactly what he was feeling, and all I wanted was to throw my arms around him and never let go, but I couldn't and it was killing me. Now he was leaving, and just the thought of possibly never seeing him again was almost more than I could bear.

"I'm so sorry," I whispered, my voice thick with tears. Why did life have to be so hard?

"So am I," was all he said, his jaw clenched as he continued with his work. When I reached out to steady my end of the board once again, he said, "That's all the help I need, Eva. You can go inside now."

My eyes filled with hot, burning tears, I nodded silently and released the board. I tried to stand and, without thinking, put my hand on Leon's shoulder for support. I felt him stiffen at my touch, and when I tried to jerk my hand away, I slipped and fell against him, knocking him slightly off

326

balance. He quickly turned and caught me before I tumbled to the ground, and I suddenly found my arm wrapped around his neck, our faces only inches apart.

There was a look of surprise on Leon's face, and we stayed frozen in that position, our gazes glued together. I could feel the beating of his heart as it quickly accelerated beneath my fingers, and when his eyes slowly drifted down to my lips, I grew breathless. There was electricity between us, sparking and sizzling like an open flame, and my body grew warm as I tingled all over. I felt my fingers wrap tighter around the back of his neck, and more than anything, I wanted him to kiss me. I yearned to feel that connection with him, to taste the heat of his lips against mine, and Leon's words from so many months ago of love having the passion of a thunderstorm suddenly drifted through my mind and finally made sense. I'd never felt this way before, and it almost frightened me a bit. It was like I was sitting on a boat in the middle of a wild and angry sea, being tossed about on the waves as wind and rain raged madly about, but through all the thunder and lightning and trembling deep down in my soul, I somehow felt safe and warm.

Suddenly, Leon cleared his throat and pulled away, breaking the connection between us and leaving me shaken and chilled. I sat silently and rubbed the cold skin on my forearms, feeling a little dazed. It would have been wrong for him to kiss me, which is why I knew he hadn't, but at least I would have had the memory to carry with me.

"Eva?"

With a startled gasp, I spun to find Asher standing at the end of the driveway, watching us. I jumped to my feet and smoothed my hands down my wrinkled dress while Leon stayed put, not even bothering to turn around.

"What's going on, Eva?" Asher asked when he came to stand before me.

I could tell he was upset, and I nervously clasped my hands together. "I...I was helping Leon fix the step," I stammered, pointing to the step as proof of my statement.

"That's why you were holding each other in what appeared to be a very passionate embrace?" Asher demanded, his voice growing louder.

With a loud *thunk*, Leon threw the hammer back into his toolbox and stood up. Facing Asher, he said, "Nothing happened, Asher, so don't make a big deal out of it." With that, he picked up his toolbox and walked away without another word.

Asher watched him go, his brow furrowed. He turned back to me then, and forcing a smile, I said, "Come...come inside for some hot chocolate. Nana has made a fresh pot every night this week."

Without a word, Asher followed me inside and hung his coat on the hall tree. I knew he was still upset and hoped he wouldn't bring the conversation of Leon back up again later. I led him to the kitchen, and as

327

he sat at the table and began conversing with Nana, I realized I'd left my purse in the car. Excusing myself, I hurried back through the house, pausing when I saw a letter lying on the floor by the front door. Realizing that it must have fallen from Asher's coat, I picked it up and started to stuff it back into one of his pockets, my hand stopping in mid-air when I saw the curly, feminine handwriting across the front of the envelope. I stared at it for a moment, contemplating whether it would be wrong to read it. My curiosity getting the best of me, I opened the letter and read what it said, the blood slowly leaving my face as my eyes widened in shock.

I could hear Nana and Asher laughing in the kitchen, and feeling the need for air, I stuffed the letter back into his coat pocket and stepped out onto the porch, taking several deep breaths. After a moment, Asher came looking for me.

"Why are you standing out here alone?" He asked, glancing around curiously as he closed the door behind him.

"I...I needed a moment to think," I said, my voice barely above a whisper.

His brow furrowing, Asher asked, "What about?"

My stomach clenching, I walked to the edge of the porch and rested my hand on the banister as I tried to sort through my thoughts. I didn't know what to say, except to tell him I now knew the truth.

Turning to face him, I took a deep breath and said, "I read the letter, Asher. The one from Lydia."

His eyes widening, I watched as the color left Asher's face, and when he swayed a bit on his feet, I suddenly feared that he might faint. After a moment, he shook his head and said in a choked whisper, "Eva...I was going to tell you."

"When?" I asked, my voice filled with disbelief. "After we were married?"

By the look on his face, I knew that's exactly what he had intended. Feeling sick to my stomach, I asked softly, "How could you, Asher?"

"Because I love you, Eva," he said as he stepped toward me, his eyes beseeching mine. "I don't love Lydia, I never did. For all of these years, you're the only one I've ever wanted, and when I came back from the war, I realized that I finally had a chance with you. Lydia meant nothing to me, Eva, I promise; she's just a poor servant girl that used to work for my parents."

"How can you say that about her?" I asked incredulously. "She's the mother of your child, Asher."

Asher flinched at my words and looked away, his jaw clenching. I could see the guilt and turmoil in his eyes, and somehow felt sorry for him. I couldn't understand, though, how could he stand there and speak so callously about the woman who'd borne his child, and I wondered if he'd ever seen his daughter, or if he'd thrown her aside just like Lydia.

After a moment, Asher sighed heavily and said, "You're right, Eva. I shouldn't have kept this from you. I just...I just love you so much that I feared I would lose you if you found out; that's why I've been rushing so to get married." His face filled with shame and regret, he stepped closer and said softly, "I guess this means you want nothing more to do with me?"

Closing my eyes, I swallowed over the lump in my throat, struggling with what to say. I cared for Asher, I always had, and I didn't wish to hurt him. I truly believed that he did love me, and I knew that I would have to choose my next words carefully.

Finally, I opened my eyes and in a kind, sincere voice, said, "You'll always be my brother-in-law and Davey's uncle, that won't ever change, and you're welcome to visit us any time you like." I paused and glanced down at my feet, unable to continue meeting his gaze. "I'm...I'm afraid, however, that it has to be over between us. I know I said that I would marry you and I always try to keep my word, but I don't think I'm bound to it now that...that I know the truth."

Looking back up at him, the pain in his eyes so real that it was almost more than I could bear, I added softly, "Lydia said in her letter that she loves you, Asher, and your daughter needs you. I know you said you didn't love her and referred to her as only a poor servant girl, but perhaps you should give her a chance because, after all, *I'm* only a poor, German immigrant."

Asher said nothing for a moment; he simply stood there staring at me, his jaw clenching. Finally, his voice barely above a whisper, he said, "I understand. I'm so sorry, Eva, for everything."

He stepped around me then and walked away, his shoulders stooped in defeat. When he got to his car, he looked back at me, and with trembling lips, I smiled softly and said, "Goodbye, Asher."

He stood there for a moment, as if he wanted to say something more, and finally just nodded, got into his car, and drove away.

I sat on the porch steps and watched him drive down our street and turn at the corner, tears burning the backs of my eyes. I should never have agreed to marry him in the first place, and if I could only go back in time and change things, I would.

Burying my face in my knees, I cried like a baby, my tears soaking through my skirt and dripping onto the pavement below. I was relieved to be free from the engagement, but saddened by how it had ended. Asher was a good man, I refused to believe otherwise, but he'd slipped onto the wrong path somehow and I hoped he'd be able to find his way again.

After a while, I stood up and wiped my face, trying to pull myself together as I turned to go back inside. Feeling drained and bone weary, I hesitated, glancing over at Leon's house. I wanted to tell him what happened, but knew that it was too soon. With a sigh, I decided I would give it a few days before I told him the news and went back into the house, realizing as I shut the door that Asher had left his coat and the letter behind.

Three days later, a "for sale" sign went up in Leon's yard and I knew it was time I told him about Asher. Feeling nervous, I went into my room and brushed out my hair, leaving it down and flowing around my shoulders. I put on some red lipstick and changed into my new, rose-colored floral dress, and then went into Mutter's room and dug through her jewelry box until I found the flower shaped clip-on earrings. I put them on and looked in the mirror, still feeling nervous but a bit more confident. Taking a deep breath, I went over to Leon's house and knocked on the door, but he didn't answer and I soon realized he wasn't home. I waited for a bit and then went back into my house to call Savannah.

"I don't know where he is," she told me when I asked about Leon's whereabouts. "Is everything okay?"

"There's something I need to tell him," I replied.

"Well, he's been a little…upset lately," Savannah stated, clearing her throat awkwardly, "and sometimes when he needs to think, he'll drive down to Fort Jackson."

I hung up the phone and got into my car, my hands shaking nervously as I took the wheel and headed towards the old, abandoned fort. I wasn't entirely certain of what I was going to say when I got there and hoped I wouldn't make a complete fool of myself.

The sun was on its downward descent by the time I arrived at Fort Jackson, and I parked my car next to Leon's beneath an old palm tree. There was always a delightfully cool breeze on the river, and as I made my way down the path that led to the open area where the fort stood, I breathed in the salty scent that lingered heavily in the air.

The pathway ended, and I saw Leon sitting several yards ahead on a broken log by the Savannah River. I walked towards him, my eyes traveling to the beautiful old fort which was built in 1808 and constructed over an old Revolutionary War battery. Later, during the Civil War, local militia units occupied its space. I'd never been here before but had heard many stories of its fascinating history. Oh, if only brick and stone could talk!

I drew closer to Leon, and still he had yet to notice me. He was facing the water and I stopped for a moment just to watch him, my heart tightening with love for this man. I thought of the first time we met when I was attempting to fix our broken shutters and ended up falling flat on my backside right in front of him; I could still see the smile in his beautiful eyes after he'd helped me up and then offered to fix the shutters himself.

330

He'd been there for me through so much, never complaining or asking for anything in return; he'd even taken a bullet and nearly died for Davey and me.

Suddenly, my mind was taken back to the first dance we had together and how he'd spoken of his quest to find true love. I'd never heard a grown man speak of such things and had realized that there was something missing in my life; I just didn't know what at the time. That same night, I'd nervously stood in front of the crowd and sang "Danny Boy", and in the song's magic, our eyes met and I'd felt the first tingle of attraction for another man since Paul's death. I could still feel the intensity in Leon's gaze as he'd watched me sing, and I closed my eyes for a moment, smiling at the sweet memory.

"Oh, Danny boy, the pipes, the pipes are calling," I sang softly, opening my eyes once more. "From glen to glen, and down the mountain side."

Leon turned around, a look of surprise on his face. He stood up and stared at me, as if seeing a ghost, and I slowly walked toward him.

"'Tis you, 'tis you must go and I must bide," I continued, my gaze never wavering from his. "But come ye back when summer's in the meadow, or when the valley's hushed and white with snow. 'Tis I'll be here in sunshine or in shadow…"

I stood before him then and gently reached up to touch his face, my heart feeling as if it would burst within my chest. In a soft, almost whisper, I sang the remaining words, "O Danny Boy, O Danny Boy, I love you so."

As my words faded off into the breeze, we stood there staring at each other, mesmerized by the magic that seemed to surround us. The sun continued to set, creating a warm glow as its reflection danced along the top of the water, and I could hear the breeze whispering through the reeds as if it had a secret to tell.

"You're so beautiful," Leon breathed, softly brushing his fingers along the side of my face. "Why are you here, Eva? Why do you torment me so?"

I opened my mouth to answer, but no words would come. I'd never felt so vulnerable in all my life, and I could barely think over the loud pounding of my heart.

"I've….come to ask you to stay," I heard myself say. Gathering more courage, I took a deep breath and softly added, "Don't go to Atlanta, Leon. Stay here with me."

"What about Asher?" He asked uncertainly.

"Asher is gone," I replied, swallowing. "It's over between us, Leon."

Leon searched my face, his gaze fervent as he tried to determine my thoughts. "And how do you feel about that?" He wanted to know.

Wrapping my arms around my waist, I sighed and said, "It was hard, but it's for the best, I know that. In the end, it wouldn't have been fair to marry him when I loved someone else."

Leon said nothing for a moment, and I began to grow fearful. Had he decided that he didn't truly love me after all? Or perhaps he'd decided to go to Atlanta and still planned to move, no matter what. I only hoped I hadn't hurt him so badly that he wasn't willing to give me a second chance.

My heart pounding, I said, "Leon, I don't blame you if you aren't willing to give me another chance. I just want you to know that I'm so sorry for everything and…"

Before I could finish, Leon suddenly stepped closer and bent his head, covering my mouth with his. Startled, I stood completely still, my heart fluttering wildly as he slipped his arms around my waist, pulled me against his chest, and lifted me off of my feet. He kissed me like a dying man, the fervency in his lips making me feel lightheaded as stars danced before my eyes. I'd never felt such passion and ardor in one kiss, and I wrapped my arms tightly around his neck, kissing him back with just as much fervency. I loved him with everything in me, and knowing that we'd finally found our way to each other was like finding a beautiful and rare waterfall after miles and miles of searching.

"I think that true love should have the passion of a thunderstorm, the sweetness of honey, the depth of an ocean, and the honesty of a child. The one you love should make you feel whole and complete, like you don't belong anywhere on this earth but with them."

Leon's words from that night at the dance suddenly rang in my ears, and I now knew what my life had been missing. I'd been missing *this*; the overwhelming sense of knowing you're finally where you were always meant to be. I never would have dreamed when I was a young girl growing up in Germany that I would travel nearly five thousand miles across the world and find my soulmate, the one that God intended me to be with. Yes, Paul had been my first love, but I knew now that Leon would be my last.

62

Vivian

It always sounded so cliché, but the last few months had flown by. I'd spent my days mostly working while occasionally going out with friends, which included both Gabe and Zachary. As agreed upon, neither man had attempted to take things further and I was content to leave it that way for now. I had my hands full with the restaurant, and during my time off, I was happy being able to just relax and enjoy life with no strings attached. I knew, however, that there was a possibility that one of them would broach the subject of courting more seriously, but I thought I'd just cross that bridge when, and if, I came to it.

Maisie and I continued writing letters to one another monthly; she loved her job at the newspaper, and had even moved into a boarding house. She was no longer seeing the same young man, but wrote to say, *"I really don't mind. Getting married isn't what I want for myself now, anyway; I'm happy to spend this time being more independent and growing in to myself."*

She seemed to be doing so well that it was hard to believe this happy, confident-sounding young woman was the same thin, frail girl who befriended me at Martinsville. We'd both come such a long way since then.

After Hitler's suicide in April, Germany surrendered the following month, and Connor was finally sent home. Savannah was overjoyed to have her husband back safe and sound, and we all threw him a welcome home party. It was good to see Connor again, and everyone hoped Japan would soon follow suit and surrender as well.

Eva and Leon were getting married in less than two weeks, and I couldn't have been more excited for them. They were absolutely perfect for each other, and even though the wedding would be small, I was thrilled to have been asked to stand up beside Eva. She and I had become almost like sisters, and I couldn't imagine how my life would be without her.

It was Friday evening when I received a phone call from my father asking me to come over. He sounded a bit strange, and I immediately agreed and hurried over to his house as quickly as I could.

"Father, is something wrong?" I asked as soon as I stepped inside.

"Please, sit down," he said, nervously adjusting the pair of glasses he'd recently started wearing.

I sat on the sofa in the living room, the clock on the mantle ticking loudly as Father quietly came to sit beside me. Clearing his throat, he looked at me and said, "It's been over a year since your mother died and frankly, it's still hard to believe that she's gone. We had a wonderful life together and I'll always miss her, but I know that she'd want me to go on with life and try to find happiness." Pausing, Father took a deep breath and plunged in with, "Vivvy, I've come to care a great deal for Lina Hamilton, and I'd like your blessing to marry her."

I stared at Father in shock, although why I was surprised, I didn't know. Mrs. Lina had been cleaning his house twice a week for nearly seven months, and I'd noticed on several occasions how much happier Father seemed in her presence. I hadn't, however, considered that they might wish to get married. How would it feel to see my father with someone other than my mother?

"I know what a surprise this must be," he said with a sigh, interrupting my thoughts, "and I'd like for you to take some time to think it over before you give me an answer."

"Father, you know you don't need my blessing to get remarried," I said softly.

"I know," he nodded, "but it would make me feel better. Please, don't give me an answer right away; I sincerely want you to think about it first."

I agreed, and as I drove back to the restaurant, I felt a little overcome with emotion and made a last-minute detour to the cemetery. As I stood before Mother's grave, I struggled to come to terms with Father's news. I liked Mrs. Lina very much, and if Father cared for and wanted to marry her, I wouldn't stand in his way, but could I handle seeing him with someone else?

With a sigh, I sank down onto a nearby bench and began to cry. It would be so strange to watch as another woman moved into the house that used to be my mother's, to see her cooking in the kitchen and sitting on the sofa sewing or reading; all the things I'd seen Mother do a thousand times. I wouldn't throw a shadow on Father's happiness, but I worried about how it would affect me personally. Would I even still want to go home to visit, or would it be too painful? Although Mother had been gone a year, the ache of missing her hadn't subsided at all.

With a sigh, I turned and went back to my car, my emotions all tied up in a knot. I was happy for Father, as I didn't wish for him to spend the rest of his life alone, but realized I wasn't prepared for this to happen quite so soon.

The next morning, Eva poked her head into my office and asked to speak with me.

"Of course, come in," I said, beckoning her inside.

She sat down and studied me for a moment, her expression that of uncertainty. "Did…did your father tell you the news?" She finally asked.

"Yes, he did," I nodded, wondering how she felt about it.

Chewing her bottom lip, Eva asked, "What are your thoughts?"

Taking a deep breath, I leaned back in my chair, the morning sun through the window casting a bit of warmth against my neck and shoulders.

"I'll admit that it took me by surprise," I said after a moment. "I want them to be happy, but it's going to take some getting used to on my part. How about you?"

Eva glanced down at her hands, but not before I saw a pool of tears gathering in her eyes. "I feel the same way," she said softly, "but I want Mutter to have a second chance at happiness, just as I've been blessed to have with Leon. I know…I know no one will ever be able to take the place of my father or your mother, but…well…" she looked up at me then, and a sweet smile spread across her face as she said, "I've always wanted to have a sister, and now my wish will finally come true."

I blinked in surprise at Eva's words. "I…I hadn't even thought of that," I said, glancing down at my hands as tears gathered in my own eyes.

I sat there in silence for a moment, wishing desperately to hold on to the past, to my mother and the memories I had of her, while struggling to face both the present and the future. Eva was right; no one would ever take the place of the parents we'd lost, but life moved on, and we had to move with it or else we'd be left behind. I looked back at Eva then, and my heart was filled with warmth at the look of genuine sincerity on her face.

With a trembling smile of my own, I stood and walked around the desk to sit beside her. Taking her hand in mine, I said, "I had already come to think of you as a sister anyway, you know, and now it seems we'll be able to make it official."

Tears flooding her eyes once again, Eva pulled me into a hug and, suddenly, the sadness and uncertainty melted from the room as peace took its place. I'd been so concerned with my feelings of doubt that I hadn't even considered the positives this change would bring; I would now have a sister and an adorable little nephew, and my father would no longer be alone.

When Eva pulled back and wiped her eyes, she said, "You know, I never imagined that when I found this job, I'd also find so much happiness."

We talked a bit more, both of us excited to tell our parents that they had our blessing, and when Eva left to go into the kitchen, I sat back in my chair and sighed.

"God won't leave us joyless. We might not be able to see the sun shining in the midst of the storm, but it's there, waiting to shine again."

Mother's words suddenly floated through my mind, and I smiled. It seemed she was right; the clouds had finally begun to pass, and through all the pain and hardships I'd endured over the last sixteen months, God had given me my joy back. Although our family would be different now, and it would take some time for all of us to adjust, I knew we could do it together.

That evening, I was ready and waiting when Gabe came to pick me up for the date we'd planned over the last week.

"You look great," he said as we drove to a cozy little Italian café that had recently just opened in town.

"Thank you," I smiled, glancing down at the sleeveless, knee length dress I wore. It was light blue with tiny little flowers all over, and I'd brought along a white sweater to throw over my shoulders just in case it was chilly inside.

When we arrived at the café, we were quickly taken to a corner booth and, after placing our orders, Gabe leaned back and smiled at me. He'd just gotten off duty and still wore his uniform, but he'd taken off his tie and unbuttoned the top two buttons of his shirt. His dirty blonde hair was soft and a bit mussed after a long day at work, and I thought the five o'clock stubble that shadowed his face made him look more masculine than usual.

"Ready for the wedding next Friday?" He asked.

"Yes, I'm so happy for Leon and Eva," I replied, nodding.

"I'm sure you'll look great in that new dress you were telling me about," Gabe replied with a wink. When I blushed and laughed self-consciously, he asked, "Are you going with Zachary?"

"No," I replied, wondering if I should ask Gabe to go with me.

Before I could dwell on it any further, however, the waitress arrived with our food and I was instantly distracted by the delicious looking bowl of spaghetti placed before me.

"My mother is half-Italian, you know," Gabe suddenly said, and I looked up at him in surprise, as he normally didn't like talking about his family.

"Really?" I asked, twirling the spaghetti noodles around my fork. "Is she from Italy, or was she born in America?"

"Her mother came to America with her husband when they married, so she was born here," he replied. "She has family, though, that still lives in Italy."

"I'd love to go there some day," I said, sighing dreamily. "I've seen photographs and it looks gorgeous."

"Maybe someday you will," he replied, smiling. "Maybe someday we both will."

I glanced up, eyeing him curiously as I tried to determine what he'd meant by that last statement. When he simply continued buttering a piece of sliced bread, his expression nonchalant, I shrugged and pushed it from my mind.

"Do you ever write to your family there?" I asked.

Gabe nodded. "Some. It's been a bit more difficult to stay in contact with the war, but I've received a couple of letters from one of my great-aunts."

"How are they fairing?"

"They're sharecroppers," he said, helping himself to another slice of bread, "so they don't have as much of a problem getting food as many of the others do. In fact, my great-aunt seemed very proud when she wrote that they never have to eat brown bread, as they can make their own white flour."

"What's wrong with brown bread?" I asked with a small laugh.

"From what I could gather, the brown bread they're currently distributing to the people is made from chaff and, at times, sawdust is even added to make it thicker. Most of the rationed foods are very low in quality."

"It would seem so," I stated, shivering slightly. "It's good that your family has the ability to get higher quality food. Perhaps now that the war is almost over, things will get better."

Once we were through eating, Gabe suggested we take a walk, and I readily agreed. It was still a bit light outside, and as we walked through Lafayette Square, I gazed around at the beauty of the city. I was so engrossed by the trickling sound of the water in the fountain and the pigeons eating nearby that I blinked in surprise when Gabe took my hand.

"Watch out," he said, nodding at something over my shoulder, and he quickly pulled me out of the way as a young boy blew past us on a bicycle.

"That was close," I breathed, smiling gratefully at Gabe. "Thank you."

He gazed down at me, a warm smile on his lips, and I suddenly realized how close we were standing.

"Have I ever mentioned how beautiful you are?" He asked, his voice low.

My cheeks flushing, I took a step back and suggested we head back to his car. Gabe nodded, and as we walked out to the road, I realized that he still held my hand.

As Gabe drove me home, he glanced over at me, the glow from the streetlights bouncing along his face as he said, "So, I know we decided to keep things casual between us, but I've really come to like you, Vivian. I don't want to push you, but if you're ready, I'd like to start courting you seriously."

My heart jumped, and I was grateful for the darkness of the car because my face immediately began to burn. I'd suspected that this would happen, eventually; I just hadn't expected it quite so soon.

Was it really all that soon, though? We'd been "seeing" each other for nearly six months, and Gabe had a right to know where we stood. I wasn't, however, entirely certain how I felt. He was very nice and I was quite fond of him, but was I truly ready to take that next step and enter into a serious relationship with someone? I suddenly felt terrified at that thought and wrapped my arms protectively around my waist.

"Can I think about it and let you know?" I finally asked in a soft voice, glancing over at him.

"Of course," he nodded, smiling, and I was grateful that he didn't push me about it further.

That night, as I cleaned my face before bed and lathered my skin with cold cream, all I could think about was Gabe and the decision I was confronted with. Suddenly, Zachary's face popped into my mind and I wondered how he would feel about my seriously courting Gabe. I'd agreed to go out with both men on a casual, friendship type basis, but now that things might progress with Gabe, I didn't know how Zachary would react, or if he would even care. I had to make a decision about Gabe, but I couldn't help hesitating, as I didn't know how Zachary felt about me.

I finally decided that I should talk to Zachary about this before I gave Gabe an answer; I felt like that was the only fair thing to do.

63

Vivian

A few days later, the weather was warm and sunny, and it seemed everyone was out and about and pouring into the restaurant. Normally, I loved having a lot of customers, but today everything was going wrong. First, one oven went out and I had to pay someone double to hurry out and repair it, and then I had to give a refund to three different customers who complained of undercooked, tasteless food. Eva had quit working at the restaurant a couple of days before, and so far, the new cook wasn't doing well at all.

Later that afternoon, I received a surprise visit from Mrs. Fitzgerald, one of the ladies I'd overheard talking about me in the church parking lot.

"Am I interrupting?" She asked, popping her head into my office.

"Not at all," I said, smiling politely. "Please, do come in."

"My husband and I stopped by for dinner and while we waited for our food, I just thought I'd pop in and say hello," she told me, the ribbon on her hat constantly flopping across her forehead as she spoke.

"How nice," I replied, trying not to stare at the bit of lipstick she had on her teeth.

After jabbering on and on about her daughter, Mrs. Fitzgerald suddenly asked, "You've been seeing quite a bit of that young doctor, haven't you?"

Blinking in surprise, I cleared my throat and said, "Uh, yes, we're quite good friends."

"He's the one with the reddish hair?"

At my nod, she pursed her lips and leaned closer, lowering her voice as she said, "Well, I know it's none of my business, and I hate to gossip…"

Sure you do, I thought, forcing my face to remain neutral.

"…but I'm not so sure he's right for you, dear. I'm afraid that you just might get hurt again."

"Why is that?" I asked, tilting my head curiously.

As if she hated to be the bearer of bad news, Mrs. Fitzgerald sighed heavily and said, "Well, it just so happens that I saw him and that nurse…I believe her name is Beatrice?…out at the park yesterday having a picnic and…well…they didn't notice me watching, but they were holding hands and kissing. I'm so sorry, dear, but I thought you should know."

By the glint in her eye, I knew she was, in fact, not sorry at all, as people like her thrived on sharing bad news and juicy gossip.

Trying to maintain an uninterested expression, I simply smiled and said, "Thank you for telling me, Mrs. Fitzgerald, but I have no hold on him; he's free to do as he wishes."

Raising an eyebrow, Mrs. Fitzgerald sniffed and stood up, stating that she should get back to her husband. After she was gone, I sat back in my chair, a bit dazed with disbelief. Zachary had told me he and Beatrice were just friends, and I hadn't realized they were still even seeing each other. I knew I didn't own him and he could go out with whomever he pleased, but the fact that he'd lied to me was both hurtful and shocking. I'd also thought that I owed him an explanation about Gabe, but apparently he didn't feel he owed me the same about Beatrice.

I tried to put Mrs. Fitzgerald's words out of my mind, but they continued repeating themselves over and over inside of my brain. By the time the day was over and the restaurant closed, I wasn't in the frame of mind to have visitors and moaned loudly in frustration when I heard someone knocking on the front door at a little past seven o'clock.

The last person I wanted to see at the moment was Zachary, and I had to force myself not to slam the door in his face when I saw him standing on the top step.

"Good evening," he greeted me with a smile. "Ready to go?"

My brow furrowing, I asked, "Go where?"

Zachary blinked, surprise flashing across his face. "To the picture show," he replied haltingly. "Don't you remember?"

It finally dawned on me that we had, indeed, decided last week to go out tonight and see a movie, but I certainly wasn't going anywhere with him now after talking to Mrs. Fitzgerald.

"I forgot about that," I said, sighing. "It's been a really long day, though, and I'm afraid I'm just too tired to go anywhere tonight."

"That's alright," he replied good naturedly. "I could come in and we could eat some of those delicious, Scotch-oatmeal Byrd cookies that I know you keep hidden in the kitchen, and maybe talk for a bit."

"I don't think so, Zachary," I stated, shaking my head.

"Okay…what about tomorrow night?" He persisted. "The same movie will be playing."

Smiling tightly, I said, "No, thank you."

I stepped back and began to close the door in his face, but Zachary reached out his hand and stopped me.

"What's going on, Vivian?" He asked, eyeing me curiously.

I raised my eyebrows nonchalantly. "What do you mean?"

"You aren't acting like yourself, and it seems you don't care to go out with me any longer," he replied. "Have I done something to offend you?"

I hesitated for a split second before asking evenly, "Why don't you just ask Beatrice to go out with you instead?"

His forehead wrinkling, Zachary asked, "What is that supposed to mean? I haven't gone out with Beatrice in months."

The fact that he was blatantly lying to me was mind-boggling. How had I been so wrong about him? I had no desire to have another dishonest man in my life and decided right then to get rid of him as neatly and politely as possible.

Taking a deep breath, I said with as much kindness as I could muster, "Look, I just think that we could both use some space."

Zachary stared at me for a moment and then, eyes narrowing, he asked, "Have you decided to court Gabe?"

"I'm considering it, yes," I stated, clearing my throat.

"I see," he replied evenly. "So, he's the one you've chosen, and this is your way of telling me to beat it? I was under the impression we were better friends than that, Vivian, and I honestly thought better of you."

I could say the same thing about you, I thought, trying to control my temper. I wanted to give him a piece of my mind, but didn't wish for him to know that I cared about him and Beatrice.

With a sniff, I raised my eyebrows and asked coolly, "What exactly do you mean by that?"

"You weren't planning on actually telling me, were you?" He asked. He was speaking in a calm voice, but I could tell by the look in his eyes that he was hurt. "You just thought if you gave me the cold shoulder, I'd take the hint and leave you alone. Isn't that right?"

"To be honest, I hadn't really thought about it, but now that you know, I hope you can understand," I replied as calmly as possible.

"I'm sorry, but I'm afraid that I *don't* understand," he stated, his jaw clenching. "I'd like to know why you feel the need to be so cool and distant? Will Gabe not allow you to be nice to me as long as you're dating him?"

At that point, I'd had enough. My cheeks flushing with anger, I said, "I don't really see that it's any of your business, Zachary, and I would appreciate it if you would just leave. I've tried to be nice about it, but I'm through discussing the matter."

"Alright," he said evenly, nodding his head. "You've got it."

Without another word, he turned and walked away. I slammed the door shut, leaning against it with a heavy sigh as I listened to Zachary get into his car and drive away. Mrs. Fitzgerald had clearly stated that she'd seen him and Beatrice together; she'd even described Zachary's appearance. She had no reason to make up such a story, and although I could hardly believe that Zachary was lying, I also knew what a poor judge of men I was. Howard had lied to me, too, and I couldn't handle another dishonest man in my life.

Feeling all tangled up inside, I locked up and went upstairs, wanting only to crawl into bed and cry for a while.

The morning of Eva and Leon's wedding arrived before I knew it, and I was running a bit late. When I finally arrived at the church, I rushed inside and immediately went into the back room to find Savannah making the finishing touches on Eva's hair.

"I'm so sorry I'm late," I apologized, plopping down on a nearby chair with a sigh. "Eva, you look gorgeous."

Eva smiled at me in the mirror, her ash blonde hair curled softly around her shoulders and pinned back on each side with two pearl combs. She wore a long, white dress with pink flowers and a matching pink sash. She was absolutely radiant, and I thought she looked just like a princess as she twirled around, the dress billowing out around her ankles.

The wedding was small, as Eva and Leon hadn't wished to invite anyone other than family and their closest friends. Savannah and I stood next to Eva at the altar, both of us wearing pale pink dresses, while Connor stood with Leon. Connor had lost some weight and looked a bit drained, but I didn't miss the warmth in his silver eyes as he watched his wife, or the way they sparkled when Savannah smiled at him. It was obvious how much they loved each other, and I was so thankful that Connor was back home.

Little Davey walked down the aisle with his mother, his angelic face filled with excitement over gaining Leon as a father. As the vows were spoken, I glanced out over the small crowd, accidentally catching Zachary's eye. He looked at me for a moment, his expression passive, and then glanced away. I hadn't seen him since our argument the weekend before, and it was apparent that he was still angry with me. I'd considered asking Gabe to attend the wedding with me as my date, but I hadn't decided yet what to do about our relationship. I liked him, but taking that next step was a huge decision, and I was afraid to take it just yet.

After the wedding, we all went into the reception hall and enjoyed the delicious finger foods that Savannah's Aunt Deborah had made. We also took a few photos, and then it was time for Eva and Leon to leave. Both Eva and Davey cried when they told each other goodbye, and my heart warmed at the scene. She and Leon were only going away for a couple of days, but I knew how hard it was to leave your child, even for one day.

We gathered at the door and threw rice at the happy couple as they ran to Leon's car, and I felt tears fill my own eyes as I watched them drive away. I was so happy things had worked out for she and Leon, but I was going to miss seeing her every day at the restaurant, and as I turned to go back inside, I sighed at the thought of having to continue searching for someone to fill her shoes.

"You know what they always say at weddings, right?" Connor asked when I came in through the back door to the kitchen.

"What's that?" I asked.

"You're next," he replied, winking.

Rolling my eyes, I couldn't help but laugh. "I doubt that," I told him.

As I helped Savannah and the other ladies wash the dishes, I noticed Zachary roll up his sleeves and help Connor put the tables away. I'd hoped he would go home, as I wasn't ready to face him yet, but he seemed determined to stay until the work was done.

Once everything was washed, dried, and put away, I untied my apron and tossed it into the dirty clothes hamper, laughing when Connor snuck up behind Savannah and popped her backside with a towel.

"Oh, you'll be sorry for that, Mr. Danes," she told him, winding up her own towel with a dangerous glint in her eye.

"Now, honey, you know I was just kidding," he said, laughing as he slowly backed away.

"Bye, you two," I called over my shoulder, grinning as Connor attempted to dodge the end of Savannah's wet towel and failed.

"Vivian, thank you so much for staying to help clean up," Mrs. Lina said, reaching out to touch my arm as I gathered my things to leave.

"That's what family's for," I told her, smiling.

Blushing, Mrs. Lina turned to pick up a rather large, square box from the table beside us and handed it to me. "This is for you," she said softly.

Surprised, I sat the box back on the table and opened it, my eyes growing wide with disbelief. There, beneath the folds of tissue paper, lay a Grandmother's Flower Garden quilt; Mother's quilt. I pulled it from the box, tears filling my eyes as I gently touched the fully completed quilt with trembling fingers. It was absolutely perfect, and even more beautiful than I'd imagined when I saw it lying half-finished on Mother's sewing table that dark day over a year ago. It was obvious that Mrs. Lina was a master quilter, and the tiny stitches around the beautiful floral fabrics Mother had chosen were exquisite. I knew that this was exactly the way Mother had wanted it to look and wished with all of my heart that she could see it now that it was finished.

She can, I told myself, closing my eyes for a moment as tears dripped down my cheeks.

"I…I hope I didn't overstep myself," Mrs. Lina said uncertainly.

Wiping my eyes, I looked at her and said in a choked whisper, "No, it's perfect. How…how did you know?"

Her own eyes filling with tears, Mrs. Lina glanced down at her hands and said, "Your father told me that your mother was making the quilt as a gift for when you returned home, and it broke my heart when I realized she didn't get the chance to complete it." Looking back up at me, she took my hand and said, "I know how it feels to lose a mother, and I wanted you to have this last gift from her."

My heart squeezing, I pulled Mrs. Lina into my arms and hugged her tightly. "Thank you," I whispered, my tears soaking her dress. "You have no idea how much this means to me."

As I walked out to my car a few moments later, carrying the quilt tightly in my arms, I heard Savannah call my name and stopped to wait for her.

"I wanted to talk to you earlier, but never got the chance," she said as she hurried to my side. Lowering her voice, she asked, "Is something going on between you and Zachary? He's seemed very upset all week at work, and I noticed the two of you didn't speak today."

Sighing heavily, I placed the quilt inside my car and closed the door, leaning against it as I explained everything that happened. Once I was finished, Savannah shook her head and said, "I don't think Zachary has been seeing Beatrice, Vivian. I don't know who Mrs. Fitzgerald thought she saw, but I don't think it was Zachary." Suddenly, her eyes widened and she reached out to clutch my arm as she exclaimed, "She must have seen Randy! He's new to the hospital, and his hair is almost the same shade as Zachary's."

Before I could respond, I heard an engine crank and turned to see Zachary pulling out of his parking space. Knowing that he must have overhead our conversation, my heart sank as I watched him drive away from the church, a trail of dust billowing out like a cloud behind his car.

64

Vivian

The next day, I went to the hospital to speak with Zachary, but he was in surgery and couldn't see me. I left a note, asking him to come by the restaurant so we could talk, but wasn't certain if he would. He had every right to be angry with me, and I felt horrible for doubting his character and integrity. After everything he'd done for me, how could I not have believed him?

Later that afternoon, I was working late in my office when I received a phone call from Gabe. After exchanging niceties, he cleared his throat and said, "After our last date, you said that you needed time to think about us. It's been over a week, and I wondered if I could stop by tonight after work so we can talk?"

I hesitated, my heart quickening in my chest. I'd made my decision, but speaking it out loud was a bit daunting.

Taking a deep breath, I said, "Yes, that will be fine," and we hung up.

A couple of hours passed, the restaurant closed, and everyone went home. It was nearing eight o'clock, and the sun was setting when I finally pushed back from my desk and put my work away. Yawning, I stretched my back and rubbed my temples, suddenly realizing I had eaten nothing since noon. I clicked off the lamp that sat on my desk, shrouding my office in darkness, and began making my way towards the door. I was halfway across the room when I heard the back door open.

That must be Gabe, I thought. *Cook must have forgotten to lock the back door when she left*. I heard footsteps treading quietly into the hallway and I stopped, suddenly wondering why Gabe had come in the back way instead of knocking on the front door like he usually did. I started to call out, but something told me to remain silent.

I stood in the dark room, listening as the footsteps drew closer. I considered searching for some type of weapon, just in case, but didn't wish to give away my location. If it was an intruder, perhaps they would go upstairs and give me the opportunity to run for help.

The footsteps stopped just outside the office door and I caught my breath, the silence screaming loudly in my ears. Suddenly, the door creaked open, and I saw a tall, shadowy silhouette fill the opening, and something about the stance of my unknown visitor warned me that this was no friendly call.

The light flipped on, illuminating my office, and I blinked from the sudden glare, squinting as I attempted to make out the face in the darkened hallway. He stepped into the light then, a sneer pulling at the scar on his cheek, and all at once I felt the blood leave my face.

"Mack," I breathed, my heart kicking into overdrive.

"Hello, Vivian," he said, the sound of my name on his lips making my skin crawl. "Have you missed me?"

I slowly backed away and clenched my hands at my side, trying to control the trembling in my fingers.

"What are you doing here?" I asked breathlessly.

Mack didn't respond at first; he simply stepped into the room, closed the door behind him, and locked it. Pulling the key from its hole, he tossed it into the air and began walking nonchalantly around the room.

"I've missed you," he finally said, his eyes falling upon the safe. He stopped walking and stared at it for a moment, eventually pulling his gaze away to direct it at me. Cocking a brow, he asked cynically, "Haven't you missed me?"

"You're crazy to have come back here," I stated, ignoring his question. "If the police spot you, they'll throw you right back into prison."

"They won't spot me," he replied, shrugging casually. "They think I'm still in Texas, and by the time they pick up my trail again, I'll be long gone." Stepping closer, his face grew cold and he said in a low, menacing tone, "With the money, of course."

"I don't have the money anymore, Mack. Surely you realize that," I said, swallowing over the lump in my throat.

"Of course, dear, I'm not entirely stupid," he snapped sarcastically. "But I will take whatever money you have in that safe, and if it's not enough, you'll just have to pay a visit to the bank tomorrow."

My stomach sinking, I scrambled to think of a way to get out of this. I hadn't been to the bank yet this week, and there was nearly three thousand dollars in that safe; the restaurant would be ruined if Mack took it.

"Why would you take the risk of coming all the way back here?" I asked, my mind searching frantically for ideas. "Why didn't you just rob someone in Texas if you need money?"

"Oh, I've been planning this little return visit ever since you decided to double-cross me last year," he replied, his eyes glinting. Stepping closer, he reached out and grabbed my arm in a painful grip, his jaw clenching as he said, "No one double-crosses me and gets away with it, girly. *No one*."

There was a sudden knock at the front door, and we both froze. Realizing that it must be Gabe, I gasped when Mack pulled a gun from his pocket and pointed it directly at my head.

"Don't make a sound," he hissed, his breath hot against my face.

The knock came again, and this time Gabe called out, "Vivian, are you there? It's Gabe."

I cringed, hoping that Gabe would give up and go away. I feared that if Mack realized Gabe was the same man who helped send him to prison, he would kill him.

I could hear Gabe rattling the doorknob, and Mack asked in a low tone, "Who is that?"

My stomach clenching, I said, "Just a friend."

His eyes narrowing suspiciously, Mack asked, "Didn't he say his name was Gabe?" When I nodded, a slow, sinister smile of recognition crossed his face and he said, "Officer Gabriel Wright, correct?"

I refused to answer, but Mack already knew, and he quickly jerked my arm and pulled me from the room. The gun remained pointed at my head as he said, "You're going to stay nice and calm and let him in, alright? No tricks this time, honey, or you'll both be dead."

Mack dragged me across the dining room and to the front door, bending my left arm painfully behind my back. He stepped to the side, and with the gun pressed into my back, nodded for me to open the door.

My fingers trembling, I turned the key and slowly pulled the door toward me. Gabe stepped inside, blinking at the dimness of the room, and before I could utter a word, Mack shoved Gabe backwards, slammed the door, and quickly locked it.

Uttering an expletive, Gabe stumbled back and crashed into a nearby table. Before he tumbled to the ground, however, he caught himself and spun around just as Mack flipped on the lights, illuminating the large room. Gabe paused when he saw Mack, his eyes growing wide when he noticed the gun held against my head.

"Don't try anything or she dies," Mack told him in a low, unnervingly calm voice.

"Mack," Gabe breathed.

As I watched the color drain from Gabe's face, I wondered how we were going to get out of this. Perhaps if I could head butt Mack or kick him in the shin, he'd let me go, giving Gabe a chance to tackle him.

"Mack, what do you think you're doing?" Gabe asked, his jaw clenching.

"You should know the answer to that, Gabriel," Mack scoffed. Pointing the gun, he said, "Walk ahead of us into the office."

Without a word, Gabe turned and walked across the room and down the hall, Mack and I following close behind. Once inside the office, Mack pushed me toward the safe and said, "Open it."

"She doesn't have the money anymore, Mack," Gabe spoke up, his voice filled with anger, and I glanced at him in surprise. So, he'd known all along about the money? I knew he'd suspected it, and suddenly wondered why he'd never just come right out and asked me.

"I know, but I'm going to take whatever she's got," Mack told him.

Looking pointedly at me, Mack cocked an impatient eyebrow, and I slowly walked toward the safe. My hands trembling, I bent over and began entering the combination, my mind running in a thousand different directions. There was a letter opener on my desk; perhaps if I could get hold of it, I could use it as a weapon. If not, I hoped Gabe would somehow be able to get us out of this mess.

"You realize if you get caught, you'll be thrown back into prison?" Gabe asked.

"By whom?" Mack asked, laughing. "You?"

Gabe didn't answer and I opened the safe, making certain to keep my movements slow. I didn't want to anger Mack further, but I had to give the two of us a chance to figure something out; I had a feeling Mack didn't intend on leaving us here alive.

"Hurry with that money," he snapped, the barrel of his gun cold against my temple.

"I need something to put this in," I said, trying to remain calm as I gathered up the stacks of bills.

Mack glanced around until his eyes landed on one of the pillows I kept on the sofa. Pointing it out, he said to Gabe, "Bring me that pillowcase."

Gabe stripped the pillow of its case and walked toward Mack, the piece of linen dangling from his outstretched fingers. Mack reached to take it, and with a quick flick of his wrist, Gabe threw it into Mack's face, throwing him off guard. I jumped out of the way just as the gun fired into the wall where I'd been sitting.

The two men began wrestling for the gun, and I glanced frantically about for something with which to hit Mack. My eyes landed upon the lamp on my desk and I quickly snatched it up, yanking the plug out of the wall with trembling fingers. I spun around, ready to strike, just as Mack punched Gabe in the temple with a crippling blow. I watched in horror as Gabe crumpled to the floor and Mack pointed the gun at his head, the trigger pulled back.

"No!" I cried, dropping the lamp. It fell to the floor with a loud crash, shattering into a million pieces, but Mack ignored it. He stood deathly still, glaring down at Gabe as his chest heaved up and down from the exertion of the fight.

"What did you think you were going to do, Wright?" Mack asked in a deadly tone as Gabe slowly sat up and shook his head. "Kill me?"

"You shouldn't have come back here," Gabe mumbled, reaching up to touch the blood that seeped from the cut on his temple.

"Why not? Are you afraid I'll tell your girlfriend about our little…friendship?"

My brow wrinkling in confusion, I looked questioningly at Gabe as he pushed himself off the floor with a wince.

"Shut up, Mack," Gabe said through gritted teeth, turning a searing glare onto his adversary. "Just take the money and go."

His jaw clenched, Mack shook his head and said, "Don't you know by now not to give me orders? I wasn't going to tell her, Gabriel, but now that you've tried to double-cross me, I'd say it's time that Vivian here knew the truth."

Gabe took a menacing step toward Mack, his hands balled into a fist. I opened my mouth to tell Gabe to stop, that whatever Mack was referring to wasn't worth getting killed over, when a growl sounded from the back of Mack's throat and without even a slight hesitation, he pulled the trigger.

65

Vivian

I covered my mouth in a scream as the gun fired, watching in horror as Gabe fell to his knees and clutched his shoulder with a moan.

"I told you not to try anything," Mack said with a hateful glint in his black eyes. "Maybe that will teach you a lesson." Turning to look at me, he laughed and said, "Don't look so devastated, honey, you don't even know the truth yet."

"You're an animal," I hissed, tears gathering in my eyes. "Why can't you just take the money and leave us alone?"

"Are you sure you want me to leave you behind with the man who helped me escape from prison?" Mack asked, raising his eyebrows nonchalantly.

My eyes widening, I looked uncertainly down at Gabe, but he refused to meet my gaze.

Chuckling, Mack said, "That's right, honey, your honorable police officer isn't who you think he is. See, he and I grew up together on the wrong side of the tracks back in Macon and, well, let's just say we both ended up with a record. When old Gabriel here decided to bail and move away, he changed his last name and got an honest to goodness job working at the police station. Can you imagine? Of all places! I guess he thought he'd try straightening up."

With a smirk, Mack looked down at Gabe and shook his head. "Once I found out where he'd disappeared to, I followed him. After all, best friends shouldn't be separated for long, should they? I managed to talk Gabe into turning a blind eye to my little racket in return for keeping my mouth shut about his past, and when his men arrested me, he promised to break me out."

"You really helped him escape?" I asked Gabe in disbelief.

"If I hadn't, he would have ratted me out," Gabe stated defensively, glaring up at Mack.

Shaking my head, I turned to Mack and asked, "So, you knew what I was up to that night in the graveyard?"

"No," Mack shook his head, his jaw clenching. "We'd agreed to not be in contact with each other, and he didn't know how to reach me. That's the reason, though, he only brought one man with him that night."

I was so shocked, a feather could have knocked me over. If not for the fact that Gabe wasn't denying any of this, I wouldn't have believed a word of it.

Another thought suddenly struck me then, and I looked at Gabe and asked, "So, all that time, you *knew* I was telling the truth about those men burning down my house, and you even knew who was responsible?"

A look of shame filled Gabe's eyes and, with a slight nod, he said, "I suspected, but didn't know for certain until I spoke with Mack later."

"I can't believe this," I whispered, shaking my head. I felt completely and utterly blindsided. And very, very angry. "You let me spend all of those months in a mental hospital because you wanted to keep yourself in the clear?" I all but yelled.

Gabe winced and said pleadingly, "That was before I got to know you, Vivian. Before...before I came to care so much about you."

"Oh, how sweet," Mack said, bursting into laughter.

"It's true," Gabe said to me, ignoring Mack. "I'll admit that in the beginning, I only cared about covering my hide, but once I started spending time with you, I found myself wanting to be the kind of man you deserve. I'm so sorry, Vivian. If I could go back and change the past, I would. You have to believe that."

"I'd say it's a little too late for apologies," I hissed.

"As much as I'm enjoying this delightful little lover's quarrel, it's time to get back to business," Mack stated, tossing the pillowcase at me. "Put the money in there and hurry."

Sighing, I walked over to the safe once again and, glancing over at Gabe, I saw the look of agony on his face. I wasn't certain if it was due to the gunshot wound in his shoulder or because I now knew the truth, but as I stuffed the money into the bag, I realized I'd nearly made the same mistake with Gabe that I made with Howard. Was I such a terrible judge of character? I'd thought that Howard was a good, upstanding man only to discover after two years of marriage that I'd been deceived all along. What if I'd fallen into the same trap with Gabe? The sad thing was, I felt that Gabe truly did care for me in his own small way.

After I handed Mack the pillowcase full of money, he turned and kicked Gabe's leg and told him to get up. "I want you both upstairs," he said as he pushed us out into the hallway. "That way, it will be less likely for you to get someone's attention outside."

We walked slowly up the stairs, Gabe's shoulder dripping blood all over the floor, and Mack told us to go into the bathroom. He pulled a roll of duct tape from his pocket and told me to wrap it around Gabe's mouth, ankles, and wrists. I did as I was told, cringing when Gabe winced in pain.

"I really am sorry, Vivian," he whispered over his shoulder.

Sighing, I said, "For what it's worth, everything I've discovered here tonight changes nothing between us; I was going to tell you when you arrived that I can't court you. I'm sorry, Gabe."

Gabe nodded but said nothing, and by the time I'd finished with the tape, his face had lost all of its color and sweat dripped from his forehead. He leaned against the bathtub, too weak to sit upright on his own, and I knew it was only a matter of time before he fainted.

"Alright, now come with me," Mack told me. When I looked at him questioningly, he said, "This ain't my first rodeo, honey. I know if you're in the same room it'll be easier to free each other."

We went out into the bedroom and Mack locked the bathroom door, placing the key in his pocket. He then told me to sit on the bed and tie the tape around my own ankles. Once I was finished, he ordered me to turn around, and jerked my arms behind my back, proceeding to tape my wrists to the bedpost.

"You know," he said, his breath on my neck sending chills down my spine as he taped my mouth shut, "now that I've had time to think about it, I've decided it would be a good idea to leave in the same way I did that very first night we met. It would be such a nice, dramatic exit, don't you think?"

My blood ran cold at his words and I shook my head, telling myself that's not what he meant.

"You don't agree?" He chuckled, running a finger along the side of my face. "I remember standing in the shadows that night, watching as you came outside in your robe and nightgown to close that barn door. You put up a good fight, you know, for a female. It's too bad you won't have a chance to fight this time."

He pulled out a box of matches then and struck one by my cheek, its flame burning my skin as it ignited. I jerked away, suddenly finding it very hard to breathe, and tried to get loose from my binds.

"Just like your husband, you will pay for double-crossing me," he whispered, leaning over to blow out the match.

The smoke drifted under my nose and I choked, desperation clawing at my heels as he threw the smoldering match onto the bed beside me and walked away. I tried to scream, to force some semblance of sound past the tape with the hope that he would come back and give me a chance to talk him out of this, but he walked from the room and slammed the door behind him, his laughter echoing off the walls. I listened as the sound of his footsteps drifted further and further away, and I began frantically trying to tear the tape from around my wrists. If he'd meant what he said, this old building would be smothered in flames within minutes.

No matter how hard I tried, I couldn't break through the tape. My wrists were raw and starting to bleed when the smell of smoke began drifting under the door and into the room. Fighting panic, I ignored the pain and continued trying, my heart pounding as an ominous feeling of death crept closer and closer.

An idea suddenly struck me, and I hoisted myself as far upward as the tape which had me fastened to the bedpost would allow. Clenching my jaw, I began slamming myself backwards against the bedpost, ignoring the pain as my backbone struck the thick, wooden pole time after time. Finally, the post broke, and I tumbled to the floor with a loud crash. The broken bedpost tore into the skin on my back, and I lay there for a moment, slightly dazed as my left shoulder and hip throbbed painfully. Moaning, I turned over and tried to push myself up, but it was nearly impossible with my hands behind my back and ankles taped together. Trying again, I almost got myself up, but came short of the mark and fell face forward to the ground. To avoid breaking my nose, I twisted and fell onto the same bruised shoulder, groaning in pain from the impact.

The smoke was growing thicker and I kept trying, refusing to give up. On my third attempt, I finally made it to my feet, and after leaning against the bed for a moment to catch my breath, I began hopping across the room toward the door. I turned around, found the knob with my hand, and managed to get the door open. As I made my way down the hall, I could hear glass shattering downstairs and the loud roar of flames.

I arrived at the top of the stairs, my heart pounding as I stared downward. There was no way I could hop successfully all the way down, and if I fell, it could kill me. Knowing that there was no other option, I turned and pressed my back against the wall, feeling around for the hand rail. When I found it, I held on as tightly as I could and began slowly hopping from one step to another. I'd made it halfway down when I thought I heard a yell coming from outside. Hoping that someone had seen the fire and could help, I continued my trek, my breathing labored as I attempted to get air in through my nose.

Feeling lightheaded from the exertion and all the smoke, I caught my foot on the edge of the step and stumbled, falling the rest of the way down. I lay in a crumpled heap at the bottom of the stairs, tears coming to my eyes as I struggled to breathe. I was dizzy, my shoulder felt broken, and I suddenly realized that I wasn't able to move any further. With a deep, heart-rending shudder, I knew that if someone didn't come soon, I was going to die.

Everything started fading around the edges of my vision and my eyes fluttered closed when, suddenly, I heard the front door crash open and someone call my name. It was Zachary and, my eyes flying open wide, I began to squirm and try to call out. Somehow he must have heard me, because within seconds, he was at my side and scooping me into his arms.

The smoke was thick and burning hot flames blazed all around as Zachary carried me through the restaurant and out into the street. He sat me on the curb and gently pulled the tape from my mouth, his eyes filled with concern.

"Are you okay?" He asked as he cut the tape from around my wrists and ankles.

"I…I think so," I choked. "Zachary, Gabe is upstairs in my bathroom."

Zachary's head shot up, and with a look of alarm in his eyes, he stared at the flaming building with dread.

"Stay here," he said, his jaw clenched with determination, and I watched as he jumped up and ran back into the burning restaurant.

My heart pounding, I pulled myself up and limped over to lean against Zachary's car. I could hear sirens blasting in the distance and prayed that they would hurry. The seconds ticked by at a snail's pace, and I couldn't seem to pull my eyes away from the front door in the hope that Zachary would emerge safely any minute. Flames had burst through the windows and were crawling up the side of the building, and I knew the ceiling wouldn't be able to hold on much longer.

My stomach was in knots as my mind went back to a night very similar to this one nearly a year and a half ago. I felt the same crippling fear now as I did then, and tears burned the backs of my eyes as the sound of my baby's cries filled my ears all over again. This couldn't be happening a second time; it just couldn't.

Suddenly, the roof gave in with an ear-splitting crash and I jumped away from the car, screaming, "Zachary!"

An ambulance, fire truck, and two police cars arrived then, but I feared it was too late. Flames licked at the night sky and I couldn't see anything for the thick, black smoke that billowed from the once beautiful building, the one Priscilla had loved so much. An officer rushed to my side and through the tears, I told him there were two men left inside.

The firemen got to work immediately, the massive streams of water barely making a dent in the raging fire. I kept shaking my head, hardly able to believe that this was happening. I couldn't lose Zachary; losing someone else I loved would destroy me. If he died, I'd never forgive myself for treating him so terribly and not telling him…

I stopped, my eyes widening as the breath left my lungs with one quick *whoosh*. I loved Zachary. I loved him. The noise and chaos faded away as I was forced to come face to face with reality all at once. Tears sprang into my eyes as I gazed at the blazing inferno; hopelessness and despair flooding over me. Why did I have to realize I loved him now, when it may be too late? What if I had to spend the rest of my life with the knowledge that Zachary died without knowing how I really felt? I'd let pride and scars from the past hold me back, and now I may have lost the man I loved; the man I would always love.

A paramedic appeared at my side, and gently taking my arm, led me toward the ambulance. The aching in my shoulder could never match the ache in my heart as I numbly followed, and I hardly noticed the hot tears that streamed down my cheeks.

Suddenly, I heard shouting and spun to see the firefighters pointing and running to the side of the building. Pushing past the paramedic, I hurried after them, the heat from the fire burning my skin as I desperately searched for any sign of Zachary. I saw movement then, and through the thick, billowing smoke, two firefighters emerged carrying a man between them, and I quickly realized it was Gabe. The other firemen followed, and I felt panic beginning to claw at my heels. If Gabe was alive, where was Zachary? Why weren't the firemen still looking for him? *He's dead*, I thought, the pain in my chest almost more than I could bear.

I closed my eyes and covered my face with trembling hands, tears dripping down my cheeks. It couldn't be true…it just couldn't…

Just then, a familiar voice overrode the sound of shouting and the crashing of timber, and I opened my eyes to see another figure emerging from the smoke. His shirt was torn and bloody, his face covered in dirt and smut, but there was no mistaking the warmth in those piercing, aqua blue eyes as he walked toward me.

My heart pounding, I ran to him, leaving all the fear and uncertainty I'd struggled with the last few months in the dust beneath my feet. His steps quickened as we drew closer, and with a cry of joy, I threw my arms around his neck, ignoring the pain in my shoulder as I relished the feel of his warm body against mine.

Without hesitation, I pressed my lips to his, kissing him fully and deeply. I felt his arms wind firmly around my waist as he kissed me back, and everything around us seemed to fade away and disappear into the background. In the midst of so much chaos and disaster, we'd found each other. We'd been through so much together, and come face to face with death itself, and we didn't hold back. We kissed each other with a fierce sense of passion and urgency, as if this was our last chance, and I could feel the pounding of his heart as it raced against mine.

In that moment of magic, of second chances and the releasing of doubts and fears, I clung to the man I knew I would love for the rest of my life and felt a wave of contentment flood over my soul. I'd been at a crossroads the last few weeks, but I now knew this was the path I was always meant to take.

"Wow," Zachary murmured against my lips as we finally pulled away.

Leaning back, I gazed into his face and he smiled, gently wiping the tears from my eyes.

"Can you ever forgive me for believing silly rumors and being such a fool?" I whispered, touching his cheek.

Smiling, Zachary nodded and said, "Yes, I forgive you."

"I don't know why it had to take a disaster for me to come to my senses," I said with a sigh, "but when I thought you might be dead, I realized something very important."

"What's that?" He asked, his eyes warm as he brushed a strand of hair behind my ear.

"That I love you," I said. Standing on my tiptoes, I slowly kissed both of his cheeks and whispered, "Fully, completely, and unreservedly."

The way he looked at me made my heart flutter, and leaning down to rest his forehead against mine, he sighed and said, "It's about time."

The firefighters ordered us to move further away from the fire, and Zachary took my hand as we hurried to the sidewalk.

"How did you get out?" I asked him as I rubbed my burning, watery eyes.

"By the time I got upstairs, busted down the bathroom door, and cut Gabe loose, I knew there was no way we'd be able to get back down those stairs," he told me, rubbing the back of his neck. "So, we climbed out your bedroom window onto the roof and jumped."

Shaking my head, I wrapped my arms around him once again and we just stood there for a moment, holding each other. I turned my face to watch as the remainder of my beloved restaurant burned and crumbled to the ground, but somehow, it didn't seem all that important. Buildings, possessions, property…none of that really mattered. All I cared about, all that truly mattered, was that the man I loved was alive and safe, and here in my arms.

As the ambulance had already left with Gabe, Zachary insisted he drive me to the hospital to get my injuries seen about. We climbed into his car, and as we rode along the quiet streets, Zachary pulled me against his side and wrapped his arm around my shoulders. I leaned against him with a sigh, exhaustion suddenly weighing on me like a ton of bricks.

"Do you remember the first time I came to visit you in Martinsville?" Zachary suddenly asked, his voice low.

His breath was warm against my ear as I nodded, my mind traveling back to that dark day only a little over a year ago.

"It was all I could do not to kill Howard myself when I returned home," he said, gently rubbing my arm. "You'd been through so much, but I could tell you were trying to stay strong, and my admiration for you only grew. When you left months later, I saw the shape you were in, both physically and mentally, but when you realized how sick your father was, you put your own needs aside and immediately stepped up and took over the restaurant."

We pulled into the hospital parking lot and Zachary parked, reaching over with his free hand to take mine.

"You're an absolutely amazing woman," he said, his voice warm as he slowly intertwined our fingers together, "and no matter what happens in life, I want you to remember this one thing: I'll always love, Vivian Oriana. I've…well, I've loved you for a long time now. I just didn't want to tell you because I knew you weren't ready to hear it. When I kissed you last November, one of the hardest things I've ever done was tell you I was content being just friends."

I tilted my head to look at him, and through the darkness, I could see the truth and passion of his words reflected in the depths of his beautiful eyes. I had no idea his feelings ran so deep, and just seeing the look of love on his face took my breath away.

My heart fluttering in my chest, I whispered, "Thank you for waiting for me, Zachary. Thank you for loving me."

He bent closer until our lips met, and as my eyes slowly drifted closed, I reached up to bury my hand in his hair and breathed a sigh of contentment. I hadn't known when I awoke that morning what the day would hold, but I knew now that I loved this man with every ounce of breath in my body, and I planned to never let him go.

When we went into the hospital, we were immediately taken back and I was told that I had a sprained ankle and dislocated shoulder, while Zachary suffered from several cuts and a couple of bruised ribs. Gabe was the worst for wear; his leg was broken in the jump, and they immediately sent him into surgery to remove the bullet from his shoulder.

The police captured Mack just outside of Albany, Georgia the following day. The police brought him back to Savannah, where I gave a full statement, and once Gabe was well enough to think and speak clearly, he admitted to everything. He told the police of his involvement with Mack and also testified to Mack's guilt for the death of my husband and baby. Mack was sentenced to life in prison, and as I watched them take him away, he turned to throw a scathing glare in my direction. I stared back without flinching, knowing that I would never have to see him again. That part of my life was finally over.

EPILOGUE

Vivian

As I walked among the grove of pecan trees, the cool breeze gently ruffling my hair, I felt oddly at peace despite my surroundings. I turned to the left and gazed out through the opening at the gate with the sign that read: Martinsville State Hospital.

It had been over two years since I left this place, and I'd never imagined that I would ever come back. As I neared Building F, the memories that flooded my mind were as real and vivid as if everything had happened only yesterday. I could see the young boy who'd been taken from the waiting room, kicking and screaming, and the schizophrenic woman that tried to attack me, her eyes wild and frizzy, black hair like the feathers of a vulture swooping down on its prey. I could hear the marching of the townsmen as they bombarded the property and killed the man responsible for murdering the nurse, and I could smell the scent of dirty, unwashed bodies in the ward.

Stepping out into the open, I turned my gaze toward another building and stopped, tears swiftly gathering in my eyes. There they were, those lost, lonely souls staring down from the windows like caged animals, their eyes empty and spirits longing to be free. I lifted my hand and waved, smiling softly when I received a few waves in return. I'd been one of them once; I knew how it felt to be on the inside looking out.

"Vivian?"

I turned my head and watched as my husband walked toward me, his gaze warm as our eyes met, and I wondered how I could feel such contentment in a place filled with so much despair. Zachary and I had been married for over a year, and I'd never experienced so much joy and fulfillment. He was my rock, my haven, my passion, and my best friend. He challenged me in ways that no one ever had, and he knew me better than I knew myself. I'd never known that a person could have such a pure, beautiful heart until I married Zachary; he always put the needs of others above his own, and I never grew tired of watching the selfless way in which he cared for others.

"Are you alright?" He asked, taking my hand when he reached my side.

"Yes," I nodded, smiling softly. "So, how did it go?"

"Splendidly," he said, excitement filling his eyes. "I'm in!"

Gasping, I squealed with delight and threw my arms around his neck, thrilled at the wonderful news. Zachary had been nominated to join the Board of Directors at Martinsville State Hospital a few weeks ago and had just officially been elected.

"Oh, Zachary, just think of all the wonderful things you can do here for these people," I said, squeezing his hand.

"I know," he replied, wrapping an arm around my shoulders as we walked toward his car, "and I intend to do my very best to make some much needed changes around here during my monthly visits."

"I want to come with you," I told him, kicking a rock with the toe of my shoe. "I'd like to try to make a difference, as well."

Stopping, Zachary took me by the shoulders and turned me around to face him, amazement in his voice as he said, "You mean after everything you went through in this place, you want to come back and try to do some good?"

"Yes," I said. Glancing over at the isolation building once again, I nodded at the figures in the windows and said, "That was me once, remember? I know how it feels to be all alone, with no hope and no one to turn to. I don't know what I can do, but perhaps I can figure out some way to help them. I've got to at least try, Zachary."

With a warm smile, Zachary shook his head in amazement and said, "You're an amazing woman, Vivian Oriana Holt. Just don't you forget that."

Sighing, I looped my arm through his, and as we continued on our way, I thought of how much had changed these last couple of years. After the restaurant burned, I decided to rebuild; for Priscilla's sake, and for mine. It had been in the family too long, and I knew I would miss the restaurant too much. After the war ended and Zachary and I were married, I asked Eva to help manage it. We were, after all, officially family now that Father and Mrs. Lina were happily married, and I wanted nothing more than to share the restaurant with her. The offer had surprised her, but she readily agreed, and we split our time evenly throughout the week. I even hired a manager to run things on the weekend so we could have Fridays and Saturdays to spend with our families.

Just before Zachary and I were married, I called Maisie and asked if she could come to Savannah and stand with me at my wedding. She agreed, and when we saw each other for the first time after over a year of separation, we held on to one another and cried. We shared something that most people didn't, and when I said my vows with my three best friends by my side, I couldn't have been happier.

Savannah still worked at the hospital and she, Eva, and I made a point to have a "girl's day" at least twice a month; we were all family now, and I loved spending time with my sisters. Eva and Leon were so happy and in love, and had recently given birth to a beautiful baby girl. Paul's parents called Eva not long after she and Leon were married to patch things up, and they'd been coming to visit at least twice a year ever since; Leon said he was happy that Davey could have a relationship with them. Time was moving on, and love just seemed to grow stronger.

As we climbed into Zachary's maroon and silver car and drove out through the gate, I couldn't help but think of the day I was forced through those same gates that February afternoon so long ago, feeling hopeless and in despair over the loss of my baby. I didn't know then that life would become even darker and my mother would soon be taken as well. I could still remember returning home and how everything had changed, and I hadn't thought it possible to find my way again.

"Life isn't guaranteed to be all sunshine and roses, and sometimes it's during our darkest hours that we realize how strong we truly are."

As Mother's words drifted through the portals of my mind, I realized once again how right she'd been. I hadn't known how strong I was until I was faced with life's storms and forced to cope. I'd been battered and bruised, stomped on and thrown away, but I'd managed to pick myself up and keep going, no matter how much it hurt. It hadn't been easy, but just as Mother had said, I could look back now and know that I'm stronger for it.

I gently rested my hand against my stomach then, sighing softly when I felt a slight flutter from the tiny, precious life growing inside, and I glanced over at Zachary and smiled, my heart full. After all I'd been through, God had replaced my grief and sorrow with joy and peace. He'd set me on my feet again and given me a second chance at life. And what a beautiful, glorious chance it was.

Before the gates closed behind us, a shadowy figure stood at one of the windows of the solitary confinement building, watching us. As we faded from view, she whispered under her breath, "I'll see you again someday, Vivian. You'll pay for what you did to me."

A note from the author:

Thank you so much for reading *The Whispering Shadows of Savannah*. I hope you enjoyed it, and I'd like to list a few details about the book that were true:

1. Most of the asylum stories are based on true events from real asylums.
2. The farmhouse that Vivian and Howard lived in was a description of the farmhouse my grandfather was raised in.
3. Asher's escape was based on a real escape from a German POW camp during World War II.
4. Since about the age of 13 or 14, I have been a sleepwalker, and I based Vivian's experiences from many of my own. I've been spotted walking around at night in my sleep, and it is said that my eyes are open and I speak when spoken to. I have no recollection of any of these episodes, but I did wake up once and was overcome with the most horrible feeling of confusion. My mother suffers from sleep paralysis; she describes the experience as being awake in her mind, but completely unable to move. It is terrifying for her.
5. "Nana's" story of how she and her husband met was a combination of two true stories. My grandparents met at a party; my grandfather played the guitar for the band, and during his break, he asked my grandmother for a bite of her ice cream. She rarely liked to share her ice cream, as it was one of her favorite treats, but he was so handsome and charming that she just couldn't resist! When she got home that night, she told her family she'd found the man she was going to marry. The grandfather of a friend of mine met his wife at a dance as well; he said it was love at first sight. He drove her home afterward and kept her return train ticket in his wallet until the day he died.

I changed the dates and some of the details to better fit my story, but I absolutely loved reading about those events and drawing inspiration from them. If you enjoyed this book, please leave a review on Amazon or Goodreads (or both!), and check out the prequel, *The Healing Rose of Savannah*. Thank you, and God bless!

Made in the USA
Monee, IL
22 December 2021

86943352R00210